MICHAEL ATAMANOV

CAUSE

FOR WAR

Wishing you safe travels on your fantasy journey,

Michael Atamanov

REALITY BENDERS
BOOK 7

MAGIC DOME BOOKS

Cause for War
Reality Benders, Book Seven
Copyright © Michael Atamanov 2021
Cover Art © Ivan Khivrenko 2021
Designer: Vladimir Manyukhin
English Translation Copyright © Andrew Schmitt 2021
Published by Magic Dome Books, 2021
All Rights Reserved
ISBN: 978-80-7619-297-3

ALL BOOKS
BY MICHAEL ATAMANOV:

TABLE OF CONTENTS:

Introduction

Horde Conference

The Vaare Star System, Meleyephatian space
Gas giant satellite Vaare I-III, Horde space docks
Mobile communication center

THE HUGE SPHERICAL ROOM which had previously served as a construction hangar for the Horde's large landing ships had been hurriedly refit as a long-distance communication center for hosting an emergency fleet conference. That was because the existing comms points on every military base or large starship could not be used due to Meleyephatian analysts' security concerns. Their formidable adversary had already shown that they could quickly trace signals to their source and send starship strike groups out to destroy Meleyephatian Horde command centers. In an effort to avoid further loss of starships and personnel, military engineers had overhauled a structure at the orbital docks of the uninhabited

Vaare system into a communications center in record time. Meanwhile, another group of military specialists had anchored a large number of gravity mines in nearby space because they had proven most effective against the adversary's small starships in comparison to thermonuclear munitions or antimatter charges.

Right on schedule, the holographic projectors on the inner surface of the hangar started lighting up. In the darkness, the glowing figures of the Horde's leaders appeared one after the next – the grand admirals of its fleets and the highest-ranked political leaders. Eleven arachnids of the twenty-one on the list... Twelve... Fourteen... Eighteen... They waited another thirty seconds, but the three missing leaders weren't showing up.

The conference had been called by Krong Laa – a level-402 Strategist, commander of the First Fleet and the formal leader of the Meleyephatian Horde – his mandibles now twitching in dismay. Although he had backed away from the demanding task of administering the huge interstellar state and had long been on the periphery of the known galaxy expanding the Horde's territory and bending ever more races to his will, he was not expecting such flagrant disobedience as skipping a conference called by the supreme leader. Was this a rebellion? An attempt to undermine his Authority in hopes of lowering his rank? Just in case, the Krong got off to a cautious start:

"I do not see commander of the Third Fleet Grand Admiral Kung Rou. Leng Tou, Vassal Race Coordinator and Kung Maa, Head of Foreign

Intelligence are also missing. Can anyone explain their failure to appear at such an important gathering?"

The answer came from Kung Paa, the Horde's Chief Analyst who had already stood unshakably in that position for one hundred seventy tongs. All biological organs and appendages of the wise and elder level-322 Analyst's once living body had long since been replaced by cybernetic prostheses, and he had only the cybernetic implants and crystal memory drives enhancing his brain to thank for his being counted among the living attendees of this conference rather than as a robot. Kung Paa had built up a reputation for always having his finger on the pulse of current events throughout the galaxy. But mere knowledge is not enough. It is much more important to use that flow of information to make far-reaching conclusions. And in that regard, the Chief Analyst surpassed even the Jargs.

"My Krong, the Third Fleet was stationed at the incursion point in the Kharsssh-O system and was first to give battle when our powerful and highly numerous foe suddenly appeared. Out of the fleet's three thousand five hundred starships, according to my data, just one hundred twenty small-class ships were able to escape. The fleet's flagship has been destroyed, and the commander's respawn point was located there."

The Krong's agonized chirr rolled through the hangar, echoing many times off its walls.

"What an idiot! I see the many tongs of peace and local quibbles with weak enemies such as the

Miyelonians and other riffraff lasted long enough that our admirals forgot to observe elementary security measures! And I suppose half of the crews were also in the real when our foe attacked, otherwise I cannot comprehend why the defeat was so crushing. I wish he and his fleet had been with us in the Aysar Cluster. Things have really been heating up out there lately! In the blink of an eye, he'd have learned extreme awareness and readiness for action at any moment. Has Kung Rou come back in the real world? If so, he should be executed for incompetence at once!!!"

"Yes, the Commander of the Third Fleet has returned. I was also able to obtain a report from him on the defeat and his losses. But after that, the main Throne World data centers were destroyed by our adversary along with millions of virt pods. And since that time there has been no word from the Kharsssh-O system in any reality. The enemy is jamming all comms channels. Coordinator Leng Tou was on the Throne World as well. He perished according to reports corroborated by several independent sources. It is unknown what became of Foreign Intelligence Chief Kung Maa. He was in the Paku-Uuu star system, which came under attack after the Throne World. But I would venture to guess that Kung Maa managed to escape, given his personal cloaked frigate has not turned up on the list of losses. Also, our Foreign Intelligence Chief is too cautious a player to get caught in such an elementary trap."

The Krong stayed silent, though he wanted to chirr in outrage. Yes, reports from the Throne

World had been of the most awful variety for the last several ummi, but to hear things were so bad... He turned all twelve of his mobile eyes on the Chief Analyst and pronounced in a flat tone:

"I have been in a hyperspace jump with my fleet for the past three ummi and cut-off from communication. The panic-monger yellow journalists in the media keep jabbering on about tens of thousands of starships of an unknown race appearing out of nowhere. And supposedly, a quarter ummi was all it took for them to wipe out all the orbital fortifications in the Kharsssh-O star system, which were constructed over hundreds of tongs and thought to be impenetrable. I trust those are exaggerations, yes? Even the Trillians couldn't fight their way through to the Throne World with their royal fleet despite the fact that, at that time, it rivaled ours both in number and firepower. Tell me, advisor that this is untrue, and our orbital artillery is still holding strong and keeping up the fight!"

"Regrettably, that is not the case, my Krong," Kung Paa understood that the ruler, famed for his quick temper, would not like that answer but at that time it was more important to get the truth across than to sugarcoat such distressing information. "We have credible reports of at least seventy-four thousand small-class enemy starships and over three hundred large ones equivalent in size to our battleships but surpassing them in firepower by approximately thirty times. The battle in the Kharsssh-O system was fast-paced and it was all over in just a quarter ummi. The enemy fleet neutralizes all starships attempting to leave the planet, while enemy battleships are now bombarding the Throne World. At the same time, no landing ships have been spotted in the Kharsssh-O System, nor any of the other systems under attack. All that has led us to believe our adversary means to destroy our infrastructure and exterminate our population rather than capture planets favorable to habitation."

The Chief Analyst's tale was picked up by Second Fleet Commander Grand Admiral Khii.

"I was receiving data on the battle in Kharsssh-O until the enemy cut off long-distance comms. They were attacking our Third Fleet, star fortresses and orbital artillery installations with total disregard for their losses from the outset. They lost over four thousand ships but destroyed all of the Throne World's defensive structures. In the first phase of attack, there were many documented cases of small enemy interceptors sacrificing themselves by slamming into our artillery or large ships at high speed and self-detonating. And that was happening in the real world, where respawn is an impossibility. My Krong, we have come up against a group of fanatics without the slightest fear of death. Whatever they are sacrificing themselves for, they must be strongly convinced of it because they do so without the least bit of hesitation, gladly even."

The Senior Psionic entered the conversation just then, all eight of his limbs weighed down with magic rings to improve his Intelligence, psionic abilities and mental fortitude.

"Our psionics have confirmed that theory.

According to the fragmentary thoughts we have managed to read, the 'Composite' as they call themselves believe us to be an ancient nemesis of theirs – something along the lines of a religious symbol of evil – and they believe themselves to be conducting a historic holy war to bring our tyrannical reign to its final end. We have yet to truly comprehend what 'ancient evil' they have taken us for. But the Composite are completely unwilling to negotiate and will stop at nothing to destroy us. They are prepared to sacrifice whatever it takes to achieve their hallowed goal."

The Krong kept silent, then spoke up, not hiding his frustration.

"All religious wars, regardless of what hokum the rulers declared at the outset about an 'ancient evil' or an 'uncompromising holy fight that must go on until total victory,' quickly lose steam as soon as the people start hearing about the heavy losses on the front. A switch flips in their brains. 'Unshakable' dogmas give way while the most notorious fanatic leaders are replaced with more flexible politicians. The Trillians were also once thought to be implacable religious fanatics, but we forced them to come to the table. However, there is another aspect of this story that's bothering me. Have we ever gone to war with the Composite before? I cannot recall such an enemy in the Horde's entire history."

The answer to that question also came from the Chief Analyst:

"No, my Krong. Neither the Meleyephatians nor our vassals have ever encountered the

Composite before. I have checked every archive. In fact, it isn't even theoretically possible because our enemy came here from a different galaxy, which is now known for certain. I believe with a high degree of probability that our race was set up by other players in the game of grand interstellar politics. I can say with a probability of over seventy-two percent that the Trillians are behind the attack. Twenty-three percent it was the Miyelonians. And I put four percent on the Geckho. In any case, we can assume that whoever was behind this invasion will be found in our galaxy, and we are most likely already aware of them."

"Grave accusations. Tell me, on what basis did you reach these conclusions?" Krong Laa's chirr clanged with a metallic edge, which did not bode well for whoever would be found at fault in the audacious attack which led to the loss of the Meleyephatian Horde's capital.

Kung Paa was eager to explain:

"As shown by battle reports and investigation of Composite ship wreckage, our enemy's main weapon is a kind of pulse emitter which triggers a quadrupolar destabilization reaction. To put it bluntly, it's a rare weapon in this region of space. However, not long before the invasion, something a lot like it was used in the Trillian-controlled Taikhirhh-o-Tsykh star system. Meanwhile a hyperspace drive identical to the kind used on the small Composite ships was patented by a Trillian corporation less than fifteen ummi ago. And that means the Trillians must have had contact with the Composite before the invasion and exchanged information with them."

The reasoning really was strong. All the Horde leaders at the conference agreed. However, Krong Laa was in no hurry to declare war on the Trillians and asked to be told the theories that could possibly implicate the Miyelonians or Geckho. The Chief Analyst explained:

"A Human Free Captain by the name of Kung Gnat figures prominently in both. A remarkable figure, I have put together a whole dossier on him. A swashbuckler with tremendous luck, he is a known confidant of Geckho leader Krong Daveyesh-Pir having completed special assignments for him in the past and engaged in them currently. He is also working for the Trillian royal family, having been rewarded by them for an unidentified outstanding feat with a functioning quadrupolar destabilizer, which is now fitted on his frigate the *Tamara the Paladin*. The best Gunner of the Trillian race was also transferred to Kung Gnat's crew to man it."

"Oh my! So, the Trillians are caught up in all this again," someone pointed out. But rather than get distracted, the Chief Analyst continued:

"Furthermore, Kung Gnat is privately acquainted with a potential ruler of the Union of Miyelonian Prides Kung Keetsie-Myau and was in fact officially considered her fiancé. I have no doubt that the Great One has also assigned this man missions of particular importance because Gnat and his crew were also mentioned in the incident on Medu-Ro IV which served as the official pretext for beginning the sixteenth space war between us and the Geckho and Miyelonians. Beyond that, Free Captain Kung Gnat is also one of the most highly regarded experts in ancient races, particularly the Relicts. We have intelligence suggesting a near one hundred percent chance that Kung Gnat is in possession of Relict technology which can perform instantaneous space travel. Indeed, Kung Gnat is the only individual known to be capable of travelling to another galaxy to carry out this special assignment from his highly placed employers. Meanwhile, the Free Captain is not an independent figure. He has neither financial nor military power of his own. He is merely a pawn and cunning agent fighting someone else's war. Anyone out there could have hired him."

"A truly remarkable personage," the ruler of the Meleyephatian Horde agreed. "The one thing I cannot comprehend is why none of you thought to try and hire this man to work for us. Diplomacy Advisor, I direct that question to you. Why is Kung Gnat not on our side? The Meleyephatian Horde would have plenty of missions for a clever swashbuckler who can travel instantaneously throughout the Universe."

"My Krong," the Diplomacy Advisor tucked in his appendages, making himself appear half as large before continuing. "Kung Gnat has in fact offered his services to the Meleyephatian Horde in the past, and more precisely to our vassals from Tailax. However, the Prelates of Tailax committed a staggering act of foolishness and blackmailed the Free Captain, making threats against his home planet and his female. Our potential partnership ended there and, soon after, Gnat was declared an enemy of the Horde. Now the Free Captain is working for the Geckho, assembling an army of vassals on his home planet for the war effort against us on an order from Krong Daveyesh-Pir. Furthermore, Kung Gnat has been granted official protection by Kung Keetsie-Myau. The First Pride intercepted a group of assassins sent by Tailax to Kasti-Utsh III and the Great One warned us that their peace treaty with the Meleyephatian Horde could be declared null and void if the Horde's vassals continue surveilling her marriage-dance partner."

The ruler's reaction was predictably harsh.

"Just what we need right now! To be back at war with the Union of Miyelonian Prides! I demand that everyone involved in that failing be executed at once! Kung Gnat is no longer to be regarded as an enemy of the Horde, and he is to be informed via unofficial channels that I wish to speak with him personally. But enough about that swashbuckler. I need a situation report about the war."

The Chief Analyst quickly deployed a three-dimensional holographic screen of data arrays and started reading off information.

"My Krong, we have lost four thousand combat ships including four battleships and two planet destroyers, which amounts to approximately fourteen percent of the Horde's total military forces. The Composite has lost around seven thousand small-class starships and two battleships. It is still difficult to comprehend how significant that is to our enemy, because there are more of them coming out of the portals in Kharsssh-O all the time, and the flow of starships shows no sign of stopping. Other than the Throne World, we have lost the three star systems closest to the invasion point. We have lost comms link with all of them. Battle is still ongoing in eleven more, but I see no chance of holding onto them. That's the bad news. Here's the good: The Second Fleet pulled off a difficult win in Larsssh-U, fighting back the Composite's attack and wiping out over seven hundred small enemy ships. The Fourth Fleet has joined forces with the Eighth and is heading toward the engagements. The Sixth Fleet has been recalled from the war against the Geckho and also redirected against our new enemy. In eight ummi's time, we will have a strike force in the Parsssh-O and Uparssshi systems of eleven thousand ships for my Krong to deploy as he sees fit. We have begun evacuating the population and manufacturing facilities from the most vulnerable systems near the fighting, for which we have deputized civilian ships. An order has been given to mobilize all our space docks to replenish the Horde's losses and all our vassals have been issued new accelerated production plans."

The rest of the Chief Analyst's report was cut-off by an emergency message from the communications officer:

"Attention! Composite ships in near space! One hundred sixty small Dero-class interceptors! They are approaching the mobile communications center!"

"Conference adjourned!" Krong Laa declared, setting an example by switching off his long-distance communications.

One after the next, the glowing holograms of the Horde's leaders went out – the participants were leaving the conference.

"They sure detected this command center quick..." the Senior Psionic spoke out in dismay, glancing at a timer and performing calculations.

He received a response from the Commander of the Eighth Fleet, who had brought up a video feed from the space dock's external cameras for himself.

"Yes, very quick. And until we figure out how our foe is doing that our flotillas will be constantly on their back foot. That's all. They're already coming this way. On the other hand, we now have a chance to take down some of their starsh..."

The Grand Admiral was unable to finish. The mobile communications center disappeared in the bright flash of a large number of high-power gravity mines exploding in near space.

Chapter One

War Between Heavens and Earth[1]

I WAS IN THE DISPATCHER TOWER at the Geckho space port standing at a panoramic window in the restaurant area. The high perspective gave me an amazing view of the terrestrial space port which was unusually cluttered with spaceships. The great number of yachts, landing modules from passenger liners and shuttles belonged to guests at the wedding of Gerd Uline Tar and Viceroy of Earth Gerd Kosta Dykhsh. They ran the gamut from the tiny-looking Shiamiru cargo shuttles to a huge Kituvaru trade ship. A couple Sindirovu interceptors were for local Geckho services while three interceptors parked in a separate group belonged to the Relict Faction. My frigate the *Tamara the Paladin* was surrounded by a scurrying brigade of technicians under the watchful eye of

---

[1] A reference to the song *War* («Война») by late Soviet rock band Kino.

14

chief Engineer Orun Va-Mart the Miyelonian and Supercargo Avan-Toi the Geckho, checking weapons systems, trading out fuel blocks and attaching proton torpedoes to suspension fittings. But all that space tech got lost on the backdrop of the three truly gargantuan large landing ships of the Third Geckho Strike Fleet, each of which was around the size of the Great Pyramid of Giza and even distantly resembling it in shape.

There was a half-mile-long line of Army of Earth troopers stretching out from each landing ship. Troops from a multitude of terrestrial factions, walking and wheeled combat robots, innumerable cargo trucks of equipment. The sight of it was majestic and I'd even say epic. Fifty-three thousand players. A bit more than the ruler of our suzerains Krong Daveyesh-Pir had demanded from Earth, but it wouldn't have been right to turn away anyone wishing to take part in the first combat operation of this scale our planet had ever seen. The troopers were bursting with pride at the fact they were representing our world and champing at the bit to prove to all the great spacefaring races throughout the galaxy what our humanity was made of.

"Captain, should you perhaps go address the troops?" suggested Gerd Ayni Uri-Miayuu the Miyelonian, standing next to me and also transfixed by the spectacle. "It will please them to see the Kung of Earth and it would be good for your Authority."

It seemed like a sensible idea, but still I refused.

"I am not in command of this operation," I

15

squinted at the pushed-together tables in the far corner of the restaurant where a group of military professionals was holding a conference. The ruler of the Second Directory, the immense General Leng Ui-Taka was gesticulating wildly and poking his fingers into an electronic tablet lying on the table as he tried in elevated tones to drive something home to his staff officers and a representative of Third Strike Fleet Commander Kung Waid Shishish, who was also attending the spontaneous gathering. Something had upset the highly experienced Strategist and he was telling the hulking Geckho officer his issues without mincing words.

Generals from the armies of Russia, Germany, China and the USA listened carefully to the representative of the magocratic world, nodding along and seeming to be in full agreement with him. The same could not be said for Gerd Avagi Dykhsh, sitting on three chairs at once in heavy shock armor and insisting on his own point of view, stubbornly refusing to listen to his opponents. I had no experience commanding troops, so I stayed out of it. But nevertheless, I would have to figure out what they were disagreeing about eventually.

It was somewhat strange to see Human-3 Faction member Gerd Alexander Antipov the "fed" Inquisitor among the highly placed military officers, but the ruler of the Second Directory approved his candidacy and even insisted on bringing the experienced counter-intelligence operative on as a staff officer. I must admit I didn't understand that decision, but still I kept my amateurish advice to myself. I felt like an outsider in general at this whole grandiose event, something of a fifth wheel. The Krong of our suzerains had assigned me the task of assembling the Army of Earth. That was done, so in theory my part in all this was over. And now I was deep in thought, not knowing what to do next.

Fly off with the rest of the fleet on my starship? First of all, one frigate wouldn't make much of a difference in battle against hundreds and even thousands of combat ships. Secondly, I wasn't even told where the landing ships were headed. When I asked that question to a representative of the Commander, Gerd Avagi Dykhsh was as delicate and respectful as possible, but he nevertheless firmly asserted that it was confidential information he was not at liberty to disclose.

Naive. Naturally, I read everything I wanted to know from his thoughts. The Third Strike Fleet's rallying point was the Ursa Star System. As an aside, I had taken direct part in its capture from the Meleyephatians and in many ways made it happen. But as for where the fleet would go next and what role the Army of Earth would play in its plans, Kung Waid Shishish's representative himself wasn't sure. Maybe they really were destined for Comet Un-Tau like the Viceroy of Earth told me in confidence during his wedding. Though now, with the Meleyephatians tied up in a new war, the Third Strike Fleet could have had different plans.

Fly to the rallying point on my own? That wasn't likely to garner a positive reception. Even though Kung Waid Shishish considered me something of a "lucky charm," he had not ordered me to join the fleet. Take care of my own business? For one, I could meet and have talks with other Geckho vassals like the Jargs and Esthetes and reach agreements for them to work together with the Humans of Earth as Gerd Kosta Dykhsh advised. Or I could get to work on the "mission of epic difficulty" from the Trillian Royal Family. But it would seem like a strange decision to stay out of the fiery space war when the army I had assembled, including thousands of my Relict Faction subjects, was preparing to spill blood. Put pressure on Gerd Avagi Dykhsh and insist on joining in? I was afraid I'd have to fall back on psionics to accomplish that, and I didn't want to go asking for trouble. The Geckho officer seemed quite overconfident and stuck-up. He looked upon us Human vassals as unintelligent children with no understanding of space warfare blurting out uncalled-for suggestions.

The only being the Third Strike Fleet representative would have listened to was Fox. Kung Eesssa, the legendary Betelgeuse Planet Devouress had centuries worth of experience conducting wars of all scales and could have moved the Geckho military officer with her indisputable Authority. But the Morphian vanished as soon as the test in the arena was over and I had yet to see her again. She just tossed out a couple sentences in parting, saying she would find me when the time came to fulfill my promise and she needed my help. The Morphian then melted into a crowd of thousands, most likely preparing to leave the planet on one of the many departing starships if she had not done so already. Some of the wedding guests had already left Earth, while combat shuttles were regularly flitting back and forth, so it was highly likely Fox had already made it far away from planet Earth.

Fame increased to 110.

Authority increased to 114!

Such game messages had become commonplace recently and I wouldn't have paid them particular attention if not for the text that followed:

ATTENTION!!! Free Captain Kung Gnat has been removed from the list of enemies of the Meleyephatian Horde. The Horde's opinion of you has improved to the level of "Neutral." Free Captain Kung Gnat may once again travel through Meleyephatian Horde space. Access to space stations and planets belonging to the Meleyephatians and all their vassals is once again unrestricted!

Now that didn't make a lick of sense... After everything I had done in the recent past – summoning an armada from another galaxy to attack the Meleyephatians and assembling the Army of Earth to go to war with the Horde – the very last thing I was expecting was for them to suddenly warm up to me. Or was this not to do with me at all? Perhaps the Horde was calling on Free Captains from throughout the galaxy to aid them in the war against their dangerous new enemy or at least offering to pay for help regardless of one's past and offering full amnesty. After all, the Meleyephatians probably needed a huge number of starships for conducting space battles, evacuating players from the systems under attack, and transporting cargo and troops.

That was the theory preferred by my personal assistant Gerd Ayni as well, who had also seen a similar message much to her own surprise. The Miyelonian assumed the Horde's affairs must have been going very poorly given they had fallen back on such extreme measures. Or had they come to a general resolution to summon Free Captains, and would later be making corrections and crossing out enemies that had been invited? In any case, my orange Translator figured there was no reason to hurry to Horde space and, in that regard, I stood in complete solidarity.

"Free Captain Kung Gnat is requested to go to the long-distance comms room!" a voice message came rolling down the dispatcher tower corridors, making me shudder.

I didn't wait around for the elevator and hurried up the spiral staircase. Meanwhile, the thoughts were racing around my head in a frenzy. Could this be someone from the Meleyephatian Horde wanting to talk to me and explain the strange jumps in my reputation? Was it even possible to communicate unimpeded with a hostile state in the midst of a bloody space war? And could it possibly backfire on me to have contact with our suzerains' adversary?

I was wrong though. I was "merely" getting a call from Krong Daveyesh-Pir, ruler of the Geckho race. I instantly fell to one knee and bowed my head respectfully before the high and mighty figure.

But I must not have done so quickly enough, or a slight look of disappointment showed on my face because the huge Geckho rumbled out menacingly:

"What, Human? Expecting to see someone else?"

The question wasn't as simple as it seemed, and I needed to think up a plausible explanation for my behavior quickly so I wouldn't seem insufficiently loyal.

"I beg forgiveness, my lord. I have indeed been expecting a call from someone else for a few ummi, which is why I experienced a moment of confusion. A member of my crew, a woman who is dear to my heart by the name of Valeri-Urla. She left my ship unexpectedly and where she has gone, I do not know. An influential relative of my business partner Gerd Uline Tar promised to figure out where the Human woman went and tell me."

The huge Geckho gave a loud growl through his teeth but it wasn't malicious at all. In fact it was approving and even contained notes of happiness.

"Ah, youth... I understand. I was the same way when I was chasing my headstrong second wife all around the galaxy, boarding her starship over and over again. I could help you look if you can't find this beautiful shrew on your own."

"Thank you for the offer, my lord, but it would be... too much or something. Like using thermonuclear warheads to hunt quail."

The Geckho liked my response and gave another satisfied rumble.

"Alright, if you say so, Human. But I have come to you for a different reason. I have been told that you completed my assignment. Ahead of schedule even. Well, I value loyal and trustworthy go-getters like you, so my reward will be generous. The choice is yours. Would you prefer a star cruiser so your ship will match your newly elevated status as Kung, or two planetary shield generators for Earth?"

For the time being, I had no need for another ship – I had no one to crew it, and a cruiser wouldn't be able to fit beneath the mobile Relict laboratory's camouflage field and thus could not travel with it through the Universe. But defensive field generators? How did the great Krong Daveyesh-Pir know exactly what I needed? I was not brave enough to ask that question aloud.

The ruler, clearly delighted by my surprise, snarled out happily:

"It would have been hard not to notice superconductor circuits, high-capacity energy storage, polyfrequency emitters, powerful generators and the load-bearing elements needed to construct planetary shields all starting to disappear from the market in this sector of the galaxy while a string of freighters lined up orbiting your home planet. Well, it's a fine initiative and I am perfectly happy to support a trusty Geckho vassal complete such a noble endeavor. The generators will be delivered unassembled as soon as possible and even unloaded at whatever point on your planet your Engineers specify."

Amazing! That made providing for Earth's defense significantly easier because now we only had to scrounge up seven more of the twelve expensive and quite hard to assemble generators rather than nine. I would designate where to install them and find the specialists required to assemble and service them. Either from my Relict Faction or one of the many other terrestrial factions. I could even pressure the leaders of the terrestrial factions into helping me find the perfect staff. At the end of the day, was I Kung of Earth or what?!

For some reason, the suzerain leader's generosity put me on guard though. Two planetary shield generators were worth around a hundred fifty million Geckho crystals. Even without having to pay for delivery, that came to eighty-five or ninety million monetary crystals. Even for a Krong, that was a substantial sum of money to just go throwing around as gratitude for a job well done. And as a matter of fact, the next few words out of the suzerain leader's mouth proved that my doubts and worries were not misplaced.

"But now, Gnat, I want to discuss more important matters. Tell me, Human, why has the Relict space tech in your possession not yet been delivered to your suzerains' specialists for study? Is that not your express duty as a member of a vassal race?"

Danger Sense skill increased to level one hundred forty-two!

How hard it is to always be talking with the Geckho Krong... I could just never get used to his wild mood swings. Just one minute ago, the ruler was heaping on gratitude for my loyal service and giving me generous gifts but now, with steel in his voice, he was demanding more out of me and clearly prepared to punish me severely for disobedience. But to give him the laboratory... No way. I needed it for myself! I started my response by carefully selecting my words with an understanding that no one would be testing them for plausibility. No, no lies. Such an experienced individual would see right through that. Only the truth. But I would be leaving out a couple things and adding in a few personal theories. And no psionics either because that could be detected and end very badly indeed.

"My Krong, I would be glad to hand over the laboratory to my suzerains, but it isn't as easy as it sounds. The mobile laboratory does not belong to me and does not obey my every command. It is controlled by its own artificial intelligence, which sometimes communicates with me and works with me because it takes me for a Relict. That is facilitated by the fact that I wear Listener armor, understand the ancient race's language, and have a living Relict on my team. But sometimes the system tells me I have failed a check or my level on the Relict Pyramid is not high enough, then the station goes out of control and even tries to kill me. There are enough security systems and combat drones in the laboratory to take down me, my entire crew and my frigate. In such instances, I have to reboot the entire system and try to reestablish our relationship from the ground up. There is a distinct possibility that one day I may find myself unable to cope with the intricate system and the mobile laboratory will eject me. But I am making slow and steady progress toward my goal, trying various methods to get the security systems entirely under my command. For now though, I am still far off. I need time, possibly a lot of it. What I can do is provide Geckho scientists with a highly detailed scan diagram of the ancient laboratory with all its hubs, modules and systems."

"Now that's a different matter entirely! Blueprints will do perfectly, Human!" the ruler latched onto my offer eagerly, and I even started to get the impression the Krong was getting more out of me than he was hoping. "Another planetary shield generator will be sent to your home planet as soon as the Geckho receive a crystal drive containing blueprints of the laboratory's technology."

I exhaled. I had seemingly squirmed my way out of a tricky situation. I even made another crucial step toward keeping Earth safe against space invaders. Meanwhile, the fearsome Geckho changed the topic again and I heard notes of sadness and anxiety in his voice.

"The Par-Poreh royal family is no longer talking to me. The Trillians didn't even congratulate the civilization of Shiharsa on our most important holiday – the day of the great unification of Geckho clans. That has never happened before. The Trillians have always sent their congratulations and their ambassador has always come bearing gifts as a token of our friendship. It is a worrying sign. My Analysts believe Krong Pino Par-Poreh the Third and his relatives are considering starting a war against my people because all Geckho and vassal fleets have been sent off to the hard-fought war against the Meleyephatian Horde. To make matters worse, based on recent intel, there have recently been secret negotiations between the Trillians and the Union of Miyelonian Prides. They must be discussing joint operations against my people. Miyelonians are famed for stabbing allies in the back soon after fighting side by side with them. I suspect that, if not for the Horde's new enemy, the point of no return would have already been crossed and they would have made their decision. By the way..."

The Krong looked at me hesitantly, knitting his furry brows.

"Tell me, Human, the Composite starships going to the Meleyephatian Horde Throne World – was that your doing?"

Well I'll be damned... My heart pricked with a sense of impending disaster. A direct question. I will not be able to quibble when answering. Deny everything? I didn't want to take on such a heavy burden, while the ruler of the Geckho race didn't have any proof of my involvement in the invasion. Even in my own crew, only a very restricted circle of players knew of our role there. They could even be counted on one hand. Or did Krong Daveyesh-Pir actually have proof of some kind? After all, my Navigator Ayukh was a Geckho by race and one of the few in my crew to know where we had been and where we jumped. Despite all his loyalty to his captain, it was easily possible the Navigator might have felt compelled to tell his people's intelligence services about an event of such critical importance. And so I decided to speak the truth.

"Yes, my lord. After making contact in a

different galaxy with the powerful and extremely aggressive Gukko-Vahe Composite, I made a deliberate decision to jump to the Meleyephatian Throne World. I did so just in case the Composite ships could track our jump and follow me to our galaxy. I thought it was a good idea to turn the Gukko-Vahe Composite against an enemy of the Geckho and weaken the Meleyephatian Horde."

"I'm glad you admitted it, Kung Gnat because it was a test of your honesty to your suzerain ruler," he buzzed out, then growled in satisfaction. "Nice move, Human! I approve! The Trillians and Miyelonians must be trying to figure out what to do next. This is the perfect time to try and talk them out of their aggressive plans. Do you understand me, Kung Gnat?"

"Yes, my lord."

"Great then. I place my hope in your diplomatic abilities, Kung Gnat. At the end of the day, Earth's Humanity doesn't want a war against those two great spacefaring races either."

The highly powerful Geckho signed off.

I found myself still kneeling in the long-distance comms room and trying to gather my scattered thoughts. Holy crap, what a little job I'd been tossed! As for the Miyelonians, sure. I could discuss the issue with Keetsie-Myau. It was not of course guaranteed I could sway the Great One's decision, but at the very least she would hear me out. But the Trillians? Krong Daveyesh-Pir was clearly overestimating my influence on them. Other than my contacts with the Hive of Tintara, and the obligation I had taken on to complete the "Mission of Epic Difficulty," there was nothing connecting me to the Trillians. So, should I perhaps get working on that mission then?

Chapter Two

To the Stars!

I DID GO OUT TO ADDRESS the troops in the end after a quick chat with my Chief Advisor Gerd Mac-Peu Un-Roi the Mage Diviner about pressing matters. We decided in the end to place the second planetary shield generator on the Chinese Human-1 Faction territory. The third on the large continent would go on a node belonging to my Relict Faction – the former lands of the Human-25 Faction. My Chief Advisor assured me there would be enough laborers to get the job done, even though it required transporting two and a half thousand players to another hemisphere of the planet on Geckho ferries and Sio-Mi-Dori landing antigravs.

As for the other three construction locations, I entrusted the Mage Diviner with selecting them and negotiating with the largest factions of both worlds himself. In theory, the La-Shin or La-Varrez factions could provide capable specialists in sufficient number as well as the American Human-12, South Korean Human-0 or Japanese Human-4 along with another half dozen terrestrial factions. I decided not to bother the Russian Human-3 Faction just yet because a significant number of their player laborers were now tied up erecting the first shield generator on Rocky Island and a thermonuclear power plant in the Centaur Plateau node, which was intended to provide neighboring nodes with electricity. In any case, there were plenty of options, so the Mage Diviner assured me it was no problem and he would handle it together with our faction's Diplomat Leng Thomas Müller.

After visiting the Geckho dispatchers and easily getting permission for the *Tamara the Paladin* to take off in half an ummi, I went with my tailed assistant Gerd Ayni and demure bodyguard Gerd Imran down the elevator to the ground-floor of the terrestrial space port. The line for loading into landing ships was just as long as before with thousands of troops sitting on their packs beneath the scorching sun. Not far away, the H3-Faction players were waiting, and I headed their way. When I arrived, the players stood up to greet the Kung of Earth.

"You're such a big deal now I'm afraid to even approach you, Gnat!" I didn't recognize the First Legion player in a heavy armored spacesuit right away, but it was Shoot_to_Kill. The hardened veteran had reached Gerd rank and been made commander of one of the squadrons waiting to ship out. With a welcoming nod to Imran and slightly wary glance at the orange Miyelonian next to me, assuming she was actually Fox who had worn everyone out so badly during training, the level-106

Gunfighter extended a hand to me. I greeted my old friend warmly and asked why this loading operation was taking so long.

"Yeah, who can say...? You're the bigwig out here, Gnat. Only you can order these furballs around. Us people are too low on the totem pole. We just do what the suzerains tell us. As far as I've heard, heavy equipment is being loaded first to get the starships balanced properly. We were told to wait, so that's what we're doing."

It was odd to sense timidity in a man I had grown accustomed to viewing as higher level and more experienced. And meanwhile, the other First Legion troops watching our conversation looked on me as a deity fallen from the heavens. It actually made me feel a bit awkward. I promised to talk with a representative of the Third Strike Fleet and figure out what was taking so long.

Authority increased to 115!

"Kung Gnat, have you heard the latest news?" he changed the topic unexpectedly, lighting up. "During a speech to the European Parliament yesterday, a representative from Austria unexpectedly started speaking Geckho and asked everyone's opinion on Earth's troopers being sent to fight in a space war. His microphone got cut off and they tried to stifle him, but several representatives from Germany stood in his support. They started asking how long we can keep the truth about human contact with spacefaring races a secret. Someone even brought up the example of antigravity drives, resonance and plasma cannons patented recently by German corporations as evidence of extraterrestrial technology infiltrating planet Earth. The uproar that kicked up was highly publicized and the broadcast of the European Parliament session was cut off. I don't even know how it all ended. What do you think? Will our politicians finally open up about the game that bends reality?"

I for some reason doubted that severely, which I told Shoot_to_Kill and the other listening troopers. In our world, over the last few weeks there had been anomalies in Antarctica and a few other areas that had "dropped out of space." Earth's astronomers had been detecting strange anomalies on the Moon and deviations in the trajectories of various astronomical bodies as well. Every day there were more and more facts to suggest game reality was seeping into our real world, and that our two parallel worlds were trying to collapse in on each other come what may. But for the time being, all that was being ignored by prominent politicians and all mention of the game that bends reality was ruthlessly censored in all mass media.

After all, for the powers that be, admitting that there exist more advanced civilizations and that our Earth is but a mere grain of sand in the scope of grand space politics would equal death. Who would pay any mind to terrestrial governments when there are much more powerful entities above them? Who would clamor over terrestrial computers, automobiles, airplanes and other 'modern marvels' when all that is hopelessly antiquated junk, many centuries behind truly modern technology? And last but not least, who would want their trillions of paper dollars, a currency that is not in use anywhere else in the galaxy?

"Stupid on their part," my orange Translator cut in, revealing a flawless knowledge of Russian. "Your politicians and ruling clans won't be able to keep silent and deny the truth forever. One day, the new reality will be revealed. There's no avoiding it. What will your stubborn politicians say when starships belonging to the Meleyephatian Horde or other invaders appear in the sky above their planet? Will they continue to admonish their subjects not to believe their own eyes, claiming that none of it is real?"

I responded to Gerd Ayni that it wasn't all so hopeless. Leading politicians and the heads of powerful corporations for the most part were very smart and insightful. They wouldn't go blindly denying the new reality. In fact, they would instead try to adapt to the new conditions and strive to retain their high status if at all possible.

Ever since my last meeting with the curators of the Dome project, I knew that the existence of the game that bends reality was no secret to the world's most prominent politicians. And now that I had become Kung and had the chance to talk with representatives of the largest terrestrial factions, I knew for certain that more and more famous people were entering the game that bends reality all the time. Politicians and their family members, business tycoons, famous athletes and celebrities. In fact, the same thing was happening on my version of Earth as on the magocratic world, albeit with a slight delay, with the powerful now competing to see who could be best at the game that bends reality. There were now even "commercial factions" like H13 and H33, where prominent politicians, bankers and CEOs of large corporations levelled their characters with tight security at an accelerated pace under the watchful eye of experienced players. There were even now companies that could boost a person's Fame to get them to Gerd rank.

"I have already seen such players," Shoot_to_Kill spat scornfully out of his cracked-open helmet visor. "There are even some in our Human-3 Faction, though they are more the specialty of the 'backup' Russian Human-23 Faction. Senators and Duma representatives along with their extended families. They're good for absolutely nothing – don't wanna work, and you can't send such famous people out to stand watch at the border. You definitely won't get them to work in the mines either. They just use the game to treat chronic ailments and take up virt pods in the corncobs under the Dome which could be used for better purposes."

"I have heard that they pay our faction good money though," Nelly Svistunova spoke up, another familiar First Legion veteran. "And they bring valuables into the game which are traded for monetary crystals to Kosta Dykhsh's dealers or sold here in the space port."

"Yeah, I know..." Shoot_to_Kill winced in dismay. "When they first enter, they bring large faceted gemstones into the game as well as gold and platinum jewelry and rare-earth elements worth millions of dollars. They've even brought purebred kittens and puppies into the virtual world. There is demand for terrestrial animals among the Geckho, though I don't know what the furballs are using them for. Those kinds of players want to become as rich in the virtual world as they are accustomed to being in our reality right away. A certain percentage of our faction's red crystals come from these noveau-riche types. In the real world as well the Dome project's financing has been improving by leaps and bounds. In fact, we now have everything you could ever ask for under the Dome. But nevertheless I believe that politicians and their spoiled kiddos are nothing but worthless ballast. Fifty decent Technicians or Engineers would bring more money to the faction in the long-term."

The conversation went no further than that. The song *In the Army Now* suddenly blared out to the entire spaceport from the speakers on the dispatcher tower. I didn't know when or how a drive of terrestrial music had been brought into the game, or how the Geckho found a compatible player, but it fit the moment perfectly so I gave an approving smile. In my personal view, though, the song *Blood Type*[2] would have been a better fit. The only problem would be that not very many of

---

[2] A very popular song by late Soviet rock band Kino about the dehumanizing experiences of the Soviet-Afghan War where one's blood type was supposedly indicated by a patch sewn on the sleeve of their uniform.

Earth's troopers would recognize or understand it unlike the highly popular hit by the groups Sabaton and Status Quo. Just as the music sounded out, the troops stood up and started moving, slowly snaking into the bowels of the huge Third Strike Fleet landing craft.

"Best of luck to the First Legion in the war against the Meleyephatians!" I sent off my old friends, to which Shoot_to_Kill assured me that his troops would not bring shame to Earth or its Kung and would never retreat no matter how grueling the battle.

In spite of everything, the troops still considered me a part of this military operation. I caught myself thinking that as well no matter how I tried to abstract myself from it and remember only the assignment from the Krong of my suzerains. But I just couldn't stay out of such a historic event. I stood on the space-port field for at least another half an hour, seeing off the endless columns of Army of Earth soldiers and getting a sense of their overall mood. They felt pride both personal and for our entire world, thirst for adventure and slight tension, confidence in their abilities and an insurmountable desire to prove to the whole galaxy what the Humans of Earth were made of.

The *Tamara the Paladin* was ready for lift-off, the whole crew had taken their seats. Every box on the pre-takeoff checklist had been ticked, the engines were warmed up and takeoff permission had been duly granted. But rather than give the final command, I was watching the clock and waiting for my wife. Princess Minn-O La-Fin had been told the Ruler of the First Directory was heading on a long-distance space voyage, and so I was expecting her to show up. And just then my wayedda's shuttle appeared from the direction of the sea, took a wide curve over the landing field and set down carefully five yards from the gangway. I went out to greet my wife and help her out of the flying vehicle.

She looked a bit pale, but she was moving with confidence and her happiness to see me was as sincere as could be. I gave Minn-O a warm hug.

"How are you?"

"The doctors say I'm out of the woods and the child is no longer in any danger. That has already gone out on First Directory news and our subjects are jubilant."

Strange answer. The feelings of our subjects were the last thing I cared about then. Minn-O and our child's health was of much greater importance. I picked her up in my arms and carried her into my ship, setting her in an armchair in the common room. Medic Gerd Mauu-La Mya-Ssa extended her a glass of water at once and the Princess accepted it gratefully, took a few sips and set it aside.

"My husband..." uncertainty and anxiety slipped though in the shaking voice of the ashen-skinned beauty. "I cannot go to space with you. If I do, I fear I might lose the child... You will have to appoint another wayedda."

Ah, so that was what had Minn-O so worried.

In the laws of the magocratic world, a wayedda was required to accompany her husband everywhere, which in her situation was a great risk. The high g-forces and hazards of deep space are not the greatest thing for a woman going through a difficult pregnancy. The Miyelonian Medic backed the Princess up.

"Calm down, I was not planning to put you or the child at risk. Stay in Pa-lin-thu under doctors' supervision and go into the game as much as you can. And as to reassure you and shut up all those in the magocratic world who wish us ill, from this very minute I name you my senior wife once again. I will make an official declaration as well."

To me, it seemed like simple words, but the Princess suddenly burst into tears. I even had to calm her down. The crew members in the room stepped out so Minn-O wouldn't be embarrassed.

"That would be so nice," she said, drying her tears. "My husband, are you aware that the uprising of Tamara's fanatics is settling down as well? After the only nonmage ruler Ui-Taka swore allegiance to you and it was confirmed that Tamara was working for the Ruler of the First Directory, the cities we'd lost control of are returning to the fold with their legal rulers one after the next. There still are of course some loony fanatics who will fight to the bitter end, but their support among the population has fallen drastically. All the news channels keep talking about the new laws Archmage Coruler Gnat La-Fin will be announcing any day now."

I shuddered when I heard the strange new

title of Archmage and figured I had misheard, but then she confirmed:

"Yes, yes, my husband! That is what they're calling you now – the only Archmage in the whole magocratic world. Even members of the great mage-ruler dynasties of La-Shin and La-Varrez have confirmed that title for you, tripping over one another to do so, forgetting about all their hostile moves in the past and swearing allegiance to you. The people expect new laws and a general thaw for the common population. Your support among the people is now greater than ever. And not only in the First Directory. I've even been thinking..."

Gerd Minn-O La-Fin fell silent, unable to find the courage to finish her sentence. I had to fall back on psionics and read what the Princess was afraid to say out loud.

"My husband, if you name yourself the sole ruler of the magocratic world, you will find enough supporters to make that an official reality. There would be resistance both from the old mage-ruler dynasties and Tamara's fanatics, but it would be possible to suppress that resistance by force. Think about it. This kind of chance comes around but once in a lifetime. My grandfather Archmage Thumor-Anhu La-Fin would have seized it in a heartbeat, as would any relative in my paternal line. Prove yourself a true ruler of the great La-Fin dynasty!"

Mental Fortitude skill increased to level one hundred twenty-five!

Danger Sense skill increased to level one hundred forty-three!

The transition from weepiness to coldly and

calculatedly suggesting I launch a great war for power was just too abrupt. I was on guard even before the system messages appeared before my eyes. No, I couldn't bring my tongue to call my wife harmless and cute. Regardless, the Princess was a member of an ancient dynasty of mage rulers. But even Gerd Minn-O La-Fin found the suggestion too extreme. That put me on guard and made me squeeze out through my teeth in dismay:

"I'll consider it. But if you try to attack me with magic again, you'll spend the rest of your pregnancy locked up in a clinic."

A look of utterly sincere panic was reflected on Minn-O's face.

"My husband, I swear it wasn't me! I never would have dreamed of doing such a thing! It was..." the Princess lowered a hand and rubbed her slightly rounded belly.

What??? Was my wife seriously suggesting my unborn son had done that? Was that even possible? Minn-O nodded to say I understood her correctly.

"Our future child possesses powerful psionic magic and already has his own opinions. Within him is concentrated the might of a great many generations of mage rulers of the ancient La-Fin dynasty, multiplied by the power of magic from your world. The Mage Diviner told me that our son's power will be unmatched. The thread of the probable future is still very thin and fragile, but our son could potentially unite the various branches of humanity under his rule. He could even make Humanity into one of the great spacefaring races.

As a matter of fact, we stand to become a dominant power in the galaxy."

Just what I needed... What I heard made my head spin. After all, the Mage Diviner hadn't told me anything like that even though we had a substantive discussion about all kinds of important matters earlier in the day. And then it hit me with abundant clarity that my Chief Advisor Gerd Mac-Peu Un-Roi was not so much loyal to me as he was to my yet unborn son who he saw as the hope for restoring the magocratic world to its bygone glory and making a decisive step forward for all humanity. I meanwhile was just a tool to provide my son a springboard for his future achievements. And I would be gotten rid of as soon as I was no longer needed.

I didn't even know whether to be happy or sad. The news was just too enigmatic. Alright, time would tell. I extended a hand cautiously and rubbed my wife's belly.

"Take good care of him, Minn-O! Our son is our greatest treasure. I will do my part by safeguarding our world against all possible invaders."

As soon as Minn-O's shuttle took off and left the space port's danger zone, I ordered the airlock closed and we took off. Time for new achievements. Distant stars awaited!

Chapter Three

Inhabited Rings

I DON'T LIKE taking off. Exiting the atmosphere is always accompanied by violent shaking and high G-forces. Your arms and legs feel heavy as cast lead, the blood pounds in your temples, it's hard to move. I wanted to close my eyes and disassociate from it all but doing so just made matters worse. I started to feel nauseous. I even had a cowardly thought flicker by that I should leave the game for twenty minutes to skip this unpleasant part of the flight. But I shooed it off – it wouldn't be proper for a famed Free Captain to act like that. It looks weak and would be detrimental to my Authority. Furthermore, this time the unpleasant sensations were at least bearable. It used to be much worse. Which was why I tried a new tactic – I opened the star map and attempted to keep my mind busy. I was most of all interested in the Rorsh star system with its space prison for particularly dangerous criminals. The deadline was ticking ever nearer, and it was not a great idea to take lightly the threats of the space mobsters from the Hive of Tintara.

The space atlas said that Rorsh was in Meleyephatian space, but it had no inhabited planets or settlements. No surprise. A secret prison had no place in a publicly available star atlas. I switched to the more complete map I had in *Tamara the Paladin*'s navigation computer. That map contained additional information from a secret crystal drive we'd captured from the Meleyephatian Horde and it did show the prison. It also depicted a Meleyephatian military base located in a nearby asteroid belt. Hmm... I was intrigued and read deeper. The map indicated the ships normally based there, consisting of a squadron of twelve Pato-Vee interceptors, ten Tolili-Ukh X modular frigates in heavy shock configuration and one Mirosssh-Pakh II assault cruiser. Not all that many if you think about it, but easily enough to take care of my twinbody. And although it may have been outdated information and that flotilla could have been called into the war with the Geckho or their new enemy, I still needed to assume the prison was under guard and I would not be able to capture it just like that.

By the way, I noticed that the Rorsh system was not all that far from the zone of conflict with the Composite. Just two ummi's flight from the Throne World for my frigate, and even less for speedy Dero interceptors. The military base staff and prison guards were probably now on tenterhooks shivering in mortal fear and expecting dangerous starships to appear from another galaxy at any moment. I suspected the Meleyephatians would be glad to see any aid sent by the Horde. Especially if it proved true that the Composite invaders were jamming comms, and orders from the Throne World and other systems under attack were not reaching the system. There was something there and the localized lack of information was something I could try to take advantage of by portraying myself as an emissary from command. Though it was still risky. The prison guards might have had clear instructions to shoot down all starships entering their zone of responsibility for example. Especially those on the enemy list. It would be better to set aside breaking Prince Hugo out of prison until the Meleyephatian Horde's true opinion of me was cleared up.

I turned my attention to other points in the galaxy that piqued my interest. The Cleopians, Esthetes, Jargs and other Geckho vassal races... Yes, I needed to meet up with all of them to establish political and military ties. I was particularly interested in the Cleopians. With many legs and arms, the clunky looking creatures had no discernable sense organs and were covered in a thick layer of green and brown skin. Something like living trees or ents from *Lord of the Rings* but smaller.

The Cleopians were famed for their dogged persistence and ability to go without food due to photosynthesis, sucking nutrients from soil, water and even air. Entirely impervious to poison and hard to kill with lasers or other light firearms, they could even survive quite a long time in a total vacuum or under harsh radiation. With no gender, they could increase their population by fission and cleavage, giving them a reproduction rate other races couldn't even approach. To split a Cleopian with a blade would mean only creating a second opponent. For the same reason, grenades and explosives were completely ineffective against them. Every chip or scrap of a Cleopian's body could live independently and would with time transform into a fully-fledged individual. Fairly languid and apathetic in their day-to-day lives, they could spend a long time in one position, not reacting to the outside world while they stored up energy. But in critical situations they could move quicker than Miyelonians while their roots and outgrowths could penetrate even the heavy armor of a Geckho. On top of that, they were very smart and had highly advanced science and culture. The Cleopians had made space flights and even explored distant planets long before they encountered the Geckho.

According to the description, they made ideal soldiers and colonists, capable of quickly spreading throughout the Universe and settling even planets other races would find inhospitable. But that was not the full picture. Although Cleopian research vessels could be found throughout the galaxy, and their traders and mercenaries were frequent guests at populated Geckho and Trillian stations, the Cleopians lived exclusively in the Serpea star system, having settled every planet within it and even all large asteroids. Serpea was the only place that interested their race, and Cleopians only felt truly at home in the system where they originated. And given all planets in the star system that could be settled had already long since been brought into the fold, the Cleopians had begun to actively build up nearby space. There were more and more homes made of old starships orbiting around their system's blue star, more and more new force-fielded palaces drifting through space all the time.

Meanwhile, though the Cleopians were at a constant state of war internally for better spots beneath the light of their blue star, they did not see particular reason to take part in external conflicts. Still, they were loyal Geckho vassals and carried out all the suzerains' orders, providing the required number of troops to the Geckho army and everything else. But the race's entire history was one of endless squabbles between members of the ruling dynasties and their clans for better places in the sun. That was how Kung Eesssa the Betelgeuse Planet Devouress got her hands on the full case of Precursor stones — it was a reward for her help getting rid of a whole list of relatives of the current Cleopian ruler King Edeyya-U. Furthermore, he knew a suspicious amount about ancient races, particularly the Relicts. I badly wanted to meet with him and figure out the reason for the Cleopian ruler's incredible knowledge. Well and naturally come to an agreement with the Cleopians to cooperate in trade and military affairs.

I was also interested in the interspace "pocket" the Relict Hierarch used after coming under siege. Rescuing him was my mission, and for completing it I'd been promised a higher rank on the Pyramid. Doing so was fraught with danger though. If Urgeh Pu-Pu Urgeh were to join up with the Hierarch and go against me, the risk of losing the mobile Relict laboratory would be too high. If it even got to the point of talking to the Hierarch and the automatic Precursor hunters guarding the ancient ship let me through to the besieged starship rather than destroying my vessel as soon as I entered space under their protection...

"Captain, we have exited Earth orbit. What are your further instructions?" the voice of my main pilot Dmitry Zheltov tore me away from studying the space map, and I closed the screen.

Yes, my method of distracting myself from the takeoff had proven one hundred percent effective. The unpleasant sensations just passed me by as the starship emerged into space. On the big screen I could see the blue ball of my home planet. Clouds, seas and continents beneath them. On that backdrop, I could distinctly make out the two interceptors of the Geckho's terrestrial services passing through the atmosphere, having taken off after us.

"Are we waiting for the Relict laboratory?" suggested my Navigator Ayukh, but I responded negatively.

"Those two interceptors aren't the only ones watching us," I pointed at the markers of the approaching Geckho starships. "All the great spacefaring races want to know if we're going to summon the mobile Relict laboratory. And if we do, they want to see how so they can do the same without us later. I wouldn't be surprised to discover a whole fleet of cloaked frigates next to us right now representing all the great spacefaring races. So we will just sit around doing nothing as if we are having a hard time establishing contact with the overly independent piece of Relict technology. And that is in fact true. For some reason, I can't sense the station responding..."

That was not actually true, and I had been mentally communicating with the laboratory, preparing it to accept coordinates for instant transport. But my Navigator and all the others in the crew could not be allowed to know that. A captain must have his secrets.

"Alright. No sense in waiting," I said out loud a minute later, straining to put a frustrated and disappointed expression on my face. "Ayukh, I want you calculating coordinates for hyperspace jumps to three systems. Write this down. The Serpea system, exiting a few thousand miles from the third planet. The Rorsh star system. There are no planets there, so just keep away from the asteroid belt. And finally, the subspace pocket we landed in once because of Precursor symbiotes. You should still have the parameters for that jump saved. Send all data necessary to complete those three warps to my monitor."

If the Navigator was surprised by his captain's strange order, he didn't show it and quickly started clacking his claws on the keyboard. Soon enough, columns of numbers appeared before my eyes. I launched a program to reformat the data for Relict computers and mentally transmitted the order to the mobile station. A response came in saying the command had been received and my link with the laboratory had been severed.

Machine Control skill increased to level one hundred fifteen!

Mental Fortitude skill increased to level one hundred twenty-six!

Psionic skill increased to level one hundred twenty-eight!

Excellent! I wiped the perspiration from my brow. That was hard work! I'm not sure anyone else currently alive in the galaxy would have been able to pull it off. Well, apart from perhaps the Relict Hierarch who I had been tasked with rescuing by the Pyramid and was currently in stasis. But what mattered was that it worked, and the priceless mobile laboratory had been sent to the coordinates I indicated to await new commands. And we would be getting on our way. I turned to the main pilot.

"Dmitry, set a course for vector seventeen – one oh four – eleven. Accept coordinates from Ayukh for a jump to the Serpea system. We will be warping to the home system of the Cleopians, a Geckho vassal!"

The pilot started rotating the frigate, watching the digits run across his screen when suddenly he turned to me with a look of surprise and doubt on his face.

"Captain, that will push our starship to the limit. The spatial disruption is too long, our power reserve will go down to two percent charge. It's a whole six ummi in hyper. We've never made such a long jump before. Just to be safe, should we break it down into two jumps?"

"No, no need. I've checked it twice," our experienced Navigator cut in, notes of offense slipping through in his voice due to the doubts voiced about his professionalism. "It's within range, though just barely."

The pilot looked again at me with worry and simultaneously hope, but I got up from my console and headed to leave the captain's bridge, showing with my whole appearance that the conversation was over. Our Jarg Analyst got up from the neighboring workstation and hurried after his captain on all six legs, trying to slip through the still barely open door – the space "armadillo," due to his short stature, was unable to reach the door opening device. I ordered the card reader on his bunk door to be placed lower than the others, but the other ones in the starship were left at the same height because otherwise the taller Geckho would start to have problems getting around.

Our Analyst picked up the pace in the hallway and caught up to me. After that, he stopped in front of me and slipped the Universal Translator around his neck:

"Captain Gnat! Needed Cleopian. Living on inhabited rings of planet. Ring three. Sector nineteen. Permission from secretary. Appointment only. Long time. Otherwise no see. Cleopian bureaucracy be scare."

It was a fully comprehensible message, and I myself had already read in a guide about the location of the space palace of the ruler of Serpea and its inhabited rings and knew where to go. But I was interested in how the Analyst knew which specific member of the Cleopian race I was headed to see. Which inputs had he used to make his conclusion that I was interested the ruler rather than one of his hundreds of millions of subjects? Or had the Jarg learned to read thoughts?

"No, not reading. Thoughts. Jargs cannot to do. But the word Serpea was just one time. Spoken. Within these walls. Meleyephatian Gerd Eeeezzz 777. Telling about work for Betelgeuse Planet Devouress. Working for Prince Edeyya-U, ruler of Serpea-III and inhabited rings. I am to hear and listen. Then I look who is now. He is Prince. Leng Edeyya-U the Sixth. Elderly King of Cleopians. Survived seven hundred eighteen assassination attempts. Now admits no visitors. Without long, long checking."

So there it was... The unforeseen difficulty. I didn't want to waste a bunch of time on bureaucratic negotiations and checks. Was I really flying to Serpea for nothing? But there was no way back now – based on the sudden brief sensation of falling and flickering lighting throughout the ship, there had indeed been enough energy and the *Tamara the Paladin* had already entered a hyperspace tunnel leading to the Cleopian homeworld.

Chapter Four

High-Profile Wards

SIX UMMI IN FLIGHT. To translate that into time units more familiar to Earthlings, it was a whole thirty-three hours cooped up in my relatively small starship. And I couldn't much go into the real world. First of all, safety regulations recommended against leaving the game in a "red zone" where one's in-game body would never disappear. And second, even if I did go into the real world, what was there for me to do on the Miyelonian station Kasti-Utsh III? Go out looking for trouble? Kung Gnat had a few too many foes these days, so appearing in public places had become a liability as proven by the recent attempt on my life in the restaurant on the Miyelonian station. But what then? Sit tight in my hotel room under guard of the First Pride and stare out my panorama window? A boring activity and unbefitting of the Kung of Earth.

Furthermore, I was totally unprepared for a possible meeting with Kung Keetsie Myau. I didn't know where the commander of the Fourth Fleet was currently, but if the Great One still was on Kasti-Utsh III, it was a very real possibility she would want to meet me. And what did I have to say to her? Keetsie Myau had unambiguously expressed an interest in the mobile Relict laboratory and even warned me what would happen if I refused. The Union of Miyelonian Prides would go to war against the Geckho, which would be the single most unfavorable outcome for my home planet, making an invasion unavoidable. I didn't want to give away the invaluable laboratory but wheedling and trying to hide behind a fog of promises wouldn't work against such an experienced Truth Seeker. That was why I had been going into the real world only when necessary for the last few days, which meant short breaks after I died in training without so much as leaving the tiny room around my virt pod.

There was one other reason I was not burning with desire to go into the real world. Of a personal nature. I suddenly had a distinct realization that, in many ways, I had been trying to reach Kasti-Utsh III because I stood to meet Valeri the Tailaxian there. Her visits to my hotel room always ended unexpectedly and often even outgrew themselves into psionic duels. But even that had its charm. The obstinate, proud beauty was grateful to me for saving her from her prison wardens and didn't even try to hide the fact that she liked me. But all the same she had issued a serious challenge to my abilities and I had to prove my power and validity. After Valeri fled, the Kasti-Utsh III space station no longer had any charm. As a safe haven for my physical body it was also a poor option and I had even considered changing my exit point into the real world.

A delicate knock from outside distracted me from the depressing thoughts and I unlocked the door to the captain's bunk. In the doorway stood my business partner Geckho Trader Uline Tar. Strange. The captain's first mate always had access to my chambers and could simply open the door with her own key, but now she had opted to knock.

"Something was telling me you were down in the dumps," Uline closed the door behind her and took a seat on the flying armchair. "Did something happen?"

"No, not really. I just feel empty or something," I poured some orange juice into a set of glasses on the table and handed one to the Trader, who was a big fan of the sour beverage. "The last few days have been a real rat race between assembling the Army of Earth and the exhausting training sessions, then handling a bunch of day-to-day issues for the Relict Faction. I've been sleeping only two or three hours a night. I'm immeasurably tired. And now that all that's over, I am too tired to even gather my thoughts. I need to compose a speech for my subjects in the First Directory and the magocratic world at large. My citizens are impatiently awaiting new laws for their planet to live by. But now I have neither the proper emotional state nor the mood."

"Then I guess I came at a very bad time," Uline rumbled out and bared her teeth in a semblance of a smile. "The thing is just that the start of every new journey in the past has been marked by a celebration for the crew. You would buy sweets, delicacies and drink and put on a feast in the common room for the crewmembers to talk amongst themselves in an informal setting. That really helped all our different races gel together. But I realized that you weren't planning to throw any sort of get-together..."

Damn! She was right. With all the action of the past few days, I had somehow overlooked a very positive tradition in my crew and forgotten to buy up everything I needed at the space port. And now it was too late, we were already in space. And even in a hyperspace jump where getting cakes and booze delivered was impossible.

"I suspect, Gnat, that you spent a good amount on my wedding and other important purchases, so now you're strapped for cash. And so I took it upon myself to buy and organize everything. The feast table in the common room is set and the team is only waiting on you. Beyond that, we now have something to celebrate."

Uline didn't say what though, expecting me to guess. Had I overlooked something again? But what? I considered it unsporting to use psionics to read the answer from Uline's thoughts, so I tried to guess on my own. There were no new crew members – Gerd T'yu-Pan hadn't taken anyone for the boarding team, which even prompted a bit of stomping from the Army of Earth troopers who dreamed of coming to join my crew. Miyelonians and Geckho weren't much for celebrating birthdays. Could it perhaps have been one of the humans' birthdays? Or maybe some kind of important state holiday for Trillians or Jargs? No, not likely. Mentally running down the list of possible reasons for celebration, I made an honest admission to my business partner that I did not know.

"Tini Wi-Gnat has become a Gerd! Come along and congratulate your ward!"

Tini accepted my congratulations and basked in the rays of glory. The once ungainly and disheveled bush-league pickpocket I had first met on the pirate station Medu-Ro IV was now a proud and capable level-106 Thief. A specialist with knowledge of three galactic languages as well as all kinds of locks and security systems, he was a skilled and fearless hand-to-hand fighter with a good understanding of electronics, particularly surveillance and password sniffing programs. And although by Miyelonian standards, Tini was still an adolescent, it was no surprise he had reached Gerd status. My ward was now a recognizable figure, and even enjoyed a certain amount of authority. From thoughts I'd recently eavesdropped on, I knew that the adolescent had bought himself a condo in the real world in a residential tower on the secure neutral planet of Porish II, which had a primarily Miyelonian population, and deposited half a million crypto into a bank account.

Now Tini was dancing with Amati-Kuis Ursssh, our Chef-Assassin whose efforts were in many ways to thank for today's celebratory luncheon. Despite their differing races and especially sizes, their dancing was harmonious and even beautiful. The entire crew was watching the couple and applauding.

"Captain Gnat, I say we have a drink!" with two glasses of alcoholic cocktail in his paws, Gerd Mauu-La Mya-Ssa staggered over to me, smiling a big toothy grin.

In my view, our Medic had already had plenty of alcohol for today. Especially considering how much trouble he got himself into last time, overindulging on liquor after the complex surgical operation to remove the bugs from Valeri's body. On the other hand, knowing about the accelerated Miyelonian metabolism, I was absolutely certain the booze would pass through his system quickly. Removing my arm from the orange Translator Ayni, who I had been embracing and was squeezed up against me, herself also exhausted after the last few days and dozing off on my shoulder, I took the glass and shared a drink with the Medic.

"My captain," Gerd Mauu-La spoke out in an utterly sober voice, lowering his voice to a whisper and giving his whiskered snout a nod toward the sleeping Ayni, "how long can you torture her with your ambivalence? You know she's up to her ears in love with you. The whole galaxy is talking about it. So take her as your *wayedda*," the Miyelonian struggled with the foreign word. "Miyelonian law permits such arrangements, and the priests of the Temple of the Great First Female are willing to give their blessing. I heard so from the mouth of the

Great Priestess Leng Amiru U-Mayaoo herself when the incarnation of the Great First Female was answering questions from pilgrims about your relationship. As a Medic I can also say it would be physically possible, though of course no offspring would result."

They just keep sliding into my life with their uncalled-for advice... If it were anyone else, I probably would have sent them on their way, quite rudely even. But this was a member of my crew who only wanted to help, so I gave a response.

"I like Ayni. I have never hidden that. But still I don't want to move too quickly and put the cart before the horse. We are both totally happy with where our relationship is right now. Furthermore..." I looked and made certain that all other team members were busy and not listening. "Ayni was given a chance to move our relationship forward and do away with all the interracial limitations. When we were here in this very room using the Precursor crystals from Big Abi's pirate treasure, that was why I suggested she take the black stone which started to glow purple when unthawed. She could have become a Human lady. But she refused."

"I didn't realize it at the time. And made the biggest mistake of my life..." the orange kitty piped up, opening her eyes to show she was not asleep and in fact listening attentively to my conversation with the Medic. "But nevertheless, esteemed Gerd Mauu-La Mya-Ssa, I ask that you stay out of my life. It's awkward enough to have every Miyelonian Pride talking about me and deciding how I should live my life and what to do. I just feel nice with my captain. I can sense his warm feelings for me, and that's all I need."

Ayni placed her head on my lap and closed her eyes to show the topic was no longer up for discussion. The Medic apologized for the lack of tact and went off to pour himself some more alcoholic cocktail. But just then... A strange silence suddenly came over the din of the party, drawing my attention. I looked up.

The reason they all clammed up was a Human girl appearing in the common room barefoot wearing shorts and a light blue t-shirt. Gerd Soia-Tan La-Varrez, a runaway from the La-Varrez Faction who had joined my Relict faction and given me magical backup during training. Had that underaged fool exited the game on my very starship?! And now after getting some rest in the First Directory, had she come back into the game to find herself in deep space aboard the *Tamara the Paladin*? Apparently so. But I ordered her to remain on earth because deep space is no place for a little girl.

Looking around, Soia-Tan locked eyes with me and walked confidently in my direction. All team members made way, letting the unexpected visitor through to the captain.

"Coruler Gnat La-Fin, I have come to join your team!" the little squirt declared in Geckho, clearly so they would all understand her, her small face poorly concealing a smirk as she relished the baffled looks on the faces of a large number of spacefaring races.

Quite the declaration... I stood up and took a skeptical look at the little knee-high. A level-sixty-seven Psionic Mage. Yes, she had of course leveled pretty well over our joint training sessions. But Gerd Soia-Tan had no spacesuit, no weaponry, and really nothing worth mentioning. She had even accidentally left her sandals behind somewhere. And what kind of help would she be in space battle? What if the starship suddenly lost pressure or had to land on a planet with unbreathable atmosphere? She would die right away. By the way... Was that not a way out of this?

"Hey kid, where's your respawn point?" I asked sneakily, inconspicuously setting my right hand on the grip of my Annihilator.

But Soia-Tan clearly saw what I was doing. A few seconds of anxiety and discomfort on the girl's face gave way to poorly concealed jubilation:

"Now it's here, in this room Coruler Gnat! I am with you, and you won't get rid of me so easily!"

So, what to do now? I took my hand off the Annihilator. No, the nice way to handle this would be to shoot her two or three times to teach her a lesson, but that wouldn't solve the problem. Now we'd have to hire a starship in Serpea to send the little sorceress back home to Earth. And she'd need a large, reliable escort team because the little Psionic Mage had both the ability and foolishness to take control of the guards' minds and escape.

"I for one like the little girl's spunk!"

The unexpected commentary belonged to Destroying Angel, which was a surprise all on its own. The German gunwoman was generally known to be tight-lipped and practically never said anything. Every sentence had to practically be dragged out of her with a set of pliers.

"Capitan. Good news. Gerd Soia-Tan. Will come in handy. Very useful. For all. If does not to die."

Uh, what the heck?! Now my Jarg Analyst was going to bat for the little pipsqueak. Then First Mate Uline Tar unexpectedly declared that she would buy a small light spacesuit for the human girl as soon as we reached the Serpea star system. After that, it wouldn't have been right for me to play the malicious monster and send the little mage back to Earth. I would have to let Soia-Tan La-Varrez join my crew...

"I'm giving you seven chores around the starship as punishment! You will scour the decks and help out Amati-Kuis Ursssh in the kitchen," I rendered my verdict. "And don't think you'll get special treatment because of your age. Around here, even Princess Minn-O La-Fin had to work just as hard as everyone else..." there I cut myself off for a second, having realized the La-Varrez dynasty girl was also a Princess by title. "Svetlana Vereshchagina and Destroying Angel will hopefully share some of their clothes and shoes with you. As for where you'll stay..."

"Captain, I request you place the newcomer in my bunk! After all, she has left her family and is also technically your ward just like me. She is also a Gerd in status, so she and I are equals."

What? This day just kept bringing me surprise after surprise. Tini Wi-Gnat, proud of his personal bunk on the starship and having categorically refused all attempts to put anyone else with him before was now suddenly offering this on his own? Come on, that just couldn't be! Unless... I looked at the Psionic Mage class of the little sorceress who was currently putting on a falsely innocent face and looking ashamedly at the floor. Was it perhaps possible that my team's unexpected gregariousness was not in fact coming out of a desire to do good, but rather mind control from the newcomer? After all, I had been told on more than one occasion that Gerd Soia-Tan La-Varrez was a true star of the ancient La-Varrez Dynasty of mage rulers and had massive potential as a psionic. She was even used actively in the war against Tamara's fanatics where the young Psionic Mage had made quite a good showing. Soia-Tan could even boast combat experience in the real world, unlike myself.

And given that, the newcomer had even more potential in my eyes as a useful team member, so letting her join Team Gnat was completely justified. I just needed to dot all the i's first.

"Listen, little one. If you use your abilities on team members without my knowledge again, you'll be tossed out the airlock to learn how to breathe in a vacuum."

By the embarrassed blush on Soia-Tan's face, I could tell right away I wasn't wrong, and she had used psionics. I frowned.

"And if you try to attack me..."

I didn't finish because the little sorceress hurried to cut me off.

"No, no, Archmage Gnat La-Fin. I won't give

you any trouble. I am not suicidal, and I understand who gave me refuge in the First Directory."

Chapter Five

Soia-Tan La-Varrez, Space Witch

I OPENED MY EYES on the cot in my captain's bunk. I finally got plenty of sleep! To feel rested after so many days of frenzied racing around was quite unusual, but very nice! The clock told me I had another two ummi in the subspace tunnel ahead of me, so there was no rush to go anywhere. Out of an old habit, the first thing I did was scan the ship using the skill – I had to figure out what was happening on my frigate!

Okay. The number of markers on the mini-map matches the list of team members, which is most important. The only one on the bridge is co-Pilot San-Doon Taki-Bu. Main Pilot Dmitry Zheltov and Ayukh the Navigator are resting up after their shifts. For some reason there was a big crowd in the bunk of twin brothers Basha and Vasha Tushihh. There I saw the markers of Gerd Uline Tar, Taik Rekh the Gunner and even Avan-Toi the Supercargo. And just how did five large Geckho fit into one small bunk? And what were they up to in there? I zoomed in. Ah, I see. They're playing Na-Tikh-U, a common way for Geckho to pass the time during long flights. This was clearly a tense match if it had amassed such an audience. The only oddity was the fact my Jarg Analyst was also taking part in the game. Ever since the Jarg outplayed twin brothers Basha and Vasha fifty times in a row, they had refused to sit across the three-dimensional holographic board from him again. But now, seemingly, the two Heavy Robot Operators had teamed up with the Supercargo and the three Geckho were together trying to beat the Analyst at this three-dimensional chess game with elements of randomness, cheered on by another two of their furry compatriots. Alright then, we'll see. I personally wanted to know how it turned out.

Chef-Assassin Amati-Kuis Ursssh was in the galley along with little Princess Soia-Tan La-Varrez. Yes, she was being punished as she should have been. Though now I looked back on yesterday's incident with a smile. Why get upset when I myself was once just as disobedient, constantly shocking H3 Faction leadership with my unexpected moves.

A whole group of people was gathered in the exercise room, including the Miyelonian Medic and Trillian Gunner Gerd Ukh-Meemeesh. Based on the positioning of the markers, my bodyguard Gerd Imran and boarding team commander Gerd T'yu-Pan were trying to once and for all settle which of them was the bigger badass. The last time they went head-to-head on the strength trainers and barbells lasted until Imran tore an intercostal muscle. That was why the Medic was standing by. And this time, the beautiful Svetlana Vereshchagina and Destroying Angel had come to watch the athletes as well. The NPC Dryad was also there, so the dispute was one of principle this time and neither of them were going to simply give up. No big deal. Exercise is good for my team's characteristics and skills, while any possible wounds would be quickly healed by the game.

The remaining crew members I found in the common room gathered around the Bard. As you might have imagined, Vasily Filippov was again playing his guitar surrounded by grateful listeners. It should be said that the professional soldier really had a knack for performing original compositions, and the game had a very good reason for awarding him that specific class. A nice activity. Overall, all was quiet aboard the *Tamara the Paladin.*

The only thing that bothered me was the Relict Gerd Urgeh Pu-Pu Urgeh, who was again sitting alone in his bunk rather than coming out to join the rest of the crew. The Relict ignored attempts by the team to get to know him and took as little part as possible in shared activities. With time, that could become a problem. All my attempts to get the Relict out of his shell and integrate him into the crew had not yet met with any success. Gerd Urgeh Pu-Pu Urgeh preferred to stay alone, going into the real world whenever he got the chance and spending a long time MIA. I knew the Technician was busy at the far away Syam Tro VII Refuge getting the artificial planetoid's systems back up and running after millennia of inactivity.

He was communicating with the sanctuary's artificial intelligence and they were trying to figure out a way to get all the equipment back online. He was seeking out failures in power supply lines, replacing inoperable elements, and sorting through spare parts for devices that had gone out of order. He was also slowly but surely draining the flooded levels, trying to get into the still inaccessible rooms of the huge complex.

Working all alone was hard on Urgeh Pu-Pu Urgeh physically, but above all emotionally. The upwelling of enthusiasm I had seen in the Technician after his successful exit into the real world had slowly faded away. He hadn't encountered any living Relicts, and it was an unbearable burden for the member of a once numerous ancient race to constantly see the hundreds of thousands of empty virt pods. Furthermore, food had become a serious issue. The hydroponic farms weren't operating because their seeds and spores had died out over the millennia, while the so-called "invar" the Technician was planning to hunt turned out to be quite dangerous and themselves nearly ate the last Relict in existence, leaving him severely injured. They bit three of Urgeh Pu-Pu Urgeh's limbs off his carapace and tore into his soft yielding belly, just about disemboweling the Relict. How these mysterious predators looked I had yet to uncover because Gerd Urgeh Pu-Pu Urgeh's explanation contained lots of vague and even contradictory elements. Somehow they were both aquatic creatures and able to move through dark narrow corridors the water had already been pumped out of. Perhaps the term "invar" actually referred to more than one biological species. Or various stages of maturity of the same creature like chrysalis – larva – adult.

Fortunately, the game healed his wounds. And given enough food in the game that bends reality, his physical body could go a long time without anything to eat. But it was mainly only to dine, heal and rest after his long grueling work that Gerd Urgeh Pu-Pu Urgeh came back into the game. The Relict didn't feel at home in my crew and avoided talking with them as much as possible.

In theory I could have sent Relict Faction players to help him out. After all, there was nothing stopping me from finding volunteers to set their exit points into the real world as virt pods in the refuge. However, that would be a potentially deadly venture. There was a serious risk my people would find themselves in complete darkness with unknown atmospheric composition and dangerous predatory invars scrounging all around. Or they could find themselves on a completely flooded level.

No, I did not want to put my people at risk. Beyond that, when I tried to discuss helping the Relict repair his shelter, he came out strongly against the idea. For Urgeh Pu-Pu Urgeh, the Syam Tro VII Refuge was his civilization's last remaining territory and he did not want to allow outsiders to visit. I read in the technician's thoughts that he was planning to use the shelter to settle the Relicts we might find on the Hierarch's ship. And the fact that the Syam Tro VII Refuge was not yet ready to receive the survivors was the only reason the

Technician had yet to insist I keep my promise and go help the Hierarch at once. Which was fine by me.

So alright, I had figured out the situation on the frigate. I got dressed and cleaned myself up. But before going to see the team, I took care of one last important thing – I needed to decide what direction to take my character. Until recently, I had been doggedly levelling my Gnat's skills toward being able to one day use the Tachyon Bender. But now that the accessory had taken its place in the ancient Listener armor suit, I needed a new reference point to aim for. I opened my stats window.

Kung Gnat. Human. Relict Faction.	
Level-109 Listener	
Statistics:	
Strength	14
Agility	18
Intelligence	39 + 7
Perception	35 + 2
Constitution	18
Luck modifier	+3
Controlled drones	3 of 3
Parameters:	
Hitpoints	2570 of 2570
Endurance points	1832 of 1832
Magic points	3187 of 3229
Carrying capacity	62 lbs.
Fame	110
Authority	115
Skills:	
Electronics	103 * First specialization

	taken
Scanning	*81*
Cartography	*90*
Astrolinguistics	*111 * First specialization taken*
Rifles	*68*
Mineralogy	*61*
Medium Armor	*104 * First specialization taken*
Eagle Eye	*113 * First specialization taken*
Sharpshooter	*55*
Targeting	*73*
Danger Sense	*143 * First specialization taken*
Psionic	*131 * First specialization taken*
Mental Fortitude	*128 * First specialization taken*
Machine Control	*116 * First specialization taken*
Mysticism	*85*
Telekinesis	*60*
Training	*47*
Disorientation	*42*
Attention!!! You have three unspent skill points.	

There was an ever-stronger slant toward psionic abilities, but guns and everything connected with them were lagging behind. I was also bothered by Scanning – though it was a skill I used all the time, every time it cooled down as a matter of fact, I had only gotten it up to eighty-one even though my character was already at one hundred and nine. I had to do something about that. Ideally, I would take an armful of geological analyzers and visit a series of asteroids in search of valuable minerals. At the same time, I would be pulling up Minerology and Cartography. However, where was I supposed to find the free time for that?

It would also be nice to start visiting the firing range regularly to bring up my lagging shooting skills. That was much easier to remedy though – we'd be in flight for another two ummi, and I could do some shooting at the frigate's gun range. Astrolinguistics I could also improve by talking with Trillians, the Relict and the Jarg in my crew.

But first and foremost my Gnat was a listener, and that class was intended to use psionics and work with mechanical devices. The total number of Magic Points and their restore speed were becoming more critical all the time. And so I invested all three free skill points into Mysticism then closed the window and went out to see my team.

"Son of a...!" I could hardly resist using psionic magic when a sinister figure wrapped in a dark robe came around the corner of the hallway to greet me with a hood over their head.

"Greetings, Captain Gnat!"

Before me, her eyes staring ashamedly at the

floor with a pile of dirty dishes in her hands stood Gerd Soia-Tan La-Varrez. She was dressed in something resembling a hybrid between a Catholic nun's dark habit and a witch's robe. I don't know where Svetlana Vereshchagina and Destroying Angel had dug up the dark garment on the star frigate, but I had questions for them. I asked the young sorceress to set the dirty dishes on the table and follow me, going straight into the gym.

When the captain entered, the team started their training exercises while Gerd Ukh-Meemeesh the Trillian helped the boarding team leader as he wheezed in tension, plucking the five-hundred-pound barbel off the man's chest using one hand without apparent effort.

I gestured for the Assassin and Gunfighter to step forward, and asked:

"I won't ask what roleplay games you were keeping this habit in your wardrobe for," I pointed at the embarrassed Soia-Tan standing next to me. "But do you really think this is any way for a thirteen-year-old girl to dress? Couldn't find any decent pants or skirts? You must be big fans of *Star Wars* given how you've dressed our Psionic Mage. She's basically Soia-Tan La-Varrez, space witch!"

"Why not? Our enemies' morale will take a hit as soon as they see her!" Space Commando Eduard Boyko laughed happily, and a few other crew members supported him.

But I didn't find this mockery of a high-level Princess from the ancient La-Varrez dynasty to be anything to laugh at. Which I told the team.

"But, Captain, she asked us to sew her that

exact outfit!" Svetlana Vereshchagina objected, clearly not understanding the reason I was bothered. " I had to sacrifice my camouflage Assassin suit to carry out the girl's request, and Destroying Angel cut up one of her dresses."

"Did you ask for this?" I turned to the little Princess for explanations and she nodded to confirm.

"Yes, Coruler Gnat La-Fin. I... it wasn't much, just a tiny bit, but I did some digging in the crew's thoughts and realized it would be a dramatic look. But that wasn't the main reason!" the girl practically shouted out the last part when she saw the frown appearing on my face. "It's just that I keep having the same dream over and over again. But this time it was especially clear and vivid. It's like a warning or a vision of the future. Here it is."

A flood of thoughts and images came crashing down on me. Indistinct, blurry. I had to relax and put my mental guard down to make sense of the "picture."

A huge room. Human guards lining the walls in power armor. Behind them... unidentifiable tall creatures that are definitely not human. Massive insects that look like praying mantises, but not Meleyephatians and not Relicts. Before them, a carved throne and seated upon it is a plump middle-aged monarch in a dark-blue army uniform with gold epaulettes. The King's face has an old jagged scar running across his whole cheek and forehead. Good thing his eye didn't get hurt. There is a young Queen sitting to the monarch's right with a doll face and pure white hair. To his left... That's odd. It's an empty chair. And above it on the wall is a portrait of a very dramatic looking woman with red hair and a bright crimson dress to match with a deep neckline. And in the middle of the room... Surprising. Two girls with their hands thrust forward standing opposite one another in identical black robes going down to their very feet while the air between them sparked and hummed with tension.

The vision flooded out of my mind and I found myself again standing in the *Tamara the Paladin*'s exercise room. But for some reason my hands were shaking, and my Magic Points were down to zero. I wiped sweat from my brow. What even was that?

Psionic skill increased to level one hundred thirty-two!

"I am the smaller of the two girls," the Psionic Mage told me. "I don't know who my opponent is. All I know is that she finds it hard to walk and barely speaks. But at that she is an extremely powerful psionic and very deadly! And this is not simply a meaningless dream. I consulted with relatives, then Gerd Mac-Peu Un-Roi the Mage Diviner. They are all of the opinion that I am seeing a vision of a probable future. A very important episode in the lines of the probable future, the outcome of which will define the course of history. And it is a battle I cannot lose!"

Chapter Six

The Price of Domination

"**C**APTAIN, DON'T BE MAD, but maybe this just isn't your thing!" the leader of the boarding team Gerd T'yu-Pan patted me condescendingly on the shoulder, taking away my last unthrown knife.

I must confess that, after spending several hours in a row shooting a light rifle at erratically moving targets and levelling my shooting skills tiny bit by tiny bit, I was fed up. I brought up my Sharpshooter by one point, but that was all. The result clearly did not justify the time wasted. Now here I was trying to take part in my troops' training session where they were learning to throw knives at targets shaped like Meleyephatians and various other spacefaring races. Some might cringe at that and ask what good are knives in battle when everyone has a modern laser weapon? But Gerd T'yu-Pan had a different opinion, saying starkly that the enemy cannot fire a gun with their hand disabled. They also can't use Psionics with a knife sticking out of their head – and the large head was in fact the weak point of the spiderlike Meleyephatians, who also usually did not wear armor there, or at least left it only partially covered. Furthermore, there was nowhere in the galaxy where melee weaponry was banned unlike firearms, which were forbidden on many space stations.

But... not on mine. Without the corresponding skills and with utterly middling Agility, my Gnat could only hit the target every other time, which was to say nothing of the fact that some of them didn't go in at all or bounced away, much to my embarrassment. Compared to the others, especially Chef-Assassin Amati-Kuis, seemingly having been born with throwing knives in her hands, I looked truly weak and at times even comical. But I didn't give up and asked to be given one more chance. This time I decided to change tactics and use Intelligence rather than Agility, which my character was much stronger in.

The six knives laid out on the table raised up into the air, hovered there for a second and went racing forward. Hit! All six targets fell, and I hit their weak spots, which were labeled with red markers. A few of the targets I actually pierced straight through, which even the strongest team members couldn't do. The condescending smiles on my team's faces gave way to looks of surprise. Another set of blades, and another rousing success.

"Ooh... ah!" my Chef Assassin shuddered in fear when the miniature poison blades attached to the top of her claws broke away from their anchors and went spinning in the air like a fanciful carousel of danger.

Go! Obeying my will, all six of the poisoned missiles stuck into the exact center of the distant target with such dense grouping that it would have been hard to do better by hand. Gerd T'yu-Pan walked up to the target, looked it over and gave a few approving claps:

"Impressive!" the huge Shocktroop suddenly got down on one knee and tilted his head. "Mage-ruler Gnat La-Fin, I beg apologies for my insolence. I forgot what powerful mages can do and allowed myself to say unforgivable things. It will not happen again! I swear it!"

Successful Authority check!

That cursed servile attitude toward mages, beaten into him since childhood... But the thing I was not expecting at all was for the other members of the boarding team to follow suit and bow as well. Even Imran, who had no relation to the magocratic world and had been with me since day one in the game copied T'yu-Pan's gesture and got down on one knee. Tini, too. Taik Rekh, as well. Even the Trillian girl Amati-Kuis lowered the front half of her body to the very floor. I could feel an invisible but undeniable wall going up between me and my team. It was as if I had fallen out of the social circle and become an outsider.

I didn't enjoy that and rebuked myself for the lack of restraint. I never should have put on this Telekinesis show and demonstrated how vast the chasm was dividing Kungs from Gerds, much less common players. I mean, what was the point? Was

I so hard up for Authority? Did I want to bolster my self-esteem and show off in front of my own team?

The only one still standing was the little Princess of the La-Varrez dynasty, Gerd Soia-Tan. The little mage on the other hand liked what she had seen and didn't even attempt to hide the smile of satisfaction. My assistant Gerd Ayni also hesitated for a few seconds, but stayed upright nevertheless.

"On your feet, friends. And get back to training," I said in the sudden silence, after which I tried to somewhat smooth over the negativity and blow down the new wall of alienation. "Gerd T'yu-Pan, let me remind you that you are not only the head of my boarding team, but also my advisor in magocratic world affairs. I expect honesty from you, not servility. And that means sometimes not only is the occasional belittling comment acceptable, but in fact necessary. When you're done at the range, come to my bunk. We need to have a talk."

The leader of the boarding team bowed respectfully, and I turned to little mage Soia-Tan La-Varrez.

"Little one, I also expect you in the captain's berth for a meeting. It is important for me to know what the old dynasties will think about my proposed changes, and you will do great as a representative of the La-Varrez mage-rulers. For you it will be a chance to prove yourself and be given a place in the future government, so I expect you to bring the utmost engagement, seriousness and openness."

The young psionic girl's eyes lit up and she

promised to give everything she had to prove herself.

I was sitting in my bunk looking through the Relict Faction's innumerable pages of financial reports and unpaid bills. I'll admit, it was enough to make me scratch my head. No, I had heard from my Chief Advisor Gerd Mac-Peu Un-Roi that finances were strained, and he even had to pawn one of the three Tiopeo-Myhh II interceptors to pay some vendors. But still I didn't think the situation was quite this dismal. We had definitely gone into the red with this explosive expansion, new nodes, many construction projects and army draft... To be precise, we were down seventeen million Geckho monetary crystals. And although the Kung of Earth's Authority and reputation as a swashbuckling Free Captain had allowed several contracts for weaponry or construction materials to be paid upon delivery, and the suppliers didn't demand payment upfront, the day was nevertheless inexorably approaching.

We would have to pay four and a half million monetary crystals just to my business partner Uline Tar for delivery of planetary shield generators on the huge Kitivaru transport ship. That contract though was for payment upon delivery and unloading, so we had another ten days before it would come due. The other issue was that I for now saw no sources of financing I could use to pay Uline in any kind of reasonable timeframe. The platinum mine on the asteroid and trade profits brought the Relict Faction and its leader money, but all that was going to paying off a snowballing expense account. And I was forced to constantly invest my personal finances into supporting my own faction. In fact, it was only thanks to those investments that the situation had not spun out of control and turned into a complete catastrophe.

The Relict Faction had been given claim to twenty-three nodes on the southern peninsula but getting them up to level two would require investment – around sixty thousand crystals a piece, not including expenses for developing the infrastructure there. Doesn't sound like much when taken separately, but in total it added up to a tidy sum. And other than the "southern strip," we were building a high-speed causeway to the Chinese Faction, oil refineries and petrochemical plants, a cargo port and a thermonuclear power plant. We also couldn't ignore the six new nodes on the western shore of the bay around the Geckho spaceport or the three distant nodes on the opposite end of the continent that previously belonged to the North American H8 Faction.

And after all, there weren't only big construction projects on the "small" continent. I also had the "big" continent of the virtual Earth to think about, and it all needed money, money and more money. Beyond level-one and -two nodes, the Relict Faction also had level three, four and even five areas. All of them needed to be developed and built up, while future development costs would be an order of magnitude higher. Another good chunk of money was going to the new ambitious'project to get together spaceships for the Relict Faction. Blueprints for them had been drawn up by the greatest Constructor of all terrestrial factions Gerd Alex Bobl after studying the technology of other spacefaring races together with a whole team of Scientists and Engineers from allied factions.

The first two Sio-Fa-Urukh corvettes ("Defender" in translation from the language of the magocratic world) were Near-Earth Atmospheric fighters and were already being assembled in hangars on a site once occupied by the plains of the Poppy Fields node. In fact, two thirds of the parts for the corvettes had been made at my Relict Faction's factories. We were only buying particularly hard-to-produce parts such as defensive shields, gravity compensators and modern computers. We had also not fitted the ships with hyperspace drives to bring down construction costs. We only planned to use the corvettes inside the Solar System anyway. The Sio-Fa-Urukhs were fitted with enhanced shields though as well as fully-fledged maneuver drives and main thrusters, along with decent laser and rocket weaponry. These starships cost no more than two million Geckho crystals, but in battle a Defender could easily go toe-to-toe with a Meleyephatian frigate in Raider or Long-Distance Raider configuration, or a pair of interceptors. At any rate, what mattered most was that the Relict Faction could produce such corvettes all on its own in the medium-term, meaning we would no longer depend on deliveries from deep space.

I didn't even consider freezing expenditures on the corvette construction lines to save money – Earth having a space fleet was of vital importance. I couldn't just stop some of the construction either because there wasn't very much time left before the countdown would be up and to successfully complete the mission of keeping both planets in existence, I needed to control more than fifty percent of the virtual planet's game nodes. And that meant ever more aggressive expansion, a constantly expanding roster of players for completing tasks, capturing more uninhabited territory and... again more expenses for building them up. Yes, with time all these acquisitions would start to turn a profit, but right now the new nodes brought only expenses.

Furthermore, the thirty-percent tribute we paid to the suzerains on all resources extracted and profits on goods sold was a heavy burden to bear. Yes, the Geckho were rubbing their hands together in glee when they saw their vassal factions' significantly higher income streams and were using these funds for nonstop construction work next to the spaceport and at other locations on the planet. But for the Relict Faction, this tribute was a heavy burden and the only possible way to be rid of it would be for Earth's humanity to be granted independence. But a step that decisive would require expanded military capabilities as well as financial and political clout.

So what to do now? Where to get money? Take out a loan from a Geckho or Miyelonian bank?

I suspected that such a famed Free Captain wouldn't be turned away, especially if I put up my starship *Tamara the Paladin* as collateral. The value of my twinbody with the best equipment was sixty million Geckho crystals minimum, so the loan was sure to be approved. However, I very much did not want to find myself in servitude to a bunch of slick-talking alien financiers. In fact, my Danger Sense skill piped up when I even considered it.

My musings were interrupted by Gerd Uline Tar, who this time used her key to come into the captain's berth without knocking. The huge furry Geckho woman plopped down next to me and growled out:

"Gnnnat, you sad again? Ever since Minn-O and Valeri-Urla left the crew, it's like there's no light in your life."

"It isn't about them... well, they are part of it. It's just that there are problems building up all around me. And the team's behavior today really upset me..."

I told my business partner what happened today at the gun range and my other concerns. The burdensome political crisis in the magocratic world. Financial problems. I couldn't spend too long in the real world. I wanted to get it all off my chest, and there was no one else for me to pour out my soul to. The Trader listened to me carefully, never once interrupting. Then she responded to every point in detail.

"Such is the price of domination, Gnnnat. The Relict Faction declared itself the hegemon of terrestrial factions, and now there's no turning back. You'd be eaten alive. You can only afford constantly accelerating forward motion, even though that is inevitably linked to expenses. And I must admit, I am surprised there haven't been any attempts on your life yet. Earth leaders both from your world and the magocratic one aren't just going to let their rule slip between their fingers and getting rid of you would be the most obvious solution. Always remember that and stay on guard in the real world. As for finances, I can help. I'll look for delivery contracts we can pick up in Serpea and see what goods are most promising for trade. Furthermore, it wouldn't be too hard for me to get thirty million loaned by relatives. In fact, they offered during the wedding to help 'build up my trading enterprise.' I could get a large amount, too... A very large amount even. But that would require a detailed project outline showing dividends and some kind of guarantee. And what about the team's opinion...?"

Uline rumbled in satisfaction, embracing me with her big powerful paws, squeezing me tight and, looking me top to bottom, bared her teeth in a happy smile.

"Don't you worry about that, Gnnnat. Such is a leader's burden. There's no way to become a big influential Kung and remain a normal player, open to a talk with anyone they come across. Even after I became a Gerd, I noticed old girlfriends who used to come to me for a chat or to gossip about their gentlemen callers started giving me a wider berth. They're afraid to bother me over minor issues, not wanting to distract me from important business as one of them admitted. Now just think how much different it is for a Kung! As far as most players are concerned, you're a legend, an untouchable star. They're afraid to even come near you. But know that you have loyal friends you can always be yourself around. I am one of those friends. And I think I have an idea for how to boost your mood..."

A measured knock at the door interrupted Uline's speech, and my business partner sharply fell silent midsentence. She even slowly covered her mouth with a broad furry paw as if she'd just said something she shouldn't have. What idea was that? I used Psionics a bit later and realized that "boosting my mood" was somehow connected with going into the real world to see my tailed orange girlfriend Gerd Ayni the Miyelonian. I didn't even try reading thoughts because I was so let down. Now Uline Tar was trying to give unsolicited advice about my relationship with the orange Miyelonian Translator. I admit, I was expecting my business partner, someone who knew me quite well, to do something less boring and predictable.

Then, somewhat ashamed, Gerd Soia-Tan La-Varrez and Gerd T'yu-Pan walked into the captain's bunk. My business partner didn't inconvenience them further with her presence and went out into the hallway. I pointed the pair to an armchair and couch, after which we started discussing the changes I wanted to make to the magocratic world as ruler of the First Directory and one of the three remaining mage-rulers and sole Archmage.

No, I was not planning to touch the fundamental principles of magocracy because that would be just too radical a step. Society wasn't ready for such big changes and would be up in arms. But repealing the majority of the utterly senseless limitations to the rights of people with no magical abilities was an obvious step. For example, common people could not hold offices such as the CEOs of large companies or banks, head scientific institutes or occupy high administrative posts such as city mayors, provincial governors or Directory leaders. The example of the very successful and respected ruler of the Second Directory General Ui Taka showed that this ban was now antiquated, was not being upheld and had to be repealed.

The ancient ban on "mixed" marriages between mages and nonmages was also begging to be abolished. With boisterous declarations about the sanctity of ancient law, mages regularly broke it when they stood to gain – an example of that were the marriages of Coruler Thumor-Anhu La-Fin's nonmagical children, or the classic example of Minn-O La-Fin, who was supposed to be forcibly married off to a mage from house La-Varrez for the sake of the ancient La-Fin dynasty's line of succession.

The two parallel judicial systems for mages and nonmages was also an outdated concept, and I suggested bringing them together. But the most important step I proposed was the creation of a parliament with members elected from the common population of all sixteen Directories. That would serve as a safety valve to release societal tension and give a chance to the most well-known and active citizens with no magical powers to express themselves in a fully legal fashion with no rebellions or revolutions. The old Council of Mage Rulers would retain the right to veto laws passed by the parliament, but I was certain the wise mages wouldn't abuse that so the peoples' uprising that scared so many would not happen again.

And at the pinnacle of the pyramid of power would be three rulers chosen from among the very strongest mages on the planet, as it was before in the magocratic world. I named myself one of the corulers. Another spot was reserved for a member of the La-Varrez dynasty. As for the third candidate, I was willing to put it up for discussion with all the ancient dynasties. I also turned down the chance to give myself more authority than the other two corulers, even though in theory there was nothing to stop me from taking such rights. Yes, I remembered my conversation with Minn-O La-Fin where she suggested I make myself the sole ruler, but I wasn't confident I could do that without a lot of bloodshed.

Despite how easily understandable my theses seemed, a bunch of minor issues and challenges cropped up, so the discussion went on for a while. For example, how to protect a judge presiding over a psionic mage's trial. Mental defense would be an absolute necessity, otherwise the defendant would be guaranteed to walk away scot-free no matter what crime they may have committed. Or the number of parliament members and a strict formula governing representatives per territory depending on population. Also how to avoid that parliament grinding to a halt if two or more

Directories found themselves at war.

We even invited another three natives of the magocratic world – Engineer San-Sano, Timka-Vu the Machinegunner and San-Doon Taki-Bu the Pilot – to join in the talks. And the longer we discussed the new changes, the finer the details and sticking points we uncovered. But then suddenly, our conversation was interrupted by a message on the loudspeaker from Starship Pilot Dmitry Zheltov.

"Kung Gnat, please report to the captain's bridge. Your presence is required," the player's voice was shaking in worry.

A few seconds before that, I sensed our frigate leave hyperspace into normal space. Had something gone wrong with our exit from hyper? A technical glitch of some kind? I instantly hopped up out of the flying armchair and dashed off to my workstation. Woah... This really was something that had to be seen in person. The blue star was so bright that even our dimming filters couldn't fully suppress its blinding light. A huge spindle-shaped space station was two hundred fifty miles from us. Other than that there were thousands of stationary and moving objects on the radar and big screen – starships, autonomous shuttles, palaces of the local elite and the hulls of old starships refitted as residential structures all hurtling through space.

Cartography skill increased to level ninety-one!

Eagle Eye skill increased to level one hundred twelve!

But that wasn't what mattered. Very near our

frigate, there was a whole flotilla of Meleyephatian combat ships. No less than two hundred of them. Frigates, support ships, a pair of strike cruisers and even one huge battleship of an unusual shape compared to normal Meleyephatian ones. I read its information. *Pikiuro*, meaning "splendor" in Miyelonian. Strange. A Horde ship with a Miyelonian name?

I looked it up in the ship search engine and read the information that came on screen. It had been captured eight tongs ago at dock in an unfinished state during the most recent conflict between the Horde and the Miyelonians. After the peace agreement, the Union of Miyelonian Prides had attempted on several occasions to purchase the huge ship back, but the leaders of the Meleyephatian Horde were unwavering in their refusal. To them it was as honorable a trophy as the severed tail of an enemy on a Miyelonian's helmet. The computer also told me the *Pikiuro* was currently serving as flagship for flotilla seventeen, a part of the Horde's Eighth Fleet, which was taking part in the war against the Geckho.

So all these ships were at war with the Geckho... And they probably had not come to the home system of a Geckho vassal by accident. The nearest of the Meleyephatian Horde ships were less than one hundred miles away, so our frigate was easily within shooting range of the flotilla's on-board cannons.

It was too late to take any evasive maneuvers. Furthermore, our equipment had already detected heightened interest in the *Tamara the Paladin* from the Meleyephatian flotilla – we were being scanned actively by several of the ships. But why wasn't the combat alert sounding automatically?! I asked that question to the officers on the bridge.

"I don't know either," Dmitry Zheltov shrugged his shoulders. "I wanted to do it manually, captain, but the on-board computer marked all ships on the tactical grid as neutral, with white dots. And the Meleyephatians really are not displaying any aggression, just scanning our ship. They aren't even targeting. Their ships are waiting in line to dock at the Serpea-III station. And the Cleopian patrol ships aren't attacking them either!"

Impossible! It sounded preposterous. Sure, I could understand about our frigate. I was a Free Captain, and basically neutral again. The Meleyephatian Horde had revoked my enemy status for some reason. But why weren't the local spaceships and defensive artillery attacking the Meleyephatians? The Cleopians were Geckho vassals, and the Geckho were engaged in a bloody war with the Meleyephatian Horde. And here Horde ships were in Cleopian space and being provided access to dock, service and repair. Had something in this life escaped my understanding? What the heck was going on?

Chapter Seven

Seeking Common Ground

I ORDERED THE STARSHIP PILOT not to make any thoughtless abrupt maneuvers and just get in line behind the rest of the ships to dock at the space station.

"Tamara the Paladin, *state the purpose of your visit to the Serpea System!*"

The message in Geckho came from the space station dispatchers and was simultaneously doubled from the fearsome space citadel. It was a simple standard question asked to all arriving starships, but how was I to respond under current circumstances? I suspected it would be stupid to announce to the local services that we had come here to seek aid in a war against the Meleyephatian Horde and establish trade and military ties as Geckho vassals. Based on the large number of Horde combat ships in the system, working with the Geckho was best left unmentioned. We hadn't brought any goods to sell, and our obviously military ship made it impossible to pose as peaceable traders. But then what should I say?

My attention was drawn by the Analyst sitting next to me – Gerd Jarg had the Universal Translator around his neck and was fervently gesticulating with all six of his appendages.

"Capitan. Very high probability. Cleopians to overthrow government. New ruler rescind vassal agreement with Geckho. War with Geckho. Found other suzerain. Think is more strong. Meleyephatian Horde. Masters. Overthrow is to take place sixteen to twenty ummi ago. This is how long Horde seventeen flotilla fly from Daal, where they to be. Small ships not enter dock. Also. So no more than twenty ummi of time. But old Cleopian ruler be alive. There not to be message his death. Still alive. Soon to execute. Cleopian tradition do not to leave competitor. For power."

I see... Or rather I don't see. Given that state of affairs, should we have been docking at the station? After all, they might not let us go after. Might the Meleyephatians want to confiscate my starship? After all, I was reminded that an influential member of the Meleyephatian Horde once demanded I return this twinbody frigate to him.

"Tamara the Paladin, state the purpose of your visit to the Serpea System!"

Same question again. It would be ill advised to keep them waiting because, according to fundamental rules common to the entire the galaxy, a ship was declared hostile after not responding to the third request from a dispatcher with all the accompanying consequences. Well, I sincerely hoped the Jarg's calculations were not wrong.

"This is Kung Gnat speaking, captain of the *Tamara the Paladin*. The purpose of my visit is to meet the former ruler Edeyya-U. I would like to speak with your former King while he's still alive. It's a personal question. Totally unconnected with the political situation in Serpea and the greater space war."

I had seemingly managed to catch the local dispatchers off guard. They took a long time to respond, seven minutes at least even though a response normally came instantly.

Fame increased to 111.

Seemingly, the local services were actively searching all possible sources and painstakingly studying all available information about Kung Gnat the Listener. For the record, the Cleopians had yet to officially announce their change in governance, so let Serpea and the Meleyephatian Hordes' intelligence services rack their brains over where I learned the old monarch had been deposed and why I suddenly wanted to talk to him.

"Denied. Free Captain Kung Gnat, state the true purpose of your visit to the Serpea star system."

Pretty stubborn... But I had also decided to display integrity and not give any other explanation for my visit.

"I repeat. My sole purpose is to speak with your former King Edeyya-U before his execution. A personal conversation. I need to ask him about ancient races. Relicts, Precursors, Mechanoids. Edeyya-U has the knowledge I require. The information is highly valuable and might help in the fight against the Composite."

This time the response came much quicker, less than a minute even.

"*Clarification required. Is the Kung of Earth also planning an official visit to the new ruler of Serpea and its inhabited rings, King Peyeru-Y the Eleventh?*"

Good question. I suspected the new ruler had already received a report about my starship's visit to his holdings, and the monarch was intrigued to have such an unexpected guest. But what need did I have for this meeting? And how would Geckho ruler Krong Daveyesh-Pir look on the fact I was holding behind-the-scenes negotiations with enemies? But a refusal would be impolite and insult the new monarch of the Cleopians. And by the way, the Cleopians had just confirmed that they really had changed rulers! Things like that justified having an Analyst in my crew. Gerd Jarg really earned his bread.

"Yes, I would like to meet King Peyeru-Y the Eleventh. If of course such a busy monarch can find the time for me. And if I don't have to wait too long for this audience. I can only spend a few ummi in Serpea and cannot stay any longer."

After giving my response to the station dispatchers, I turned on the frigate's loudspeaker.

"Avan Toi, go into the real world and inform the Geckho the government has been overthrown in Serpea and the Cleopians have sworn allegiance to the Meleyephatian Horde. The Geckho may not yet bet aware. Gerd Ayni Uri-Miayuu and Gerd Ukh-

Meemeesh, you do the same. Tell the Miyelonians and Trillians."

As soon as I'd given my orders, the dispatchers came back with their answer:

"You have been permitted to access the station. Dock eight. Welcome to Serpea, Free Captain Kung Gnat!"

"The only ones coming with me to the ruler's palace will be Gerd Ayni the Translator and Gerd Imran to pilot the shuttle and serve as my bodyguard. All others have leisure time. Keep the frigate guarded, but nothing more. Our goal is to project an air of relaxation, emphasizing with our behavior that we are no enemies to the locals. I have transferred five thousand crystal bonuses to every team member. Stroll around the shops in the spaceport zone, see the sights, go to bars and entertainment areas. Basically, let loose and get some R and R. Don't get into any disputes with members of spacefaring races whether political, religious, historical or otherwise. Basically behave with pride and confidence. Remember you are part of the team of a famed Free Captain, you are the best of the best, a true space elite. Any questions?"

"Captain, what about the Geckho?" asked Supercargo Avan Toi. "Can we also go onto the station?"

"Well, why not? Our starship is neutral, we are not involved in this war. So if you come across any Meleyephatians, no need to reach for your blasters or get into a firefight. Just walk past and don't give in to any possible provocations. But if there is a conflict, call me on the radio. The palace of the ruler is very nearby, on the top of the station on the bright side. A five-minute flight. So I'll fly over quick and figure things out."

Authority increased to 116!

The team believed in their captain and had no doubts about my abilities to sort out any possible trouble. Ugh, I wish I had their confidence... I put on a steely calm for the team, but inside cats were scratching. What could I talk to the Horde's new vassal King about? I saw no common ground whatsoever.

Gerd Imran walked up to me in his red armor suit and, putting up his face shield, reported:

"Captain, the shuttle is ready. But the gift couldn't fit in the baggage hold, so we had to put the box on the back seat. I hope the Miyelonian can fit next to it. Otherwise, I'm afraid Gerd Ayni will have to climb into the baggage hold..."

I walked up closer to the small shuttle. Yes, practically all the space in the back was taken up by a large plastic container that held a special gift for King Peyeru-Y the Eleventh. It just felt wrong to fly off and meet a crown ruler empty-handed, so we had to hurriedly prepare a present befitting the title of the ruler of the Serpea system. However, now it was taking up too much space. Even the scrawny, short Miyelonian couldn't fit on the seat next to me, especially in a space suit. Bring the gift unpackaged? I didn't want to because that would mean losing the element of surprise.

"I can stand!" the Miyelonian assured me, but I decided otherwise.

"You'll sit on my lap. The whole galaxy is gossiping about our 'close relationship' as it is, so let's toss them some more grain for the rumor mill."

The shuttle lifted off, slowly starting up and carefully slipping through the forcefield separating our dock from the vacuum of the long maneuver corridor. The Cleopian dispatchers assigned my *Tamara the Paladin* a very honorable parking spot — a large hangar that could easily fit three starships of its size. And most importantly, it was the very first in the eighth maneuver tunnel, so our frigate didn't have to endure a snail's-pace crawl down a miles-long shaft behind other starships.

"Turn on dimming!" I advised Gerd Imran, and my timing was impeccable.

Even with the armored glass set to maximum light filtration, the blue star of Serpea was blinding. Despite all his usual restraint, the shuttle pilot uttered a string of curse words, covering his eyes with a hand and complaining he basically had to fly by touch. Nevertheless, Gerd Imran steered the flying vehicle confidently along the hull of the space station, trying to keep inside the artificial gravitation zone and directing us around all the protruding elements. Within three minutes, we could already see the glimmering sphere of the forcefield on the very tip of the spindle-shaped station. And there, the most prestigious location, was where the new monarch of the Cleopians had his dwelling place.

Two local interceptors headed out to cut us off but, obeying an unheard order, turned sharply and made way. The low-speed shuttle slipped through the force-field and set down on a totally vacant flying vehicle pad.

There was someone waiting to greet us. Four Meleyephatian troopers in attack armor surrounded the shuttle and, making no attempt to hide it, scanned us with a device that looked like a blow drier. One of the troopers chirred something out.

"We have been requested to leave our weapons in the shuttle," Gerd Ayni translated, removing her helmet and shaking out her mane of orange hair. "And they are asking what the big thing we brought is."

"Tell them it's a gift for the ruler. Also tell them I must keep the Annihilator with me – it is a ritual weapon to which all Listeners are entitled by status, and I cannot go without a mandatory element of my Relict armor."

In fact, I simply didn't want to leave my priceless weapon unattended because I wasn't totally sure it would be there when I got back. Furthermore, the Annihilator served as something of a guarantee the Meleyephatians couldn't capture me if they decided to turn hostile. I had yet to change my respawn point, so shooting myself once in the head was a surefire way to get back to the Geckho spaceport on Earth in fifteen minutes' time.

And another thing...

Scanning skill increased to level eighty-two!

"Ayni, tell them to have the other troopers reveal themselves. It isn't polite to greet a high-status Kung while cloaked, especially when I can see them just fine as is. And have them help carry the gift. It's too heavy for my bodyguard to carry on his own."

Successful Authority check!

There was a slight delay, but five seconds later another thirty eight-armed troopers appeared around us. Large and draped in the distorted light of their camouflage suits, their weapons were at the ready and they looked upset to have been unmasked. Two of the "spiders" took the box obediently and dragged it to where I pointed.

We walked along a path made of small porous granules toward the middle of an odd park, which was packed densely with identical short and spiny greenish brown little trees, which had short, seemingly trimmed branches. Growing plants bearing a strong resemblance to Cleopians must have been a local art form. An odd suspicion cropped up in my head and I took a closer look. Yes, that's right. They actually were Cleopians, but for some reason they were inactive and somehow dormant. There were several hundred, perhaps even a thousand.

"They're dead, but not all the way," my Miyelonian companion said in Russian, clearly not wishing for the Meleyephatians to understand us. "All their brain nodes and sense organs have been removed. Just their bodies remain. Without minds, the bodies cannot make the conscious decision to leave the game, and the player dies in the real world in short order. Here the body remains as a trophy to please the eye of the victor. With good lighting and regular watering, Cleopians can grow in this form forever. For the most part, they are former rulers and famed political leaders that lost power struggles."

It's cruel, but such is the price of defeat. And there is the lone living Cleopian in this corpse park – in the middle of a shallow water basin there stood a greenish-brown gnarled "cactus" whose long limbs were untrimmed and shifting around. He was staring pensively with his sole black eye at a big round raft floating on the surface of the water, which was topped with an interactive screen depicting differently colored markers. There were several shades of red, a dozen varieties of green, a few yellows, a lone orange and many dark blue dots. They were revolving on the screen in endless circles and arcs around a bright blue center. A map of the Serpea star system?

I read the hydrotherapy patient's information though I had already guessed who it was.

Leng Peyeru-Y. Cleopian. Dark Red Faction. Level-189 Aristocrat.

Just a Leng? Not the Krong of his people, not even a Kung? I looked over at the round screen. There were a lot of the dark red markers, but they were nowhere near predominant and even got lost in the sea of dark blue and pink ones. If my understanding of the political situation was correct, the new ruler who had just overthrown the previous King was in quite a shaky position. And meanwhile the King turned his eye from the interactive board to me and my companions. Considering the possible consequences, I nevertheless did not bend the knee and limited myself to a polite standing bow. Imran and Ayni followed my lead.

The ruler buzzed out a long emotional message and Gerd Ayni got straight to translating it into Geckho:

"His Majesty King Peyeru-Y the Eleventh is pointing out the Human trooper's Geckho officer armor. In fact, it has an honorary inscription from Second Strike Fleet Commander Kung Waid Shishish on it. And he asks whether Kung Gnat the Human knows how to kill members of the Cleopian race."

What? Is he afraid of me and Imran? Yes, I could sense the ruler's fear. And it was strong, verging on uncontrollable panic. Does he think the Geckho sent assassins to get revenge for the betrayal and defection? Our suzerains would of course appreciate the gesture, but after such an attack we would never be able to leave this park and we'd have to kiss our frigate goodbye. I was also glad that I had left my Small Relict Guard Drones back on the frigate, otherwise the King would have had a stroke.

"Tell him that your captain had yet to contemplate that issue because there was no need to do so. And also ask him who needs killing? Advise him that my services do not come cheap. And if it will mean having to sacrifice my neutral status, they will be VERY not cheap."

By the way the Cleopian started shifting around and blinking his lone eye before my companion finished translating, it was clear he was quite familiar with the language of his former suzerains and my response calmed the King down quickly and even amused him. But... what is that? My head felt heavy for a few seconds.

Mental Fortitude skill increased to level one hundred twenty-nine!

Is someone around here trying to read my thoughts? It couldn't have been the monarch himself – Cleopians weren't known for their great psionic abilities. It was probably one of the innumerable Meleyephatian bodyguards assigned to the usurper. Or even a few of them. I couldn't hide the smirk when the three Spiders standing at the edge of the pool stumbled and one even pulled in his limbs, falling into the water with a great splash. It would be stupid to try to attack me mentally without enhanced Intelligence! Considering the two Intelligence rings on Gnat's fingers, I now had that stat up at forty-six. And if none of the Meleyephatians here had Intelligence of at least thirty-seven, even trying to dig into my thoughts was a laughable notion!

Telekinesis skill increased to level one hundred twenty-nine!

The head of the stunned Meleyephatian and a large part of his body was underwater and before the unconscious "spider" drowned, I used magic to lift him and drag him onto dry land. A Medic dashed straight over to bring his soaked compatriot to his senses, but the show of mental force made a big impression on the other Meleyephatians. The troopers took a few steps back. A few even took a pill of some kind. They had to be improving their resistance to mental effects – in the world of the

Meleyephatians where everyone had psionic abilities, it was far from an unnecessary precaution.

"I can take care of my political opponents on my own. Or I will get help from my new friends," Leng Peyeru-Y spoke in clean-accented Geckho, pointing with a branch-arm at the eight-legged troops. "But what have you brought in the box?"

I asked Imran to remove the top and unpack the plastic container. Before everyone's eyes came a large white spiral shell adorned with a beautiful glimmering gold engraving in Cleopian reading:

"To the ruler of Serpea and its inhabited rings from the Kung of Earth as a sign of respect and symbol of the inevitable victory over the Composite."

"This is the shell of a Gukko-Vahe Composite pilot I shot down. His Dero interceptor was foolish enough to attack my frigate *Tamara the Paladin*. I imagine there will be more trophies like this with every ummi the war against Composite goes on, but this one is remarkable because it was the first. One day, this shell will be given pride of place in the Victory Museum. If of course King Leng Peyeru-Y the Eleventh wishes to give it up instead of keeping it as a unique trophy, which collectors throughout the galaxy would be willing to kill for."

Just in case, I reinforced my fine words with psionics so he would properly appreciate my gift and the true spirit of the historic moment. But I was probably worried over nothing. As it was, the trophy had the King of the Cleopians very intrigued. The Meleyephatian guards (or supervisors) felt the same.

Authority increased to 117!

Fame increased to 112.

"The shell is in mint condition! How is that even possible in space battle?!"

"Yeah, it took some doing," I didn't get into the technical details of capturing the small interceptor or how I got my hands on the big shell. "I tried to take the pilot alive for an interrogation. Unfortunately, the soft tissue was too severely damaged, and the captive didn't last long. My Medic cut out the body for study, and I took the shell as a trophy."

Authority increased to 118!

"What can I say? I am flattered. This is truly a gift befitting a king and will raise my status in the eyes of other Cleopians. I see no obstacle to Kung Gnat speaking with the previous ruler. Edeyya-U really was interested in the history of ancient races and was assembling a lavish artifact collection. But I was not able to determine where he was hiding it. And if Kung Gnat can help figure that out, I promise my guest any item from my predecessor's collection he wishes to take."

One of the Meleyephatians behind the Monarch's back shuddered and suddenly chirred out something in dismay, but the King of the Cleopians didn't alter his decision.

"I am King here and I do not require the Horde's permission for such minor issues. I have made my decision and have no intention of going back on my word! You will be taken to see the prisoner Edeyya-U. That concludes our audience."

Chapter Eight

Heather Ale

"**C**APTAIN, WHAT THE HECK was that? Are we siding with the Horde now?" Gerd Imran seized on a moment when the Meleyephatian troopers went ahead of us down the corridor to break up a group of Cleopians to ask a nagging question.

I could tell by the way he phrased the question and his upset tone that Imran didn't like the idea of turning whichever way the wind blew like a political weathercock.

"Our wise captain is maintaining his neutrality," the orange Miyelonian spoke up for me, responding to the Gladiator.

I didn't risk answering out loud. Three minutes earlier I had used Telekinesis to remove a miniature bug of Meleyephatian origin from Gerd Ayni's ear. When it had been placed, I did not know. I discovered another on the sole of my right shoe. I switched off both of the bugs using my Machine Control skill. And although a further Scan did not reveal any other tracking devices, I was still afraid of unnoticed microphones in the walls or other systems tracking us, so I sent my response mentally to both Gerds Ayni and Imran.

"Did you not notice how pitiful the new ruler is? He was so scared! Fear had his mind in chains. It was keeping him from thinking properly. Peyeru-Y saw every newcomer as a potential assassin. Peyeru-Y the Eleventh threw in his lot with a new suzerain, overthrew the old ruler and... lost. In the last few days, the political situation has changed drastically. A new enemy has attacked the Meleyephatians and the Horde no longer has the resources for some squabble in far-off Serpea. And so the other Cleopian leaders do not support the mutiny. Peyeru-Y the Eleventh has no support among the Cleopians. Even his bodyguard is composed exclusively of Meleyephatians. The only explanation for why the other more popular Cleopian leaders have not overthrown the usurper or made him yet another decoration for the park is the Horde's seventeenth flotilla. And it will not remain in Serpea forever. One day it will have to leave. And on that day, Peyeru-Y the Eleventh's rule will come to an end. The Cleopians understand that and are simply biding their time rather than getting into a tussle with the more numerous and powerful combat ships of the Horde. So I am very glad we didn't engrave Peyeru-Y the Eleventh's name on our gift, and the trophy will also be acceptable to the future ruler we will in fact be building a relationship with."

We reached the end of the corridors, and a high-speed elevator brought us to the opposite end of the huge station. It was crowded inside the elevator due to the dozen large Meleyephatian troopers crammed in with us. They were tense and keeping their hands firmly on their weapons, clearly feeling discomfort on the occupied station. My presence was also making the Meleyephatians nervous. They were afraid of mental trickery from the Listener and had taken pills. But I was staying peaceful and studying the messages coming in from Gerd Uline Tar on my communicator.

My business partner had discovered several potentially profitable contracts to deliver various kinds of cargo and had sent them over for me to sign off on. I even marked one of the contracts as interesting and told the Trader to take it – an urgent delivery of automatic drilling equipment to the neutral GF-111K System. One million five hundred thousand Geckho crystals for delivery within a ten ummi timeframe. It wasn't all that much, but the elegance of this job was that the GF-111K system was right next to Rorsh, which was where Prince Hugo – the "embodiment of absolute evil" – was rotting away in a space prison. At the very least now our coming to Rorsh wouldn't cause too much surprise.

The elevator door slid silently aside, and we went into the fairly poorly lit corridor. Light was a vital necessity for Cleopians, so it would not be a pleasant environment for them, and station inhabitants would not be able to spend much time here. Scanning and studying the information on the mini-map revealed that we were on a prison level normal Serpea citizens were not allowed to access.

Scanning skill increased to level eighty-three!

Cartography skill increased to level ninety-two!

And again... I am getting very sick of this! I don't know how our escorts did it, but I found eight microscopic Meleyephatian bugs on myself, Imran and Ayni. And at that, this time I was unable to remove the spy implements with Telekinesis. They were stuck dead with an adhesive that had already set.

Oh well! I started putting the espionage devices out of commission one after the next using my Machine Control skill. The chance of success in each case was ninety-eight percent, so I handled it no problem.

Electronics skill increased to level one hundred four!

Machine Control skill increased to level one hundred seventeen!

Training skill increased to level forty-eight!

You have reached level one hundred ten!

You have received three skill points!

Not bad! The guards that had been assigned to us had helped me level up without even suspecting it! After level one hundred, every subsequent level came harder and harder, so I had come to appreciate such things. I perked up and even felt an urge to play a little prank and show my mettle at the same time. I chose the one of the twelve escorts whose emotional background levels were slightly different and turned toward the large lemon-yellow Meleyephatian. No, I did not read his thoughts. But even without that I could tell who was behind the attempt to spy on me because, other than the anxiety and apprehension they were all feeling, this Meleyephatian also had an air of confusion and fear of expected punishment for failing his job.

"Ayni, have that level-89 Saboteur come over here!"

The Meleyephatian heard the Miyelonian Translator's trill and obediently walked over, deftly shuffling his jointed appendages. Looking right into the constellation of large faceted eyes on his head, I sent the Meleyephatian a mental threat:

"Listen up and listen good! If you try to stick any more espionage devices on me or my companions, I will no longer take pity on you for being low-level and weak. I will split open your armor and stick every last one of your eight arms all the way up your butthole. Do you understand?"

I even tried to say that out loud in the Saboteur's native language, but I lacked the vocabulary. Also, many of the high-frequency sounds in the language of the Meleyephatians were something the human voice box was not adapted to reproduce. But still he understood me, despite my linguistic stumbling.

Successful Authority check!

"I understand (unclear, but something meaning 'perfectly' and also indicating that this individual was female), Kung Gnat. I promise (unclear) will not happen again."

Astrolinguistics skill increased to level one hundred twelve!

"That's just peachy! Now take me to the prisoner."

The lemon yellow Meleyephatian was leading the group. The corridor got darker and darker. It became hard even for a human to make out anything in the gloom, so Imran turned on his helmet light. An endless number of cameras. Security systems and active combat drones. Forcefields... Finally, our procession came to an end in front of an unremarkable armored door with no words or numbers on it, exactly the same as the hundreds of others before it.

The Saboteur's crystal key opened it to reveal a small dark room with a forcefield giving a tense hum and holding the prisoner tight in the middle. And in fact, there were two prisoners, both Cleopians by race.

Krong Edeyya-U. Cleopian. Light Green Faction. Level-265 Scientist.

Gerd Eda-No Edeyya. Cleopian. Light Green Faction. Level-117 Historian.

Both of the captives were badly burned, the usual thick and solid surface covering almost completely removed from their bodies to reveal the pink color of their very faintly pulsating flesh. There were just a few small charred patches of broken "bark" left on their bodies, but they practically didn't cover any of the vulnerable flesh beneath. Furthermore, the Krong had all his lower and upper appendages amputated and a forcefield was suspending him in midair. I was left with no doubt that the prisoners had been tortured brutally in an attempt to uncover some kind of important information. The torture theory was confirmed by the Meleyephatian Torturer in the chamber, probably there to keep the prisoners from exiting the game. It was perhaps precisely because he wanted to hide the dark side of the space power struggles from outsiders that the new King was so reluctant to allow us here.

Nevertheless, both of the prisoners were conscious, and their two black eyes immediately focused on the newcomers. I also noticed the greed with which the remaining charred scraps of their covering started taking in the bright light of Imran's helmet light, covering over with a frothy slime before my very eyes. The regeneration process had clearly begun.

"We have a quarter ummi before Krong Edeyya-U will be executed," Ayni translated the Saboteur's trill after which the Meleyephatians all left the chamber and the doors closed.

Before starting the conversation, I waited for my Scanning ability to reload and took a closer look at the situation. Thick metal walls. Four microphones and an infrared camera on the ceiling. Torture implements lying on a three-legged table. The only source of light was Imran's headlamp. The device to switch off the forcefield was not to be found in this chamber. We would be allowed to speak, but not set the prisoners free.

I walked up to the mutilated Krong and, not ashamed of the cameras, got down on one knee before the former ruler. Let the new ruler throw a tantrum because I showed more respect to his predecessor. I was not afraid of possible hysterics from a Meleyephatian puppet.

"These are not the circumstances I expected to meet you in, Krong Edeyya-U, but we will not get another chance to talk now. The new authorities consider you dangerous and it was very difficult for me to secure this audience."

The prisoner kept silent, just looking at me and my companions attentively. The way the Cleopian looked at my Relict armor and ancient weaponry, with both curiosity and clear knowledge, did not evade my attention. Imran's armor suit bearing an inscription from the Geckho fleet commander did not go unnoticed either. Good, let him see that we have no ties with his tormentors. I asked Gerd Ayni to translate my words into Cleopian.

"I was sent here by Kung Eesssa, the Betelgeuse Planet Devouress. The legendary warrior woman told me you are one of the galaxy's most authoritative experts on the history of ancient races. I understand that these are not the greatest of circumstances, but I very much need information on the Relict Pyramid, the ancient war and Precursor artifacts. Kung Eesssa claimed you are very knowledgeable on this topic and would be able to help. Unfortunately, I have nothing to offer you personally in exchange – I can neither grant you freedom nor stay your execution. But this information is necessary for our entire galaxy in the war against the invading throngs of Composite ships. Necessary for my planet Earth. Necessary for the Cleopians, who you ruled for many tongs. And necessary for me personally. I need to reach a new rank in the Relict Pyramid hierarchy. That way I can do more, and it will help my home planet a great deal."

I wasn't using psionics, because I understood perfectly well that doing so unnoticed in the Krong's case, given his certainly high Intelligence would not be possible. The Meleyephatians hadn't been able to get anything out of the captive either, which meant Krong Edeyya-U's mind was well defended against psionic attacks. I must admit, I wasn't especially counting on a response, and so I was surprised when the disfigured captive spoke up. Ayni translated.

"Don't bother, Human. The Relict Pyramid was destroyed more than ten thousand tongs ago. It cannot be built back."

And now that the discussion was moving, I pushed it along.

"The Pyramid isn't a material object with a singular existence. It is a huge system of nodes distributed throughout the Universe that stores the knowledge of the ancient Relict race. Some of the nodes were spared. Hidden outposts, mobile Relict laboratories and at least one refuge with a hundred thousand virt pods have also survived. And some of those pods contain living members of the ancient race. I actually have a living Relict in my crew and have seen the race's ships with my own eyes. The Pyramid is also the governmental structure of the Relicts with its own laws and rules, access levels and duties. The Pyramid continues to function.

Communication with the Pyramid has been severely encumbered, but it is still possible. I was able to send and receive messages from it and was assigned a certain rank and access level to the Pyramid."

Fame increased to 113.

Authority increased to 119!

"Sounds like you know more about the Relicts than I do, Kung Gnat. What help could I be to you in that case, Human?"

"Any information about locations that have yet to be looted by modern researchers. Any valuable artifacts. Data discs. Devices that can read them. Any information that could help advance my study of the ancient race. Relict technologies that could help fight back the intergalactic invaders."

The imprisoned Krong closed his eyes and droned out piteously.

"Human, do you understand how severely you have just worsened my position and multiplied my suffering? The torturers wanted only information about my supporters, access keys to financial shares and the locations of caches of valuables. But now my assistant and I will be tortured all the more cruelly to beat information about ancient races out of us..."

"I understand that and beg apologies. But still I believe it would be frustrating for such a recognized specialist in the history of ancient races to have the invaluable information you collected so painstakingly vanish and do nothing to help your descendants. For the purpose of your entire life to come to nothing."

The disfigured Krong fell silent for a long time. But eventually, he surprisingly agreed to help.

"Let me tell you, human, where the answers can be found. But I do have a nonnegotiable condition. Take your Annihilator and kill my assistant. He barely knows anything, but they're still torturing him to cause me even more pain. It's terrible to watch him suffering. Do that, and I will help you!"

I turned my attention to the Historian, who was suspended in the forcefield. During my talk with the Krong, he didn't utter a single sound, just staring blankly all the while. I placed a hand on the grip of my Annihilator, but still was in no hurry to do the bidding of the mutilated Cleopian ruler. There was a cautionary tale that was just reminding me too much of this situation...

"Ayni, translate this. My people have an ancient legend. In it, long ago, a miracle elixir was created in a secret laboratory that could restore strength, cure any ailment and cause a state of euphoria. A highly powerful neighboring faction found out about it and attacked the laboratory, killing all who worked there. Only the senior head of the laboratory and a young technician survived. The captors promised to torture them cruelly to learn the formula and production technique of the miracle elixir. The old leader was afraid of the torture, so he agreed to help the enemies. He asked them only to kill his inexperienced technician first, saying he didn't know much in the first place, and as the leader he was ashamed to become a traitor in the eyes of an underling who had shown more bravery. The young technician was tied up and suffocated in an autoclave. And then the old man told the enemies he had been training resistance to pain and mental attacks his whole life so there was no use torturing him. His junior colleague, though, was not prepared the same way and might have revealed the secret. But now he could be comfortable knowing the information would remain safe. After that, the laboratory head died without ever revealing the secret formula to his foes."

"An interesting story. Kung Gnat is wise and keen, and the analogy is of course plain to see," the former ruler agreed. "However, I have nothing more to offer you than what I've already said. If you want information on the Relicts, kill my assistant!"

It looked like a dead end. Although... Was it just me, or had the mutilated Krong been staring stubbornly for a while now into the face guard on my helmet as if to offer eye contact? I raised the guard to reveal my face and looked closer into the Cleopian's lone eye, black as night. A flood of thoughts came crashing down on me.

"Well, well. Finally figured it out! Yes, Human, the story you told is indeed cautionary here. But there is one key difference. I actually want you to save Gerd Eda-No Edeyya, not kill him. He is my last remaining child. Help me! My heir knows many things about the ancient races, almost as much as I do. He can help you in your quest. Kung Gnat, pretend you trust me and shoot Gerd Eda-No Edeyya with your Annihilator. But don't actually kill him! A few shots to the chest, then at his lower limbs. Go ahead and take his right or left upper limb

after that and take it with you out of this chamber, then plant it somewhere with light and water. You can easily find information on how to regrow the body of a Cleopian in a nutritive medium. The virt pods belonging to me and Eda-No have been destroyed, so my child cannot leave the game until changing faction and being given another virt pod. Help him do that! His knowledge will repay you many times over, and the Light Green Faction will support you with troops. When power changes hands again, you will have the gratitude of all Serpea. And here's a down payment for the time being..."

An unintelligible blurry picture. The Cleopian seemed to be trying to send me an image he had seen with his own eye, but my brain couldn't interpret visual information from a creature with such different vision.

"Ah... Human, without knowing the precise location you will have a hard time interpreting it. But alright, commit this to memory. The Pmee System, Miyelonian space. First dwarf planet from the star. The surface is molten, the radiation is harsh. At a great depth beneath the surface magma there are subterranean structures of Relict origin. Ship locators can detect them. It is a base that has not been looted and is in good condition as you requested. But I was never able to find a way inside. Perhaps you will have more success, Listener. I wish you luck. Consider this a down payment for saving my heir."

Chapter Nine

Formation Number Nine

SECURITY CAME STORMING into the chamber, but they were far too late. I had already stashed the Annihilator in the special main weapon slot on my armor suit and heard a snide note from the imprisoned Krong that Kung Gnat had made the very same error as the villain from the legend he recounted. The lemon-yellow Meleyephatian took a thoughtful look at the hole in the ceiling where the security camera had been, then at the scraps of flesh floating in the forcefield – all that now remained of the Historian. I was somewhat afraid they would be displeased I had killed the Cleopian, but there was nothing of the sort. The Meleyephatians were interested in something else entirely.

"Couldn't get any information?" the eight-legged Saboteur revealed a knowledge of Geckho.

"As you can see... But still it was worth trying."

Authority reduced to 118!
Authority reduced to 117!

Not nice. The Meleyephatians were very disappointed, clearly having expected me to be somewhat better at extracting valuable information from the prisoners. But I didn't give a crap about their unfulfilled hopes. It was a done deal. I had pulled off the branch I needed with Telekinesis and hidden it in my inventory. I headed to leave the chamber, the very embodiment of dismay and frustration. I didn't even have to fake a bad mood either – the two Authority drops in a row really had upset me because that parameter was not easy to bring up, while improving my Rifle skill by one was poor compensation.

The Meleyephatians crowding up the doorway made way without anyone even trying to stop me or my companions, much less searching anyone. Once in the prison corridor, I turned and met eyes with the prisoner.

"Krong Edeyya-U, I admit your bravery has impressed me. It's a shame we couldn't meet earlier under more favorable circumstances. I wish you an easy death." I turned my attention to the crowd of Meleyephatians around me. "There's no need to show me the way. I can go back to my frigate on my own. You can bring my shuttle to the bay area next to dock eight. I don't think the Cleopian monarch will want to see me in his palace again after what happened."

Successful Authority check!

My companions at my side, I walked down the darkened corridor until I reached the elevator.

"Shall we go back to the ship?" Gerd Ayni suggested, but I shook my head no.

"I have a little piece of business to attend to first. I need to visit the Miyelonian embassy. Could you figure out where it's located?"

The orange kitty opened her communicator and looked up the information.

"Floor seven hundred six is completely dedicated to the embassies of spacefaring races. The Miyelonian embassy is there as well. We can take this very elevator there."

We didn't waste any time and headed for our target. There were no Meleyephatians on floor seven hundred six. In fact, a general air of silence reigned – the corridors were empty, there wasn't a single local or visitor. After three minutes, we saw a huge set of heavy doors decorated with the emblem of the Union of Miyelonian Prides and guarded by a pair of fearsome Miyelonians crammed into shock armor. Both guardsmen immediately pointed their infantry resonators at me, sending an unambiguous message.

Danger Sense skill increased to level one hundred forty-four!

The pair were fully serious about their intent to shoot if I crossed a bright yellow warning line painted on the metal floor. I had no more doubts. With the system being occupied by Meleyephatians and ambiguity about who now ruled Serpea, the Union of Miyelonian Prides had ordered their guards to shoot to maim any outsider trying to enter their embassy without a scheduled meeting. I stopped a step away from the line and took a small plastic box from my inventory, handing it to my Translator.

"Ayni, go in alone. Security will let you through. Hand this package to the ambassador or any high-ranking employee of the diplomatic mission. There is a crystal drive here containing encrypted information. The file is to be sent via secure channels to Kung Keetsie Myau. It's very important. The password for the file will be sent in the real world. And warn the embassy workers that any attempt to open the file will cause valuable information to be irretrievably destroyed and whoever is at fault will be executed along with their entire family by the Great One."

The orange kitty nodded and crossed the line fearlessly. Security did in fact let the Miyelonian through, and my companion was soon out of sight behind the embassy's armored doors. Imran and I meanwhile wandered the empty corridors of floor seven hundred six while awaiting our Translator. But everywhere was desolate. The doors of the alien race diplomatic missions were all closed. The only place bustling with life was the wing containing the Meleyephatian Horde embassy, but we didn't want to go back there.

Then suddenly, the headphones in my helmet flipped on.

"Captain, we have problems," the alarmed voice belonged to Eduard Boyko the Space Commando. "There's a fight going on in a bar called Blue Glow. Our guys got into a big scrap with the crew of another starship. Tini's been stabbed. Basha Tushihh got his head bashed in."

Based on Gerd Imran's shudder, he had also heard the alarming radio communique.

"Hang on! I'll be there soon!" I promised and ran back to the elevator, opening a station map as I did. Imran hurried after me, not a step behind.

Blue Glow... Yes, there was a restaurant by that name next to the space port. Floor eleven. Pretty far... I might not make it in time... On the other hand, how could I call my crew the "best of the best" if they couldn't hold their own in a regular old bar fight? But just in case, I got in touch with the frigate and requested backup. They were much closer to the scene of the fighting.

We got there at the same time. The huge armored Trillian Gerd Ukh-Meemeesh spilled out of the neighboring elevator accompanied by Amati-Kuis Ursssh, Destroying Angel, Grim Reaper, Svetlana Vereshchagina and... Gerd Soia-Tan La-Varrez. The outrage left me speechless.

"What the heck is wrong with you?! You psychos brought a little girl to a bar fight!"

But it was too late to change anything. The bar's brightly glowing neon lights were right next to us and even from over by the elevator we could hear commotion, shouts and fighting. We hurried ahead, unceremoniously pushing our way through a crowd of onlookers belonging to all kinds of crazy races. A huge Cyanid bubble standing in the doorway was sent flying aside by my Telekinesis, the vacuoles, mitochondria and other organelles within his transparent body shifting around wildly. I read a bit too late that this was a Diplomat of his race. Not a great guy to get caught in the crossfire.

Authority reduced to 116!

Yes, I would have to apologize for this later. But now was not the time. The interior of the restaurant was dominated by chaos and destruction. Overturned tables, broken dishes, aromatic cocktails and trampled food littered the floor. Squeezed in the corner of the big room, my crew was holding the fort down. Vasha Tushihh was brandishing the leg of a table in his huge paws. Next to him, his brother Basha Tushihh was waving the torn-out spiked limb of a Meleyephatian. Though his head was bloodied, it bore a look of determination to fight. They were supported by the Miyelonian Gerd Mauu-La Mya-Ssa, one of his paws hanging limp, and Avan Toi the Supercargo, who was hardly able to stand. I didn't see Tini or any other team members. I didn't see Eduard Boyko, who had called me for help either.

Up against my troops was a big group of aliens from many different races. Geckho, Cleopians, Meleyephatians, Miyelonians and even Humans. The diverse crowd had one thing in common − the badges on their spacesuits, which all came from the same starship, the *Udur Vayeh*. They seemed to all be from the same crew. There were no less than forty of them and they were pressing in on my friends with their numbers and mass. I couldn't say exactly what sparked this conflict, and it didn't matter right now whatsoever. The most important thing now was to help my crew!

"Avast ye scurvy dogs!" I shouted out to the whole room, and my microphone-enhanced voice echoed off the walls. "That means anyone not taking part in the fight – scram before you get caught in the crossfire!"

The crew of the *Tamara the Paladin*, barely holding on, shuddered and their cries of joy heralded to our foes that the captain had arrived, and their troubles had just begun. The crowd stumbled back and dispersed. Many hurried to the exit. The brawlers from the crew of the *Udur Vayeh* started turning to the new challengers. Stepping over the groaning and writhing bodies on the floor, we hurried to our friends. I had to use Psionics to stun the two most hardheaded – a big Geckho and a very drunk human, before we could join our friends.

"Formation number nine! Basha, Vasha, Avan Toi and Ukh-Meemeesh, link shields. United front! Gunfighters to the back. Imran, back them up. Nonlethal weaponry!" I warned the two Assassins and tossed my Paralyzer to Destroying Angel. "Medic, go check up on our Bard," I pointed at Vasily Filippov, who was lying against the wall. "Little one, give me mental support! Go!"

We advanced on our enemies, who were now confused and disorganized. They were having a hard time coordinating their actions after six large Geckho from their group suddenly turned on their comrades, dealing out blows with their huge fists. I had chosen to target the Geckho in particular because that race was renowned for having immense strength rather than stellar defense against mental attacks.

Psionic skill increased to level one hundred thirty-three!

Mental Fortitude skill increased to level one hundred thirty!

Gerd Ukh-Meemeesh the Trillian was dealing out beatdowns so hard even Cleopians weren't standing back up. Not to be outdone by our "crocodile," Basha and Vasha were wielding their heavy weapons and whacking opponents left and right. I took two nimble Miyelonians out of the game temporarily by hitting them with Disorientation. The spiny Cleopian in front of me I threw back against the far wall with Telekinesis. In the air he even felled a few of his comrades.

Telekinesis skill increased to level sixty-two!

Mysticism skill increased to level eighty-nine!

"Captain, I am with you!" clambering out from under a pile of bodies, Eduard Boyko's face was smashed and bloodied with his nose slanting noticeably to the left. He went over to join our "tanks," holding in his arms a heavy metal pole he'd scrounged up somewhere. "Link shields with the rest!"

"Bard in formation!" said the Medic, putting away the med kit and taking out in its place a pistol that shot tranquilizing needles.

A heavy tabletop flew over and froze six inches over my head. The Tachyon Bender in my armor suit triggered! I used Telekinesis to send it right back into the very thick of the enemy party. My first impulse was to launch it at two

Meleyephatians standing slightly to the side who I considered most dangerous, but the pair seemed to be merely observing rather than intervening in the fight. Their armor suits bearing Seventeenth Flotilla emblems told me just in the nick of time that these Meleyephatians were from another starship and only here to watch.

We kept pushing in on our opponents, gaining ground with every step. The unknown Miyelonian froze with his blade next to me but flew away after a powerful blow to his earring-laden ear from our armored Gunner Gerd Ukh-Meemeesh.

Disoriented! Disoriented! The man now next wielding the neck of a broken bottle seemed dimly familiar, but I wasn't able to get a good look at him because Destroying Angel took him down with the Paralyzer, while his incapacitated body was sent flying by a left hook from Imran.

"Vasily Andreyevich, hit us all with a speed and regen buff! Where's Tini?"

"Gerd Tini was sent to respawn," the Medic told me, and my face went dark with fury.

These guys had killed members of my team? This wasn't just a bar fight between groups of itchy-knuckled brawlers wanting to blow off steam? They were committing murder? I simply could not forgive that!

"No mercy! Kill every last one still standing!"

Laser lights flickered. A fireball cast by the Psionic Mage exploded in the thick of the enemy group, sending them flying and scorching them. The last of our enemies, and by that time there were no more than six or seven remaining, fell dead to the floor engulfed in flame. A second later the fire-suppression system turned on and foamy water came flooding down from the ceiling.

ATTENTION!!! Action violates rules for neutral stations! Free Captain Kung Gnat's Danger Rating has risen to two.

Fame increased to 114.

Authority reduced to 115!

Not good... The fireball especially was overkill. I would have to give the little one a talking to later. In any case, the picture we presented to the local news channels was unambiguous – Free Captain Kung Gnat and his team are engaged in drunken debauchery and trashing Blue Glow, disfiguring and killing its patrons. After all, that was exactly how the local authorities would see things if they wanted to pressure me. But I didn't see any other way – I couldn't just let anyone kill members of my team unpunished, especially my ward. I glanced up at the ceiling and looked around, running a scan at the same time.

Machine Control skill increased to level one hundred eighteen!

All the video cameras in the restaurant seating area had gone out of order. I of course should have done so straight after entering but better late than never. Standing in the midst of the foam-coated living and dead bodies, I turned to my companions.

"Who started this?"

"Who started it...? uhhh..." Basha Tushihh looked around and pointed a paw at the body of a conked-out man in a spacesuit, still squeezing the neck of a bottle in his hand. "There he is! Denni Marko, you should remember him. He used to be in our crew. He was drunk and let himself say some things he shouldn't have. He was saying very nasty stuff about you and Valeri. There were some insults about Ayni as well, so he took a well-deserved smack to the face from our Bard. Tini tried to break up the fight, but Denni Marko stabbed the Miyelonian adolescent with a knife. And it only got worse from there... There were too many of them. The Meleyephatians and local security tried to break us up, but it was no use."

Denni Marko? Yes, I remembered him perfectly well. A former admirer of Valeri's, he never fit in with our crew and left. Yes, he could indeed have been hiding hurt feelings. I was not expecting to meet him here.

"Who is captain of these thugs? Find where his starship is parked. I would really like to have a word with him and get compensation for the attack on my team. Plus someone is gonna have to pay for the damage here and I don't want it to be us."

I was in fact heading to the *Udur Vayeh*'s dock to voice my complaints, but a large number of law enforcement officers arrived and interfered with my plans. Before it was too late, I got out ahead, hinting to the Cleopians the right way of viewing the situation – my team was attacked, my crewmember was murdered. We were just defending ourselves.

Psionic skill increased to level one hundred thirty-four!

It worked! The Cleopians started

"apprehending" the thrashed the *Udur Vayeh* team members, clinking plastic handcuffs over arms, legs and various other appendages. There hadn't yet been any complaints directed at me or members of my team, but it was clear that we wouldn't be left alone for long.

"Let's get out of here!" I commanded my crew and sent a message straight to the frigate to prepare for an urgent departure from the station.

But we didn't make it out so easily. No, the Cleopians hadn't yet gotten over the mind control. They didn't stop us. But the Meleyephatians from the Seventeenth Flotilla who had stayed on the sidelines suddenly stood decisively in my way.

"Free Captain Kung Gnat, we kindly request you not resist and come with us. Someone wishes to see you on the flagship. We also insist you take the Translator with you. A shuttle will take you to the *Pikiuro* battleship."

Chapter Ten

A Game of Chess with a Cardinal

THERE WAS NO USE in arguing here. Yes, I had lost control and screwed up, turning a bar fight into a bloodbath, so the fact the Meleyephatians, who had captured the Serpea system, would react to the incident was completely expected. There was no avoiding a serious conversation with the occupation authorities, but still I was hoping to uphold my fairly strong position. My ward had been killed, my team was at a serious disadvantage and only defending themselves. That could be seen on the security camera footage, and there were lots of witnesses. I was unlikely to get away scot-free, but still I wasn't expecting the Meleyephatians to place any prohibitively serious sanctions on me.

I called Gerd Ayni Uri-Miayuu the Translator to the flying vehicle pad near Blue Glow, then sent the rest of my team back to the frigate. I was also able to hand off the bundle containing the Cleopian

Historian's branch to our ship Medic, telling him to plant it in a nutritive medium with good lighting. I also got in touch with my business partner and asked Gerd Uline Tar to apologize on my behalf to the Cyanid ambassador I had accidentally pushed and, if necessary, pay compensation for emotional distress. I also had one more little snag I needed to fix before it turned into something serious.

A large Reesssh-10 landing shuttle, which could hold up to fifty Meleyephatian assault troops in heavy armor suits was provided to me and my Miyelonian Translator alone. No one flew with us, there were no pilots on it and the vehicle was completely on autopilot. I didn't just sit with my arms crossed though and walked through the shuttle. An interesting vehicle with a streamlined shape that could land on planets with dense atmosphere and take off from them. With powerful energy shields in the front hemisphere, it even carried antirocket defense mechanisms. It carried a whole arsenal of firearms and boxes of ammunition in niches along both walls, including a miniature recon drone and two mine clearing robots. In the cargo hold in the back there was a mobile shield generator folded up for providing cover in the landing zone after setting down. Ah, if only Earth's Constructors could see this. They would probably pick-up new ideas for their designs.

Scanning skill increased to level eighty-four!

Unfortunately, I had to limit myself to the skill alone, not using a Prospector Scanner to see a higher detail blueprint of the flying vehicle. The Meleyephatians would probably not approve of such technological espionage. It also wouldn't be the greatest outcome for this flight to get stranded on a deactivated shuttle with all its systems off.

The Miyelonian trailed behind me in silence, doing her very best to put on a look of ambivalence even though the orange Translator couldn't hide the predatory glimmer in her eyes – very few of her compatriots had probably ever gotten such a close look at a competing spacefaring race's modern military technology before. I had long been aware that Gerd Ayni Uri-Miayuu was closely linked with Miyelonian intelligence, despite not being officially in their employ. She made a valuable informant in the inner circle of Free Captain Kung Gnat, being present at negotiations with influential players of different races and taking part in every venture I could conceive of. Furthermore, I had quick information relay channels with Kung Keetsie Myau and enjoyed the Great One's particular favor.

I didn't see anything scandalous about Gerd Ayni working for her native government. It was normal behavior for a patriotically inclined citizen. I myself was regularly sending new technologies and information about the goings on in deep space to Earth. Furthermore, I had read the Translator's thoughts hundreds of times and knew how sensitive she was with my personal interests. Gerd Ayni would never reveal information that could disadvantage her captain. On top of that, my tailed companion was provided personal security in the real world by Union of Miyelonian Prides intelligence for her activity, and she needed that to protect against the various criminal groups, space pirates and religious fanatics who still had yet to forget the story of the murder of the incarnation of the Great First Female Leng Amiru U-Mayaoo.

In general, I turned a blind eye to my Translator's spying. But when I saw my tailed friend candidly photographing the Meleyephatian landing shuttle's interior, I stopped Gerd Ayni and switched off her camera using my Machine Control. I sent my companion a mental reminder that we were neutral, and those shots were simply not worth the Meleyephatians possibly accusing us of espionage and declaring us enemies of the Horde yet again.

"Sorry, Captain. I wasn't thinking. I could have hurt you. It won't happen again."

We sensed the flight come to an end by the changing tonality of the thrusters before a magnetic crane grabbed the shuttle and pulled it into the battleship's hangar. The doors slid silently aside, and Gerd Ayni and I emerged into a brightly lit huge room containing thirty other identical Reesssh-10 landing shuttles.

There was someone waiting for us. A large group of eight-legged troopers surrounded our shuttle and stood stock still, not taking out their weapons. The group leader stepped forward – a large Meleyephatian with light gray coloration.

Gerd Rwazzz 1024. Meleyephatian. Renegade Nest Kiko-78. Level-142 Psionic.

Renegade Nest? Among the troopers surrounding the ship, I saw another few renegades from various nests. As far as I knew, renegades generally refused to take part in the Meleyephatian

Horde's innumerable wars for territorial expansion and subjugation of other races. But obviously here they were taking active part in the war with the Geckho, which for the Meleyephatians was defensive.

The Psionic stared at me with his constellation of black eyes. I tensed up inside, expecting an attempt to read my thoughts or another psionic attack, but my Mental Fortitude skill kept silent, just like my Danger Sense. Perhaps our escort had requested orders from his superiors about us and was receiving them. Finally the Psionic turned his head toward my companion and started to chirr. Gerd Ayni got straight to translating:

"Gerd Rwazzz 1024 welcomes the esteemed Kung Gnat to the Seventeenth Flotilla's main ship and asks you to follow him to the long-distance communications room. You're expected."

Well, well... Looks like this summoning to the Horde battleship was not linked to the fight in Blue Glow at all. Some Meleyephatian Horde bigwig just wanted to have a chat with me. Alright then. I guess I'm about to learn why my enemy status was revoked and what the Horde wants with me.

The troops made way and our escort hurried down a nearby corridor. At a quick pace, I went after the scurrying eight-legged Psionic, trying to remain dignified and not flee. The Miyelonian on the other hand had to start running. Why such a rush?

Our escort stopped short and pointed a hand at the door.

"The long-distance comms room. Hurry up. The man on the other line does not like waiting and is not known for his patience."

The door slid aside, revealing a round room with mirror walls. Ayni and I stepped inside. Curious. I had never had the chance to use a mirrored long-distance comms room with anyone else. I was always alone before. Well, to be more accurate, I had managed to communicate with the real world in the Pyramid Contact Hall together with my team, but that was a somewhat different situation. But now, the reflection was freaking me out. I saw myself and the Miyelonian from all sides at once, duplicated an infinite number of times. By the way, the Miyelonian could pose a problem if I would be speaking with a powerful psionic. Sure, my thoughts were fairly well protected, but I was worried about the information in my companion's head. I personally could read the orange Translator's thoughts like an open book. A powerful Psionic with good Intelligence could probably also do so with the same level of ease.

The light in the room went out and before us appeared a glowing holographic image of a large Meleyephatian in matte-black armor. Fascinating, very fascinating... The hologram was wearing a Relict Listener armor suit refit for a Meleyephatian. My companion for some reason also instantly fell into a low bow, her knees on the floor and her head hanging low. It was odd to see the proud Miyelonian in such a degrading pose. What was happening? I didn't copy her servile gesture but did get down on one knee and bow to the seemingly important member of the Meleyephatian Horde.

"Do you know who I am?" the Miyelonian translated the Meleyephatian's chirring without raising her head.

I had to read a hint from her thoughts.

"The immortal Krong La Ush-Vayzzz, leader of the Meleyephatian Horde, commander of the galaxy's strongest fleet and perhaps the most powerful being in the entire Universe."

I did my best to hide the flood of emotions. How about that! Sure, I was expecting an important figure in Horde hierarchy wanted to speak with me, but the very leader of the Meleyephatians? Meanwhile, he listened to Ayni's translated response and chirred back.

"The largest, but not strongest fleet. The Trillian royal fleet surpasses mine in terms of combat potential. The fleet of the distant Elvinians is also strong. There are at least another two fleets commensurate with mine in strength. I am speaking of the Composite fleet and that of the Humans. And that is exactly what I wanted to talk to you about, Human."

I didn't have a clue what the Elvinians were. As for the Trillians, sure. The Composite, too. But the fact that Humans somewhere had a mighty space fleet was big discovery for me.

"For starters, I'd like to have a talk about this Composite. They appeared out of nowhere, destroyed my capital and spread out through my whole territory faster than the speed of light. I have been made aware that you brought about their invasion. I also suppose you know a lot about these invaders. What forces does our intergalactic enemy possess? Who is behind the invasion? Answer honestly, Human, and you will escape my wrath. You have my word!"

Danger Sense skill increased to level one hundred forty-five!

I could sense that the Krong of the Meleyephatian Horde would have been all too happy to strike me down, but something was holding him back. For some reason he needed me. Either that or my death would have led to political consequences the Horde leader wanted to avoid. But I couldn't just say nothing. I had to choose my words very carefully.

"The Composite invasion happened with the full knowledge of the suzerain of my people, Geckho leader Krong Daveyesh-Pir fully approved."

"So it was the Geckho then..." Krong Laa hissed out the fury spilling out of him. "My advisors considered that option even though the Geckho normally behave in a more straightforward manner."

I didn't clarify that the order of events was somewhat different, and that I had informed the leader of my suzerains after the fact. I knew perfectly well that admitting that would mean signing my own death warrant. I hurried to continue.

"I read the thoughts of the pilot of a Dero interceptor we captured alive and discovered that the Vahe-Gukko Composite has been preparing a very long time for this 'Final War.' More than two hundred tongs. They were looking for a reason to finish off their 'ancient enemy' and that they had twelve thousand flotillas ready to invade our galaxy with a total of more than half a million starships."

"Half a million???" the Horde leader was shocked and not hiding it. Obviously, his sources had been indicating somewhat lesser enemy forces.

He spent a long time in silence, digesting the new information. Then he spoke up, not hiding his frustration.

"The foolish Geckho! Do they really not understand the power they're playing with? My fleet, regardless of how fast it hurries to the scene of events, will take another twenty-eight standard days. By that time, considering the Composite's might and how fast they can spread, hundreds of inhabited star systems will fall. That puts many systems in jeopardy – Urmi, historical capital of the Union of Miyelonian Prides and Shiharsa, the Geckho homeworld are among them. Do the Geckho really believe they can hold back the power they've unleashed?!"

Danger Sense skill increased to level one hundred forty-six!

Astrolinguistics skill increased to level one hundred thirteen!

I was shivering, my heart pounding in my chest in worry as if I was having a vision of some deadly peril. Seemingly, the very mighty figure was having a hard time holding back his fury and not lashing out at whoever had the misfortune to fall in his field of view, much less the man ultimately behind all the worrying events. My mood did not go unnoticed by the Krong.

"I can sense your fear, Human. Fear not. You gave an honest answer and I promised to have mercy on you. I always keep my word. Furthermore, your safety is guaranteed by Kung Keetsie Myau, and war with the Union of Miyelonian Prides does not fit into my current plans."

This just keeps getting funnier... Kung Keetsie Myau had guaranteed my safety? I wonder when that happened? And why hadn't anyone told me so before now? Meanwhile, Krong Laa continued:

"The Meleyephatian Horde is strong and capable of handling the Composite. But grand space politics is not a one-on-one game. The other players must always be taken into account. The Trillians have been suspiciously ramping up activity and have announced general mobilization even though the Composite has yet to threaten any of their systems. The Miyelonians took heart from their recent success and are not averse to tearing off a few more chunks in the expected chaos. But what has me most bothered is the yet unfinished conflict with the Human race. The distant 'Empire,' as they call themselves has a surprisingly strong fleet, and a war on two fronts, regardless of the ten or so minor conflicts we are also engaged in, is not exactly what the Meleyephatian Horde wants. And so I have a special mission for you, a Human by race. Communicate my peace offering to your compatriots. If you're able to put an end to the war, you can expect a generous reward and a favorable attitude from me. Meanwhile, if Emperor Georg the

First agrees to support my fleet in the war against the invaders from another galaxy, I officially guarantee that the Meleyephatian Horde will remove your home planet of Earth from its list of targets. So what do you say, Human? Do you accept the mission?"

How about that! The enemy my home planet had to fear most of all was offering a way of avoiding conflict. Billions of lives were at stake. Such historic chances didn't come around every day. I gave my agreement right away with no hesitation.

Authority increased to 116!

"That's just great! You can get the details from my advisors. Best of luck to you, Human. I'm sure you're going to need it. That concludes our audience."

The holographic image vanished and, the light turned back on. I suddenly realized I was drenched in sweat and my arms were shivering. Yes, the sense of tension during that brief conversation was colossal. It was probably the same as how D'Artagnan felt after his chess match with Cardinal Richelieu. However, unlike the famed musketeer, I did accept the offer to fight for the other side. Whether that was good or bad was hard to tell. The Army of Earth, which was currently fighting against the Meleyephatians, would probably not approve of my choice.

But time would tell.

Chapter Eleven

You Don't Talk to Your Food

"AYNI, YOU ARE NOT to tell a soul about that audience! For the time being, even my business partner Gerd Uline Tar has no reason to know. The official story is that the Meleyephatians called us in for a disciplinary hearing after the bar fight to teach us a lesson."

The orange Miyelonian nodded in understanding, but then suddenly shuddered and looked at me in worry.

"But Captain, what about the threat to the Geckho and Miyelonian star systems? Star City will soon come under attack by the Composite. Is it wise to hide that information from my people?"

"It seemed to me that Krong Laa Ush-Vayzzz was intentionally creating panic and mentioned the threat to the Geckho and Miyelonian capitals for the purpose of gaining support from those races in the war against the Composite. A wise and experienced politician such as him could not let slip such a convenient chance to turn the attention of two spacefaring races against an enemy of the Meleyephatian Horde. Speaking of that..." I recalled what my Chief Advisor Gerd Mac-Peu Un-Roi the Mage Diviner had said about the probability of a war with the Miyelonians and Geckho rising, which would make the situation for my home planet Earth worse. "Yes, I agree. We must inform Kung Keetsie Myau of the threat. The Commander of the Fourth Fleet has greater awareness of the military circumstances and, if necessary, will take measures so the Union of Miyelonian Prides will not be caught off guard. At the same time, you can tell the Great One the password to open the file she was sent."

I read the tailed lady's thoughts and found approval for my actions. And not just mere "approval," but COMPLETE APPROVAL, verging on unlimited devotion. Her loyalty to her captain was absolute. The pretty Miyelonian was prepared to carry out any order I gave and even to die for me for real, not just in the game. I admit, that made me feel somewhat ill at ease. I was no saint and did not deserve such blind devotion from my assistant.

Together with the Translator, I left the long-distance comms room in search of the "advisors" Krong Laa had spoken of to learn all the details of my upcoming diplomatic mission. And in fact, I didn't have to look far. The familiar Meleyephatian Psionic and cleanshaven tall human girl in a black uniform bearing the emblem of the Seventeenth Flotilla were waiting for me not far from the corridor. A human on a Meleyephatian Horde battleship? I was of course intrigued and read her information.

Gerd Ruwana Loki. Human. Ar Syndicate (Second Recruitment). Level-162 Psychologist.

When I left the comms room, which was shielded from outside comms, I also got three messages at once from my business partner Gerd Uline Tar.

#1. Captain, the conflict with the Cyanid ambassador has been quashed. The condition was that Kung Gnat must come to the Cyanid homeworld in the Kukun-Dra system in the near future for an official visit to establish ties.

Authority increased to 117!

Fame increased to 116.

#2. Tini respawned next to the frigate. He received a sanction from Gerd T'yu-Pan for careless behavior and was sent off for enhanced training.

#3. The captain of the large container ship the Udur Vayeh *came by for a visit. A Human by race from the Gilvar Syndicate. He tried to throw his weight around, acted rude and demanded compensation for the attack on his crew. He threatened to sue us and bragged about his connections with Serpea's new rulers. Grim Reaper and Eduard Boyko sent the wise guy somersaulting down the gangway.*

The last message was worrying. It wasn't as if I feared aggression from the roguish but peaceful cargo ship, but I didn't want to ruin my relationship with the new ruler of Serpea King Peyeru-Y the Eleventh, which was already getting rocky. And now that my ward had respawned and was back in the crew, I sent an order to the *Tamara the Paladin* to leave the station and wait for me in near space. After that, I headed out to the two waiting advisors.

I greeted the psychologist with a curt nod and she immediately extended me a crystal memory drive. As she did, she was staring me intently in the face. Was it my glowing blue eyes again? I knew they could be disturbing and even scary to people seeing them for the first time. However, that didn't last long and soon the Psychologist looked like she'd just come to after nearly drowning, gathered her thoughts and started her speech. Gerd Ruwana was speaking the language of the Horde though and quite hastily, so I needed translation.

"Kung Gnat, we have prepared you an information packet about prior contacts with the 'Empire,'" Gerd Ayni translated the fast clicking and chirring coming from the Human woman. "A chronology of encounters, the sector of Empire space our scouts have mapped, a beacon map, video footage of battles and brief summaries, as well as work by our translation department to decode the messages we've intercepted. For a more detailed rundown, I ask that you come with us to the briefing room."

Both of the advisors turned and headed down the corridor. Before stashing the crystal in my inventory, I nevertheless scanned the suspicious object. Nope, all clear. It was indeed a simple data crystal containing no bugs, explosives or other unpleasant surprises.

"Beacon map?" I asked, having heard an

unfamiliar term.

"Yes, Kung," Gerd Ruwana replied without turning around. "The Empire's starships use a network of stationary beacons placed at spatial weakness points for quick transport. It allows hyperspace jumps to be made over significantly greater distances, speeding up travel between star systems by dozens of times. The beacons also reduce the energy required for activating a hyperspace tunnel. It is a highly useful technology and has already been studied by Horde scientists. The unequalled Krong Laa Ush-Vayzzz ordered a tong and a half ago to begin construction on two beacon chains in Horde space intended only for combat ships. It has allowed the Horde's fleets to bring down their travel time significantly. Now, going from the central systems to the Aysar Cluster no longer takes a tong and a half as before, but thirty times less. However, when the Composite invaded, the majority of the beacons were turned off so the enemy couldn't use them."

Our escorts stopped in front of yet another door, and the Psychologist used a keycard to unlock it. She gestured to invite Ayni and me inside, then entered the small room with three soft plush armchairs. The Meleyephatian stayed outside. As soon as the doors had closed, the young woman turned up the brightness on the ceiling lights, took the farthest-away armchair and turned it so she could see me and the Miyelonian at the same time.

"Kung Gnat, I have been authorized to answer any questions you might have related to the diplomatic mission. I have been to the Aysar Cluster twice. During the second and third contacts I was charged with establishing relations with representatives of the Empire. Unfortunately, I was not successful. Nevertheless, I am prepared to tell you everything I saw with my own eyes and what I was able to find out."

She was still speaking Meleyephatian and that was exactly what spawned my first question.

"I have a fairly easy time learning other races' languages. I am fluent in Geckho and Miyelonian, conversant in Relict and have a basic comprehension of Trillian. I can even pronounce a few phrases in their language. But I am unable to reproduce the high-frequency sounds of Meleyephatian. I must admit, I actually thought humans were incapable of doing so. How can you speak it?"

"I had a surgical operation on my vocal cords," Ruwana pointed at a barely visible thin white scar on her neck. "Every child in our colony receives it in infancy in order to be able to learn the Horde's main language. The language of the Meleyephatians is the only acceptable mode of communication in the Ar Syndicate. The use of other languages is strictly forbidden."

I see... I was not willing to go so far as to have my vocal cords manipulated. Alright, I would have to keep using a Translator for all my conversations with members of the Horde. I asked Gerd Ruwana to tell me about the first three "contacts," as she put it, with the Human Empire without going into detail. Most likely, all this information was on the crystal drive she'd given to me, and I was planning to study it in my free time. But now I wanted the condensed version.

The psychologist responded eagerly.

"First contact. Approximately three tongs ago. Reconnaissance flotilla two hundred eleven discovered an unusual anomaly. A hyperspace beacon as we later realized. Ships were sent to the Aysar Cluster to investigate. The beacon was studied, but beyond the beacon itself nothing of interest was found. However, another three beacons were visible from the system. The flotilla continued on and encountered a large fleet of starships belonging to an unknown race. Around three hundred enemy ships headed by a huge flagship. Here it is."

Gerd Ruwana activated a palmtop, and scenes shot from what seemed to be a very great distance appeared on a three-dimensional holographic screen in the middle of the room. There was barely a hint of the small-class ships, just slowly moving dark splotches. However, the dark giant made an impression – a huge flat-disk or rather puck-shaped ship. There was no way to determine its linear dimensions with nothing for scale, but the starship was without a doubt huge.

"The Horde's ships were immediately hit with a barrage of powerful psionic waves. They caused a state of panic and feelings of despair which very few captains could withstand. At the same time, the enemy fleet went on the attack, easily destroying the recon flotilla's helpless ships. Very few escaped, mainly cloaked frigates. And that was the end of the first contact. Then the Meleyephatian Horde began preparing for the next encounter with its newly discovered space neighbor."

The psychologist turned off the hologram, crossed her legs and continued her tale.

"We made great preparations before the second contact. Three thousand ships, among them one hundred fifty cruisers and a whole five battleships. It was assumed that would be sufficient forces to suppress any possible resistance and subjugate the new race. I found myself on one of the small ships of the fleet being sent to the war. I was given the task of communicating with prisoners. It was my first serious assignment. Command had studied materials from the first expedition and so all crews underwent enhanced preparation to resist mental attacks. We were trained doggedly to stand up against mind control, be able to tell hallucinations and induced images from reality and forced to take pills by the handful. So much time has passed, yet I can still recall the vile flavor in my mouth..."

Most likely, Gerd Ruwana was referring to the pills Horde troopers had swallowed in my presence before. I asked the Psychologist to pause her story and tell me more about these tablets.

"Yes, here they are," she extended me a blister pack of blue pills. "They are issued to every Meleyephatian trooper as part of the standard army kit. They provide base resistance to psionics and improve the Mental Fortitude skill by a third for those that have it. But the tablets didn't prove necessary. There was no mind control. As soon as our fleet exited warp near the beacon in the Aysar Cluster, it was attacked by enemy stealth bombers. The nuclear and gravity bombs landed with great accuracy. Before we even realized what was going on, we had lost two thirds of our ships. My frigate was also destroyed along with hundreds of others while just two of us managed to get away in an escape pod. I was very lucky to have the pod picked up before the enemy's main forces arrived because, after that, they stopped trying to rescue survivors. But I survived the first phase of battle and saw what happened next with my own eyes. My observations formed the basis of the report on the events in the Aysar Cluster system, which were sent to the unequalled Krong Laa, Commander of the First Fleet. That was how I was deemed a valuable staff member by the leader of the Meleyephatian Horde and given permission to bear children."

Astrolinguistics skill increased to level one hundred fourteen!

Of course the phrase about the Humans of the Ar Syndicate needing to have permission from their Meleyephatian masters to bear children jumped out at me. But I didn't interrupt her tale and continued listening carefully.

"The Empire didn't send that many starships, just around three hundred. There were no heavy ships among them, just light cruisers, frigates and interceptors. But those starships were very distinct from the ones we saw on first contact. What happened next is hard to call a battle. The enemy was constantly on the move and slicing our fleet to bits with the ease of a skilled butcher, destroying all ships that broke off from the main group. Meanwhile, attempts to join together in a dense group led to more stealth bomber strikes at the core of the fleet. All attempts to contact the Empire's ships and conduct negotiations proved fruitless. It was all over in a quarter ummi. No one escaped. My ship was also destroyed, and I respawned far from the scene of events..."

Gerd Ruwana was speaking very emotionally. Using frenzied gesticulation and heavy breathing, she was capably playing with her voice and facial expression, taking strictly measured pauses at the exact right places in her narrative to inspire empathy in her audience. I found myself unwittingly admiring the capable work of the master rhetorician and the story itself had pulled me in. On top of that, she was not bad to look at... I never thought I'd find a bald woman pretty, but Ruwana Loki seemed to be an exception.

Mental Fortitude skill increased to level one hundred thirty-one!

Shuddering as if I'd seen a ghost, I mentally got on guard and put up my bristles like a hedgehog. I even checked if psionics had been used. No, there was no magic from Gerd Ruwana. Just the expert vocal work, professionally set light, favorably emphasized pretty facial features and precise movements of a skilled predator on the hunt. But that was not all. I could barely hold back a smile when I looked at the data of the gas analyzer built into my ancient armor suit. There we go! Traces of a narcotic gas known to induce a relaxed state. The same one used in Miyelonian casinos so their patrons would let their guard down. As well as pheromones. The psychologist was well prepared for this meeting and was trying very hard to catch my eye. For some reason she needed me. I wonder why.

But when I tried to reach out to her thoughts, a response came straight away.

"You shouldn't do that, Kung Gnat! I am well protected against mind control and am currently on tablets. Plus why read my thoughts? I'm answering your every question honestly as is."

"Every question? Alright, then tell me what all this is for," I said with a broad gesture at the room. "There are drugs and other chemicals in the air."

After I said that, my Translator Gerd Ayni put her helmet on and activated air filtration. I did not follow the Miyelonian's lead, though I was prepared at any moment to defend myself against her control and charms by putting down my spacesuit helmet's mirrored faceguard as well.

"This?" If Gerd Ruwana was ashamed, she didn't express it at all. "I was ordered to attend the negotiations with the Empire, but the only way to do that is to join your crew. And doing that would be very difficult without such little tricks because Free Captain Kung Gnat, despite all his neutrality does not accept members of the Meleyephatian Horde in his team. Which is very strange, because he is no longer an enemy of the Horde and has been granted complete freedom of action."

"But why should I want you on my frigate? I

have a full crew. As it is there are no internal conflicts, and the crewmembers all obey their captain rather than any outside curators. Your joining would upset the balance. Plus, why do I need a foreign observer playing her own game and revealing our secrets to the outside? Furthermore, we speak Geckho on my ship, which you do not know."

"That is not entirely true, Kung Gnat. I do understand Geckho, but I don't speak it. But that of course is not my greatest virtue. I am an experienced Psychologist, and I can find the keys to communicate with any player regardless of race. With me around, there will be no conflicts. Furthermore, I can serve as your pass to any star system or facility belonging to the Meleyephatian Horde. The people of the Ar Syndicate colony have earned the Horde's trust and are nearly equal in rights to the Meleyephatians. Furthermore I have the trust of the brilliant Krong Laa. You will have available repair and modernization of your ship at our military facilities, dock on our motherships and even quick travel via the Meleyephatian Horde's beacon system. You will have access to the market of the most modern equipment and a military contract database. You will also have the cooperation of local authorities in thousands of star systems in our galaxy. If I were in your crew, Kung Gnat, none would so much as dare to glance sidelong at a member of your team in a restaurant in the Serpea system."

Gerd Ruwana's speech was well-composed. Even though the Horde's beacons were of little interest to me, much less help solving conflicts with authorities. The most modern equipment? Interesting of course, though I assumed the price of truly new stuff would be exorbitant. Not for my current financial state. But the Psychologist had said something else that really caught my attention. Access to the Horde's secret facilities. I had seemingly found the key that could open the door to the space prison that held the "embodiment of absolute evil." As soon as Ruwana mentioned the possibility, as far as I was concerned, her fate was decided. However, I was afraid she might not look too kindly on my plans.

"I'll think about it," I said, not getting ahead of myself. "First I want to hear the rest of the story. On the basis of what facts was it concluded that the Horde was doing battle with Humans specifically in the far-off Aysar Cluster?"

She seemed to be expecting more in response to her listing off the advantages of letting her join my crew. Gerd Ruwana had a hard time keeping the smile on her face and didn't allow the frustrated expression to slip through. But still the Psychologist got her emotions under control and continued the story.

"After the battle, the enemy picked up our escape pods in space. In accordance with instructions, given the threat of being taken prisoner, the Horde troopers killed themselves in order to respawn in a safe location. But a few of them, holding poison at the ready, waited around to try and learn something about the enemy. As a rule, the escape pods were opened by large six-legged creatures. Strong, fast and covered in a tough layer of natural armor just like the Meleyephatians, they had two huge faceted eyes on the sides of their head. And the brutes had long and sharp front appendages, which they put into action at the slightest sign of resistance. But the Horde's psionics still read the thoughts of the six-legged creatures and found that they were just obedient foot soldiers of their commanders, who were Humans by race. They even read the names of a few captains and commanders. Among them was the name of the Human woman commanding the Empire's fleet in that battle. Admiral Nicole ton Savoia. 'Hero of the Alien War,' 'headquarters tactics instructor,' 'feisty bitch,' 'the Emperor's finest hound,' 'Georg the First's darling,' and other such glowing epithets."

"Feisty bitch?" I shuddered. It's hard to call that praise for a woman commander. I was also interested in the etymology there. After all, a bitch is a female dog. The word "hound" was also a reference to dogs. How did the Meleyephatians know about Earth animals? Although... Valeri the Beast Master from a far-off quarantine planet had a big creature with her that was very similar to a panther. Maybe there were also dogs elsewhere in the Universe.

At any rate, I had more important questions. I put all the nonsense about space dogs out of my mind and asked to be told about the third "contact."

"Third contact..." Gerd Ruwana Loki started retelling readily. "The events in the Aysar Cluster system during the second contact are top secret because such a crushing defeat could damage the Horde's authority on the political arena. But Meleyephatian Horde command has conducted a very thorough analysis and conclusions have been drawn. Almost a third of the First Fleet was sent to put down our insolent neighbor, eight thousand starships. Unfortunately, the beacon system had not yet been constructed, so Krong Laa was unable to take part in the operation with the core of the First Fleet, but the Meleyephatian Horde had plenty of experienced admirals without its greatest Strategist. That time, underestimating the enemy was completely out of the question. We had conducted deep recon in the Empire's space and held never-ending training sessions. The fleet arrived in the Aysar Cluster system at full battle readiness and... just sat there for eleven days, unable to work up the nerve to go further. Our scouts were constantly telling us about enemy ship movements. We spotted three fleets at once, so we waited for the enemy to arrive and prepared surprises, placing thousands of space mines along all possible attack vectors. But..."

The Psychologist shook her head sadly and I realized right away that the third "contact" had also ended in tragedy for the Horde.

"A new beacon turned on right in the middle of the system and the Empire's fleet of seven hundred ships appeared right there. It was again composed of speedy light starships and catching them was no simple task. That was the start of a long carousel situation. Short clashes where our fleet lost a few ships, then another explosion of distance. And so it went many times. We tried to get in touch with our foe to talk, suggested they surrender and promised to spare them. And once we even got a response. Here is that message."

The Psychologist again activated her communicator, calling up a holographic image. A large creature similar to a praying mantis chirred out a short trill. Gerd Ayni, seated next to me, spoke out in surprise:

"That's Meleyephatian, even though it's a strong and unusual accent. The message says 'You don't talk to your food. You eat it.'"

"Yes, that response really stumped our admirals. They still thought they were dominant on the battlefield and were just about to crush their puny adversary, but the enemy didn't even seem to perceive the Horde's fleet as a serious opponent, just playing tag and bringing down our ship count."

Wait! I asked for the video to be rewound to the very beginning, then put on pause. I had seen such creatures before! In the strange "prophetic" dream Gerd Soia-Tan shared with me there were "praying mantises" like this one standing around the perimeter of the big room. So those were the Emperor's bodyguards!

"Something the matter?" Gerd Ruwana Loki wanted to know, but I shook my head "no" and asked her to continue her story.

"At a certain point, it seemed our adversary made a mistake and was in a tough spot. Our fleet latched into our prey with all its arms and legs but... it was a trap. At first there was a stealth bomber attack, and we lost a large number of small ships. After that, from out of nowhere the EMPIRE'S TRUE FLEET joined the battle, taking over for the lure that drew us in and killed time. What's surprising is that our scouts totally overlooked that fleet, having spent the last few days observing the little distraction flotillas and not noticing the main armada. A great number of enemies arrived, around twenty thousand starships. And that one was definitely a HEAVY FLEET. Two colossal black motherships, a huge destroyer, forty carriers, three hundred battleships and as many as two thousand cruisers. Our adversary released over one million combat drones, tied down all of our heavy ships with stasis webs and blocked our hyperspace engines, taking our targeting systems out of commission with radio-electronic equipment, and then the beatdown began... Eight thousand of the Horde's starships were blasted to smithereens like clay pigeons. In the course of the whole battle, our adversary only lost thirty-four small-class ships. On an order from Krong Laa, all senior commanders in charge of the third 'contact' were executed for incompetence and expansion was declared forbidden for the Meleyephatian Horde in the direction of the Empire..."

The cleanshaven woman fell silent, then finished her story.

"The Meleyephatian Horde possesses truly limitless industrial potential, and all the losses we sustained were quickly replaced. The First Fleet was even made stronger and fully modernized. But no attempt was made for a fourth 'contact.' Although the unequalled Strategist Krong Laa Ush-Vayzzz was himself personally leading the whole first fleet toward the Aysar Cluster beacon, and no one in the galaxy could possibly stand up against such a force, a series of political events changed the wise Horde leader's plans. Furthermore, our scouts have reported that we wouldn't be able to pull off a sudden attack – the Empire's main fleet was at full readiness and anticipating an invasion. Meanwhile, Human frigates have now been spotted even in Horde border systems. And so the unmatched and unerring Krong Laa made a decision to spare his forces and sign a peace treaty with Georg the First."

I see... I myself would find it interesting to catch a glimpse of the force that made the Meleyephatian Horde put its tail between its legs and retreat. Earth could really use such a powerful ally. I looked thoughtfully at the Psychologist woman awaiting my response, weighing everything in my head again and voiced my decision.

"I have two conditions. The first, which is nonnegotiable: no crew members can know about my conversation with the leader of the Meleyephatian Horde. If you talk, you'll be sent out to learn to breathe in a vacuum. Second: you will not constantly nag me to complete the diplomatic mission. I cannot go to the Aysar Cluster right this minute. I have some urgent tasks to complete, including waiting for my 'transport' to come back from its sojourn through the Universe. In any case, that will make things go much quicker than flying via a chain of beacons, especially given some of the beacons are switched off. If you accept my conditions, you may go pack up your personal items, and I'll see you on the *Tamara the Paladin.*"

"I have no personal items. So I am ready to go, Captain!"

Chapter Twelve

Urgent Delivery

"I DON'T TRUST HER!" the Miyelonian whispered to me as soon as Gerd Ruwana Loki asked us to wait a bit and walked away to discuss with shuttle hangar security.

"Me neither. She is fanatically devoted to the Horde, and all her actions are aimed at helping her masters. But for now we need Gerd Ruwana, and the plusses from her presence outweigh the minuses. At any rate we'll keep an eye on her."

Our escort came back somewhat distraught, saying we had gone to the wrong hangar because the Meleyephatians had directed the *Tamara the Paladin*'s shuttle to a different one, and that was how our group would be getting back to the frigate. However, we had to traverse the several-mile-long battleship on foot to get there.

"Check out that level of trust, Kung Gnat. You should appreciate it. To pass through the inner rooms of a flagship requires Ro-III clearance. Not even all Horde space fleet officers have that. But you and the Miyelonian are being let through."

With those words the Psychologist took a yellow and red ribbon with a constellation of small red crystals forming an unfamiliar complex hieroglyph out of her inventory and clipped it onto the right sleeve of her light spacesuit. The Miyelonian's eyes went wide in surprise, and the Translator answered my unasked question.

"That is a Komisho badge. It is given to high-rank officers of the scouting or diplomatic corps from Meleyephatian Horde vassal races. The correspondence isn't one-to-one, but it approximately lines up with colonel rank in terms of Earth military titles. But if I understand the restrictions linked with wearing the Komisho correctly, Gerd Ruwana does not have the right to bear or use arms. At all. Even a knife. And she cannot give orders to troops. She is only to observe and pass information up to analysts who are authorized to process it."

"Yes, that is true," Gerd Ruwana demonstrated with a trill in Horde language that she was also familiar with Miyelonian. "I am merely an observer, not a trooper or commander. But I am a high-rank observer. To speak the honest truth, the number of Meleyephatians in the whole Seventeenth Flotilla that outrank me can be counted on one hand. All the rest are required to defend me with their lives and cooperate with me on any issue however I require. And there by the way is the support I requested."

In the end, we didn't have to stomp through the endless halls of the combat ship on our own two. The eight-legged trooper drove over a light flying vehicle made for two Meleyephatians. Or two people and one Miyelonian. Gerd Ayni and I took the second row, Gerd Ruwana sat in the driver's seat, input a destination on the console and sat back in the chair, letting the autopilot steer the vehicle itself. The flying car dashed off as fast as a racecar, pressing me back in the seat. Corridors and rooms flickered by. Armored barriers automatically opened just a fraction of a second before we went slamming into them. Eight legged troopers flashed past, having just stumbled out of our path. The light gave way to darkness, rooms, corridors, hangars for armored landing craft, then more corridors...

Cartography skill increased to level ninety-three!

Eagle Eye skill increased to level one hundred thirteen!

I had to grab the handle with both hands so I wouldn't fly out on sharp turns. The Miyelonian also felt uncomfortable and latched into me, her teeth clenched to the point of crunching so she wouldn't accidentally start squealing and bring down her Authority in front of a stranger. I suspected Gerd Ruwana had chosen for the flying vehicle to travel this fast on purpose to stop us outsiders from seeing something valuable or even confidential on the flotilla's flagship. Given that, the Psychologist's recent statement about the "trust being shown" to me seemed somewhat less than genuine. But then a minute and a half later the flying vehicle braked abruptly and quietly set down on the floor five feet away from the *Tamara the*

Paladin's familiar shuttle.

We moved into the shuttle, and I took the helm. Thankfully, the shuttle hangar forcefield had turned off, and the classic shape of the twinbody frigate was impossible to confuse with anything else even at great distance. I found it somewhat strange to see Cleopian interceptors spinning loops around my frigate. But still they didn't display any aggression, just demonstrating their presence, so I decided to simply ignore them.

Machine Control skill increased to level one hundred nineteen!

Telekinesis skill increased to level sixty-three!

I hadn't so much as touched the helm and, seemingly, Gerd Ruwana had yet to realize the shuttle was not on autopilot. Three minutes later, our flying vehicle reached the frigate and was snatched up by the gravity crane. Geckho Supercargo Avan Toi was there to greet us but stopped with his mouth agape when he saw a representative of the Meleyephatian Horde on board. So I wouldn't have to explain it to every team member individually, I activated the loudspeaker.

"Attention, crew! We have a passenger! Gerd Ruwana Loki, a Psychologist by class and observer from the Meleyephatian Horde. Her presence on board is to serve as confirmation of our neutrality, which is very important to maintain. Furthermore, Gerd Ruwana has helped us settle some issues connected with recent events on the station. She will be with us to observe for two or three voyages. Her status is that of a guest of the captain. Gerd Ruwana can understand the Geckho and

Miyelonian languages but reserves the right not to respond in them. You are not to load her down with work, but you should feed her and give her a place to stay. And Tini, no practicing your thief skills on her! At any rate, our guest doesn't have anything of value. I checked with a scan. And you, little one, don't go digging in our guest's thoughts! No other limitations. You may and in fact must speak with our guest. I am counting on you all to treat her well."

As far as I could tell from a cursory skim of the team's emotional background, no one was feeling negativity over the message. The Psychologist then said something, and Gerd Ayni got straight to translating.

"Gerd Ruwana says she can be given work assignments. And that she would like to join the crew with an official work contract for three to five voyages."

"Denied. We only take the best of the best, and the right to join Team Gnat has to be earned."

I handed our guest off to my assistant Gerd Uline Tar, then listened to a report from Supercargo Avan Toi. The containers for urgent delivery had been placed in the cargo hold, aligned for weight and strapped down tight.

"Captain, trust my experience. These guys are up to no good. Either they're smugglers or something else," the Supercargo said quietly, activating his tablet and poking a claw into the lines on screen. "The cargo manifest indicates two automatic processing plants, but we were in fact given a vertical layer fracturing device, deep subsurface sapper robots and several *megatons* of explosives. No one that really owns an ore deposit would ever use such a method to harvest such valuable resources. Only troublemakers looking to make off with a big jackpot and bail before the real owners show up."

"That is exactly what they want – to make money as quickly as possible and pick up as much as they can load. The GF-111K system will find itself in the midst of the war with the Composite any day now, and all valuables left behind will be taken by the intergalactic invaders. And that's why the owners of the ore deposit are in such a rush. And so we are also hurrying to deliver the cargo, then escape the danger zone."

The sullen Supercargo scratched the back of his head in thought. Such a possibility had truly not even crossed to his mind. I then gave the Geckho an approving shoulder pat and headed to the captain's bridge. My attention was drawn by some Cleopian interceptors that were interested in my ship. Ayukh the Navigator explained:

"Captain Gnat, message from the station dispatchers. They are demanding we return to dock. The captain of the *Udur Vayeh* has sued us over the events in Blue Glow. Hearings are scheduled for the day after tomorrow, and the local authorities are demanding that Free Captain Kung Gnat attend in person. They even sent interceptors so you won't try to run away and dodge the court session."

Have they completely lost it?! I have a contract for urgent delivery of drilling equipment, and I have to be in the GF-111K system in ten ummi or risk finding myself blacklisted as an unreliable transporter. Looks like I'm about to find out just how much the Horde observer's words about her high status and extensive capabilities are worth...

"Do we really have to pander to the whims of any old stranger? Ayukh, have you calculated a route to our destination?"

"Of course, Captain. It's pretty far, to be honest. Eight ummi underway. But we can make it on schedule."

"Excellent! Dmitry Zheltov, set a course for the GF-111K system. Accelerate for hyperspace jump." I turned the loudspeaker back on. "Gunners, man your weapons! Target the Cleopian interceptors. Do not open fire, simply demonstrate readiness to do battle."

After that, I activated the comms system and made an announcement to the dispatchers and everyone else observing my starship.

"This is Free Captain Kung Gnat. Docking command denied. I am carrying out a mission for a representative of Krong Laa aboard my ship. I request the captain of *Udur Vayeh* be told 'screw you' and advised to stay out of my way on the space highways."

My frigate went into motion, working its maneuver thrusters and turning toward the distant GF-111K system. After that, the main thruster switched on. Any outside observer could have clearly seen that the *Tamara the Paladin* was not planning to obey the Cleopian dispatchers' order and was taking a vector in the opposite direction of the nearby space station. I was sitting at total readiness, expecting aggression at any moment from the Cleopian interceptors and preparing in that case to immediately engage the frigate's combat electronics and command the Gunners to eliminate our enemies. However, not one of the four interceptors activated a stasis web or disruptor or even tried to point their cannons at my ship. We were in fact being let go. And that was strange because such blatant disobedience from a foreign spaceship would surely have a detrimental effect on the local ruler's Authority.

ATTENTION!!! Failure to comply with government demands! Free Captain Kung Gnat's danger rating has risen to three.

ATTENTION!!! The authorities of the Serpea star system have named Free Captain Kung Gnat persona non-grata. You have two ummi to leave the Serpea star system.

ATTENTION!!! A bounty for Free Captain Kung Gnat's head has been set at two million Geckho crystals.

Fame increased to 117.

Fame increased to 118.

That seemed to be the extent of what my foes could do – flip out in impotent rage and attempt to harm me without explicit violence. Two million crystals? They must not think I'm worth all that much! I also suspected the "persona non-grata" status would go away as soon as the Cleopian ruler was overthrown. In any case, I had nothing more to do here.

"Let's jump out!" I commanded and at that very second the stars shifted, and space rolled up into a bright tunnel.

The new rulers of Serpea had in fact not been brave enough to tangle with a Meleyephatian Horde observer and bite the hand that fed and protected them. They just showed that I had upset them, but their approval meant nothing to me.

I was eating a meal in the frigate's common room seated at a table with Vasily Andreyevich Filippov the Bard and Dmitry Zheltov the Starship Pilot. Today the Chef Assassin felt called to experiment and Amati-Kuis Ursssh had prepared "Earth delicacies," as she told me with unabashed pride while setting the table. I thanked the six-legged girl for thinking of me and her terrestrial crewmates, though it was tough to guess what dishes from my home planet she was aiming for with her heap of purple seaweed doused in transparent gluey sauce, or the baked two-foot-long trilobite. Still, it was all edible and even surprisingly tasty. In fact, the Miyelonians and Geckho at the neighboring table were stuffing their faces with the "Earth delicacies" and praising Amati-Kuis's cooking.

"Well, guys let's have a little drink to calm our nerves after Serpea," the Bard took a bottle of vodka made by "time-honored technique" from his inventory and poured us each a single shot.

I didn't object and the Starship Pilot was just

coming off a shift, so he could afford to let himself unwind a bit.

"So Gnat, I heard our guys were sent to Un-Tau as you were saying," Vasily Filippov shared the latest news from under the Dome. "They landed on the comet an ummi ago. If you can call what they did a landing. It's probably more accurately described as a 'crash' or 'disaster.' One of the large Geckho landing ships was blasted to smithereens by Meleyephatian anti-space defense systems, while two more slammed to the comet's surface with no shields and engulfed in flame, so they aren't likely to be able to take back off. The landing group disembarked under heavy fire and, at the cost of massive losses, made its way into a multi-level underground complex. I think they were saying it's some kind of important spider shrine."

"You can say that again!" I snorted mockingly, stunned by how little the participants in the operation actually knew. "It is only the origin point of all life in the Universe. At least, Meleyephatian scientists came to that conclusion a few centuries ago. For renegades of many nests, the temple carved into the glaciers of Un-Tau is the most important shrine in existence. Furthermore, there is a place of power there where Psionics experience epiphanies and previously hidden abilities of the mind are awakened. For Meleyephatian political leaders, a visit to Un-Tau temple is de rigueur. They cannot be considered fully fledged political leaders until making the pilgrimage. So the Horde will fight like mad for that shrine, showing no mercy to either their enemies or their own."

I set down my glass as the soldier poured us a second round.

"Yeah, I guess so," Vasily Andreyevich continued. "They say it's a living hell down there. Everywhere crawling with spiders, the Army of Earth's troopers are paying for every captured corridor with hundreds and even thousands of lives. One good thing is that the Meleyephatians aren't using heavy weaponry or nuclear explosives in the shrine. But even still our guys are dropping like flies. One hole in their spacesuit and it's all over, they get sent to rez. The landing team will be lucky if they can hold their position for two days. Then after they respawn, the Geckho are forming them into new squadrons and preparing to ship them back out to the ice comet."

"Yeah, sounds gruesome... But as far as I understand, the Army of Earth was not tasked with capturing the shrine. That would be practically impossible. They're just supposed to serve as a distraction for the Horde to untie our suzerains' hands for the real attack on other star systems."

"That is true, Captain. But still it isn't nice that Humans are made to serve as cannon fodder..." the Bard fell silent sharply because Gerd Ruwana Loki came up to our table with a dish in her hands.

There were plenty of seats at the neighboring tables, but the Horde observer chose ours and, not asking permission, sat down next to the three of us. We scooted over to make room.

"Captain Gnat, you've got pretty good chow

on your ship. No comparison with the stale rations they serve on Horde starships."

I had a hard time pulling up my dropped jaw. Had the Horde representative just spoken Geckho? Although... What choice did she have? Gerd Ayni the Translator was now in the real world, while no other crew members would understand our guest's whistling and trilling. Seeing our astonishment, the Psychologist broke down laughing.

"There's no need for such surprised looks. I am not forbidden from using other languages to communicate. The same way no one forbids humans from walking around on all fours or crawling. Still it's more comfortable to stay on two feet and walk upright. In the same way, I find it more comfortable to speak the galaxy's most common language especially given it is my native tongue. But I had to do something to break the linguistic isolation. And now that the conversation has started, give me a splash of whatever you're drinking!" Gerd Ruwana swallowed a glass of compote in one big swig and pushed the empty glass toward Vasily Filippov.

The Bard looked at me dubiously, awaiting his captain's decision. But I just shrugged my shoulders, not knowing what to do. I didn't want to hear complaints that we were getting our observer drunk. But still, Gerd Ruwana was an adult woman, and you shouldn't say no to a guest. Vasily Andreyevich split the last of the vodka between our four glasses with droplet-level accuracy, as if using a burette in a chemistry lab.

"To the meeting of different branches of

humanity!" the Starship Pilot looked happier as soon as our guest came and even stood up while giving his toast. "May this meeting be beneficial and educational for both our peoples!"

We drank. Gerd Ruwana also tried to drain her glass to the bottom but choked and coughed. Tears welled up in her eyes. Once finished coughing, the cleanshaven Psychologist apologized.

"I have drunk alcohol before. Twice. But those were sweet Miyelonian cocktails. I wasn't expecting such a strong beverage... I apologize again."

"Don't the Meleyephatians drink alcohol? I have seen them in bars many times on different space stations."

"Kung Gnat, those were most likely civilians. Horde military does not allow alcohol or any other psychoactive substances for that matter. Furthermore, I am a human by race so I have to be more of a 'proper Meleyephatian' than they do. Such is the price of fitting into a more numerous and powerful society."

We sat in silence for a bit, unhurriedly slurping down the contents of our plates and singing the chef's praises. But then Dmitry Zheltov inquired:

"Ruwana, so what is your role on Horde ships? You carry no weapon, so you must not be taking part in combat operations. Do you work for intelligence, exposing unreliable elements and potential traitors?"

"Not at all," she laughed happily. "I am not to be looked upon as a component of the punishment system. I am a Psychologist. I am tasked with helping troopers keep up the faith that they're on the right path. I answer questions, soothe frustrations and help avoid conflicts, which are an inevitability on overcrowded starships undertaking long space flights. But I am first and foremost an observer. I note interesting details, quirks and deviations from the accepted norm, and bring to light potentially capable players who could improve their abilities or rank if given the right push or additional training. Having an observer on a starship is seen as a good thing because the common soldiers and commanders see it as a chance to prove themselves and advance their career."

"I suspect you will have seen a ton of 'deviations' from the patterns typical on Horde starships on our frigate," the Bard chuckled.

"Indeed," the Psychologist didn't hide it. "This place breaks the mold. I see many quirks and mysteries that leave me perplexed. You have many races under one roof, but there are no conflicts in the crew. It isn't something you see often. I have also seen two Mechanoid repair bots. They are rare and independent-minded machines, and you have two on one small ship? Odd. Then there's an NPC creature on a combat ship. That is a great rarity. As is the Jarg. Members of that race are generally found working in large analytical centers rather than roving the galaxy in the crews of Free Captains. I was also struck by the Miyelonian adolescent. Tini I believe he was called. His race has a tradition of showing off important life events with trophies and decor attached to their heads...”

That perked my ears up because I myself didn't know much about this Miyelonian tradition. Still it was true that every Miyelonian in my crew had a whole set of trophies and all kinds of decor on their helmet and furry ears. Tini the little thief and our Medic, even our Engineer had a striking abundance of little chains and earrings. Ayni the Translator, too. I would be curious to know what my tailed assistant was trying to communicate to her compatriots with them. Meanwhile, the observer continued.

“Anyway, the little thief has three earrings in his left ear bearing the emblem of the Great Priestess. Those are handed out personally by Leng Amiru after her sermons, and few of the thousands of pilgrims in attendance are lucky enough to get one. And so I'm just lost in guesses. Has Tini really traveled through the galaxy following the Priestess long enough to be selected three times? That would be odd because the adolescent is not particularly religious otherwise...”

The conversation was getting onto shaky terrain. A bit more of this and Gerd Ruwana would guess that Tini was closely linked to the incarnation of the Great First Female and working for her if she hadn't already come to that conclusion. Fortunately, our guest was distracted by the Bard.

“So, is there anything else you can say, for instance, about me?”

She cast a long look at the middle-aged man and started to choose her words carefully.

"Your military past jumps right out, no hiding that. As does the fact that the captain treats you with great respect. You once had a high rank in the military. Actually, no..." I can't say what emotions the observer was reading on the Bard's face, but she corrected herself at once. "You're active military. And proud not only of a heroic past, but also of your present. I think you're an observer like me, but from Earth military command. And you were promoted recently, likely sometime in the last few days."

Vasily Andreyevich gave a few approving claps.

"Bullseye! The day before yesterday I was promoted to colonel."

Well, well! Why was I, the captain of this starship, always last to hear this kind of news? I wonder what valuable information my crew member had told the Dome project curators to earn himself a promotion.

"So that means you know more about all of us than we know about you," came a comment from our Starship Pilot. "Can you tell us about yourself? Because we've never met Humans from the Ar Syndicate before and know absolutely nothing about you."

I would also have liked to hear that, but Gerd Ayni appeared in the common room doorway, found me with her eyes and beckoned. Had something happened? I apologized and got up from the table.

"My Captain, Kung Keetsie Myau would like to see you in the real world. The Great One asked me to say that she is delighted with the gift and really appreciated the information about the Composite's forces and movements. Her Fourth Fleet will be departing Kasti-Utsh III tomorrow. And for that reason, Keetsie would like to invite you to a 'small friendly gathering,' as she put it. In a quarter ummi in your hotel suite."

I must admit, I was somewhat perplexed. Leave the game in a "red" zone? Safety instructions were categorically against that. But still, there was absolutely no way to refuse. As if able to sense my doubts, the orange Translator added:

"Kung Keetsie promises not to make you answer any tough questions such as about the claim to your home planet or the mobile laboratory situation. Just a friendly dinner. She also has a special gift waiting for you!"

Chapter Thirteen

A Special Gift

HERE WAS PRECIOUS LITTLE TIME to arrange a meeting with such an honored guest, so Gerd Ayni and I were rushing. We ordered alcohol, drinks and all kinds of fruit for express delivery directly to my room. I turned down my tailed translator's idea to order in food from a restaurant, considering such a solution too boring. Instead of that, I bought the fresh meat that most strongly resembled Earth's lamb, marinades and spices along with an electronic grill. I cut and marinated it all myself while Ayni met the delivery people and set a table for four.

By the time the doorbell chimed, everything but the main dish was ready. I wiped off my hands, took off the apron and went over to meet Kung Keetsie Myau. As it turned out, the hotel hallway was packed full of First Pride troopers all tall and strong "tomcats" in white assault armor and holding their weapons at the ready. In comparison with her bodyguards, Keetsie looked dainty and waifish even though the commander was average height for a Miyelonian and just half a head shorter than me. But what surprised me most was that the Great One came alone without even her fiancé Gerd Lekku. She was wearing a perfectly white, short frock and a white sparkling half-mask covering up the dark spots on her muzzle, as well as light sandals and a small bag over her shoulder.

I greeted the ruler of the Miyelonians and kissed her fluffy white paw with its manicured claws. By the way the bodyguards twitched and the "kitty's" pupils went wide in surprise, I realized a bit too late that his gesture was unfamiliar to members of the distant spacefaring race. At any rate, Keetsie reacted positively and smiled, revealing a set of sharp little teeth.

"Humans do not have a venomous bite, you can relax," she said to her guards and walked through the doorway, open wide for her in a gesture of hospitality.

"Won't your fiancé be coming?" I asked, locking the door behind her.

"Gerd Lekku has being sanctioned and his status has been temporarily downgraded to that of a first-circle admirer. He became too predictable and boring. I grew tired of him. So let him think up ways to stand out from the group of admirers and prove himself again."

She walked into the room, looked around and read the messages left on the tabletop by herself, Valeri and Ayni with a smirk. Not a single cleaner had dared erase the marker scrawling.

"What an amusing artifact this has become! One day this table will be in a museum and our descendants will discuss what we were referring to."

Kung Keetsie took a seat in a deep armchair and good-naturedly accepted a glass of fizzy cocktail from Ayni's paws. She removed her mask, but before drinking, said:

"Tomorrow, following a decision of the Council of Rulers of the Union of Miyelonian Prides my fleet will be departing for the border to meet the Composite starships sprawling through the galaxy. So Kung Gnat, it will be some time before we meet again. If we are in fact fated to do so. The Composite is very strong and extremely murderous. Furthermore, there are many more starships invading our galaxy than we originally assumed. The enemy is capturing system after system from the Meleyephatian Horde and, at this rate, will reach the Miyelonian border within eight days. If we are unable to halt the invaders, in eleven days Composite starships will be in the Urmi system bombing Star City in both the virtual and real worlds. In an address to the nation today, I promised to move my virt pod to the capital and swore to share the fate of my millions of subjects living there. Victory or death. I will not retreat."

Ayni got down on a knee before the Great One and pronounced with trepidation in her voice:

"But milady, why put yourself at risk? Can the Union of Miyelonian Prides not find anyone else to defend it?"

"I asked the Council to send me. You see," Kung Keetsie tenderly stroked the orange hairs on her subject's head. "Being a ruler does not merely mean honor and respect. Nor is it only luxury and having an army of servants at your beck and call. It also means taking responsibility for the lives of my two hundred forty billion citizens. And I as the strongest Strategist of all the fleet commanders figured I would have a better chance of handling this than anyone else. So then, friends," Kung Keetsie raised a glass, "let's drink to the power of cannons and good fortune in battle. I get the sense I will soon be needing both of them!"

We drained our glasses, but Keetsie was not satisfied and extended her empty vessel to Ayni.

"Pour me another! And get something stronger. This may be the last peaceful night of my life. And so I want to cut loose like never before!"

The nuclear swill Ayni brought on the ruler's request was too strong for me and I set my glass aside after just the slightest taste. A beer and vodka "yorsh"[3] seemed like a light aperitif in comparison with this top-blowing beverage. I probably would have dropped dead if I'd drank the whole shot. But both Miyelonians drank theirs down, though their eyes began to shimmer and the foolish laughter they were both trying to suppress showed that the alcohol was in fact having an effect on the two space cats.

"Humans, what good are they...?" came Ayni, sparking another wave of laughter in them both.

While I placed the first portion of steaks on

---

[3] Literally meaning wire brush, this is the name of the aforementioned drink in Russian, usually containing a hefty dose of vodka.

the grill, the Great One threw off her sandals, climbed up onto the table and put a sticker over the smoke detector, saying, "this way no one will stop us from having a good time." After that, she took smoking sticks from her bag and offered one to the Translator. Falling back on the couch in an embrace, the two Miyelonians lit up. They offered me some too, but I recalled my previous unfortunate experience being carried out of a party thrown by Kung Keetsie in an unconscious state, as well as what Gerd Mauu-La Mya-Ssa the Medic said after about the smoking mixture being deadly to humans.

"I am very happy with your gift!" the Great One suddenly spoke up when I came back to the table again. "I sent the decrypted data to our head scientist and he confirmed the blueprints can be used to make a device just like it for instant travel through the Universe. But it will take time. Half a tong. Maybe even more. So the new technology won't be able to help in the war against the Composite. It will all be over before that one way or another. But say, Kung Gnat, given how quick you move and your shady ways, you probably also sent the same technology to the Geckho, Trillians, Meleyephatians and all the rest, eh?"

"Only the Geckho," I admitted because lying to such an experienced Truth Seeker would be impossible. "Krong Daveyesh-Pir was very insistent, and my race are Geckho vassals and very dependent on our suzerains. In return, I was rewarded with yet another shield generator for my home planet."

"I can't promise you a planetary shield generator. we are currently experiencing a big shortage there," the Commander of the Fourth Fleet blew a thick wisp of smoke at the ceiling and suddenly looked me right in the eyes. And meanwhile I didn't see the slightest sign of impairment. The Great One was concentrated and utterly serious. "But it is possible I will die soon, and I do not want to be in debt to anyone if I do. You need money now. So you will have money. Ten million crypto. I hope that will be enough so you won't think me less generous than the Geckho ruler."

Woah... I didn't know how the Miyelonian had learned about my financial problems. Had my business partner shared this issue with her best friend, then Ayni relayed it to her patron? Or was the Great One able to read my thoughts? I'm reminded that she once did so with ease. Although since then I had gained a lot of experience and levelled my mental defense skills quite a bit. In any case, Kung Keetsie guessed right about the gift – ten million crypto not only covered all my current debts, it also left me a solid chunk of cash to bring my Relict Faction to a higher level of development. Honestly, I was not expecting such generosity. I picked up the glass of nuclear swill and took another sip. My head went spinning, so I had to drink some juice and eat a bite of fruit. That made it a bit better. Meanwhile, Kung Keetsie carried on, observing my reaction closely.

"You can tell the ruler of your suzerains that he can relax. The Union of Miyelonian Prides will not attack the Geckho even though I cannot hide that we did have plans to do so. Krong Laa made us an offer... the specifics aren't important. You don't need to know. But the Council of Rulers agreed, and we will be joining the Meleyephatians as allies in their war against the Composite. But only with the Composite, not the Geckho or any of the Horde's other enemies. We definitely won't be going to war with the far-away Humans of the Empire. But enough about politics. Fill us some glasses! Put on some music! Let the good times roll!"

Alright then, there we were in complete agreement. I had just settled a very important problem Gerd Mac-Peu Un-Roi the Mage Diviner had warned me about − keeping the Geckho and Miyelonians from going to war and thus eliminating the very worst line of the possible future for Earth. I also fixed the Relict Faction's financial issues, which had been weighing heavily on me for the last few days. And so I was fully entitled to relax, forget my concerns and let myself fully sink into the party atmosphere!

My memory of what came next is foggy. It was all in a haze, and I mean that both literally and figuratively. Maybe it was the alcohol, and maybe it was the narcotic smoke seeping into every nook and cranny of the hotel suite and making far-away objects look blurry. At any rate, with every passing hour of raucous partying, my memories became less and less distinct and more fragmentary. I remember for sure that we danced to music. First me and Ayni, then I had the Great One as a dance partner.

After that, I put a second round of steaks on the grill because the first batch got eaten up in just a few minutes. And while the meat cooked, we gambled on a game suggested by Kung Keetsie – something like electronic roulette with sectors showing the number of gold-shaded tokens won by each player. At first we just played normally but then... we shifted to strip-roulette. I have no idea why I even agreed to it, but still I had enough good sense to stop when the pure white Miyelonian was down to just her underpants and the orange one could not boast of even that. I though had better luck.

The drunken Kung Keetsie was insulted that I ended the game and threw a couch pillow at me. I responded in kind, which led to a pillow fight, and both of the ladies worked together against me. It didn't go too well for me. The nimble, tailed beauties backed me into a corner and pushed me to the floor. Even using telekinesis to throw soft objects at my opponents wasn't much help. But then I realized the Great One was terribly afraid of tickling and Ayni came over to my side, so Team Gnat ended up winning an uncontested victory.

After that we... bleached the Great One's snout hair with hydrogen peroxide. Why? With a sober mind, it hardly seems possible to explain. I personally liked the dark "mask" set in front of her white fur. It gave Keetsie a peculiar charm. But the

Miyelonian opened up to us all of a sudden, admitting that she had been terribly embarrassed of the black spots on her face ever since childhood – if not for them, Keetsie Myau would already have been the recognized Incarnation of the Great First Female of the Miyelonian race with all the accompanying honors. We found peroxide in a first aid kit in a wardrobe, so we decided to fix that "flaw," and soon enough we had created a "new incarnation of the first female."

After that, we drank something else and the Miyelonians had another smoke. Then Ayni and I gave a four-hand team back massage – the Great One was hurt or pulled a muscle during the pillow fight. Either we were overdoing it or Keetsie managed to read some of the salacious thoughts my mind was subjecting me to, but we had an unfortunate misunderstanding – her body temperature rose and she entered an erotic trance. I remember that moment fairly clearly because I was deeply embarrassed and afraid of the possible consequences while Ayni also just about died out of fear. But the ruler soon came to her senses and just laughed at our bewildered state. Then, going out into the hallway in just her underwear, she ordered the First Pride troopers to summon her fiancé Gerd Lekku, and also bring the "special gift" she had waiting.

Soon enough, a heavy metal box was brough in exactly like the one my team found at the pirate captain's treasure cache. I knew perfectly well what was inside and remember how exasperated it made me – like I had already refused such a "gift" once, and now even with an intoxicated mind I still am not going to change my race. To that I received the bizarre response that it was "not for me." I probably should have figured it out then, but a strange apathy washed over me. The thoughts were barely moving in my drunken head, so I just reassured myself with the fact that no one was going to physically force me to become a Miyelonian.

The party seemingly continued, but I have no confidence about that. I think we turned the heavy couch around and the two tailed beauties and I sat embracing while we watched the sunrise over the planet Kasti-Utsh III through the panoramic space station window and the fearsome Brawler Gerd Lekku cooked us some more meat. But at a certain point I just passed out and don't even remember going to bed in my bedroom. In my sleep, I could hear music playing and the party must have carried on without my direct participation.

But the way I woke up was unforgettable. My head was splitting, I felt unwell. My memories of the previous night's party seemed like total nonsense – I mean the ruler of a great spacefaring race couldn't really have let that loose and gone that wild around me. She was behaving like a college student. I probably just drank too much... Yes, the very severe hangover confirmed that theory. It was a struggle to move even a finger. There was nothing that could make me stand up in that condition, but I wanted horribly to go to the bathroom. With immense effort I unstuck my eyelids... and woke right up because on the bed next to me there was a sleeping naked woman I had never met before! Her fire-red long hair was spread out on the pillow with one leg hanging off the bed. And most surprisingly of all, my bedmate was a Human by race! On a Miyelonian station!!!

Already guessing what happened last night but not yet believing it could be real, I walked on shaky legs out of the large room. Yes... the drunken delirium and all its fantasies were real. The living room was completely trashed. Clothing laying loose in puddles of wine, piles of dirty plates on the table, Keetsie's underwear on the bathroom door handle. The Great One herself I found sleeping on the couch embracing her fiancé. But most importantly, the box of Precursor stones was open! So it wasn't just a crazy dream! She really did give me the "special gift!"

Ayni Uri-Miayuu had changed race. And now I needed to grapple with the possible consequences of my girlfriend's action.

Chapter Fourteen

Unforeseen Circumstances

THE FRIGATE WAS STILL in a hyperspace jump and flying on autopilot. The fact someone was on duty on the bridge was really more down to tradition than necessity. But still I headed to the bridge to check in on the officer keeping watch because it was currently "night" on the starship and the rest of the team was sleeping in their bunks. Other than the Engineer as well – based on my scan, the Miyelonian Orun Va-Mart was working on something in the right power unit of my twinbody frigate, aided by two of the Kirsan repair bots. I opted not to distract them.

"What happened while I was gone?" I asked co-Pilot San-Doon Taki-Bu, who was looking bored by the solitude.

"It's all been appallingly quiet, Coruler Gnat La-Fin. The only noteworthy incident happened three hours ago. Your guest attempted to gain access to the bridge without proper clearance. But I didn't let Gerd Ruwana Loki in."

What reason did the Horde observe have to come here? Was she snooping and trying to learn something about the frigate's tactical and technical characteristics, or perhaps our current route and past flight logs? Or was she just bored at night and wanting to talk with the only team member still awake? In any case, it had to be looked into. I sat at my workstation and called up the security camera footage. Let's see... by all appearances, my guest had gotten up to a storm of activity, not sitting calmly for even a minute. She inspected every room on the frigate, spoke with every team member and even tried to get the Relict to open up for a long time, though he was stubbornly ignoring her. Even the repair bots couldn't escape the observer's attention – Gerd Ruwana spent a long time following the white Kirsan through every room on the starship until the flat metal millipede hid in a ventilation slit she was unable to crawl into.

My guest also entered the Medic's room and subjected the Cleopian appendage planted in soil in a transparent autoclave to particular attention. She even took a picture of it. She knocked insistently at my bunk door, but I was in the real world and naturally did not open. After that, she spent a long time listening to the Bard perform then spoke with Vasily Andreyevich for a while. The Psychologist even suggested the experienced soldier fill out a questionnaire on a holographic screen. She looked noticeably happier after seeing the test results and jotted them down in her palmtop.

At lights-out, when the crewmembers split up

into their own bunks to sleep, Gerd Ruwana didn't go to bed though and kept strolling around the frigate. She visited the galley, where she helped the little sorceress load plates into the dishwasher. She spent around an hour working out in the gym, favoring the stationary bicycle and treadmill, then went off to the showers. We had no cameras there due to ethical concerns, so I fast-forwarded. After that, the Horde observer made another attempt to catch the repair bot but again to no avail – all three Kirsans went their separate ways and hid as soon as they noticed the bald-headed Human woman. Then she did indeed hang around the closed door to the captain's bridge for a while, and only after being refused entry did she head to her assigned bunk. But even now she was not sleeping, unlike her roommates Destroying Angel, San-Sano and Svetlana Vereshchagina. She was just sitting upright on her bed in the dark bunk and staring blankly at the wall. Why isn't she asleep?

I mentally sent a message to my guest, saying I wanted to see her in the common room and also headed there.

"Welcome back, Free Captain Kung Gnat!" the bald-headed lady was plainly happy to have a chance to speak with someone and eagerly took a seat next to me.

"You've been on your feet for five ummi already. Tell me, why aren't you asleep?" I didn't beat around the bush, leading with a direct question.

"I'm used to the days being longer on Horde ships, so I'm not tired yet. It's also a side effect of the pills. My brain is in active mode, I'm overstimulated and am having a burst of adrenaline. So I couldn't sleep either way."

"You could have gone to the Medic. Gerd Mauu-La Mya-Ssa would have given you a sleeping pill."

But the Psychologist just waved off the suggestion, assuring me she had enough pep left to make it another whole twenty-four-hour cycle.

"But now that you're back, Captain, may I ask you a few questions?"

"Go ahead," I allowed, and she perked straight up.

"I have spoken with every crewmember, but I have yet to determine which of them is the Morphian," Gerd Ruwana admitted. "Think you could clue me in? I've been racking my brains over it."

"What makes you so sure there's a Morphian hiding out on my frigate?"

For my part, I was crystal clear that there were no Morphians on my team currently, but I was in no hurry to share that information with the observer.

"Well, how could there not be?!" she jumped enthusiastically to prove her theory. "Recently, a Morphian has appeared at Kung Gnat's side as if by magic on several occasions even though the dangerous predators are nearly extinct and very, very rare. I'll grant you could have coincidentally encountered one, or even two... But three or more? The laws of statistics say such a thing is simply not possible unless there is a Morphian disguising itself as one of your close associates. My main suspect was Gerd Urgeh Pu-Pu Urgeh the Relict – he appeared out of nowhere, doesn't talk to anyone and asks only to be left alone. It's suspicious, isn't it? Who could possibly confirm this was a member of a race that was thought to be extinct rather than a clever predator taking an unusual form?"

"Interesting theory," I agreed, gratefully accepting a paper cup of coffee from the many hands of the white Kirsan, who had made it for his captain, "but it doesn't stand up to basic scrutiny. The Meleyephatian Eeeezzz 777 who was once in my team saw us find the Relict with his many eyes and probably told the Horde. Eeeezzz 777 even sacrificed his life in the game to save our ancient crewmember."

"Oh yeah? I was not aware of that. In any case, the Relict exited the game that bends reality, so he can't be the Morphian by definition. Same goes for Gerd Ayni the Translator, even though she was my second suspect. The Morphian has appeared in her form far too often."

I couldn't resist a smile when I pictured the look in the Psychologist's eyes after Gerd Ayni the Translator came back a different race. What "iron-clad proof" that she belonged to a race capable of changing form! I had left the now Human woman in my room so she could sleep it off and went back into the game alone. Some might say I "chickened out." So be it. I was just not ready for the serious conversation I would have to have with my girlfriend.

Gerd Ruwana accepted a cup of coffee from

the metal hands of a Kirsan with a certain amount of surprise and even trepidation. She cautiously sniffed the contents and, pointing a finger at the millipede, looked at me expressively, awaiting my commentary.

"This is Kirsan, a self-teaching Mechanoid repair bot. It's been alive for more than ten thousand tongs, seen a lot in that time and, if you hand it a Universal Translator, it can tell you lots of interesting stories from the past. But that doesn't happen often. It's usually pretty quiet. By the way, the melt hole in its middle segment is a recent combat wound from when my crew tried to take a Vahe-Gukko Composite pilot alive. The repair bot is very proud of that distinguishing feature, as well as its nonstandard coloring. To my eye, the white Kirsan is the cleverest of the three on my frigate. And not long ago it noticed that, when the lights start turning back on, people from the crew slowly lumber over to the coffee machine, after which they wake up properly and get started on their normal daily activities. From that the repair bot concluded that Humans have to restore their energy in the morning using this black, bitter liquid. So if there's no other work to be done on the starship, the Kirsan will 'repair' Humans, helping them to achieve a state of normalcy."

The Psychologist took a cautious sip of the coffee, tasted it and set the cup on the table.

"A stimulant drug of botanical origin. I don't need it. I have other ways of keeping my activity levels up. But, Captain Gnat, I still have a few questions. Above all about the Cleopian. He hails from the Green clan. I assume this is the Historian and the Free Captain is rescuing him this way. Do you not fear issues with the Serpea authorities? The Meleyephatians won't be too happy to see such an unfriendly act, either."

"I don't care about the new authorities of Serpea, much less after they declared me an undesirable element. But the information about ancient races contained in that Historian's mind is of great interest to me and I wanted to use him to get it even though the former monarch wasn't much help. As for the Meleyephatian Horde..." I considered it an appropriate time to make my next move. "I am prepared to prove my worth to your masters. We are currently heading to GF-111K, a system with no owner. But the one next to it belongs to the Meleyephatian Horde and, as far as I understand, all its inhabitants will die in the next two or three days because all combat starships are tied up while Free Captains are fleeing the war so there is no one to evacuate the residents before the Composite arrives. I could help the Horde with evacuation. What do you say? Would that work to cement a good relationship with your masters?"

"Without a doubt," came the Psychologist, delighted. "It would be the exact right move on your part, Kung Gnat! I will help you reach an agreement if such a thing becomes necessary. And let me ask you a second question right now, this time of a more personal nature. There is an NPC Jeweler on your frigate who makes items that raise statistics. She looks like a Human, but she isn't one. By the way, are you aware that she is expecting a child and the Machinegunner and Space Commando had a shouting match yesterday over who is the father? Anyway, it doesn't matter. That wasn't my question. All your crewmembers are wearing rings she made, and they are a great boon. I have learned the Jeweler is selling rings giving +2 to any statistic through Gerd Uline Tar the Trader at a rate of ten thousand crypto a piece. And five times less for team members. I have two thousand crypto, enough for one ring, but the Trader refused to sell it to me at the reduced rate. She said I am not a team member and not entitled to a discount. Could you assist me with this? Or at least tell me what I can do to temporarily achieve team member status?"

Just that? How little she needed to be happy in the end. I wanted to reply that I would have a talk with my business partner, but then the little sorceress Gerd Soia-Tan La-Varrez walked into the common room all groggy and yawning as she ambled toward the galley to help our Chef-Assassin cook breakfast for the crew. But I had a better idea. I called over the Psionic Mage and pointed the Psychologist to her.

"Wanna make yourself useful? Here's your chance. And it will benefit the overall mission, too. You see, the way it turned out, I already know how my visit to Emperor Georg the First will begin — some freaky sorceress is going to attack my companion Gerd Soia-Tan right in the throne room and do their very best to kill her. And so, before that happens, the kid has to level her magic abilities. I'm not a good fit as a sparring partner.

My Intelligence is too high, so she will have zero chance of doing anything to me. Meanwhile, the majority of the crew is ill suited for the opposite reason – Soia-Tan will have a one-hundred-percent chance of taking their minds under control. But you make the ideal partner! First of all, with Gerd status and elevated statistics, you must have high Intelligence. And second, you were trained in resistance to mental attacks, so you'll have the corresponding skills at a high level. Plus you can take your tablets if it comes to that. If you help train Soia-Tan, you'll get a stat-boost ring in return. Two even. Furthermore, you won't even have to spend your own money. I'll buy them for you. What do you say?"

The Psychologist spent a while considering it, then agreed.

"I'll take a +2 Perception and a +2 Constitution," Gerd Ruwana Loki announced her conditions. "And only mental magic! Because I know the kid can throw fire, too! I don't wanna get sent back to my respawn point or walk around with a scorched face."

I nodded and turned to the little sorceress, who was listening closely.

"Tell Amati-Kuis Ursssh that she'll have to get by without your help in the kitchen today and tomorrow. After that, run to the gym and no lollygagging! I'll be checking on your progress myself. After that, we'll work in a link but this time I'll be feeding you mana!"

Gerd Ayni Uri-Miayuu came back into the game just seven hours later. I assumed her arrival would cause extreme surprise and discomfort among the team, but... the only ones actually surprised were myself and Ayni. The Translator came back into the game looking like the same orange, tailed Miyelonian she left as. I saw no changes to her appearance at all. But how?! She changed race!

"You missed a training session I informed everyone of in advance!" boarding team commander Gerd T'yu-Pan came at my fluffy assistant sounding peeved. "There were a few formations and techniques we couldn't practice today because you weren't there!"

The bewildered Miyelonian just lowered her snout guiltily to the floor and batted her lashes, so I had to speak up on my personal assistant's behalf.

"Not so loud! She had a good reason. Gerd Ayni was carrying out a very important diplomatic mission on my request – helping avoid a great war between the Geckho and Miyelonians. It's in both of our interests, T'yu-Pan because planet Earth was on the Miyelonian fleet's hit list. So then, has the Fourth Fleet departed from Kasti-Utsh III?"

"Yes, Captain Gnat," the Miyelonian bowed with dignity. "Kung Keetsie Myau has taken her fleet to the Meleyephatian border as promised. There will not be a war with the Geckho."

Authority increased to 118!

That instantly changed everyone's opinion of

the tailed lady's "skipping class." The Translator was congratulated, given approving shoulder pats, and asked the details of her diplomatic mission. I asked Supercargo Avan Toi to go into the real world and tell the Geckho military that the assignment I was given by Krong Daveyesh-Pir was complete and the Union of Miyelonian Prides has decided against their aggressive intentions toward the Geckho. I asked Eduard Boyko the Space Commando to bring the same message under the Dome so it could be sent on to Geckho Viceroy Gerd Kosta Dykhsh.

"As for you, Ayni, I ask you to come to the captain's quarters in ten minutes. I'm just finishing training with the little one. You can tell me the details."

My part in Gerd Soia-Tan and Gerda Ruwana Loki's practice session could hardly be called fully fledged training though – I was just feeding mana to the little sorceress and giving her the odd piece of advice. In the meantime, I was sitting on a bench in the corner of the room and studying an extensive report from my Engineer Orun Va-Mart. The frigate's right power unit had started failing occasionally for no good reason, losing twenty to forty percent of its energy, which was bad enough all on its own. But given the twinbody's two power units were supposed to be synchronized, it was downright dangerous. My main Engineer was busy trying to find the root cause of the failure with his assistant San-Sano and the repair bots. Their conclusions were not comforting – in the best case, the safety fuse had blown on one of the energy circuits. In the worst, the energy storage or hyperspace propulsion systems would need to be repaired. In any case, there was no way to fix it while travelling – we needed to disassemble the starship at a decent repair bay outfitted for the purpose.

Mysticism skill increased to level ninety-two!

Psionic skill increased to level one hundred thirty-five!

Gerd Soia-Tan La-Varrez the Psionic Mage walked up to me all soaked with sweat, very tired but smiling in satisfaction.

"Coruler Gnat La-Fin, we're done training!" the kid told me with clear pride. "I even 'broke through' the Psychologist's defenses a few times, though it wasn't easy."

After making sure the Horde observer had left the gym and was not eavesdropping, the little sorceress continued barely audibly:

"If you like, I can tell you what Gerd Ruwana thinks of us, this whole mission and you in particular, Captain."

"Is it something important?" I clarified but received a negative response.

"No, it's nothing. I was only able to overhear a few fragmentary thoughts. Mainly she misses her home colony of Ar and is mad that she's wasting time distracting a little kid rather than flying somewhere far away to complete some important mission. She's also interested in Colonel Filippov the Bard. Out of the whole team, she considers only the colonel worthy of speaking with her. She is enamored with his abilities and doesn't understand why Vasily Andreyevich Filippov is a common player rather than the leader of our whole group. In the Meleyephatian Horde, he'd be offered a commander position straight away. Gerd Ruwana has to struggle to tolerate the others and is actually scared of the Jarg and tries her best not to cross paths with him. Even you, Coruler Gnat La-Fin, she views as a wannabe even though you are dangerous and possibly useful. I was unfortunately unable to read any more – Gerd Ruwana hides her thoughts and emotions very skillfully."

Wow, great job kid! She was really doing awesome today. She levelled up three times in just one training session. I ran my hand tenderly through the child's hair and perked up the young sorceress:

"Tomorrow you'll be working with +2 Intelligence rings. I ordered you a pair from the NPC Dryad and Nefertiti is already working on them."

"Awesome!" Gerd Soia-Tan giggled in delight and even clapped her hands together. "Tomorrow I'll show you what I can really do! And give you a full report on what the Horde observer is hiding!"

I wanted to respond that it wasn't appropriate to subject our guest to such scrutiny, or to try and dig down to her private thoughts, but a message popped up before my eyes and distracted me.

ATTENTION!!! Leader of the Human-23 Faction Leng Vinogradov the Academic proposes unification with the Relict Faction on the following terms: the Human-23 Faction shall join the Relict Faction in its entirety. Do

you accept? (Yes/No)

Very strange. It was not so very long ago that the "backup" Russian faction wouldn't even hear talk of unification and in fact refused to even speak to my Diplomat Leng Thomas Müller. In light of their low numbers, the faction was not even required to muster players for the Army of Earth. As far as I knew, the H23 Faction was engaged in selling services to "very demanding" individuals – shipping quick-acting medicines from deep space (including those for curing cancer), bringing government figures and other people vested with great authority or money into the game, then levelling them at a rapid pace. Something extraordinary must have happened for the faction to get out of that game and agree to be swallowed up. And so, not in possession of all the information, I didn't rush and headed to my bunk.

Gerd Ayni was waiting for me in the hallway, even though she had the privilege to open the door to the captain's quarters by herself. As soon as we were left alone, I demanded an explanation from my tailed assistant.

"I'm also in shock..." Ayni admitted. "When I swallowed the stone, a character editor opened before my eyes in the real world – exactly the same as the one I saw the first time I entered the game that bends reality. It was not possible to change statistics or age, nor could I change my level from 111. However, there were thousands of races to choose from! I could hardly even find Human in the endless list, and when I did there were lots of varieties. Some even had wings on their back. I had never heard of such a thing before. I just about chose the Human subrace from Tailax because I remembered how much you liked Valeri-Urla and her huge eyes. But still I chose a different type. I didn't change anything else and left it all as it was. I even kept my game class even though it was possible to change. But I decided you needed a Translator more than yet another Trooper or Engineer."

I nodded affirmatively and the tailed girl continued.

"And then... I didn't feel so good – humans have a different metabolism after all, and I had drunk too much alcohol. I fell on the floor. When I woke up on your bed in the bedroom, the hotel suite was already empty. You were gone, Keetsie Myau and her fiancé as well. There was just a robot cleaner hard at work in the great room, cleaning up the aftermath of our debauchery. I could barely fit into my shorts, and I actually had to leave my boots behind and walk barefoot. A few times I nearly fell over because I wasn't accustomed to walking without a tail. How do you Humans do it? I walked around the suite, getting used to my new body. I read the new messages left on the table, took some hangover medicine and hurried into the game. And now here I am, but for some reason I'm Miyelonian again."

"I see the Precursor-made stones don't work exactly as intended and are considered forbidden artifacts for good reason," I suggested because no other explanations were coming to mind. "They changed your body but had no impact on your virtual avatar stored in the game's memory. By the way..." it dawned on me. "One could make a big conclusion from that. Perhaps our reality is just another virtual world and some game laws apply there, too."

"That seems to be the case. In fact, there is a theory that the game world is the prime reality and everything else is a mere projection." Ayni raised her snout, looked me right in the eyes and asked timidly. "But tell me, Kung Gnat, do you like my new appearance? Or... did I do something wrong? After all, I don't have much understanding of Human beauty standards."

"I liked it a lot!" I reassured her and even embraced the tailed lady, and she didn't object. "You can check for yourself. I really appreciated what you did. Red, I promise you we'll have a lot more time to talk it over in the real world..."

A knock at the door interrupted our conversation. I had to open up. The Space Commando was standing in the doorway looking agitated.

"Captain, here's the deal... I was talking to Leng Tarasov under the Dome and he asked me to tell you a request for help has come in from the Human-23 Faction and the Human-2 Faction, which is the UK."

What? Two factions at once? And of course I noticed that Eduard mentioned the H23 Faction, which sent a request to merge with the larger and more powerful Relict Faction just a few minutes ago. Circumstances really must have been squeezing in on them.

"Tarasov was very mad and didn't mince words. With all the swearing removed, here's basically the situation. The son of a Russian oligarch living in London entered the game that bends reality and became a member of the UK H2 Faction. After that, he brought so many valuables into the game that he was able to buy his own starship – a somewhat antiquated Omi-Chee class yacht. No weaponry, antediluvian thrusters. You wouldn't even care to look at such a crumbling old bucket. Meanwhile, the rich bastard put together a team of his acquaintances, most of whom are also the sons of Russian politicians and oligarchs living in London. But there was also a guy and two girls who were UK citizens, though they also came from a rather well-to-do background. And that group of young slackers loaded up their ship with booze and valuables to sell, hired the first Pilot they found and a couple Bodyguards hanging around the Geckho spaceport, then set out to 'take the cosmos by storm.' The first place they went was Poko-Poko, a neutral station beloved by smugglers of all kinds. There the 'golden boys and girls' rested up, dropped some cash in a casino and went into the real to brag to their friends about what an awesome time they were having on a space station, and what 'mindblowing smokes' they found up there."

"Poko-Poko?" I asked in surprise, having heard the name of a station with quite a nasty reputation. "They should have headed straight for Medu-Ro IV if they wanted to go looking for trouble so bad..."

"Well, they certainly found trouble," the

Space Commando agreed. "Where they went next is unknown. They haven't left the game for three days. Then, two hours ago, one of the English girls climbed out of her virt pod in hysterics saying their group had been kidnapped by a group of lowlife scumbags. Using mind control, they forced all of them except her to change their exit point from the game. And now they're threatening to kill them one-by-one if their rich parents don't pay ransom for their idiotic offspring. One of the Russian guys has already been killed."

"Well, what does this have to do with me? They jetted off looking for trouble, and now they found it. Let their rich parents bail them out. Have the kidnappers named a price?"

"They have," Eduard confirmed and for some reason gulped nervously before continuing, "they want the Relict mobile laboratory!"

Chapter Fifteen

A Stick in the Spokes

I DIDN'T FEEL BAD for those idiots. They did everything in their power to get themselves into such a tough spot and they had only themselves to blame. It's basically the same as sticking your hand in a wild lion's cage despite the obvious danger, then screaming in pain and whining that you have nothing but a bloody stump after. In a situation like that, there would be no blame to place on the animal. And so, to be frank, even if the kidnappers shot or even ate alive all the prisoners, I wouldn't shed a single tear.

But the idiots were Humans from Earth, and I was their Kung in this big game. And so I would be the one catching sidelong glances if I ignored the message about terrestrial faction Humans in trouble. I would have to rescue them or at least get revenge. Furthermore, I really was the only person who stood a chance of helping them. I had the Relict laboratory the blackmailers were demanding and a starship that could bring me and my team of elite troopers wherever we wanted.

There was one other reason to take a very serious view of this event. There would be more and more starships from Earth as time went by, and so I needed to definitively show all kinds of space gangs that Humans from Earth were not to be attacked. And this demonstration of force had to be perfectly clear and extremely brutal to beat the very idea of such attacks out of their heads for the future. Whether these hostages would live or die was secondary. It would be nice if they survived. But if not, their deaths would serve as a lesson to the young scions of other elite families. Yes, it was cruel. But how else was a true Kung supposed to think and act?

And that was the very position I outlined to my team. Yes, we would certainly get involved, find and punish the kidnappers. But we would not be giving up the laboratory under any circumstances especially given how difficult it would actually be to do that. The Relict Laboratory was now performing random null transports throughout the Universe and would be appearing in certain locations known only to me for very short spans of time. The next such contact was planned in seventeen ummi. We of course would try to be there to meet the intricate Relict vehicle, but there was no guarantee the laboratory would listen to me or allow the *Tamara the Paladin* to enter its camouflage field. In the Solar System, although the ancient laboratory's artificial intelligence took it to the agreed-upon location and even responded to my message, it didn't want to pick up our starship, which was why we then had to travel around the galaxy on our own.

Of course, the true situation wasn't exactly the way I described it to our crew. But the image of the 'stubborn laboratory' was very beneficial because it significantly reduced pressure on me from the great spacefaring races. Meanwhile, the only team member that could expose my lie was the Relict Gerd Urgeh Pu-Pu Urgeh who was again missing in the real world, busy with the Syam Tro VII Refuge. The other team members then had no reason to doubt their captain's words, especially given I was generously adding psionic suggestion when saying it.

Psionic skill increased to level one hundred thirty-six!

Mental Fortitude skill increased to level one hundred thirty-two!

Mysticism skill increased to level ninety-three!

Yes, I approached the address to the team with all due seriousness and had put everything I had into it, even burning though all of my Magic Points. However, the result was plain to see even with no magic – every last member of my team approved of my position, including the Horde observer who was at the crew gathering and had also been affected by my magic, ready to fly off and save the unfortunate hostages on Kung Gnat's first command. And I should say so! The unfortunates were Human, just the same as her. How could she sit idly by! Meanwhile, Gerd Ruwana didn't even understand I had made it through her defenses and considered the thoughts authentically hers.

On my request, the Space Commando told

the rest of the crewmembers all known details of the affair, but there wasn't much:

"The girl who told everyone about the kidnapping is very scared. Furthermore, she was high on drugs and drunk for the attack, then her brain was worked over very professionally with psionics. And so, the hostage had very little worthwhile information that could identify the kidnappers. She wasn't even certain exactly where they were at the time of the attack – on their space yacht, Poko-Poko station or some other location. All she remembers, and hazily at that, is that a group of quick-moving shadowy figures appeared around her suddenly, slammed her to the floor, injected her with something and she passed out. She woke up in a very dimly lit room with her hands and legs bound. Next to her, there was a lot of blood on the floor and the corpse of one of the boys, cloven in two by a sharp blade. She hasn't seen her other friends and doesn't know what happened to them. She said the location has reduced gravitation. And so it has been theorized that the Humans were taken away from Poko-Poko station, but that isn't for sure. They only communicated with her mentally. She hasn't seen any of the attackers, so she doesn't even know what race they are."

"Quick moving... using blades... this looks like Miyelonian handiwork. Some pirate gang. There are plenty of them hanging around Poko-Poko," Gerd Tini suggested, but I didn't agree.

It was possible the sliced-up corpse was shown to her on purpose to make us focus on Miyelonians specifically, because it was just too obvious a conclusion. But blades were also used by Human Gladiators, and really anyone at all could have used a bladed weapon to kill the prisoner. Furthermore, all Miyelonian pirate clans other than the real lowlives would think twice before tangling with a Human from Earth because Kung Keetsie Myau had given her protection to the Kung of Earth, and every Miyelonian was aware of that.

"Navigator, get me all data on Poko-Poko station. Amati-Kuis Ursssh, I need you to go into the real world and delicately ask the Hive of Tintara if they're behind this. Tini, I need you to ask the same question to your old buddies from Medu-Ro IV. It isn't likely. This isn't their style. But you should ask anyway. Gerd Uline Tar, get in touch with your husband and figure out which Pilot and Bodyguards those people hired at the spaceport. Everyone else get back to your tasks, but don't leave the game. In half an ummi we'll be unloading goods for our urgent contract. After that I'll tell you where our frigate is going next."

This time, I brought only the Trillians in my crew to my bunk – Chef-Assassin Amati-Kuis Ursssh and Gerd Ukh-Meemeesh the Gunner. The two large "space crocodiles" made my bunk feel cramped, so I pushed the table into the very corner and sat on the couch with my legs crossed to free up a bit of space so the Gunner could stretch out to his full length. For the time being, I was still having a very hard time understanding Trillian and the girl could barely speak Geckho. But still I didn't invite the Translator because the topic we were discussing was very painful to Gerd Ayni. Just in case an unsurmountable lack of understanding arose, I had borrowed the Universal Translator from the Jarg. But still I was hoping I wouldn't need the device because I could use psionics to send messages and the Gunner could help us translate things we both didn't know.

Above all, I heard Amati-Kuis assure me the Hive of Tintara was not involved in the attack on Earth Humans at Poko-Poko and was overall totally unaware of it. Furthermore, the space mobsters assured my companion that they would never put a stick in the spokes of Free Captain Kung Gnat while he was working on an important job for them.

I didn't get everything the Trillian girl was saying, so Gerd Ukh-Meemeesh translated the tough spots. At a certain point, the Gunner shuddered and asked what exactly linked his captain with the notorious Hive of Tintara. Before answering that question, I asked both crewmembers to tell me as frankly as they could what they thought about Prince Hugo from the Par-Poreh royal dynasty.

"Prince Hugo is a national hero!" the young female hooted out. "The Prince set himself the goal of restoring the glory and ancient traditions of the various Trillian groups, tried to shake up the rigid political system which was no longer up to the challenges of modern reality, and to settle internal conflicts between Trillians of different colorations.

Hugo Par-Poreh is such a brilliant and powerful figure that he could have brought the Kingdom of the Trillians to a totally new level in the Galaxy. Other spacefaring races saw him as a threat and their villainy made them capture Prince Hugo. They say he's been killed. Or neutralized somewhere on the outskirts of space. But his cause yet lives, and the Prince still has many supporters! I myself am one of them!"

Astrolinguistics skill increased to level one hundred fifteen!

Training skill increased to level fifty!

You have reached level one hundred eleven!

You have received three skill points (total points accumulated: six).

That's nice, God damn! My character was having a harder and harder time with every new level despite my gradual progress in the Training skill. I was actually frightened by the thought of how hard it would have been to advance had I not taken that highly useful ability.

Noting to myself that the young Chef-Assassin was an ardent supporter of Prince Hugo, I asked Gerd Ukh-Meemeesh his thoughts. The Gunner was more cautious.

"Captain, don't be offended but you're a Human, so you see the situation with Theologian Gerd Hugo Par-Poreh from 'the outside.' That means you have a different view of his role in modern Trillian history. I have spent a long time in space among Geckho, Cyanids and Miyelonians. I understand perfectly well that members of other races could easily hate Prince Hugo Par-Poreh for the cruel deeds ascribed to him..."

"But none of it is true!" Amati-Kuis objected, interrupting. "It was all made up by Prince Hugo's political opponents, who didn't want such a strong leader rising to power, trying to use their made-up scary stories to bring down his Authority so he wouldn't be able to reach the rank of Leng, then Kung and then Krong."

An interesting story. To be frank, I was myself surprised at why a figure with such fame throughout the galaxy was still a Gerd, and not higher status. The situation actually made me think of my Translator Gerd Ayni Uri-Miayuu. She had enough Fame for five, but her Authority had been totally slain after the assassination attempt against the incarnation of the Great First Female was broadcast to the whole galaxy and was now sitting at around negative two hundred.

The experienced Gunner didn't argue with the fanatic supporter of the "embodiment of absolute evil." He just asked me why I had all these questions about a member of the Par-Poreh royal family.

"Let me tell you. But I need you both to guarantee you won't talk because this topic is top secret. The Composite is quickly making its way through the galaxy, so every star system at risk of capture is being evacuated urgently. It is very likely that our *Tamara the Paladin* will soon be deputized to transport particularly dangerous criminals from a secret space prison. And one of the figures locked up there is a famed Trillian accused by the governments of several spacefaring races of bloodcurdling crimes and who has been sentenced to life in prison. And so it is important for me to know how you will behave if Prince Hugo is on my frigate. Is that going to be a problem for you, friends?"

Both Trillians sat in stunned silence, staring at one another. First to speak was the Gunner.

"I won't make any trouble, Captain Gnat. I don't count myself among the supporters of the bloodthirsty Theologian, nor am I an opponent. To me, Prince Hugo will be just another prisoner, same as the rest."

"Captain, my loyalty to you is infinite. You are my master and have the right to give me any order you wish. But in case of a possible confrontation between my master and a member of the Par-Poreh royal family, I would kill myself because I would not be at liberty to choose a side."

I was using psionics actively while listening to my team members' answers. They were both saying their true thoughts.

"Alright then, that will be plenty. I don't ask anything more from you. Let me remind you again that this conversation was strictly confidential and no one else can know about it, not our team and especially not outsiders. We're done here. Return to your duties."

The Trillians both bowed in perfect time and left the captain's berth. I turned over the still unused Universal Translator in my hands and went off to the Jarg's bunk to give him the device back. The Analyst was alone and greeted me with a strange hissing sound. I didn't realize right away, but Gerd Uii-Oyeye-Argh-Eeyayo was asking me to close the door so we could talk privately. As soon as I'd locked the door, the Jarg clipped on the Universal Translator and began:

"Captain. Complex calculation. I finished. Tell. When Jarg should. To kill observer. From Horde."

I must admit, I just sat down on the cot because I hadn't come anywhere near telling anyone my plans for Gerd Ruwana Loki, but those were in fact the very thoughts I had been having. We could not under any circumstances allow the Horde observer to see us helping the "embodiment of absolute evil" escape from prison, where it had been so challenging to get him locked up in the first place. That threatened such serious consequences that it even made me scared. It would at the very least earn me enemy of the Horde status again and might lead all the way to war against Earth. And one thing was for sure. I could say goodbye to any possible aid from Krong Laa and would get no reward for succeeding at the diplomatic mission (and there I remind you my homeworld was promised immunity).

I didn't deny it. I just asked the Analyst to explain how he reached those conclusions and why he specifically had to kill the observer.

"Strange contract. No benefit. Lots of time waste. Little profit. Means money. Not main reason. Reason is system. GF-111K. Think hard. Nothing. Means next system. Looking map. Nothing. Full map. In computer Navigator Ayukh. Rorsh. Prison. Many evil criminal. Remember. Captain go to speak. Trillians. With Hive of Tintara. Think. Prince Trillian. Escape. Meleyephatians cannot to know. Gerd Ruwana. To talk. Must be gotten rid of. Captain can no afford. Scandal. Very bad. Jarg maybe. Jarg bad reputation. Short temper. Anger. Emotions. Explosion. Happen. Sometimes. Accident. No one fault."

I understood it all. And I was even prepared to agree that the Jarg was the ideal candidate for an "accident" with the enquiring observer who was constantly interrogating members of my team. No one would be surprised, because Jargs were indeed famed for their ability to explode in stressful situations, killing everyone around.

I extended a hand and carefully ran my palm over the space "armadillo's" spines.

"You're a real genius! You'll blow yourself up after we take Prince Hugo on board and undock from the space prison, but before we link up with the mobile laboratory. And tell me right now where to pick you up. You really are an amazing Analyst and my lifeline. I would not want to lose you."

"Jarg staying. Point. Respawn. On frigate. Risky. Not supposed to. But a little is okay. I trusting. My. Captain."

Chapter Sixteen

Asteroid Field

THE *TAMARA THE PALADIN* stopped just over thirty thousand miles away from the edge of the asteroid field. On the big screen, I could see the half-mile-long *Ovi-Uro VII* starship drifting among the asteroids in great detail – a joint design of Miyelonian and Trillian constructors, the giant space factory was used to process valuable minerals. With dozens of automatic mobile processing plants stuck to it delivering mineral concentrate to the ship, it could store up to a billion cubic feet of ore in its belly. As far as I could tell, only seven starships like it had ever been built in the galaxy and four of them belonged to the Par-Poreh royal dynasty. I was unable to determine the ownership of the other three because the data was classified, but they must have been VERY far from simple players.

Which of the seven titans was now before me I could not tell. It had no number or even name. At any rate, payment had been promised in Geckho crystals, and we communicated in that language, which only made things less clear.

"Captain, the client has requested we drop off the containers right here in space," came Gerd Uline Tar, who was conducting the negotiations.

I had no objection. If anything it was easier for us. No need to waste time docking at the space factory.

"They're being secretive. They don't want to show us the asteroid that caught their fancy and which they are planning to blow up with the nuclear charges we brought," Dmitry Zheltov chuckled.

Yes, that seemed to be exactly it. Although... that was of course naive of them. I turned on the *Tamara the Paladin*'s scanning apparatus and had the computer search all nearby asteroids. The number of objects was off the charts, but I used the filter to take away all the little stuff, leaving just the large bodies with linear dimensions greater than a thousand feet. Anything smaller than that and the clients of our urgent delivery wouldn't have needed so many kilotons of explosives. Smaller asteroids could even be pulled into their cargo bay for further processing. There, that makes it much easier to understand. There were just fifteen natural objects remaining in a million-mile radius. Now I wanted the data on their average density and composition.

Machine Control skill increased to level one hundred twenty!

Scanning skill increased to level eighty-five!

Mineralogy skill increased to level sixty-two!

"There it is," I put a marker on a gnarled rock weighing eighteen billion tons that was slowly drifting its way through space. "The core is made of ruthenium and palladium. Total potential extractable minerals – one hundred forty thousand tons if you play by all the rules and take a couple tongs. But if they just blow it up, they'll be able to get a thousand or so tons of precious metal and escape the Composite fleet."

"Two thousand tons of palladium and ruthenium would make a great haul," Dmitry Zheltov said thoughtfully, zooming in on the mothership on his monitor and carefully studying the four interceptors docked on it, as well as two heavy laser cannons. "But I would be interested in dropping through here in a few days when the miners have already loaded their take and melted the ore down into metal..."

"What's this I'm hearing?" I chuckled happily, turning my spinning chair toward the Starship Pilot because I was not expecting such provocative and criminal ideas from the prim and proper graduate of the Space Military Academy. "Dmitry, your idea is of course tempting but I suspect this system will be stuffed to the gills with defense forces in two days' time. Plus, they won't be able to smelt it all down before then. They'll just load chunks of the asteroid into the belly of their huge ship and run away from the war. Plus look at it," I pointed at the Trillian symbol for "execution" on the hull of the gigantic starship. "I don't know whether that beaut' belongs to the royal dynasty or not, but these space prospectors have a patron that is not to be messed with. They could find you in any part of the galaxy."

"Well yeah, I wasn't suggesting we attack. We

aren't pirates or anything..." the Starship Pilot said in embarrassment, then added barely audibly in the silence that it was of course tempting. Potentially, the *Tamara the Paladin* could easily take down the four interceptors while the flying factory's artillery did not cover all sectors and could be worked around. But we wouldn't be able to make away with such a large prize and would run into the same problem as the most successful pirate in the history of our humanity, the Englishman Francis Drake, who was forced to throw dozens of tons of silver bars overboard because his ship was sitting below the waterline and could not sail.

But I didn't respond because my attention was completely wrapped up in another asteroid. Enormous, unevenly shaped. One mile long and up to half a mile thick at its widest point. The computer determined that its mass was eleven billion tons, but most surprisingly almost fifteen percent of that mass was tantalum. Not the rarest and definitely not among the most expensive or precious minerals, but it also wasn't the most common metal in outer space. Normal asteroids, even metal-rich ones contained practically no tantalum. There I saw more than a billion and a half tons of it. I had never heard of the metal being widely used in space industry, so that titan could totally cover tantalum requirements for hundreds of years of production.

Electronics skill increased to level one hundred six!

Mineralogy skill increased to level sixty-three!

"Captain, the cargo has been jettisoned!" the

Supercargo reported back on the internal comms, and a message followed almost at once from the Trader that payment had been received.

Okay, nothing more to do here.

"Ayukh take down the coordinates of this place. Maybe if we get the chance to come back, we'll find the vandals on the *Ovi-Uro VII* left something of value behind. And maybe we'll find room for the large tantalum deposit. Done? Then calculate a route to the Rorsh star system. You should have the coordinates saved. I gave them to you earlier."

I ate lunch with Horde observer Gerd Ruwana Loki. The Psychologist had just finished her second training session with my ward Gerd Soia-Tan and this time was even sweatier than the little magess. As far as I could tell, the "living target" had done much worse this time and the observer's mental defense was splitting at the seams. Even her pills weren't enough.

"The girl is making progress; her skills are improving quickly and her psionic attacks have become much more dangerous. On top of that, with the Intelligence rings, the sorceress can now perform more sophisticated actions."

"By the way, speaking of rings," I remembered and set the promised reward on the table. "Nefertiti has finished up, so here's what you ordered. But I would ask you to do another couple training sessions with the kid. We can discuss payment in a bit."

She nodded and suddenly asked why the Relict Gerd Urgeh Pu-Pu Urgeh hadn't been on my ship for seven ummi. His game avatar was sitting motionless in his bunk, inactive because he had exited into the real world. Was his captain perhaps granting him too many liberties as a team member?

Good question... I had to admit I myself had already started worrying because the long absence was out of character for the Technician. Gerd Urgeh Pu-Pu Urgeh had been missing in the real world for almost two days. Had something maybe happened to him? But still I assured the observer that everything was fine, the Technician would soon return, and she would have a chance to speak with him.

The Psychologist was completely satisfied by that response, but then abruptly changed topic and asked the results of our visit to the GF-111K System. We had left too quickly. Did something happen that wasn't to plan?

What was this? Simple curiosity? Or were my guest's masters demanding the Psychologist monitor our every move? I got on guard, but still had no problem telling the truth.

"No, it all went smoothly. We dropped off the cargo and received payment. And we didn't bother the client by sticking around and keeping them from mining platinoids. Even still it's an interesting little place. Lots of ruthenium, palladium and gold too. And as for tantalum, there's enough to process here for a hundred tongs."

"Tantalum?" she shuddered for some reason. "Actually, I just remembered something about tantalum... Kung Gnat, I never said it before because I didn't think it mattered, but there was something unusual that caught the attention of the Horde commanders after the first three encounters with the Empire's ships. The thing is that the hulls of all Imperial ships from the smallest to the very largest were made of a special tantalum alloy that's very difficult to produce. The question was even raised at meetings where they asked why the Humans were bothering with such a difficult process. Would it not be easier to use more common metals?"

"Yeah? And what conclusions did the Meleyephatians reach?" I asked, and Gerd Ruwana nodded.

"Horde scientists have replicated the alloy and studied it. Most likely, that specific tantalum-based alloy was chosen by the Humans due to its unusual properties – it has zero magnetostriction and at the same time a surprisingly low thermal expansion coefficient. The hull of a starship made of such an alloy will not suffer serious mechanical damage when hit with a combat laser or subjected to electromagnetic weaponry, which of course makes them harder to damage in space battle. Furthermore, it will not deform when moving through layers of space with highly variable magnetic fields and massive temperature fluctuations. After all, you must be aware, Captain Gnat, that stars and other massive objects express themselves in different layers of space and create expansive areas that are lethal to fly through in hyper, necessitating detours to calculate a safe route. Meanwhile, the Empire's starships are capable of using any hyperspace tunnel they like, not only the safe ones we're accustomed to. That allows the Empire's ships to move between distant star systems much quicker than the Horde's because they are taking 'shorter' paths which would destroy a normal starship due to the highly powerful deformations within."

Interesting. So, what would happen if we made our usual starships out of this wonder alloy? Would we also be able to travel quicker through space? But the Horde observer didn't know the answer to that question. She said only that there would be lots of technical problems, and the price of starships would go up by at least an order of magnitude.

"But after all, the Composite's ships don't use the special tantalum alloy. Nevertheless, they can travel between star systems with striking speed."

The observer just shrugged her shoulders.

"It should be said that our new enemy has much more advanced technology than the great spacefaring races we are familiar with. We don't yet know much about the Composite. How are they able to jam comms both in the game and the real world? How can their small ships carry such powerful cannons? Where do they store enough energy to use them? How is the Composite able to detect the use of long-distance comms in neighboring star systems and how does it send its flotillas to our command ships relaying the comms so quickly and accurately? For now we only know that coordinating between our fleets will be much harder."

The Composite can determine where long distance comms originate? Interesting. Although... I had seen that before in the other galaxy. As soon as I used long-distance comms, there were suddenly too many Composite starships to breathe. The only reason my frigate was able to escape was the mobile Relict laboratory's excellent camouflage field. That had to be taken into account...

"I see..." I considered it a good opportunity to change the topic and ask a question about Vasily Filippov the Bard. Just what did the observer see in him to keep her circling around the middle-age crewmember, running test after test?

"I am performing my usual duty, uncovering talented and promising players. And Vasily Andreyevich is very talented. He passed a strategic thinking test with the highest possible score. He has indisputable talent as a commander and a great deal of experience planning and conducting combat operations on his home planet. As is, Vasily Andreyevich would be capable of commanding a landing party of thirty thousand troopers and independently planning operations to capture well defended targets, such as planetoids, space stations and megalopolises. And at that, he isn't even a Gerd in rank. What would he be capable of if his status went up to Gerd, or even Leng?! I put in a request to our Analysts and was given permission to invite him to come work for the Meleyephatian Horde. Colonel Filippov would be guaranteed total immunity, fast levelling and skill improvements as well as a high salary and the very best living conditions. The Bard promised to think it over. Vasily Andreyevich must now be consulting with his commanders. I'm certain he'll make the right choice – my offer is a bit better and more attractive than stagnating here as a musician and entertaining the crew of a small starship."

So there it was... The observer had such a low opinion of me as captain and of Team Gnat as a whole. I of course noticed that the Bard didn't inform his captain about the unusual offer as well. Vasily Filippov must have decided for himself already and wanted to present me with it as a done deal.

"Doesn't it matter that the Humans of Earth are currently at war with the Meleyephatians? Won't the new Horde commander then have to go to war against his own people?"

"The landing on comet Un-Tau was an operation Humans were forced into. It was up to your suzerains. Humans have no greater objectives there. Furthermore, as far as I know, the landing was a devastating stroke of bad luck and the last remnants of the landing party are holed up in the depths of the ice comet with no way of continuing the attack or evacuating. I'm sure that, in a day or two, the remaining hotbeds of resistance will be suppressed, the last commandos will be taken down, and your Humans will be free of your obligations to the Geckho."

Mental Fortitude skill increased to level one hundred thirty-three!

The Psychologist was speaking with such confidence that I just about bought it. Yes, I had heard from other sources that the landing party was in a tough position, had suffered huge losses and would supposedly be taken down within half a day or so. But it had been more than two days since then and the landing party was still holding strong. Beyond that, the Humans were not exactly looking to retreat. Instead they were going deeper and deeper into the ice temple and clearly General Ui-Taka must have had his reasons for that. My personal opinion was that the Ruler of the Second Directory was at least as good a Strategist as Vasily Filippov and probably in fact better. Furthermore, General Ui-Taka had achieved Leng status, which gave him more advantages compared to the Bard on my ship. So if the Human landing party was still at the shrine, the Meleyephatians would be on the receiving end of more headaches. I had no doubt of that. But I didn't share my thoughts with the observer – let her keep thinking the Humans on Un-Tau could be written off.

Meanwhile, the Psychologist seized on the pause in conversation to change the topic, asking a question I was sick and tired of hearing about glowing blue eyes, both mine and those of little sorceress Gerd Soia-Tan. In the observer's words, she first noticed them back in Serpea and called up all known information about the strange mutation but had yet to get a response from her leadership. And that was very strange because the Horde's Analysts were usually quick to answer all such requests.

"Clearly the Meleyephatians didn't yet have enough to go on, just me and the little sorceress, and that was why they didn't want to say anything definitive. But I can tell you that glowing eyes are a telltale sign that a Human has inborn magical abilities. Only people like us have glowing eyes as an option in the character editor – blue, green, orange and red – and can choose them. After that, there are also corresponding changes to the body in the real world."

"Interesting, interesting..." Gerd Ruwana put that down in her palmtop. "We can check that against a selection of humans from vassal colonies with strong magical traditions."

The observer wanted to ask another question, but San-Doon Taki-Bu's voice rang out over the loudspeaker to say that we would be reaching the Rorsh star system in one minute.

"Now the time has come to prove just how much influence you have over the Meleyephatian Horde and negotiate with local leadership. I'm reminded that you recently were trying to get onto my starship's bridge. Okay then, please follow me. Now you can see it with your own eyes."

Chapter Seventeen

Space Prison

THE TALKS PROVED to be very difficult. There was no comms link with the central systems of the Meleyephatian Horde in the game or real world, so prison warden Gerd Avusssh knew nothing of the tough situation on the front in the war against the Composite. He didn't know that I was no longer on the list of Horde enemies either because his information was out of date. And although Gerd Ruwana had demonstrated her colored bands to the stubborn war dog on the monitor and assured him that Kung Gnat was working for the leader of the Meleyephatian Hord Krong Laa Ush-Vayzzz, the prison warden couldn't get in touch with his superiors to check the observer's authority and didn't want to take personal responsibility for the emergency evacuation of prison staff.

At least the Meleyephatians didn't shoot at us. We were also fortunate to discover that all the starships in this system had left the military base and gone to the Throne World on the very first day of the Composite invasion, so they would not be getting in the way of my plans. The flotilla never returned though, and none came to replace it, so I figured the starships sent off to help defend the capital had been destroyed along with the thousands of others taken down by the dangerous intergalactic invaders. On the backdrop of all the chaos and overall panic about the secret prison, either they had forgotten or simply had no way of sending starships here because the ships were more needed elsewhere in the galaxy. But if there was any method of evacuation left other than my frigate, the negotiations would surely have gone nowhere. But as it was, Gerd Ruwana Loki and I were able to sow a seed of doubt in the Meleyephatian prison guards' minds, and the colony leader continued negotiating rather than sending us away.

But actually reaching an agreement was slow going, and Gerd Avusssh would start denying already settled understandings and we'd have to start all over again... At a certain point I got sick of it all and told the observer that I did not intend to spend any further time here in the Rorsh system and would be leaving. I was indeed trying my very best to demonstrate that I had come here by random chance and evacuating the Meleyephatian garrison from the threatened star system was just a spontaneous good-will gesture and nothing more. If they didn't want to be rescued that was their problem, and I would be washing my hands of the whole affair.

Psionic skill increased to level one hundred thirty-seven!

"Wait, Kung Gnat!" the Psychologist started to worry. "Give me your shuttle and a quarter ummi. I will speak face to face with prison warden Gerd Avusssh and try to convince him."

"Alright. But no more than a quarter ummi."

The observer made it happen much faster than that. Before even half an hour had passed, a call came in to the frigate from the space prison. The satisfied Gerd Ruwana Loki spoke in Horde tongue, and Gerd Ayni got straight to translating:

"I managed to convince the Meleyephatians. Ready docking node. We are to link a small autonomous module to the *Tamara the Paladin* after it detaches from the main station and ferry it to the nearest safe Meleyephatian Horde system, which is Meesh-Mo, approximately a five-hour flight. The Meleyephatians are currently mining their station and will detonate the charges as soon as all the troopers get to the module. This is a green zone, so all Meleyephatians other than the warden and two or three bodyguards will go into the real world. Gerd Avusssh himself then will keep an eye on their special cargo. The other guards will come back into the game five ummi later when their autonomous module is safe and sound in Meesh-Mo."

"What exactly is this 'special cargo?'" I asked with curiosity even though I had of course already guessed exactly what they were referring to.

The Horde Observer's words only strengthened my theory:

"That is classified, Captain Gnat. I am not at liberty to disclose that information to players not in possession of Ro-VI clearance. And believe you me, it is in your own best interest NOT TO KNOW what is being transported off this station."

I didn't argue. And of course I noted that Gerd Ruwana Loki had at least Ro-VI level clearance – almost the maximum if I understood the Meleyephatian system of eight confidence levels for members of vassal races correctly. I was also struck by the ingenuity of the Meleyephatians themselves – the fifty troopers, which was the exact number stationed at the space prison's garrison, took turns entering the green zone of the little module in small groups and leaving the game. Their avatars then disappeared thirty seconds later, making room for the next batch of troopers. And clearly, they would also be adhering to a strict schedule when coming back into the game so they wouldn't crush one another in the cramped space. Of course all that required excellent coordination, but it was a way to transport even very large squadrons using small-class ships.

I sent an order over the loudspeaker for the Supercargo to prepare the docking node and get ready for our shuttle to return. I myself was very upset. Damn! It wasn't coming together at all the way I was planning. The cautious and untrusting prison warden had decided to personally accompany the valuable prisoner from the Par-Poreh royal dynasty, which must have been because he would answer for him with his head. Beyond that, he kept a few experienced Bodyguards with him... Not enough to completely mess up my plans, but I would now have to put more effort forward. As long as I could break through the prison warden's mental defenses, I wouldn't have to tangle with his security.

I drank down a Magic-Point restoring cocktail and mentally made contact with Gerd Soia-Tan La-Varrez who was working in the kitchen, telling her to feed me mana. I also turned to the Analyst sitting next to me and gave him a furtive nod. Gerd Jarg understood perfectly without a word and hurried out into the hallway. The shuttle the observer was coming back on had already been snatched up by the magnetic crane, so Gerd Ruwana would soon be back inside the frigate. I hope the Jarg will be careful and no other team members will get hurt...

After that, I sat back in my seat and started watching the small space station just five hundred feet away from my frigate start preparing to undock a cylindrical module, which was currently having its maneuver thrusters checked. Not big at all – twenty feet long and seven feet in radius, it was more like an escape pod than a true ship. A module like that could not travel between the stars, and couldn't even do much inside one system but, in case of a crash or other emergency, it would allow a few team members to survive and wait for help to arrive.

Alright, they were ready to go. But Gerd Avusssh would not detonate the abandoned station while the autonomous module was still docked and in the blast radius. And that meant it was time for me to take action! I closed my eyes and concentrated.

Machine Control skill increased to level one hundred twenty-one!

Got it! The docking mechanism jammed. Yes, you won't be leaving the station just yet. So, who do we have here? Almost at once I sensed four minds inside the autonomous module. I have to make sure I don't mix them up... Prince Hugo Par-Poreh's mind was of no interest to me, same for the two Meleyephatian Bodyguards. But the prison warden I did want to take full mental control of. Let's get started!!!

Psionic skill increased to level one hundred thirty-eight!

Mental Fortitude skill increased to level one hundred thirty-four!

It was surprisingly easy. I was expecting somewhat stronger resistance. Now I was seeing the world through the many eyes of a "spider." It felt strange to see everything around all at once like a panoramic camera, but still I got my bearings. I had seemingly chosen the wrong target. The prison warden was next to the "spider" I'd taken over, holding a remote control in his hands and gazing out the porthole. Next to the leader there were another two large "spiders," both armed and ready for action. One of them poked a spiked hand into a button on the door and nervously pulled at a sliding lever, trying to figure out what was taking so long.

Does that mean the Trillian prisoner is not in the autonomous module?! Four conscious minds, and they're all Meleyephatian? Although... the fifteen-foot-long metal container on the floor, which barely fit in the small evacuation pod was easily big enough to fit a large male Trillian. There was no one in the container, I would have been able to sense another active mind. Was the Prince stunned? Drugged? Or had the "embodiment of absolute evil" been forced to exit into the real world to make transporting such a dangerous prisoner less problematic. Any of those options were fine by me as long as they weren't leaving the Prince behind on the doomed station.

Second attempt. I tried to take control of the prison warden's mind. This time it was much tougher. I could sense strong resistance as if I were trying to push my body through a thick sticky substance. This Gerd Avusssh was a tough nut to crack! And seemingly he was also taking pills to bolster his mental defenses. I released the controlled guardsman and concentrated everything I had on the new target.

"Gerd Soia-Tan, help me!" I ordered the little sorceress, and suddenly felt a flood of power.

My quickly dwindling Magic Points started to fill back up, and my mental power was boosted. I could feel it was working and the enemy growing weaker. Come on, a bit more... One last push, breaking through... Got him! It worked!

Psionic skill increased to level one hundred thirty-nine!

Mysticism skill increased to level ninety-four!

Now the warden of the secret prison was entirely under my mental control and had become an obedient puppet. Still, I must give him his due – Gerd Avusssh was the very strongest opponent I had ever faced off against. However, in this case, unlike my attack on the low-level Meleyephatian, I was not able to conceal the mind control. When Gerd Avusssh came to his senses, he would surely remember that he was attacked with psionics and would sound the alarm in the Meleyephatian Horde. I could not allow that under any circumstances. My part in the operation to break absolute evil out of prison had to remain a secret to the Meleyephatian Horde. And so, unfortunately, the high-status Meleyephatian's fate was sealed from that very minute – with the safety of my entire home planet at stake, I simply could not leave such a dangerous witness alive and had to do something cruel. But I decided to take mercy on the three guards.

I sent a mental order and Gerd Avusssh chirred out to his Bodyguards:

"Troopers, your presence is no longer required. I order you all to exit into the real and come back in five and a half ummi. Now step to!"

All three Meleyephatians obediently followed their fearsome leader's order. Including the trooper I used to spy on them earlier. That low-level Bodyguard hadn't even sensed my mental presence, so I let him keep his life. The prison warden himself then, holding a remote, turned around, quickly opened the airlock and walked back onto the station. Before that, I read his thoughts and made sure Gerd Hugo Par-Poreh was indeed in the metal container. Yes, the Prince had been temporarily knocked out with a dose of neurotoxin because, with his immense physical strength, the large Trillian could easily break free of his chains, open the box and attack the guards.

Obeying my commands, the autonomous module closed up, undocked from the station and headed into space to meet the *Tamara the Paladin*.

Machine Control skill increased to level one hundred twenty-two!

Telekinesis skill increased to level sixty-four!

Electronics skill increased to level one hundred seven!

Just then I heard a strong thunder from the direction of the hallway. The Navigator, Translator and Starship Pilot also heard it and turned toward the door. A look of extreme confusion was stuck on all their faces.

"What's happening?" came shouts on the radio from many voices.

I first read the information on my captain's tablet to make sure no serious damage had been sustained, then turned to the security camera, which had fortunately survived the Jarg's blast, and examined the scene. Lots of blood on the walls and floor, the dead body of the baldheaded woman pin-cushioned by sharp spines... The Jarg had pulled it off.

I turned on the loudspeaker and made an announcement to the team:

"Our guest must have unwittingly upset our Analyst, causing him to accidentally explode. Both players have been sent to respawn. Frustrating. And very bad timing because we needed Gerd

Ruwana to talk with the local Meleyephatian garrison. I also had a lot of other plans for her to help with. But I will apologize to the Horde observer and try to smooth over this unpleasant incident. But now, Gerd T'yu-Pan, assign a group of troopers to clean up the aftermath of the explosion. Just tell them to be careful and use their spacesuits – Jarg spines are venomous and there could be toxic vapors in the air. All others get back to work. Pilot and Supercargo, allow the module departing the space station to dock on our ship."

I listened to the team's emotional background. All good. Only Gerd Ayni next to me had put the facts together and realized what happened. She glanced at me with mute reproach. Little Gerd Soia-Tan suspected something, too. But as far as everyone else was concerned, the captain's explanations were totally satisfactory. Yes, they were all sorry it happened, but for the most part they considered the observer to be at fault, saying she shouldn't have been bothering the Jarg with her pointless questions. Didn't she know they were famed for their ability to explode? Furthermore, I got the sense that many team members even breathed a sigh of relief because the outside observer had been getting on their nerves. None of them would have admitted it out loud, but they were still treating the Horde representative guardedly and Gerd Ruwana Loki had never been truly accepted on our frigate.

"Docking successful!" Starship Pilot Dmitry Zheltov informed me.

"Excellent. Set course for vector eighteen-four-three. Away from the mined station and toward the second planet."

"Captain, are we not even going to try to rescue the inmates of the space prison?" the question was asked in the language of the magocratic world, which no one else on the bridge understood except for Gerd Ayni Uri-Miayuu the Translator.

I looked the orange kitty in the eyes, hesitated for a few seconds but nevertheless sent the mental command. The prison warden changed his respawn point to the station which was now about to blow (I didn't know where it was before, but it was safer this way), activated the console and the space station disappeared in a flash of bright white light.

You have reached level one hundred twelve!

You have received three skill points (total points accumulated: nine).

You have reached level one hundred thirteen!

You have received three skill points (total points accumulated: twelve).

You have reached level one hundred fourteen!

You have received three skill points (total points accumulated: fifteen).

You have reached level one hundred fifteen!

You have received three skill points (total points accumulated: eighteen).

I was rocked. The world in front of me went blurry for a few seconds. Five levels in one go! My Gnat had never experienced such a thing before and I was utterly unprepared for such a powerful and, why hide it, pleasurable experience. In one moment my Health Points, Magic Points, and Endurance Points all shot up. But what mattered most was the flood of euphoria and surge of power. The effect was so stunning that I could barely resist screaming in overstimulation. Then I checked myself – a great number of space prison inmates must have just died, given there was enough experience to level-up five times. I could never do such a thing again, otherwise I was not far from a terrorist murdering just for the thrill.

Struggling to catch my breath, I discovered the Miyelonian standing at my side and looking at me judgmentally. Seemingly, Gerd Ayni was the only one on the bridge to notice her captain's suddenly level jump. I hurried to don the null ring so the other crewmembers wouldn't line up my rapid advancement with the destruction of the space station. Meanwhile, I explained to the Translator:

"Sorry, Ayni, but I couldn't afford to risk it. The mission is strictly classified, and you remember what the Hive of Tintara's Analyst said. Our heads will roll if anything leaks. If those people were simple peaceable citizens, I'd have given it more thought. But my life along with yours and Imran's are worth immeasurably more to me than the lives of hundreds of space ne'er-do-wells sentenced to rot out here for their heinous crimes. Think of it like this. I just took out the trash, making our world a little bit cleaner..."

Authority reduced to 117!

Out loud the Miyelonian didn't say anything, but she turned around and walked into the hallway with an unhappy look on her snout. Seemingly, her loyalty to the captain had been shaken to the core. I must admit, I myself was not liking any of this one bit. I felt vile having to commit murder, but I didn't see any way to complete the space mafia's "mission of epic difficulty" without getting my hands a bit bloody...

"Captain, the little magess Gerd Soia-Tan La-Varrez has suddenly lost consciousness! Cardiac arrest! I'll perform resuscitation!" the alarmed voice ringing out in my headphones belonged to our Medic Gerd Mauu-La Mya-Ssa.

Seemingly, Gerd Soia-Tan had also been overwhelmed by the sudden flood of experience from helping me, and had some trouble digesting the abrupt change in state. And given her level was significantly lower than mine, the experience shared with her was probably enough for even more level-ups than I got. Her heart couldn't take it. I hope he can save the girl, and I won't have to go get her at her respawn point. Those painful thoughts just about made me miss something extremely important.

"Dmitry, brake!" I shouted. "Stop! Now the very slightest advance and just a hair to the right with maneuver thrusters. Yes, like that."

Our ship crept slowly beneath the mobile Relict laboratory's camouflage field. The ancient station's artificial intelligence responded eagerly to my request. The station was at full power and ready for an instant transport.

"Ayukh, look up the farthest-away Trillian star system. On the very edge of known space. The kind of place it would take a normal starship a tong or even more to get to. But make sure it's also calm and free from rowdy pirates and political turmoil."

Yes, I wanted to get this assignment from the Hive of Tintara off my back as soon as possible, but I also wanted to release the dangerous "embodiment of absolute evil" somewhere on the outskirts of known space. That way, Prince Hugo couldn't cause too much damage and would take years to return to a more inhabited region of his huge state. The conditions put forward by the space mafia said nothing about the drop-off point having to be convenient for the Prince, so let him struggle a bit to make it back!

And although Ayukh was surprised to hear such an order from his captain, he didn't ask questions and delved into studying the star map.

"The GG-666 System," the Navigator suggested a minute later and pointed at a red star somewhere unimaginably far from our current location. I even had to zoom out the map on my monitor and scan over a couple of screen-lengths to see it. "The Trillians only established sovereignty over it half a tong ago. Based on the data in the atlas, it's a desert planet and terraforming has just begun. There is also a tiny mining colony on its satellite. Using its own thrusters the *Tamara the Paladin* would need two tongs to get there."

"Sounds perfect! Calculate coordinates and I'll translate them into Relict format. But now I need to drop by the Pyramid Contact Hall. I want to use its long-distance comms to test a theory. Orun Va-Mart and Gerd Imran will be coming with me to the laboratory in a shuttle. All others be ready for combat! Gunners standing by! It's entirely possible that Composite starships will be showing up!"

Chapter Eighteen

Heart-to-Heart

IDEALLY, I WOULD HAVE BROUGHT the Relict Technician with me. He could have helped setup the long-distance comms, not to mention the other complex systems on the ancient station. But Gerd Urgeh Pu-Pu Urgeh was still not back in the game, which was starting to look more and more like flagrantly bad behavior. Whatever concerns required the Technician's attention on the Syam Tro VII Refuge, he was still a member of my team and had to take part in the life of the ship. And so I was planning to have a very serious talk with the Relict as soon as he showed back up.

The second our shuttle left the frigate's hangar, the normally taciturn Gerd Imran turned to me suddenly from the pilot's seat:

"Gnat, you said Relict Faction players could change their exit point into the real world before. Is that offer still good?"

I admit, I was taken aback by that question but of course answered that it was still in force.

"It's been getting uncomfortable under the

Dome," the Dagestani athlete admitted. "Whether they're trying to get me to spy on you and tell them everything Team Gnat is up to or making awkward attempts to bribe me with easy women, I can't even relax in my own room anymore. Recently, I practically had to physically kick two particularly brazen skanks out of my room. They just wouldn't take no for an answer. Then yesterday, these people I didn't know who also weren't Human-3 Faction players tried to give me a hard time and pressure me to get you to go off and rescue the people on Poko-Poko."

"Did you figure out who they were?" I asked in alarm and the Gladiator nodded.

"Surrogates sent by the rich kids' parents. At first they offered me money, a whole briefcase stuffed full of cash. But when I refused, they started threatening me. I can say for sure that the unsavory characters also approached Dmitry Zheltov and Svetka Vereshchagina. I don't understand how they got let into a secret facility with no clearance either. I filed a complaint with Leng Tarasov, but the leader of the H3 Faction refused to kick them out. After that, he even said that 'Gnat had too quick a takeoff and that made him full of himself. We have lots of questions for him and the faction he leads. So let him work for the good of his country and solve the hostage problem to prove he's the real Kung of Earth.' I think Tarasov is being pressured, too. And I think it's coming from someone even higher up than the curators of the Dome project."

Ahem... Too quick a takeoff... What is that?

Basic envy or a statement of fact that the Russian faction and its curators had lost their leverage over me? The Human-3 Faction leadership no longer had any way of pressuring me. I didn't depend on them financially or politically and my real body was safe on the far-away Miyelonian station of Kasti-Utsh III. But my friends were left very vulnerable. Of course I promised to help Imran, as well as all my other friends being subjected to external pressure and threats.

I suggested several different places he could move his virt pod: the Miyelonian space station Kasti-Utsh III, the German city of Dusseldorf, the megalopolis and capital of the First Directory Pa-lin-thu, or the Canadian military base in the province of New Brunswick. I didn't even suggest Novosibirsk, which was where the former Human-25 Faction had its corncobs because I had some unresolved issues there even though I could choose their corncobs in my settings. And naturally the Syam Tro VII Refuge was also a no-go at the very least until the situation with the missing Technician was settled, and we had solved the problem of the predators living there.

"First Directory," Gerd Imran chose. "The Second Legion guys are there to help me settle in, plus Gerd T'yu-Pan and San-Doon. San-Sano also invited me to visit the magocratic world..."

The last part made the Gladiator very embarrassed for some reason, which did not escape my attention.

"San-Sano? And here I thought you were more into Svetlana Vereshchagina."

"Svetka is a good friend. We can talk about anything and she always listens and supports me with advice. She's also an excellent sparring partner in the arena. In one-on-one fights she beats all our Miyelonians and even the leader of our boarding team. She's not bad to look at either. She has a nice body and she's really pretty... The only thing is that Svetka is married to Denis Tormashyov, the Senior Engineer from the Prometheus who we entered the game with. Two weeks ago they got it officially registered. It's all legal now."

Imran breathed a heavy sigh. The shuttle had long since docked on the ancient laboratory and the Miyelonian Engineer had gone out ahead to check on the station's systems. But I had yet to leave the flying vehicle because I didn't want to end the rare heart-to-heart with my bodyguard.

Imran meanwhile took advantage of the fact we were still alone and shared his own plans:

"Gnat, if the dangerous job for the Hive of Tintara space mafia ends well, I am planning to make an official proposal to San-Sano. I like her. Even when she's wearing a greasy jumpsuit, she's a hundred times more feminine than any glamorous beauty with puffy silicon lips. She's small, delicate and modest. The kind of girl you want to protect and be a rock for. I have only spoken with San-Sano about this topic one time, but even then I made up my mind. Ah, if only San-Sano lived in our world. I would take her to Dagestan to meet my parents. I would show her Derbent, drive her up to the Naryn-Kala fortress. Archeologists say it's eight thousand years old at least, maybe even thirty thousand! Get this, Gnat. It might be older than the Egyptian pyramids! That fortress on the banks of the Caspian Sea was already standing before our Earth had split between the one we know and the alternate magic world. I would really like to take San-Sano there to see it! But now I have to go to the world where my chosen one lives..."

Because Imran fell into a deep thoughtful silence, I patted my friend on the back and tried to cheer him up.

"The mission for the Hive of Tintara is nearly complete and Prince Hugo is already aboard the *Tamara the Paladin*. But there's no way to avoid publicity now, and the inhabitants of the galaxy will instantly realize who released the ghastly reincarnation of Jack the Ripper, Freddy Kruger and the Joker in one package. And the least I can expect then is to have my Authority drop to Leng or even Gerd. I could even find myself on a list of wanted criminals forbidden from accessing all reputable systems. That wouldn't be a death sentence, of course, but I see nothing pleasant if that does come to pass. And so I'm going to try a different way."

Gerd Imran looked at me inquisitively and made an expressive gesture as if slitting an adversary's throat. He was obviously suggesting I quietly dispose of the "embodiment of absolute evil" on some far-off asteroid, then tell our employers that I was unable to free the blood-thirsty Prince. I gave an awkward smile.

"That would be nice... But the thing is Gerd

Hugo Par-Poreh is of royal blood, and it would not only be the Hive of Tintara seeking revenge, but the whole Trillian ruling dynasty. We'd be getting more than we bargained for. Our Earth, too..."

"What, commander, you got a better idea?" the Gladiator shuddered.

"That's the thing. I do. But to pull it off I need to test if I can use long-distance comms in star systems neighboring the Composite. So here, Imran... Go under the Dome one last time. Igor Tarasov wants to talk with me? Alright, tell him I'm ready. The Human-3 Faction has a device that displays location parameters for establishing a long-distance comms link. Memorize these digits and tell them out there. And meanwhile, Orun Va-Mart and I are gonna get the equipment ready."

This time my interaction with the ancient laboratory's artificial intelligence system was peaceful. I'd even call it friendly and trusting. The computer program controlling the laboratory's intricate machinery no longer had any doubts about my authority and, given the Pyramid was unreachable, it recognized me – a Listener and acting leader of the Relict Faction – as the most authoritative possible player in the ancient race's hierarchy.

The artificial intelligence suffered from a critical lack of knowledge about the modern world and I was all too eager to share that information while also setting reference points and priorities. We were weak. Our enemies were strong and numerous. A direct confrontation with modern great spacefaring races would spell death for us. And so we needed to be very cautious and even delicate, proving our worth to the others but at the same time not giving them a reason to treat us with aggression. Regaining our former might and seeking political allies was our first order of business and top priority. We also had to obtain peace in the protracted war with the Precursors, who found themselves in a similar situation to the Relicts.

There were no objections, the artificial intelligence was totally fine with my proposed agenda.

Astrolinguistics skill increased to level one hundred sixteen!

Electronics skill increased to level one hundred eight!

Training skill increased to level fifty-one!

Because it wasn't very comfortable to talk to an invisible voice surrounding me on all sides, I suggested the artificial intelligence manifest itself in the form of a hologram. The computer mind liked that idea, and soon a glowing semitransparent Relict was at my side. And although it bore a certain resemblance to Gerd Urgeh Pu-Pu Urgeh the Technician – two round spherical eyes on the sides of a flat head, six jointed appendages on a cephalothorax and a huge abdomen dragging behind –this individual nevertheless looked very different from the Relict I was used to. Its head was three times bigger than the Technician's with noticeably smaller eyes. Furthermore the appendages were a bit shorter – try as it might, a creature like this one couldn't even reach halfway down its disproportionally long abdomen and it would also scarcely be able to walk. Upon seeing the Relict, I was for some reason reminded of ant queens, which also couldn't take care of themselves independently.

"This is my creator. An inventor. His name was Paa Um-Um Paa," the computer mind eagerly explained.

It was very compliant today in general and was trying to help me in every possible way with hints and whatever else it could provide, also eagerly answering any question I could ask. It was much easier to communicate with a visible partner, because now I could see body language in addition to a voice and even certain emotions which also carried useful information and aided the conversation.

Unfortunately, the laboratory's artificial intelligence knew nothing about any diplomatic channels to contact the Precursors, but it did note that any diplomatic actions by a Relict of lower level than Hierarch would not be taken into serious consideration. And so to achieve peace with the Precursors I would have to at least find a living Relict of that rank somewhere in the galaxy. At most, I could become a Hierarch myself. It would be a long mission fraught with difficulty but, given how few Relicts remained, it was easily within reach. And the most obvious way forward was to continue feeding the remaining nodes of the Pyramid information about the modern world, thus raising my value and influence.

The fact I had successfully sent packets of information to the Pyramid bore witness to the fact that this data was being processed somewhere, which meant the Universe-wide distributed network was still functioning, though in an unstable emergency mode. And if I continued refilling the Pyramid's knowledge base, and my contribution to the overall inflow remained high, one day I would be promoted and my Listener class would be changed to something higher. How much time would that take? The program didn't know. Maybe a tong. Maybe ten or a hundred tongs. But one day my work would pay off.

I must admit, that answer didn't satisfy me one bit. I couldn't wait so many long years and a human life could well reach its end before I saw any tangible gains. And so I asked about other ways of raising my standing with the Pyramid.

"Due to the state of war, we would appreciate destroying Precursor starships and automatic hunters, as well as enemy outposts or any other military victories. It would also be possible to repair the damage and turn the dormant Pyramid nodes to active mode. Such actions would be looked on very highly," the semitransparent Relict suggested.

I didn't want to tangle with Symbiote ships even though I knew where they could be found. But as for repairing Pyramid nodes... Interesting. Very interesting in fact! There we could get our hands on valuable artifacts and find out more about the

Relicts. The only thing was that the station didn't know of any remaining Pyramid nodes in repairable or even inactive condition. As for the Syam Tro VII Refuge, the artificial intelligence had heard of it, but knew nothing about its coordinates either in the real world or the game. It also couldn't provide a description of the "predatory invar" living in that refuge – for some reason there was no information about them in its database. Too bad. I changed the topic.

Now I wanted to know about the mobile laboratory's defenses and whether it had any weaponry systems. I was reminded that, on our first meeting, the station threatened my frigate with destruction if I didn't provide a comprehensive response about who I was and what authorization I had to enter a secret Relict mobile laboratory. What was that? A bluff or an attempt to scare me? Was the laboratory really fitted with weaponry that could easily destroy a frigate-class starship? The second option would be nice, but neither I nor my two Engineers had detected anything of the sort in the mobile laboratory. Furthermore, the Technician Gerd Urgeh Pu-Pu Urgeh who was servicing the laboratory had told me nothing about the combat abilities of the laboratory he was entrusted with.

"Listener, this is after all a science center and not a military outpost, so the station does not carry serious weaponry. But still the laboratory is not defenseless. The distortion screen can absorb damage, and many types of weaponry are not able to damage a target without visual contact. I have analyzed the data on your frigate's current weaponry. The laser cannons cannot damage the laboratory, the beams would be deflected. The quadrupolar destabilizer on your frigate would also be useless. It would not be able to focus energy streams on a fixed point to trigger the matter destruction process. The gravity and nuclear bombs could be dangerous, but the laboratory would be able to escape the blast zone before detonation. So if modern starships only have weaponry like that, they do not present a serious threat to the Relict laboratory."

"What about the Mechanoid spatial cutter?" I asked. "Are you familiar with such weaponry? As far as I understand, it cuts space from its fabric and a camouflage screen could do nothing to stand in its way. And for that matter, could the spatial cutter be installed here on the laboratory?"

"Yes, I am aware the Mechanoids use such a weapon. It would be dangerous and present a serious threat to the laboratory," the artificial intelligence agreed. "If an enemy with such a weapon has an approximate idea of where to aim, they could in fact destroy the mobile laboratory. But as for your second question, Listener, yes. It could be installed but the reactor only provides enough power to either keep up the defensive screen and fast transport systems or use the spatial cutter. Calculations show that the station would be vulnerable and helpless for quite a long time after shooting it. I cannot allow that. It contradicts the most basic security protocols. The survival of this station is of critical importance given the lack of active Pyramid nodes and is top priority."

I see... So the spatial cutter could be installed, but I would have to turn off the laboratory's artificial intelligence to use it because it would stop me from using a weapon with such high energy requirements. I didn't share my thoughts with the computer mind. Furthermore, the question for now was purely theoretical because the spatial cutter was back on Earth. I asked about its offensive systems.

"There is an EMP system, which can damage enemy ships and fry electronics. The instant transport system can also be used to take low-mass starships in close proximity along for a ride. If they are outside the distortion screen, they would be so badly damaged when transporting they would not be able to continue to function at full capacity. There are also security drones."

I knew about the drones. I was already in control of the Small ones anyhow. Of the two large drones, one was in a nonfunctioning state and even the Mechanoid repair bots couldn't fix it. The second was also badly damaged and already belonged to me anyway. Too bad. So the only thing I could count on in battle was the EMP system. And when fleeing the battlefield I could try to damage nearby small-class enemy ships. Not much to be frank...

I had to wrap up the fascinating and beneficial conversation with the artificial intelligence because Gerd Imran had come back into the game. And before he forgot, the Gladiator shot out a series of digits. I turned on my palmtop, jotted down the coordinates and translated them into the Relict numeral system.

"Now I am going into the Pyramid Contact Hall to start a long-distance contact session," I warned the computer program. "However, there is a high probability that we won't be able to talk with our far-off partners for long because hostile Composite ships could show up at any second. You have seen them before in another galaxy. If that happens, terminate the session at once. And be ready to jump away to the coordinates the Miyelonian Engineer is about to enter into the navigation system."

"Will do, Listener! Safety first. The station will be ready to perform an instant transport."

Chapter Nineteen

The Curators Again

I ACTUALLY THOUGHT that Igor Tarasov, leader of the Human-3 Faction would be under the Dome in the real world or in one of the nodes belonging to his faction. And just maybe at the Geckho spaceport. So I was very surprised to see a familiar room at the top-secret Onega-3 military facility, which was used for meetings with the project curators. But this time for some reason half of the seats in the room were not occupied by military specialists and representatives of various national security agencies, but unfamiliar civilians. Some of the middle-aged paunchy men wore stylish suits, while others stuck to jeans and t-shirts. I saw many women ranging in age from young to advanced age. One of them was up on the stage with a microphone in her hand and seemingly planning to conduct the conversation with me.

"Kirill Ignatiev, as a member of the concerned public I demand that you go at once to resc..."

She didn't finish her sentence though,

instead wriggling her speechless lips in bewilderment, trying to squeeze out even a single sound. She was too pompous to greet me, or even identify herself. She went straight on the verbal attack and got what she had coming. Plus she was trying to make demands. Sure, I'll be right on my way. In the entire galaxy, just two entities were entitled to make demands of me – the official master of Earth Kung Waid Shishish and his superior, the ruler of the great spacefaring Geckho race, Krong Daveyesh-Pir. This wretched woman with tousled hair didn't much look like either one of the influential Geckho.

The speaker's sudden predicament stirred up a commotion. A middle-aged man ran out on stage wearing a Federation Council[4] badge on an expensive custom-made dark blue designer suit. He took the microphone from the rabblerouser, who was still standing in silence with her mouth agape and wanted to say something incendiary as well. But I didn't let him insult me and damage my Authority. On my mental command, the senator handed the microphone to the leader of the Human-3 Faction standing next to him on the stage, got down on his belly and started doing push-ups. He was wheezing, and it looked tough, but a man of his girth could use a bit of physical exercise.

I meanwhile searched for the speaker I normally saw conducting the meetings.

---

[4] The upper house of the Federal Assembly of Russia, equivalent to the US Senate.

"Major Kudryavtsev, why have these outsiders been allowed to enter a restricted facility?!"

The stunned military man bleated back some gibberish about how he "didn't have the authority to get rid of such important individuals," to which I flashed my burning blue eyes in anger.

"Major Kudryavtsev, have you forgotten your oath, charter, honor as an officer and job description? Since when can civilians freely stroll around a top-secret facility in Russia simply because they are 'important?' If you lived in the First Directory, you'd have died this very second. As it is, I give you three minutes to get your act together and clear the room of outsiders. If it takes you even a second longer, your heart will stop beating. The countdown is ticking!"

Kudryavtsev instantly hopped up and started moving in a frenzy – he summoned security and even personally ran over to push the outsiders out of the room. That's what the proper motivation can get you! Meanwhile I noticed that many of the military men sitting in the hall were helping the major actively, and they weren't precious with the most stubborn and disobedient of the intruders, dealing out kicks and restraining hands behind backs.

"How dare you?" shrieked a hysterical middle-aged woman. "I will crush you all! Do you have any idea who I am?!"

"Yes, we do," I answered for everyone with a calm voice. "A corrupt civil servant, head of the

Moscow Oblast land relations department."[5]

I read into the thoughts of the lady who was indignantly refusing to allow herself to be removed and continued:

"You are also a member of a crime ring made up of civil servants from Moscow and the surrounding area who were behind the biggest fraudulent land grab in human history, which is known as 'New Moscow.' You purposely bankrupted collective and freehold farms, pestering them with never-ending inspections and fines. Then you bought up massive plots of land at private 'invitation-only' auctions for practically nothing, gaining thousands of square miles of land stretching from the Moscow Ring Road to the Kaluga Oblast, officially labelling the properties marginal and unproductive land. After that, your accomplices passed a law to expand Moscow's borders to match the lands you now owned by 'complete coincidence.' And then with a stroke of the pen, you rezoned your new properties as urban residential areas, raising their value by a minimum of six hundred thousand times!!! The members of your gang are now among the richest people in the country. You make the oligarchs, oil barons and scrap-metal tycoons look silly with the scale of your fraud, putting yourself in control of land worth in the trillions of rubles!"

The accusations were very serious, and the

---

[5]*Author's note. In reality, there is no such government body. But this is fiction, so any possible similarities with a real person are pure coincidence.*

commotion immediately settled down. Even the military men busy conducting the outsiders out of the room and the outsiders themselves all froze in silence and looked from me to the corrupt civil servant and back.

"How do you know all that, Gnat?" clarified one of the H3 Faction curators. "Were you gathering information on her?"

"No, I have never seen her before in my life and didn't so much as suspect she existed until today. I read all that from her thoughts just now."

"You're a dead man!" the lady promised me in the sudden silence. "You little snot, you have no idea the kind of forces standing behind me! The prosecutor's office can't do anything about it! Even the President himself cannot stop me!"

At first, I twitched in fear – in the game, such flagrant threats and boorishness right in the face of a high-profile player usually led to a serious Authority drop. And if my Authority had in fact fallen even one point after what she said, I'd have killed her on the spot. But she got lucky. Nothing changed for me, while her threats didn't frighten me in the least. No matter how rich this con artist may have been, she didn't have the reach to get her grubby little hands on me way out in outer space. And so I continued reading information from her thoughts.

"Right now, you and your husband are buying up whole city blocks in the UK and planning to flee there in the next few months. Meanwhile your little son who you sent off to study at Oxford got punch drunk with all the easy money, bought his very own starship in the game that bends reality and took a group of his jerkoff buddies out to party in space, where he got himself into trouble."

Before the woman could respond, security pushed her very unceremoniously out the door. After that, the 'gym rat' senator was taken out all red and wheezing. I glanced at the timer. Two and a half minutes. The major had pulled it off.

"Gnat, what are you doing?!" Leng Tarasov jumped in. "You're really getting carried away today! You don't seem like yourself."

I turned to look at my old acquaintance. I could tell by the faction leader's sunken eyes and exhausted appearance that this "member of the concerned public" had absolutely fried his nerves today.

"Well, what do you think? I was pulled away from the front lines of the war with the Composite where I just watched hundreds of players die real deaths with my own eyes, and my starship could be attacked at any moment by the menacing intergalactic invaders. I was told I needed to have an important conversation with the leader of the Human-3 Faction to discuss neighborly relations and smooth out some sharp edges. I dropped everything to be at this meeting. But what do I see? Instead of a relevant conversation, I am met by a bleating herd of corrupt civil servants that shoved their way into a military facility trying to order me around!"

Leng Tarasov didn't respond. instead one of the curators in civilian garb took over – the very same one who asked me how I knew about the land scheme.

"Kirill, I promise you my agency will be looking into all the facts you mentioned today. But setting aside emotions and negativity toward a select few individuals, what do you know about the events on Poko-Poko? After all, citizens of our country are in trouble. We have to react somehow. What actions are you planning on taking in connection with the crisis? And what possible help might you need from us?"

I tried to give as much detail as possible in response to those questions, even though I warned everyone in the room in advance that the conversation could end at any second if enemy starships showed up.

"I have already determined that the largest criminal syndicate in the galaxy is not involved, nor are the Miyelonian pirate prides. Even the Pride of the Bushy Shadow, which I have a strained relationship with, has assured me they are not behind the kidnapping of Humans on Poko-Poko. The fact they are demanding none other than the mobile Relict laboratory as ransom is food for thought. The criminals must realize that I will not give up Earth's humanity's only trump card, which means they aren't interested in the ransom. No, these criminals must have a different goal in mind. So what are they trying to achieve? The most obvious answer is that their true goal is to damage my Authority as Kung of Earth and make me look incapable of protecting my own civilians to clear the way for another leader. In that case, it could be the leader of one of the large terrestrial factions from either our or the magocratic world behind the kidnapping. We also shouldn't throw out the option that this whole kidnapping is being faked and the debauched rich kids are just hiding out and not responding to comms requests."

"But how? The girl saw one of her friends' dead bodies with her own eyes!"

"So what? Someone who died in the game could have respawned long ago, so his bloodied corpse is nowhere near proof of kidnapping and murder. Don't overlook the fact that the dead player hasn't left his virt pod in the real world in the UK, which means one of two things: either he managed to change factions, or the leaders of the Human-2 Faction are hiding something."

When I said that, Leng Igor Tarasov shuddered sharply and said what he thought:

"You know what, that's an interesting idea! The Brits might just be trying to shake down the parents of these 'Russian rich kids' for tens of billions of pounds! It would be a hard temptation to pass up!"

But I just shook my head, reigning in his enthusiasm:

"Such fraud would be uncovered sooner or later, and the resulting scandal would be bigger than we can even imagine. So I am still in favor of option one because enough time has passed for the players to be able to change their exit point. It would of course be nice to figure out the name of the new faction the rich kids joined, it would give us a thread to pull on that might end up unraveling the whole ball. To do that, we'll have to get the hostage to see one of her friends in the game. We could also try to figure out what happened to the starship they bought, a fairly old Omi-Chee space yacht. I already know there is no such ship on Poko-Poko right now. But a space yacht is no needle in a haystack, and sooner or later it will turn up. At any rate, it can't have gone very far with its low speed. But for the time being it's still at large, so I went a different route and tried to find out about the Geckho the 'golden boys' hired at the spaceport..."

"Yeah? Turn anything up?" came a hopeful-looking Vinogradov the Academic, leader of the Human-23 Faction. "The spaceport managers refused to give me that information, making reference to space travel privacy rights. But when I told them a group of people got themselves into trouble, appealed to their conscience and begged for help, the Geckho just threw me out of the dispatchers' tower. Quite literally. That sent my Authority on a four-point tumble."

Leng Vinogradov the Academic breathed a heavy sigh and threw his arms up as if to say he tried to help but got nowhere. I had a hard time hiding a smirk. It must have been a funny scene in the spaceport, showing in full color just how poor a grasp the leader of the Human-23 Faction had on space diplomacy. One cannot speak with the suzerains in such a fashion. If a one starts to fawn and grovel, the Geckho will only hold them in contempt for their weakness, certainly not help them. He should have offered a favor in exchange for the information, or invoked an influential common acquaintance – for example Viceroy Gerd Kosta Dykhsh, or even myself. Then the spaceport workers would have reigned in their attitude and helped like good little boys. But I didn't say what I thought about the middle-aged academic's behavior, just answered his question.

"I am familiar with two of the Geckho. We used to fly on the same Shiamiru shuttle captained by Uraz Tukhsh. That also leads me to certain ideas, though it would be premature to speak of any specific conclusions just yet. In any case, we are investigating and the special services of the Geckho, Miyelonians and Trillians have all joined in. Even the Meleyephatian Horde observer was intrigued by the events and promised to bring the Horde's capabilities to bear. If need be, I will go to Poko-Poko myself. But then it wouldn't be for a friendly meeting with the owners of the space station. No, I would bring a logistical support force with me, and we would turn everything there inside out searching for clues!"

Authority increased to 118!
Authority increased to 119!

Well, well! I was speaking with people from the real world, but the game functions were working as usual – I could use my Psionics, while my Authority figure was dependent on their thoughts. Although why be surprised? After all, some of those in the room (for example Leng Igor Tarasov on stage or the head of the Human-23

Faction Leng Vinogradov the Academic) had characters in the game and my Authority already depended on their opinion of Gnat.

By the way, I wasn't even slightly bluffing about the possible violent resolution. Geckho leader Krong Daveyesh-Pir had promised me a reward for solving the diplomatic crisis with the Miyelonians and certainly wouldn't refuse me such a small favor as sending a few hundred enforcers to Poko-Poko. Plus Kung Keetsie Myau might also want to find out who was going to such lengths to frame the Miyelonians by showing off a human body cut to shreds with a blade. Such weapons were something of a calling card of the Miyelonian race. Everyone in the galaxy knew that. But even if the Great One didn't want to interfere, I already had enough resources to hire a squad of hundreds of notorious cutthroats, who could turn Poko-Poko into a living hell for a few million crystals and explain to the pirates and smugglers that the Humans of Earth were not to be messed with!

Now that the curators had gotten a detailed answer on the Poko-Poko issue, I suggested we get to the main topic I had come to this meeting to discuss. What were the Human-3 Faction's problems with the Relicts?

And there the floor was taken by faction head

Leng Igor Tarasov.

"Gnat, there are two main issues. The first is territorial in nature. My people came through the passes to the south of the Yellow Mountains based on long-ago settled and confirmed expansion plans in order to construct a fort on Centaur territory. But we were surprised to discover that node already occupied by the Relict Faction and furthermore already possessing a level-two claim! The neighboring nodes are also all occupied by your faction! How can that be? You were still with the Human-3 Faction when you heard we held a claim to those southern territories. I am positive I remember that you were at the meeting a month and a half or two ago when we discussed development plans!"

Honestly though, I didn't know whether to laugh or cry at these preposterous complaints. What was he saying? Had they just now figured out that the entire southern peninsula with its twenty-six game nodes was occupied by my Relict Faction? Had they not noticed that thousands of NPC-Centaurs, Minotaurs and Dryads had already been hard at work for three weeks in those swampy tropical forests, building roads, forts, an airport for heavy antigravs, the city of Phyliragrad (named after the Centaur ruler), metallurgical factories and lots of other infrastructure? If not, then what was H3 Faction intelligence even good for?

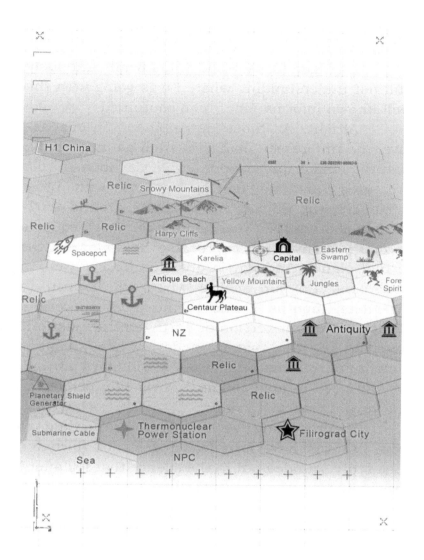

No, I didn't laugh at my neighbors' lack of information. And I took the long way to answer.

"When I only just started in the game that bends reality, the Human-3 Faction had five game nodes. Now it has nine and you were thinking about moving into a tenth. Is that right? Correct me if I'm wrong."

Leng Igor Tarasov shook his head cautiously, still not understanding where I was going with this well-known information. I then continued.

"Alright. At those development speeds and given no unforeseen obstacles such as inaccessible natural landscape, dangerous NPCs such as sea creatures, and no border conflicts with other neighbors, the H3 Faction will have around thirty game nodes within a year and a half, which equates to one percent of all capturable hexagons on the virtual planet. And now a question for everyone in the room. Do you realize what will happen in seventeen months if one of the most successful factions from our version of Earth controls just one percent of the game nodes when realities synchronize? To make sure our world stays around, we will need to hold claims on over fifty percent of the virtual planet's territory."

"If everything goes perfectly according to plan, we will have forty-five nodes, not thirty," a lone reply sounded out in the silence that fell after I finished. "Furthermore, the Human-3 Faction is nowhere near the only one representing our world, so there is a chance."

I shook my head, not hiding my skepticism.

"You're forgetting about the magocratic world. Their factions are also numerous and developing quickly, and they are much less fragmented than we are. For now, as far as I know, the alternate world leads ours in the race for survival, and their advantage grows with every passing week. And that's leaving out my Relict

Faction. That is another serious topic for discussion."

"Kirill, I agree, we aren't growing fast enough," the head of the Human-3 Faction spoke up again. "And that just so happens to be the second issue I wanted to discuss with you. Gnat, we have a serious shortage of players. We can't even properly work on all our projects, even though we have technically hit the limit for number of corncobs under the Dome. We have already constructed fifty-four of the tall towers and building more would mean tearing down the other facilities. The soccer field has already been removed along with the tennis courts. Next on the chopping block is the model Labyrinth, then we'll have to start axing residential buildings."

Oh wow... A problem I was not expecting. I'll admit, I didn't even suspect such a thing would be possible. And meanwhile, Tarasov delved into the explanation.

"When the Dome was built to study the game that bends reality, our priorities were secrecy and security. And that was why we put the base underground. At the time it seemed like more than enough space for our potential needs. After all, no one suspected we would need to bring hundreds and thousands of people into the game in the future. Anyway, the construction of new corncobs is currently in question, but we have no more free virt pods. Meanwhile, eight hundred seventy virt pods are occupied by players that have switched to your Relict Faction. I suggest we transfer all of them to Novosibirsk, where corncobs were built for the former H25 Faction along with everything your players could need to work and unwind."

Novosibirsk? In theory, I was not opposed. If necessary, I could even transfer all these people to the First Directory of the magocratic world. However, not everyone was comfortable there. After all the language was unfamiliar and the culture and laws were completely different. But first I nevertheless asked why the curators and heads of the Russian factions didn't want to take the most obvious path – for the Human-23 Faction to be absorbed by the larger Human-3. It was easy to do in the game's faction management settings, then the smaller faction's corncobs would all become available to choose.

"We didn't want to mix players from two factions with such radically different purposes, which would be impossible to avoid if they merged completely," Igor Tarasov pulled a wry face. "Anyhow, the Human-23 has quite a few... how to put this delicately... demanding individuals. They expect a certain level of comfort and are often busy in the real world, only coming into the game from time to time. We cannot count on them to take full part in the life of the faction and the players themselves are uncomfortable crossing paths with common citizens. Plus it wouldn't be safe."

"Yeah, I get it. I agree that certain protocols must be upheld when it comes to high-level state actors, and they can't always be observed easily. The one thing I don't understand is why I was sent an offer to absorb the H23 Faction into the Relict. No one can shirk their duties in my faction. All players must do their part according to their game specialty, or they're sent packing. I have no interest in ballast. I even have noble Princesses working on equal footing with the rest!"

Vinogradov the Academic looked embarrassed and turned to the room for a few seconds in search of support, and explained:

"You see, Kirill... Well, we thought there would be a much higher probability of you going to help the people on Poko-Poko if some of the hostages belonged to your faction. But now their game faction has changed... so I agree it seems inappropriate... I will withdraw the diplomatic offer."

I see. I didn't wait for Leng Vinogradov the Academic to reach his virt pod and myself chose "refuse" in response to the diplomatic annexation offer. Then I told them all that my assistants and administrators would talk to the Relict Faction members living under the Dome and offer to let them choose other exit points into the real world. And in fact, the problem Imran was complaining about solved itself. The Relict Faction players would be transferred out from under the Dome in a centralized fashion to different locations of their choosing.

I was inspired and retook the initiative in the conversation.

"I say we go back to the border conflict and expansion into empty game nodes. My Relict Faction is no enemy to the Human-3 Faction and makes no claim to territory which does not belong to it. But as Igor Tarasov noted correctly, it has been more than a month and a half since those plans were discussed, and a lot has changed. There is now an independent Relict Faction uniting the players of the two alternate worlds. At first my faction only controlled one island in the middle of the gulf. But we quickly obtained nodes on both sides of the gulf, then around the Geckho spaceport and to the northwest of it reaching all the way to Chinese territory and to the south and north of the H3 Faction. After that, we expanded onto the opposite end of the small continent and the large continent. Other than continuing to grow in those directions, my faction soon plans to make a sea landing along the entire southern coastline of our continent and occupy seventeen nodes reaching to the lands of the La-Shin Faction."

I took a short pause to allow the listeners to digest and come to grips with what I'd said, then continued.

"Every day we have less and less time remaining before synchronization, and the goal we have in front of us is very important: to keep both parallel worlds safe along with their shared population of around seventeen billion people. That's why we're in such a hurry. We're developing as fast as we can and taking control of all we can reach including nodes our neighbors have not yet occupied for whatever reason. Yes, we were the first to take the node to the south of the Yellow Mountains. By the way, it now has been named Snake Paradise. I'm sure you understand why. As compensation for the potential inconvenience, I am prepared to offer the Human-3 Faction one million crystals."

I saw Igor Tarasov's eyebrows shoot up in surprise – he was seemingly not expecting such generous monetary compensation. In fact, I immediately was assured by the head of the Human-3 Faction that our border incident was settled and his faction no longer had any qualms with the Relict.

"Alright then. You'll need money to expand to the east beyond the swamp nodes. We left you a development corridor there on purpose. Let me remind you once again that we are no enemies of yours and the Human-3 Faction's expansion is also in our interest because our factions are currently part of a military and political alliance, so your nodes will also count toward our total."

"So Gnat, how much territory does your faction currently control?"

The question belonged to the curator that promised to handle the rude civil servant. In theory, I could have refused to answer because such information was legally classified. But I decided to tell the truth so they would see the true state of affairs in virtual politics.

I opened the faction management tab and read the information out loud:

"As of right now, the Relict Faction has forty-one level-one nodes, thirty-four level-two, eleven level-three, three level-four, two level-five and one level-six node. That's a total of ninety-two hexagons giving a maximum player limit of sixty-three thousand three hundred thirty-six. The Relict Faction's total number of owned and rented virt pods is..." I turned to another tab in the game menu and read that data, "four hundred eleven thousand five hundred thirty. So my faction's ability to bring more players into the game that bends reality is very, very extensive."

Meanwhile, I did not clarify that the lion's share of those virt pods were in the Syam Tro VII Refuge, and so currently not available. But in any case, the reaction in the room was a sight to behold! A bomb going off would have had less impact!

"So there is an exhaustive answer to a question that has been asked many times within these walls. Now we know the fundamental difference between Kungs, Lengs and other faction leaders..." Igor Tarasov said, visibly shaken.

Authority increased to 120!
Authority increased to 121!
Authority increased to 122!

Unfortunately, I didn't have time to savor my moment of triumph. The meeting with the curators suddenly vanished and I found myself standing in the middle of the Pyramid Contact Hall again.

"Have Composite ships appeared in the Rorsh system?" I asked the nearby Miyelonian Engineer Orun Va-Mart with worry.

"No, Captain Gnat. But I had to perform an emergency shutdown of long-distance comms because an alarm is going off on the *Tamara the Paladin*. Gerd Ayni Uri-Miayuu asked that the captain be told immediately that 'you know who' has come to his senses, broken all his chains, thrashed his way out of the box and is currently wreaking havoc in the escape pod."

Chapter Twenty

Getting to Know Absolute Evil

"WHAT'S THE STATUS," I said to my tailed Miyelonian assistant as soon as I got back on the frigate.

"The team is shaken up and wants explanations," Gerd Ayni told me, her voice tearing in anxiety as she ran. I noticed my Translator's tail shaking and her ears pinned back. Ayni was afraid. In fact she was terrified and verging on uncontrolled panic. "Gerd Uline Tar ordered the airlock not be opened and for us to await our captain's return. Gerd Jarg the Analyst respawned and also counselled us not to do anything without Kung Gnat's awareness."

Wise decision! The last thing I needed now was for my troopers to kill a prisoner we'd exerted so much effort to get our hands on, or for Gerd Hugo to cripple a member of my team. I could hear the knocking and heavy blows to the barrier from far away. And when I got closer to the docking bay,

I could even feel the starship vibrating. The huge muscular Trillian was enraged, slamming into walls and crushing everything. And another thing... it's hard to put the unpleasant sensation into words, but it was like a wave every two seconds of baseless clammy fear, and the intensity of the waves grew quickly the closer I came.

Mental Fortitude skill increased to level one hundred thirty-five!

Danger Sense skill increased to level one hundred forty-eight!

Indeed, we had a problem. If even I was experiencing discomfort from the powerful psionic pressure, then what could be said of the remaining crew members who did not have the same psionic defenses? My Danger Sense skill also was sending clear signals. And that was strange. What could one unarmed prisoner do against my two dozen cutthroats with skills and combat abilities that made me proud? Okay, I could figure that out when I got there.

In the narrow corridor, the boarding team troopers were all piled up and wearing full armor with their weapons at the ready. Half of the crew was also on the scene. The Humans, Miyelonians and Geckho were scared, so they were trying to stick together. My appearance was greeted by all with clear relief. The crew believed in their captain's ability to handle any issue.

"Captain Gnat, unknown threat from the escape pod!" Gerd T'yu-Pan reported with military crispness. "Something big and heavy is trying to get onto our frigate. It also has magic and is exercising mind control! So far we have observed: fear, baseless panic, desire to give up and flee or leave the game. But my troops have held strong."

As if in response to the Shocktroop's words the ship was rocked by a powerful blow on the other side of the airlock door and a new wave of ghastly fear rolled through the starship. I saw the peoples' faces go pale and the NPC Dryad squeeze up against her husband Kisly, running out of her jewelry workshop for security and support. Nevertheless, no one ran or threw down their weapons.

In an exaggeratedly peppy voice, I promised to get to the bottom of it, pressed the Scanning icon and... to be honest chickened out a bit when I saw our adversary on the mini-map: a Trillian Theologian of level 370!!! What??? No one had warned me the bloody Prince Hugo was such an incredibly high level! And just how were we supposed to handle this newly freed monster? Nevertheless, I didn't let my bewilderment show and ordered the team to switch to nonlethal weaponry. At the same time, I sent away the two small Relict guard drones, which had raced to the scene. The last thing I needed was to accidentally kill a member of the Trillian royal family.

"Vasily Andreyevich, put speed and bravery bonuses on everyone! Formation five! Tanks link shields! The biggest and strongest stay with me: Taik Rekh, Basha and Vasha, T'yu-Pan and Eduard Boyko. You five get ready. I'll be opening the door in one minute. Take strength and regeneration elixirs now. I repeat: nonlethal weaponry only. Shockers, batons and Paralyzers. Gerd Ayni..." I looked around for the Miyelonian Translator squeezed in behind the rest, "I'm gonna need you, too. To translate. Everyone else, get out of here and stay out of it. We'll handle it! I know who our enemy is, and what to do with him! So get back to your duties or wait in the common room."

Psionic skill increased to level one hundred forty!

Yes, I purposely did not take the Trillian Gerd Ukh-Meemeesh with the assault group even though he was the very strongest, heaviest and sturdiest of my troops. I figured this was not a good enough reason to ruin my Gunner's life. He would have to live in Trillian society after this, and every other member of his race idolized the rebellious Prince Hugo and would ferociously hate all those who dared oppose him. For the same reason, I tried to keep the Trillian girl out of it as well.

ATTENTION! Immunity to fear received! Duration: 230 seconds.

Oh! That's much better! Vasily Andreyevich Filippov made a clear demonstration of how beneficial a skilled Bard can be. I don't know if the other members of the assault group got full immunity or just increased their resists to mental attacks, but the troopers perked up right away and started looking at the locked hatch impatiently, burning with desire to get the problem under control as quickly as possible.

Ugh, now I would like to know what could be done with a creature of such enormous mental power... I drank down a mana-restoring cocktail, then looked at the mini-map in search of the Psionic Mage. A partner would come very in handy for me right now. The little sorceress Gerd Soia-Tan La-Varrez was found in the med bay working with the Miyelonian Medic. And for the record, Soia-Tan had already hit level ninety-three! She was progressing fast. But for some reason the Psionic Mage was not responding to my mental call. I sent another, but again got nothing. I asked the Medic and was told the Human girl was currently in a medically induced coma. Too bad. I would not have an easy time standing up against the mental power of such a high-level opponent on my own. And by the way...

I quickly spent up my free skill points. A whole fifteen of the eighteen went into Mental Fortitude, bringing it up to one hundred fifty. And I immediately chose a second specialization, which unlocked at level one hundred fifty: 20% boost to psionic defenses. That would make things somewhat easier. But still I had no confidence I could stand up to the ghastly Theologian. He was just too far beyond me in level and skills. How could I resist the horror he was sending down?

A phrase popped unwittingly into my mind, which I had long ago heard from Human-3 troopers: "When Tamara's around, I'm not afraid." Yes, Leng Tamara and her ability to provide group members an impenetrable defense against psionics would be a great help right now. The only thing was that my courageous friend had died in the far away and foreign magocratic world. The Second Legion's troopers had already verified that. Her remains were now in Pa-lin-thu, capital of the First Directory awaiting a dignified burial. I ordered them not to rush it. I was planning to inform the nation of Leng Tamara's demise and the location of her funeral ceremony in a public address.

And so I had to get by without the defense the Paladin could have provided. I took out the tablets the Horde observer gifted me. The blister pack contained six more of the blue pills. I took one myself and gave another to the Translator who was still shaking like an aspen leaf. The remaining four I split between the tanks. Unfortunately, there wasn't enough for Vasha Tushihh to get one.

ATTENTION! Resistance to psionic damage increased by 50%. Duration: 43 minutes.

I finished my preparations, placing my remaining three skill points into Psionics to raise the attack ability to one hundred forty-two.

"Captain, you said you know who is on the other side of that door. Could you tell us?" asked the huge Taik Rekh, looking imposing in his assault armor.

I showed the whole group a visible target marker. Our opponent was standing right on the other side of the door and seemed to already be aware we were planning to attack.

Targeting skill increased to level seventy-four!

"Yes, I already know. He is a dangerous criminal the Meleyephatians kept behind bars for almost twenty-three tongs. They couldn't afford to kill him though – he was from the Trillian royal dynasty and that would have threatened very serious diplomatic consequences. So instead of a well-deserved execution for his heinous crimes, the villain was sentenced to life in prison. And now the prison guards have foisted the monster on us. And to make it so we wouldn't refuse and couldn't put him back in his cell, they blasted the space prison to smithereens."

"The Par-Poreh royal dynasty..." Vasha Tushihh droned and tried to thoughtfully stroke his head through the metal helmet with an armored glove. "Don't tell me this is..."

The large and powerful Geckho was not brave enough to speak the name of the rebel Prince. Perhaps he also believed in the old wives' tales that every time the name of Prince Hugo was uttered, the day of his return to the galaxy drew nearer.

"Yes, the same..." the Miyelonian said fatedly. "So we're already as good as dead. The Prince leaves none alive. Ever."

I hurried to intervene so the Translator's despair wouldn't transfer to the others. Ugh, I didn't want to waste such crucial Magic Points to inspire my team, but it didn't look like there was any other way.

"So then, listen up. Here's the plan of action. I'll open the hatch and walk in first. Maybe we'll be able to settle this by negotiation. After all, we just have to deliver Prince Hugo to his destination. Our mission ends there. There's no need to fight the Theologian. But if the large Trillian does attack me, run in after and try to push him up against the wall with all your mass or pin him to the floor then subdue him. In case of aggression, you not only can beat the Trillian. You must. Just don't overdo it! I remind you that the 'embodiment of absolute evil' is not to be killed! We need him alive!"

All my troopers confirmed that they understood the mission. Only the Miyelonian was still wavering.

"Captain Gnat, why should we even open the hatch? Why don't we just take the escape pod with this monster inside where he needs to go, then send it off and make a quick getaway?"

The troopers took an immediate liking to Gerd Ayni Uri-Miayuu's idea, but I came out against it.

"According to my data," I pointed at the captain's tablet with a flickering emergency message, "this mad Trillian has already damaged the escape pod's hull. There's a leak. Right now, Prince Hugo's life is not at risk because we're inside the Relict laboratory's defensive screen, which is filled with breathable air. But we cannot dock with the laboratory, nor land on a planet. And as soon as our frigate leaves the defensive screen, air will start leaking out of the escape pod. Then the valuable captive will suffocate, and we will be charged with murdering a member of the Par-Poreh royal family. So, let's get started!"

Before the moment of decisiveness had passed, I twisted the latch, abruptly threw open the hatch and stepped forward.

Inside the escape pod, all the lighting had already been smashed and the only source of illumination was the light on my helmet and those of the assault group troopers in the doorway. Woah... A set of fearsome teeth in a huge wide open Trillian mouth appeared suddenly out of the gloom and froze mere inches from my head. The Tachyon Bender triggered! The second of delay was long enough for me to dodge and throw my opponent back with Telekinesis. Although "throw back" was probably putting it a bit too strongly... the target was too heavy to move very far. I managed to send the Trillian just a foot backward. With the clang of a closing beartrap, his ghastly jaws clamped shut on thin air where my head had been just half a second before.

Gerd Hugo Par-Poreh. Trillian. Pink Trillian subrace. True Values faction. Level-370 Theologian.

ATTENTION!!! Prince Hugo Par-Poreh is one of the Galaxy's most wanted space criminals. Danger rating: 15 (maximum).

ATTENTION!!! A bounty for Gerd Hugo Par-Poreh's head has been set at three hundred seven million one hundred twenty thousand Geckho monetary crystals.

The embodiment of absolute evil turned out to be a long six-legged "crocodile" of pale pink coloration with a whitish belly the color of a dead fish. Both of the Trillian's upper legs and his powerful jaws were caked in blood – he must have hurt himself trashing and smashing the escape pod hull's thin walls. I was also struck by his eyes – red and orange, they glowed in the dark like two menacing flames.

Danger Sense skill increased to level one hundred forty-nine!

Time slowed down again. The clawed foot Prince Hugo was trying to use to grab me stopped next to my torso. I jumped back while also shooting the Paralyzer practically point blank. The green ball of paralyzing mixture spread out in a sticky blot on the armored light hide of the Trillian's chest without affecting him whatsoever.

Rifles skill increased to level seventy!

Sharpshooter skill increased to level fifty-seven!

And again I had to dodge and put some distance between us, this time somersaulting away from the heavy long tail the Trillian was using to try and trip me. The negotiations had clearly failed before they even got started. I was left with plan B – to take this monster down while doing my best not to kill him.

I shot the Paralyzer from five feet away. And again, and again! All three balls missed the mark – my adversary was proving surprisingly light on his feet, able to react and remove his fifteen-foot-thick body from the flight trajectory of my missiles. I could hear jubilation and self-satisfaction in the loud roar the Trillian let out. Prince Hugo seemed to be enjoying the battle and was certain he would prevail. The last shot I took from the Paralyzer's clip also missed.

Mental Fortitude skill increased to level one hundred fifty-one!

Woah... The psionic blow was too powerful for even my mental defenses, which were nowhere near weak. I was flipping out, so I missed the next attack. Even the second granted by the Tachyon Bender didn't help – the clawed foot struck me right in the chest causing an immediate burning and electric shock sensation. Ow!

Medium Armor skill increased to level one hundred five!

I flew backward and slammed into the wall. That hurt! My Listener armor energy shield's seventeen thousand or so points of defense were reduced to less than nine thousand. To make matters worse, a portion of the damage had gotten through to my character and I had lost almost a thousand hitpoints as well. Of my two thousand seven hundred Hitpoints I now had just one thousand seven hundred thirty left. Despite the fall and pain, I couldn't hold back a malicious smirk when I saw the look of extreme bafflement on the villain's snout. He had used his "ult" on me, a combat ability that would take a very long time to cool down, and here I had the gall to still be alive! Furthermore, Prince Hugo had also made a serious investment into the psionic attack, spending a solid chunk of his Magic Points, yet the effect was so minor I wasn't even incapacitated. So that was the upside of investing in Intelligence. No matter what, a Gerd would always be lower in that figure than a Kung.

"Een Psssh Khowo Va!" my opponent cursed, seemingly unable to believe his eyes.

"Yes, yes. It didn't work. Try bringing your Intelligence up a bit first," I responded cheerily, already on my feet and completely ready to deflect more attacks.

And they didn't keep me waiting. But this time, I was ready and dodged a basic poke of his claw into my chest, followed by an attempt to bite off my head. I tried to attack as well and for some reason it didn't work either. For some reason, the Disorientation I placed on the Prince didn't seem to have any effect, while my opponent's psionic defenses were simply impenetrable.

But then where was my support group? And just then the troopers, wearing heavy and clumsy exoskeletons squeezed one by one through the doorway, attacking all together and dashing forward with a roar. I put on Disorientation again and tried to take Gerd Hugo Par-Poreh's mind under control – sure it came to nothing, but it did distract the Prince from the new contenders on the battlefield. The five troopers piled on all at once, knocking the Trillian off his feet and pressing him up against a wall. No matter how strong the high-profile Trillian may have been, he couldn't cope with nearly two tons of metal and flesh crashing down on top of him.

Gerd Hugo wasn't giving up though and tried to escape. Vasha Tushihh howled in an ugly voice and fell when Hugo's heavy tail swiped at his legs. Seemingly, that broke both of the Geckho's legs. But that was the last thing our adversary managed to do. With a hail of blows raining down on him from shockers and clubs, Gerd Hugo went limp and fell silent. Half a minute later, all the hands and feet of this "absolute evil" were bound up tight using strong metal cords and tied tightly to his body while I unloaded another Paralyzer clip right into the "crocodile's" slightly opened mouth just to make sure.

All five of the balls burst, flooding the "crocodile's" maw with a viscous paralyzing substance, but even that couldn't knock Prince Hugo out and he was still conscious. Flickering his fearsome orange eyes, he honked menacingly:

"Two Humans. Three Geckho. One Miyelonian. I will remember you all." I understood the muted words squeezed out through his muzzled jaw before Gerd Ayni translated it. "You will all die a horrible death. I promise you that! I am evil incarnate, and I do not forgive those who wrong me!"

Fame increased to 119.

For the first time, I was not pleased to see a Fame growth message. I even had a cowardly thought flicker by that I should put on the Null Ring so my menacing opponent wouldn't be able to read my character data and get revenge. Still, Gerd Hugo would have an easy enough time finding me based on the names of the others, plus there was almost certainly not another Human in the galaxy with such an incredible Listener armor suit. So that ship had sailed. I had been sentenced to death.

And such a fury came over me at that moment that I couldn't hold back and kicked the monster's snout with force.

"Human, I will make a goblet out of your skull," the ghastly Trillian promised, wincing in pain. "The Geckho I will dissolve in acid. They will die slow, so they will suffer. And the Miyelonian I will kill last, after I've had my fun with her. I am so fond of her fear. It really stirs my emotions. I always love killing Miyelonians. It's so funny to watch the fluffy little creatures beg for mercy and debase themselves before dying. Yes, yes. Quiver, tailed one! If you piss yourself in fear, I might even have mercy on you."

Gerd Ayni stared back at the bound Trillian with eyes wide in horror, shaking in fear and just about to pass out. For a second it seemed that the Miyelonian might even give in to the degrading suggestion. So I turned the Translator's snout my way and looked Gerd Ayni right in the eyes.

"Calm down. He's no longer any danger. What do you say I give you an anti-fear amulet?"

I had to ask that question twice before Ayni heard me and nodded.

"Hey Eduard, lend me your hatchet!" I demanded and the Space Commando extended it.

I walked up to the "crocodile's" snout and used the butt of the hatchet to break a long front fang from his upper jaw in a few calculating blows. I looked at the bloody foot-long curved tooth.

Fang of Gerd Hugo Par-Poreh, level-370 Theologian (trophy).

"A valuable item! You could sell it for a lot, or our Dryad Nefertiti could turn it into an excellent anti-fear amulet! Y'know, I think I'll take another for myself."

Paying no mind to the bound "crocodile's" whining in pain, I popped out a second fang with the hatchet and put it in my inventory. The bound prisoner groaned and lost at least half of his fighting spirit. The auras of fear also stopped coming. I saw the assault squad troops shudder as the flood retreated and, instead of a ghastly lethal monster, they saw nothing but a crying Trillian begging not to be crippled.

ATTENTION!!! Gerd Hugo's danger rating has fallen to fourteen!

The ghastly monster, who had terrorized the galaxy and subjected his helpless captives to cruel humiliation many times, was proving very sensitive to pain. I can't say for sure. I've never had a tooth pulled. But nevertheless, I don't think I'd be humiliating myself quite this much in such a situation. And I wasn't the only one to notice. The other players next to me also took note.

Vasha Tushihh, sitting on the floor and giving himself an injection of painkiller from the med kit, suddenly spoke up:

"Captain, I want one, too! I have earned it in memory of the encounter with the legendary ancient evil!"

His brother Basha also supported the idea and, after that, three other members of the assault squadron also suddenly wanted trophies from the prostrate Prince. Gerd Hugo had already lost all his verve and was whimpering, actually begging to be let go. I looked at the dangerous creature's pocked maw and commented to my troops:

"There are no more big fangs. I can only get little teeth now. Or I could rip out some claws. Actually, does someone maybe want his penis? Why not? It would make a great gift for a lover. Or it could be turned into an amulet to increase male potency!"

"Please don't, I'm begging you..." Gerd Hugo whimpered. But I wasn't listening and continued to spook him and paint pictures.

"In fact, we should invite the rest of the team. We can take this 'absolute evil' apart bit by bit for spare parts! Six feet, teeth and a hide must be worth something. Then we can kill him for the rewards and experience! Why treat this guy with kid gloves? He's promising to have us all killed. And here we came to his prison with every intention of setting him free, only to get such base ingratitude in response."

"Set me free? Human, just who are you? And why aren't you the least bit afraid of me?" the surprised six-legged "croc" honked out.

"Me? How can you not know me? Ah, yes. You've been in prison for the last eighteen years, so you're behind on life. Well in that case, I'm your replacement. A new evil. Eviler than you ever were. Plus my team is composed of the biggest scumbags this side of the Milky Way. My ex-girlfriend blew up the whole ruling council of a planet, taking down all their leaders in one fell swoop and clearing the way for me. This Miyelonian you were just scaring is famed throughout the galaxy for disemboweling the Great Priestess of her own race in full view of a large crowd and during a live broadcast to billions of citizens of the Union of Miyelonian Prides. I also sometimes travel with Kung Eesssa, the legendary Betelgeuse Planet Devouress. I'm sure you've heard of her. Vaa the Morphian as well, who was behind the attempt to take over the Meleyephatian Horde, the bloodiest single event in the history of our galaxy. As for me, I caused the Composite to invade from another galaxy. They have already destroyed the capital of the Meleyephatian Horde and show no sign of stopping! Now I have come here to break you out of prison. But after what you said about turning my skull into a goblet, I might change my mind and just bury you on a distant asteroid for the experience and rewards. My decision will depend on how you behave."

Fame increased to 120.

Authority increased to 123!

Psionic skill increased to level one hundred forty-three!

Some might say I had lost my mind or was playing with fire by mocking and frightening the "embodiment of absolute evil," but I saw no other way out. I had been sentenced to death. There could be no doubt that if I just let the Prince go, he would do everything in his power to track down me and my companions. But this way I had a chance to change my fate... Yes, it worked! And now before Prince Hugo got a chance to respond, I had already realized from his changed emotional background that he would be offering peace.

"Human, I am prepared to make an exception for you and your team. I didn't know the whole picture and made a mistake. I beg forgiveness for my harsh words and promise not to track you down in the future if you stop maiming me and just let me go. And when I become ruler of the Trillians, I will have highly paid work for your team. In fact, I have just the job for you."

I pretended to think and responded only half a minute later, which made the Prince very nervous.

"Alright, Gerd Hugo. I agree. But just in case, I will hang you up on a gravity loader outside my starship for the remainder of this flight so you can't keep trashing stuff. Don't worry. All the air around is breathable, so you won't die. I just wouldn't suggest leaving the game. The station where your body is located in the real world will be destroyed any second now. But in around three ummi, I will let you out in Trillian space and tell the Hive of Tintara to come pick you up."

After that, I turned to the assault squad troopers and threw my arms up bitterly.

"Too bad. There won't be any more trophies. Everyone who didn't get one will be compensated monetarily."

Chapter Twenty-One

Cards on the Table

THE COMPOSITE STARSHIPS took a whole forty minutes to reach the Rorsh system and, by that time, we had already deployed the gravity loader and suspended the "embodiment of absolute evil" inside the space station's camouflage field. The pink crocodile twitching his legs and hovering in the air looked so awkward and silly, that I had to ask my team to stop whinnying at the royal and recording videos. Any high-profile player would be very sensitive to drops in Authority, and now that we were on the vindictive Prince's good side, I didn't want to anger him again.

I even took Gerd Ayni and had already gone to Nefertiti's jewelry workshop to give the NPC-Dryad the two-foot-long fangs I'd knocked out of the "crocodile's" mouth. I had already cleaned the blood off them and told the quickly progressing NPC lady to make the rare trophies into pendants to be worn around the neck with fear protection spells. But the jeweler turned the fangs over in her hands and put forth an alternate suggestion:

"Captain, I could of course make pendants. But these two long teeth would be better used to make a pair of blades. In that case, beyond the spell each could be imbued with, there would be an additional set bonus. And it just so happens I could make that be immunity to fear. I have already learned how to craft pretty and more importantly effective bladed weaponry, and here the raw materials were taken from a level-370 creature, so the damage modifier will be crazy. It should be a true masterpiece: a weapon that could crush even gods. And I'm just burning with impatience to get started! I won't need any pay either. I myself would like to see how it turns out."

"Alright, make them a pair of blades. And in that case, let's put a gilded engraving in Miyelonian hieroglyphs on the bone. Ayni, write this on something for the Dryad so she can copy it onto the weapon. Here it is: 'I must not fear. Fear is the mind killer. Fear is the little-death that brings total obliteration. I will face my fear. I will permit it to pass over me and through me. And when it has gone past, I will turn my inner eye to see its path. And where the fear has gone, there will be nothing.'"

The Miyelonian jotted that down on the tablet screen and looked at me in surprise.

"A powerful passage. Is that a curse of your people?"

"You might say so. It is a litany against fear. It was written by the famed fantasy writer Frank Herbert and millions of people have used it to overcome fear since. And if it is indeed true that everything a large number of intelligent creatures believe in will become real in the game that bends reality, perhaps somewhere in the endless virtual Universe the desert planet of Dune with its giant worms has already appeared along with other worlds dreamt up by famous writers. By the way, I'll be giving the set of blades to you. I think I've let you down badly several times today. So let this serve as my apology."

Ayni looked down.

"No, Captain Gnat, you didn't let me down. It was more like you scared me. You have killed too much today. You were too calculating and ruthless. And it even looked like it made you happy. Then you were talking about being the new embodiment of evil, even ghastlier and crueler. Of course you said it to the vile Prince Hugo to take the initiative in the conversation, but I got the impression..."

The pretty orange Miyelonian didn't finish, dashed over and pushed herself up against me, little tears glimmering in her eyes. I embraced the tailed lady and tried to calm her down, but Ayni burst into tears.

"Captain, please don't turn evil. I'll follow you to the end either way of course, but still, I beg you..."

Our conversation was interrupted by Dmitry Zheltov, whose voice rolled down the starship's corridors:

"Combat alert! Enemy ships at a million and a half miles!"

Half a minute later I was seated at my work console. With a silent nod at the respawned spiny

Analyst, who was also now sitting in his seat, I didn't make any audible commentary on his successful operation to get rid of the Horde observer.

"Took them long enough. And they exited pretty far away," noted Ayukh the Navigator, zooming out the star map and trying to determine their arrival vector. "By the looks of things, they came from the unclaimed HU-786 system. What if they maybe they aren't here for us? They could just be passing through. What do you think, Captain?"

"It's possible," I shrugged my shoulders. "The Meleyephatians warned us that the Composite reacts quickly to every use of long-distance comms in nearby systems and sends out strike groups. But this is just three small ships, and they popped up in a random spot..."

"Maybe our comms equipment is more advanced, and the Composite is having a hard time reading our coordinates?" the very plausible theory belonged to co-Pilot San-Doon Taki-Bu. "But the scattered space station debris has clearly caught their eye. They're turning our way. Gaining speed."

"Those Dero interceptors have crazy acceleration! Impressive!" Dmitry Zheltov looked at the lidar output and couldn't believe his eyes. "They're experiencing G forces around one hundred and thirty. Nothing alive could survive in such conditions. Captain, we need the same kind of gravity compensators on our frigate! Then we'd be uncatchable!"

"We have a model, but Orun Va-Mart has yet to get a handle on the complicated technology. And we'll need several such frigates, but the only way to get them is in battle." I turned on the loudspeaker and made an announcement. "Combat alert! Gunners standing by. Shoot only on my command and only at targets I indicate. When they enter the kill zone, I'll put on stasis webs and target markers."

The three starships came over quickly, accelerating more and more with every second. One million miles is quite a respectable distance, but the computer was showing that the three Dero interceptors could overcome it in just eight minutes.

And then a message in Relict lit up on my helmet screen.

"Listener, danger. It is recommended you use instant transport to leave the field of battle at once."

I realized the message had come from the station's artificial intelligence, which also saw the approaching Composite interceptors. Leave? But why? I tried to reassure the computer program and told it I could see the enemy perfectly well but was expecting to come out on top. Three little Dero interceptors were not exactly the kind of enemy one had to run from.

"My mass detector is picking up the displacement of a large number of small objects. Visual contact cannot be established, but there are around seventy. They're on all sides. They've formed a thirteen-lekk-radius sphere with our mobile laboratory inside. The sphere is slowly constricting. There is a chance they may use the weapon that cuts out a section of space."

What? Those three interceptors were just a lure to distract us while the true danger was sneaking up in invisibility? Entirely possible. I suspected the Composite had noticed a difference in the type of long-distance communication system, and perhaps even lined it up with the uncatchable invisible station they had been chasing around a star system in their own galaxy. And so they took a different tact – instead of sending a strike force, they sent a group of cloaked ships to uncover and destroy the uncatchable adversary.

And by the way, how much was a "lekk" in miles? Usually, the game system automatically translated units of measurement but, in this case, there had not been a recalculation. And so I couldn't tell whether the enemies were thousands or even millions of miles away or right next to us. Should I ask the security program about these "lekks?" But might that question lead to another upwelling of mistrust toward me if that was a basic concept every Relict was supposed to know?

In any case, the station defense program's suggestion warranted serious consideration. Was time to move my butt? Battle with three little Dero interceptors was one thing. They didn't have weaponry that could damage us. But it was another thing entirely to fight seventy unknown cloaked starships.

Danger Sense skill increased to level one hundred fifty!

Attention!!! You may choose your second specialization in the Danger Sense skill.

The sudden pop-up game message forced me

to make a choice.

"Let's get out of here!"

The picture on the viewing screen changed right away. The station debris disappeared. The positioning of the stars changed. There was a reddish orange planet a few thousand miles from our frigate. Right next to my frigate there was either more fire-damaged debris or asteroids drifting through space. Unfortunately, a stream of system messages ran before my eyes, blocking my view and stopping me from identifying the nearby objects.

Machine Control skill increased to level one hundred twenty-three!

Cartography skill increased to level ninety-four!

Eagle Eye skill increased to level one hundred fourteen!

You have reached level one hundred seventeen!

You have received three skill points (total points accumulated: six).

You have reached level one hundred eighteen!

You have received three skill points (total points accumulated: nine).

You have reached level one hundred nineteen!

You have received three skill points (total points accumulated: twelve).

Three levels at once? But what for?! And then, when I dismissed all the poorly timed pop-up hieroglyph columns from my screen, I finally recognized the debris. It was not asteroids as I first thought. It was four starships twisted and crumpled into droplets of metal, each of which had once been at least as big as my twinbody. The nearest one was just nine hundred yards away. They really snuck up close! But no matter how advanced the Composite starships' gravity compensation technology may have been, they were unable to withstand an instant eight-parsec transport.

"So, where are we?" the furry Navigator looked in surprise at the flickering screen and even slammed his huge fist against the instrument panel in frustration.

"You're the one who's supposed to know that. But for your information, we jumped to the GG-666 system. You provided the coordinates."

Just then the navigation system "came to" and confirmed that our frigate was in fact in the GG-666 star system. Technically the frontier of space, the final Trillian-inhabited system. All systems past this one were either neutral or unexplored.

"Perfect!" I lit up with glee. "Ayukh, get in touch with the miners working on one of the moons of that planet. Have them point us to a landing site, or better yet send out a shuttle for their Prince."

I then headed to my business partner Gerd Uline Tar's bunk. The Geckho woman had shot a few clips for news channels, boosting her Fame and even earning her a healthy buck from selling the interesting footage. Well, I now had something for the Trader that would not only generate interest throughout the galaxy but would also spark lively discussion – the "embodiment of absolute evil" had reemerged after twenty-three tongs in obscurity and was now on Kung Gnat's frigate! Yes, I decided not to try and conceal my participation in setting the bloodthirsty Prince free, and instead be the first to tell the galaxy the news. That way I could put the proper accents on the information in order to avoid or at least mitigate the expected negative reaction which threatened to send my Authority on a nose-dive.

"Won't that be just too short a timeframe?" Uline Tar clarified after writing down my message while also filming scenes of Gerd Hugo to confirm what I was saying. "Gnat, you are addressing the leaders of the great spacefaring races and saying you expect their decision in two ummi and, if they don't react, you intend to do whatever you see fit."

"Yes, that is exactly what I want – to share responsibility with the political leaders. Let them explain the decision to their subjects, whatever it may be. Then there won't be so much pressure on me. I'm just doing a job, carrying out their decision."

I was in fact able to present the events in a light favorable to myself, claiming I had simply been evacuating forgotten players from systems under threat of Composite invasion. In the Rorsh system, I took on board the staff of a small space station. But I didn't evacuate them alone. They took some "secret cargo" with them to my ship, which they warned me in advance. I wasn't particularly surprised. So they had some extra luggage. Nothing out of the ordinary. It could easily have been data drives of secret information or space currency in cash. In any case, it was none of my business. But then things started to get weird. First, the station head who had led the negotiations with me decided at the last moment only his underlings should be saved, himself wanting to stay behind. And as soon as the escape pod made it out to a safe distance, he detonated the space station with himself inside.

After that, my crew noticed rattling and commotion inside the docked module. And when we opened the hatch to find the source of the strange sound, a high-level Trillian came charging out at me and my team. He maimed a member of my crew and was just acting aggressive overall, throwing around threats, behaving rudely, and trying to kill me. And the ruffian turned out to be a member of the Par-Poreh royal family, Gerd Hugo, who was serving a life sentence at that unremarkable station in the Rorsh star system. The Prince turned out to have been the very "secret cargo" I had been warned about. After a big struggle, we managed to get the hell-raiser tied up. And then we barely managed to turn tail and escape when a group of Composite starships arrived to the Rorsh system. More than seventy ships, of which I was able to destroy four.

Now I was in a safe location and faced with a difficult choice: what to do with Prince Hugo? It wasn't me that sentenced him to life in prison twenty-three tongs ago. And really, it was not for me to judge how plausible the tales of his long-ago villainy were, because they were so far in the past by human standards that I wasn't even born yet. I was not planning to ferry the dangerous "passenger" around, so I asked the rulers of the great spacefaring races for advice about what to do with this member of the Par-Poreh royal dynasty. Hand him over to local authorities? Execute him? And I promised to do exactly as majority decision dictated.

I thought my words through very meticulously so any check by even the best of Truth Seekers would show that I spoke nothing but the pure truth. And given that, how could this be Kung Gnat's fault? I acted nobly, saving a group of doomed players. It was not my fault the Rorsh system was host to a secret prison for particularly dangerous criminals. I was also not planning to decide the bloody Prince's fate myself, instead putting that decision on others. This way if Gerd Hugo broke free, it wouldn't by my Authority that suffered.

Plus I was naturally hoping they would tell me to hand him over to the local authorities, which was equivalent to releasing him because this was Trillian space, and most members of their race practically worshiped the rebel Prince. I wasn't the least bit worried they would decide I should execute, which would put an end to my "mission of epic difficulty." The Geckho didn't want to ruin their already rocky relationship with the Trillians, so Krong Daveyesh-Pir would order the prisoner set free. The Miyelonians also wouldn't care about old half-forgotten scary stories of "absolute evil" with the capital of the Union of Miyelonian Prides at risk of invasion, and their military alliance with the Trillians as vital as air. I didn't know if it would come down to Kung Keetsie Myau personally or the council of rulers, but the Miyelonians would definitely decide to hand over the criminal to the local authorities. As for the Trillians, there was nothing to say – the Par-Poreh royal dynasty had asked to have their relative set free, so they would be glad to see the story ending well. The leader of the Meleyephatian Horde Krong Laa I couldn't predict so easily, even though they were also going through tough times and thus would not want a war with the mighty Trillian race either. But even if Krong Laa did vote for execution, one vote would not be the deciding factor.

Chapter Twenty-Two

Space Refugees

I WOKE UP IN A GREAT MOOD in my own bunk and the first thing I did was study my Gnat's figures. I was still a Kung. Whew. That was a load off my mind. Even though my Authority took a three-point dip to one hundred twenty, it was not a huge deal. I was fearing much worse consequences from this whole nasty and slippery story of "absolute evil." In fact, it brought my Fame up by a whole seven points! I was not wrong. The news that Prince Hugo had surfaced had in fact elicited massive interest from the galaxy's residents, and the Free Captain who told them about his return was now recognized by significantly more powerful figures.

I looked at my characteristics and skills. Overall, a picture was coming together of a quite good and very resourceful character:

Kung Gnat. Human. Relict Faction.	
Level-119 Listener	
Statistics:	
Strength	14

Agility	18
Intelligence	39 + 7
Perception	35 + 2
Constitution	18
Luck modifier	+3
Controlled drones	3 of 3
Parameters:	
Hitpoints	2786 of 2786
Endurance points	1986 of 1986
Magic points	3716 of 3716
Carrying capacity	62 lbs.
Fame	126
Authority	120
Skills:	
Electronics	108 * First specialization taken
Scanning	86
Cartography	94
Astrolinguistics	117 * First specialization taken
Rifles	70
Mineralogy	63
Medium Armor	106 * First specialization taken
Eagle Eye	115 * First specialization taken
Sharpshooter	57
Targeting	74
Danger Sense	150 * First specialization taken Attention!!! You may choose your second specialization in this skill
Psionic	143 * First specialization

	taken
Mental Fortitude	*151 * First specialization taken* *Second specialization taken*
Machine Control	*123 * First specialization taken*
Mysticism	*95*
Telekinesis	*64*
Training	*53*
Disorientation	*43*
Attention!!! You have twelve unspent skill points.	

I had to invest those twelve points quickly because the first of them had been received almost 24 hours before and could soon "burn up" if I died all of a sudden. What to improve? Of course Psionics. That was my primary skill, main weapon and tool. So six points went straight into Psionics, raising that ability to level one hundred fifty. When I saw I could take a second specialization for that skill, I didn't even think because I had already long since made up my mind – of course I would take the ability to work in a "mental link!" Now Gerd Soia-Tan La-Varrez would be able to take full part in my attacks, and I could also aid the little sorceress with my power. And if I could track down Beast Master Valeri and get her back, with her Psionic skill over level one-hundred and the "mental link" specialization as well, we would become unbeatable an unbeatable trio of mages. I suppose we could even try to take on the Relict Hierarch.

After that, I invested five more points into Mysticism, bringing it up to one hundred. I had also long had my eye on a specialization for

Mysticism: increase maximum Magic Points by 20 percent. That brought my total mana up to 4586 points in one go. Excellent! Now I'm basically a monster in the art of magic! Very few mages could boast of such stellar Magic Point reserves, and when two sorcerers did battle, it was often mana reserves that decided the outcome. Beyond that, I invested the two remaining points into Cartography – a very useful skill, but recently it had been levelling too slowly and I had already started getting impatient to choose a specialization, of which there were in fact very many interesting options.

As for the second Danger Sense specialization, I took a long time to choose. I felt like I needed all of them. I could have it specify the threat, increase warning time, or have my character react automatically to possibly eliminate threats to my life. I opted for the time improvement. Another couple extra seconds to get ready would always come in handy!

After closing the characteristic tab, I activated the Scanning ability and looked at what the mini-map was now showing. All was quiet aboard the *Tamara the Paladin*. Gerd Hugo had already been picked up, so both him and the gravity loader were no longer drifting around under the camouflage shield. The Relict was still not aboard, and I had already stopped doubting that something had happened to Gerd Urgeh Pu-Pu Urgeh in the real world. He was past due to return, and if the Relict Technician didn't come back in the next two or three days, we would have no choice but to officially declare him dead.

Dmitry Zheltov took charge on the bridge. The boarding team troops were training hard in the gym. Both Engineers were in the mobile Relict laboratory dismantling a nonfunctioning large Relict guard drone, and they were being helped by one of the Kirsans. The little sorceress Gerd Soia-Tan was working in the galley alongside Chef-Assassin Amati-Kuis, preparing lunch for the team. Gerd Mauu-La Mya-Ssa the Medic was attending to Vasha Tushihh in the med bay, seemingly giving the giant Geckho injections of healing nanites to help the bones in both his legs heal faster. Nefertiti the Dryad was tucked away in her workshop with co-Pilot San-Doon while her husband Kisly was exercising with everyone else in the gym. Not great, of course. But still, one couldn't expect much else out of the amorous and provocatively half-dressed NPC Dryad, who drew strength and inspiration from curious glances and male attention.

I didn't peek at the erotic show, closed the mini-map and turned to the financial tab. I had already paid back Gerd Uline Tar, just like I had many vendors but now I needed to figure out how much I could send to my Chief Advisor Gerd Mac-Peu Un-Roi for the Relict Faction's development. I glanced at my account balance and my eyebrows crept up onto my forehead! Over the past two ummi, other than a charge of ten crypto as a "multicurrency account service fee," there had been two massive deposits. One hundred fifty million crystals from the Hive of Tintara with a note reading "For a job done excellently. We are willing to provide more work, Kung Gnat." That made me flinch – nope, enough. No more dealings with space mobsters! The second bundle came from the Shiharsa system, the Geckho race's homeworld. Forty-five million crystals – exactly the amount Geckho ruler Krong Daveyesh-Pir must have believed I deserved for settling the conflict with the Miyelonian race.

I looked at the positive balance in my account – two hundred thirty-seven million, and the excitement was so intense my heart was about to jump out of my ribcage. What a fat stack of cash! That could get Earth a fully outfitted battleship, or a whole three assault cruisers! Although... despite the fact my homeworld did need a space fleet, it was more important to provide defense for planet Earth itself. That was plenty to buy up three defensive field generators with twelve million crystals left over. It would take at least another eight generators to turn on a planetary shield, and twelve more for complete and reliable defense. Together with the three I could now buy, we already had nine. Amazing news! If these nine generators could be built quickly enough, my home planet could no longer be taken in one fell swoop. Even enemy battleships would need a few days to get through the planetary shield. That would be enough time for help from the suzerains to arrive.

Yes, it's decided. I'll spend the money on three defensive planetary field generators. Now I had to come to an agreement to buy and deliver everything we needed. I summoned my business partner Gerd Uline Tar over the loudspeaker. The Trader showed up in an excellent state of mind, even humming a tune to herself. But before she made it through the cracked-open door, Timka-Vu the Machinegunner flew in. Overheated from exercising in the gym, he dashed over at full speed as soon as he heard his captain was on the ship. After apologizing to Uline Tar, Timka-Vu entered the berth then even closed the door in front of my taken-aback first mate. This behavior was very out of character for the large and muscular but fairly reserved man from the magocratic world. Something really out of the ordinary must have happened for Timka-Vu to be in such a hurry to talk to me.

Getting down on one knee respectfully before his mage ruler, the magocratic-world native reported:

"Coruler Gnat La-Fin, General Ui-Taka has requested that you be sent an urgent message. The situation on Un-Tau is critical. The reinforcements the Geckho promised have not shown up for several days now. The Army of Earth's last eight hundred troops are engaged in an uneven fight against seventy thousand defense forces in the under-ice temple. The ruler of the Second Directory swears he is doing everything both possible and impossible but says he cannot hold the position for longer than two ummi. After that, the Army of Earth's last troops will surely fall and the landing operation will end in complete failure. The General begs the Kung of Earth to help, and urgently at that!"

After saying that, Timka-Vu straightened up, opened the door, apologized to Gerd Uline Tar again and hurried to get back to exercising with the other boarding team soldiers. My business partner ran a surprised gaze over the team member, then walked into the captain's bunk and sat on an armchair. Without asking my permission, she poured herself some apple juice in a two-liter mug she still had yet to take back after her last visit to my bunk. And she said with contentment in her voice.

"Captain Gnat, it couldn't have gone better! All leaders of the great spacefaring races voted unanimously for Prince Hugo to be handed over to the local authorities. A shuttle has already come from the planet to get Gerd Hugo and now we're rid of the dangerous passenger. My fame went up three points right away, and my Authority is now up to forty! With the way this is going, I could be a Leng one day! I must admit, I never even dreamed of such a thing!"

I didn't upset my friend and tell her she was never going to make the new rank as long as she was still in my Relict Faction because we already had players with much higher Fame and Authority. Instead, I asked about the news. The woman eagerly got to talking.

"The biggest piece of news being discussed on every channel is that the Meleyephatians suffered a devastating defeat in the Apree-U System, where the Composite wiped out their entire Eighth and Fourth Fleets. The Horde's losses totaled over six thousand starships and all their battleships and planet destroyers were all lost. Reports are saying Krong Laa ordered the admirals executed for their failure. And what's most important, the Horde no longer has any large fleets in their central systems that could halt the Composite's advance. The Second Fleet has taken serious damage, while the Third retreated without a fight, leaving billions of Meleyephatians to the whims of fate. And until the main armada of the Meleyephatian Horde headed by Krong Laa himself has returned from the outskirts of known space, there is simply no one to defend the Meleyephatian Horde's star systems. The Composite is occupying system after system without encountering serious resistance. Meleyephatian Horde news is dominated by panic. Everyone who can is trying to evacuate and get as far away from the war as possible."

The information was very worrying. The Meleyephatians had suffered defeat after defeat, surrendering their densely populated and industrially developed star systems to invaders from another galaxy. They had also lost a significant portion of their combat fleet and completely ceded the initiative to their enemy. If the Trillians didn't join the war, I saw no force capable of stopping the Composite.

"And still the Meleyephatians don't want to make peace with the Geckho?" I asked, but the Trader answered negatively.

"I haven't heard about any peace offers. In fact, there have been serious battles on the front, and Kung Waid Shishish's Third Strike Fleet has driven back the Horde's Fifth Fleet and is now besieging the planets of the Ria star system. Both sides suffered significant losses, so Kung Waid Shishish has stopped at besieging Ria instead of advancing further. It is of course not for me to judge, but it looks like my race's counteroffensive has stalled. Furthermore, Geckho ruler Krong Daveyesh-Pir is sending all forces to systems closest to the Composite offensive, and Kung Waid Shishish is not likely to receive reinforcements."

"In such conditions, it would be logical to sign a ceasefire and join together against the common enemy from another galaxy," I suggested.

The Trader responded that such a thing would not happen. Kung Waid Shishish was known for his stubborn streak and would continue the war until the balance on the front was in his favor and enough combat ships were under his command. After all, losing half of a fleet without getting anything in return would be a death sentence for his military career.

"There are three more pieces of news, Captain. Remember how my relative promised to figure out where your girlfriend Valeri-Urla flew off to? Well, he just sent me a message saying she has been spotted with her panther in the spaceport on planet Shiharsa. There Valeri got a ticket heading for Ponty IV, a space station in a star system bordering the Gilvar Syndicate. Your friend's passenger liner will be arriving in Ponty IV in three days."

Highly interesting news and I thanked Uline for the information. Seemingly, Valeri-Urla was going back to her quarantine planet home in the Zeta Reaper system, or at least somewhere in that region of the galaxy. I would really have liked to intercept Valeri and get her back after her sudden departure from my team. I really needed the

Tailaxian as an experienced psionic with unique abilities, and I was very much hoping for her support. Well and, what's to hide? I also wanted her back as a pretty girlfriend. Although in light of recent events with Ayni I had to admit I didn't much see how the two could coexist.

"General Leng Ui-Taka was also looking for a way to talk to you. He told me it's important."

I nodded and confirmed that Timka-Vu had already told me the news.

"So that's why he was running like a bat out of hell!" the Geckho woman buzzed out happily and poured herself more juice from the pitcher. "And well, the last piece of news, Captain Gnat. My husband sent a message saying another of the Human hostages captured at Poko-Poko has been executed. The same girl who the kidnappers are using for negotiations told them. She didn't see the body with her own eyes, but she was told by friends from the group of hostages her kidnappers allowed her to visit. And by the way, some food for thought – all the Human hostages have joined a clan called Pri-7865."

I shuddered. We finally had a thread to pull at to figure out this whole confusing situation with the hostages taken at Poko-Poko.

"Have you figured out what sort of clan it is?"

"Of course. We don't know who leads it, or their numbers, but the clan was formed in the last few days. The office is registered on Poko-Poko station. Its line of business is listed as 'virt pod rental.' And as far as I am aware, there would be no way to pull off something like this without the station administration's awareness. All the station's virt pods and rooms belong to them no matter who they might have signed a contract with. The owners of Poko-Poko will definitely be familiar with the kidnappers."

I squinted my eyes unsavorily. If the owners of the pirate station were behind the kidnapping of Earth Humans, they would come to regret it fearsomely!

"Uline, I need your help. Tell me, there must be Geckho mercenary clans that engage in dirty work, right? I need a tested group with a proven track-record that can field at least two hundred well-equipped troops. I am willing to pay handsomely."

Uline considered it briefly, then responded cautiously.

"Of course there are Geckho mercenary clans. But two hundred troopers won't be able to capture a space station no matter their level. They have thousands of guards, combat robots and defense systems. On top of that, there are many pirates and smugglers based on Poko-Poko who will also stand to defend the station owners."

"I wasn't planning on asking the mercenary group to capture the station. Their mission would be to wreak havoc in the dispatcher area for at least a quarter ummi so we can dock a landing ship at Poko-Poko. My Humans will do the rest. What do you think, will fifty thousand elite troopers do?"

"As far as I can tell, you're referring to the Army of Earth. But will Kung Waid Shishish allow you to take an army under his authority away from the front? I have my doubts. The Humans on Un-Tau are holding back massive Meleyephatian Horde forces, which is giving the Geckho Fleet room to breathe."

"The Kung sent the Humans to die as cannon fodder. He promised support and regular reinforcements but left them with no supplies or additional troops. Without speedy intervention, it will all be over in two ummi. And a failed landing operation won't exactly raise Kung Waid Shishish's Authority. So I'll have a chat with the fleet commander. Maybe I'll be able to talk him into it. Especially if the Meleyephatians promise to send the freed-up troops to the war with the Composite rather than against the Geckho."

I wanted to tell my business partner in greater detail about my suggestion, but a game message jumped in suddenly, distracting me.

ATTENTION!!! Leader of the Tush-Laymeh Leng Torish-Khe proposes unification with the Relict Faction on the following terms: Clan Tush-Laymeh shall join the Relict Faction in its entirety, Relict shall provide territory to resettle members of the clan. Do you accept? (Yes/No)

Tush-Laymeh? Based on the clan's name, they were Geckho of some kind. I asked Gerd Uline Tar what she knew about a clan by that name. The Geckho woman considered it and even turned on her palmtop to look up information.

"A small clan of star traders, most likely even freight forwarders. Many tongs ago, after the second to last war with the Horde, they found themselves in the Meleyephatian occupation zone. They didn't abandon their property or reasonably profitable business ventures and refused to evacuate to Geckho space. Instead, they accepted the new order and kept working as a component piece of the Horde. The guide says Clan Tush-Laymeh numbers slightly over seven thousand Geckho. Their holdings include three space container ships and five escort frigates. What makes you ask, Gnat?"

"That group of Geckho are asking to join my Relict Faction in search of calmer waters. The Meleyephatians must be putting pressure on them during the war with Geckho. They suspect them of working for the enemy and won't let them do their job. Maybe they're even trying to expropriate their starships. You yourself said the Horde has been overtaken by panic and the Meleyephatians are looking for any method to escape the Composite offensive. Trader container ships can be used to evacuate a civilian population if necessary, plus the Horde's military has to procure ships, so it's easy to explain why they might want to confiscate these Geckhos' ships."

"Sounds about right. I have heard that the Horde is buying and even forcefully confiscating civilian ships for military purposes. The only strange thing is that Clan Tush-Laymeh is not reaching out to the Geckho to arrange their return. Do you think they fear a cold reception after betraying their homeland and agreeing to work for the enemy? Do you see you as a calmer and more advantageous patron? Anyway, what is your decision, Captain?"

I thought very briefly and gave a crooked smirk, having made up my mind:

"I must admit, I don't give a hoot about their long-ago decision to abandon the Geckho and join the Horde. But our faction could use seven thousand players. Plus three space cargo ships we could use for our own interests would come in very handy! They would be especially helpful if Kung Waid Shishish refuses to provide his own landing ships for the Army of Earth. So I'll take these refugees under my wing!"

Chapter Twenty-Three

Comet Un-Tau

KUNG WAID SHISHISH did not wish to speak to me long distance even though I sent an urgent request through Supercargo Avan Toi who went out into the real world. The commander of the Third Strike Fleet must have guessed the conversation would be about the fate of the Army of Earth, and the influential Geckho could not help the troubled Humans. Or didn't want to. Alright then, that untied my hands and I decided to figure things out myself without looking to my suzerains, who were proving quite useless. Yes, taking such liberties might displease the Geckho, but I could always make excuses saying I tried to coordinate with them, but they wouldn't even take my call.

The mobile laboratory made its null transport and exited two hundred feet from the surface of the ice comet. Ahem... That cleared things up right away. It was a trash situation, and the Third Strike Fleet wouldn't be able to reach the ice comet without huge losses. The shrine's space defenses were being held down by almost seven hundred

Meleyephatian ships. For the most part they were Tolili-Ukh X modular frigates in various configurations as well as larger clusters made of the same ship. There were also a large number of Meleyephatian interceptors and even five Mirosssh-pakh II assault cruisers. I winced unwittingly, having remembered how easily one such cruiser had taken down my twinbody in the H9045/WE star system. Our escape back then was simply a miracle. And here there were a whole five of the dangerous ships with massive firepower. One of those five cruisers was most likely the flagship of the whole squadron. I only wished I could tell which one...

Still, I also saw positive aspects in the Meleyephatians concentrating such serious forces in Un-Tau. These seven hundred starships were probably needed on the front of the war with the Composite, and the captains of this flotilla were probably frustrated with the fact that they had been stuck here for days doing nothing rather than defending their people and bravely fighting back the intergalactic invaders. I could try to take advantage of that in the negotiations.

But in addition to this flotilla, the shrine also had plenty of defense on the ground. I saw heavy artillery towers through powerful optics, along with a large number of rocket launch sites. On top of that there were herds of combat robots roving around the surface of the ice comet, which did not inspire optimism. On top of that, the amount of starship debris on the surface of Comet Un-Tau boggled the imagination. And the fresh remains of

Geckho Third Strike Fleet landing and support ships stood out as black specks of soot on the white ice. There was also lots of slightly snow-covered debris from Meleyephatian and Miyelonian ships – evidence of the recent heated battles which eventually resulted in the Union of Miyelonian Prides capturing Un-Tau. And even deeper in the ice was yet older wreckage from prior conflicts. By the looks of things, this shrine regularly played host to space battles.

Cartography skill increased to level ninety-seven!

Eagle Eye skill increased to level one hundred sixteen!

"Captain, that Akati U interceptor is dangerously close," Dmitry Zheltov told me in a whisper, as if he thought our conversation on the bridge might be overheard and pointing at a small ship thirteen hundred feet away. "Maybe you should order the Gunners to give it a buzz before it accidentally uncovers us?"

"No, I don't want to give up our location. I'll handle it quietly," I promised and closed my eyes.

I had already done this a few times in the past. Before the interceptor pilot could even get startled, his mind was completely under my control. Following an unheard order, the Pilot turned on the maneuver drives then flipped the main thrusters to full power, pointing his small starship directly down at the surface of the ice comet. On the flotilla's public channel, his parting words slipped through: "How I tire of wasting time here when my children are in danger and might die!" after that, the fiery flower of an explosion bloomed on Comet Un-Tau. One more starship fragment was added to the collection...

Psionic skill increased to level one hundred fifty-one!

Machine Control skill increased to level one hundred twenty-four!

That wasn't so bad! But I guess I'll have to repeat that trick, because a Tolili-Ukh X Meleyephatian frigate in raider configuration was also getting worryingly close. The only thing was that it had a bit larger crew than the little interceptor, so I was afraid of slipping up and exposing myself.

"*Little one, help me out!*" I ordered, and Gerd Soia-Tan La-Varrez eagerly joined in the attack.

There it is! I detected the Pilot. He was frustrated and agitated, listening to a flurry of discussion between the flotilla's ships. But the problem was that the Pilot was not alone. There was another Meleyephatian next to him in the cabin. Either a Navigator or a copilot, to be honest I couldn't tell. But he would be able to take control of the ship and mess up my plans.

"*Little one, I will take control of the Pilot and block the doors. You take the other one,*" I mentally sent an "imprint" of the intended target's mind. "*No need to get fancy. Just knock him out or hold him under control. Ready? Begin!*"

The Tolili-Ukh X frigate started moving and, spinning along its lengthwise axis with ever greater speed, headed down for the surface. They tried to stop us. Other Horde ships placed a stasis web on the oddly behaving frigate, then two more. But that just added a few seconds to the inevitable finale. It went up like a roman candle!

Targeting skill increased to level seventy-five!
Telekinesis skill increased to level sixty-five!
You have reached level one hundred twenty!
You have received three skill points.

It ended up well, but I figured that was enough. The other ships were somewhat farther away, and I couldn't guarantee the success of mental attacks against them. Furthermore, after the strange demise of the first two ships, the others were on alert and paying close attention to all other ships.

I raised my head... and was actually baffled to see the two pilots and Navigator looking at me with their eyes wide in wild terror. Even the spiny Jarg was glancing at his captain with a certain trepidation. Yes, what I'd just displayed went far beyond what a normal human was capable of. But was that any reason to fear me? I tried to break the tense silence quickly.

"Ayukh, ready comms. I will send you the Army of Earth's channel settings and encryption key."

Of course we didn't use normal radio. The signal would have been too easy to intercept. The secure comms system based on quantum entanglement was a technology I had been gifted by the Prelates of Tailax, but now we had figured it out and it had been implemented successfully by all terrestrial factions. It was not possible to track the signal to its source.

"Kung Gnat speaking. We have reached the Un-Tau system. General Ui-Taka, situation report."

For a few seconds, my only response was silence, but then a signal came through saying message received. And a second later, I heard a familiar voice.

"Shoot_To_Kill speaking. General Ui-Taka is severely wounded. All senior officers were KIA, so I have assumed command. I have four hundred sixty troopers left. The First Legion, Japanese, Germans and one hundred thirty survivors from the magocratic factions. I have put them into three combined squadrons, and we are holding six rooms on the eighth floor underground. We have no more heavy equipment, we're running out of rounds, and we'll be lucky if our oxygen lasts five hours. So pull us out, Gnat! You're renowned for your ability to make miracles! Let's see what you can do!"

Authority increased to level one hundred twenty-one!

I see. The situation was indeed critical, even worse than I was expecting. I told the troopers to hold and break through to the surface on my signal. Meanwhile I ordered the Gunners to target the laser cannons of the nearest two interceptors and aim the quadrupolar destabilizer at an assault cruiser. As far as I could tell, no energy shields or armor could help the cruiser if it was able to focus streams on the hull and trigger the matter destruction process. But still I decided to hold off on the attack and tried to negotiate my way out of it.

And my mental call was soon answered by

one of the Meleyephatian flotilla commanders.

"Kung of Earth? This is seventy-second flotilla commander Leng Ovaz Ussh. I must admit, I've been expecting you a long time. I was actually wondering what was taking you so long. Have you come to formalize a surrender and save your soldiers?"

"Surrender? Don't make me laugh! I have come to sign a mutually-satisfactory peace agreement."

"What is there to discuss if one side is capable of completely wiping the other out? We have a colossal advantage in numbers and firepower. And the fleet has complete superiority in near space. So I will only be satisfied with the complete surrender of the little Humans trespassing where they don't belong. Don't want the shame of being captured? They can shoot themselves and respawn far from here. In any case you've lost. Our shrine is not yours to take!"

I sensed the man's emotional background. Self-satisfaction. Scorn for a weak adversary. A feeling of complete superiority. By the way, Leng Ovaz Ussh turned out to be quite a strong psionic, even compared with other members of the Meleyephatian race, which was known for its skill in mental attacks. But he unwittingly gave me a clue about what I needed to do to make him reckon with me. If one party is capable of wiping the other out? Okay then, I'll try and take him by surprise.

"Ayukh, get me the coordinates of another point near here. Preferably on the other side of the comet. Just in case we accidentally expose ourselves."

The Navigator clacked his claws in the instrument panel and ten seconds later rattled off a series of digits. I initiated the processing program to translate them into the Relict coordinate system. After that, I contacted the station's artificial intelligence and ordered it to prepare to transport to that point.

"Gunners standing by! We will attack the cruiser with quadrupolar destabilizers and that interceptor with laser cannons. I've marked them. Fire!"

A second after the volley, our laboratory had moved to the other point where I watched the scattering wreckage of both the targeted starships with great satisfaction.

Targeting skill increased to level seventy-six!

Targeting skill increased to level seventy-seven!

Electronics skill increased to level one hundred nine!

You have reached level one hundred twenty-one!

You have received three skill points (total points accumulated: six).

"Leng Ovaz Ussh, you still alive out there? Tell me which cruiser is yours. I'll be sure to destroy it last. That way you can enjoy the show as your flotilla's starships die ignominious deaths one after the next. And after all, they would surely come in handy for the Horde and fight valiantly on the front in the war with the Composite."

The Meleyephatian didn't respond, though I could tell he could hear me. And for that matter, several starships were speeding off toward where we had just been. So they had detected where the shots came from. I ordered a new jump point prepared.

"Gerd Ukh-Meemeesh, are the weapons recharged?" I asked on the loudspeaker and the Gunner responded that they weren't yet, and the quadrupolar destabilizer would need another forty seconds. "Alright, we'll wait. For now, aim at that heavy laser cannon battery on the ground. Taik Rekh, you're on that interceptor. For some reason it's just sitting there motionless, so it will make a great target."

Forty seconds later, the ground cannon was no more along with the Meleyephatian interceptor.

Targeting skill increased to level seventy-eight!

Now from a new position, I indicated another set of targets for the Gunners. But first I tried to talk to the Meleyephatian commander again.

"Leng Ovaz Ussh, remind me, what was it you said? If one side is capable of wiping the other out? Well, I'm having a great time up here wiping out your starships and ground-based defense systems. But still I'd like to go back to the start of our conversation. Shall we discuss peace?"

No response came for a very long time, so my Gunners gave them what for again. And only after that did I get a mental message from the flotilla commander.

"Your terms, Kung Gnat?"

"That's more like it. You should have started that way. So then, first of all, I need landing ships to

take the Humans off the comet. I see a couple in your fleet. They'll do just fine. Don't think anything bad. I won't be taking the starships for good. As soon as my troops are unloaded, I'll give them back. Second, I want to go down to Un-Tau myself to visit the great shrine. And third, I have forty Meleyephatians with me here that I saved from a doomed station. I promised to deliver them to a safe location somewhere in Horde space, and Un-Tau is about as safe a place as one could hope for. Plus they can visit the Temple of the Dawn of Life. Not every Meleyephatian gets so lucky. That's all. I have no other terms. But perhaps a piece of advice: get in touch with the commanders of the other Horde fleets. Your seven hundred ships could help them in the fight against the Composite. There's no point having such a force go up in smoke when the Horde needs every starship it can get until Krong Laa's First Fleet shows up."

The response kept me waiting a fairly long time. I think Leng Ovaz Ussh was checking my words over and over again, unable to believe he got away so easily. Finally, the commander responded:

"Kung Gnat, I agree to your conditions. But let's get one thing out of the way for the future. Next time you want to pray in the great Temple of the Dawn of Life, you don't need to send thousands of Human troops in advance. You can just fly over, no trouble. Security will let you enter the shrine."

Chapter Twenty-Four

The Shrine

T HE LANDING PLATFORM was on the side of the comet opposite the local star, but it had been cleared of ice and debris and was well lit by spotlights, so the Starship Pilot and his partner had no issues. Dmitry Zheltov and San-Doon reduced speed, rotated the twinbody frigate one hundred eighty degrees and set us down with surgical precision in the very center of the circle of landing lights.

Our people were waiting for us. All that remained of the Army of Earth after nearly six days of constant fighting was three hundred fifty troops. They were lined up in grand rows around the perimeter. At a respectful distance, more than a quarter mile from the humans I could see the temple's numerous defenders. But I wasn't expecting any provocations or treachery out of the Meleyephatian troopers. If this were taking place in my real world then sure, some Earth commanders and leaders wouldn't have been able to resist the temptation to take out such exposed enemies on the well-lit platform. But Meleyephatians stood by their agreements. You couldn't take that away from the great spacefaring race. And so they just observed the Kung of Earth's arrival from a distance.

Accompanied by Gerd Imran and Gerd T'yu-Pan, I came down the gangway and stopped in front of the greatest representatives of the human race, all standing at attention. Yes, today I took only Humans with me down from the starship. Uline Tar, Tini, Ayni and all the other members of alien races in my crew would have to forgive me. Today was not their day. I didn't even take the Small Relict Guard Drones so they wouldn't distract with their presence and throw me off.

The pressure gauge on my spacesuit read twenty thousand Pascals, surprising for such a large space object – almost a fifth of the terrestrial average. The gravity of 0.18 G also allowed me to walk around without risk of hurtling off into space. But the temperature was negative two hundred Fahrenheit, and just three percent of the air was oxygen, so I didn't even think of taking off my spacesuit helmet. But still, sound did carry in this atmosphere, and I could use that to my advantage.

Turning up my microphone to maximum, I pronounced in a jubilant voice:

"Brave souls! Allow me to congratulate you on your first victory! And although it came at the cost of lots of blood, the importance of this victory is hard to overstate. Our Earth just made its debut in grand space politics and you held your own admirably, forcing your enemies to reckon with us and our interests. As Kung of Earth, I am proud that our planet has birthed such worthy representatives of the human race. You didn't shiver in the face of death, didn't retreat and didn't surrender even though your enemy was strong and surpassed you in number. You held out and earned this triumph fair and square!

"You may object, saying the arrangement I reached with Leng Ovaz Ussh hardly constitutes a victory. It was more like a tie. We both went back to our initial positions and agreed to go our separate ways. But still I consider it a victory. The Army of Earth proved its validity and fulfilled its duty as vassal to our suzerains. No one – not Kung Waid Shishish, not even Krong Daveyesh-Pir – could accuse you Humans of slacking off in the war or fighting poorly. You fought like hell! You held onto every foot of hallway by your teeth, and even when up against a one-to-two-hundred disadvantage, you kept defending your positions. Plus we negotiated for starships to bring you to anywhere in the galaxy. On top of that, there's nothing stopping us from gathering the many trophies strewn about the battlefield. The right to visit the sacred temple can also be considered a plus. So it wasn't a tie, and certainly not a defeat. This was a victory, plain and simple!"

The more I said, the more I felt the emotional background changing. Just a few minutes earlier, the people standing before me looked dead tired and barely able to stand on their feet. They had just been pulled from a combat position where the Army of Earth's last forces were holding a defensive line without any hope of rescue. And although the commanders assured their subjects that the enemy would no longer shoot, and the many-day nightmare was over, only after my words did it start to reach the troopers that they had not merely survived to the end of the battle but won! I felt their sense of impending doom retreating, replaced by exhaustion and pain. The blunted feeling of all the sleeping and fear medicine they had taken over the last few days was fading away. I saw the formation of troopers start to adopt a proud upright pose. Then smiles spread like wildfire through their faces, some even crying tears of joy.

Psionic skill increased to level one hundred fifty-two!

Mental Fortitude skill increased to level one hundred fifty-two!

Mysticism skill increased to level one hundred one!

Yes, there was no getting by without Psionics here. And it wasn't so much to control the troops magically, but more down to practical considerations. I had discussed this with the team back on the starship. We argued for a long time until reaching the opinion that we could not provide simultaneous interpretation into all the languages spoken by the Army of Earth. And so I was speaking in my native Russian but pouring in generous amounts of mana at the same time to communicate the same things mentally to make sure they all understood.

"The Humans of Earth do not yet have any medals or awards for successful space operations but, as Kung of Earth, I promise to settle that vexing oversight as soon as possible. All fifty thousand troopers will be given a commemorative decoration. Beyond that, all the survivors will get a special bonus from me of three thousand Geckho monetary crystals."

Authority increased to 122!

Authority increased to 123!

I was slightly knocked off course because I wasn't expecting such a strong reaction. But I quickly got myself together and continued.

"Starships are landing now to ferry you away to a safe station. Take your rest, heal your wounds, be merry, carouse and celebrate your victory. But get ready for another combat operation because the Army of Earth will find its next job soon. The time has come for Earth's Humanity to show the galaxy what it's made of. And this time not in our suzerains' war but working for the good of our shared home planet! And may the Universe shake with the stomping of your boots!"

Only Gerd Ayni, Gerd Imran and Gerd Soia-Tan wanted to accompany me to the under-ice temple. The little sorceress took a lot of convincing and practically had to be dragged down by force. Only when I said it was a unique place where players with the magical gift could improve their abilities was the young enchantress convinced to go with me. The other crewmembers all refused. Furthermore, a few of them admitted that the ghastly appearance of the ice comet was weighing on them and pushing them back to the spaceship. Strange. I felt the exact opposite – a huge burst of strength. My legs even seemed to be dragging me into the ice temple all on their own.

Leng Ovaz Ussh himself came to serve as our

"tour guide." For the record, I was mistaken before. The flotilla commander was not on one of the cruisers during our brief firefight. He was actually with a large group of eight-legged Shocktroops preparing for the final decisive attack on the Human position. And now that same large Meleyephatian in heavy assault armor greeted me at the entrance to the under-ice shrine, which had suffered lots of damage in the recent fighting. He bowed down respectfully, lowering his cephalothorax, then pointed with four arms at a hole in the ice mountain.

"Kung Gnat, please. After me. Pilgrims normally visit three locations in the Temple of the Dawn of Life. First and foremost is the main sanctuary – an ice cave which is where all life in the Universe began. Then there is the Hall of Visions and the Hall of Fear. Some are brave enough to go further down into the Hall of Death, where epiphanies descend on visitors and they can witness the moment of their death. But that hall is not as popular among pilgrims and is not considered a must-visit."

Astrolinguistics skill increased to level one hundred eighteen!

Gerd Ayni translated the Meleyephatian's chirring even though I understood about a third of it on my own.

"To be honest, I am not exactly champing at the bit to see the circumstances around my own death. Such knowledge brings only strife and does nothing to bolster one's power to achieve all that they want in this life."

"I understand, Kung Gnat. I myself have never visited that gloomy location in the depths of the ice temple. We have robots to maintain it, as well as the few Meleyephatians who are utterly devoid of psionic abilities. But even for them it's a grueling ordeal. Technical malfunctions happen an order of magnitude more often in the Hall of Death, while living creatures often lose their minds if they spend too long in the gloomy depths of the ice comet."

Our conversation took us down a long corridor that was littered with the wreckage of both Human and Meleyephatian combat tech. In some places, the piles of twisted metal even reached the high ice ceiling. I saw five shredded Peresvets with Human-3 First Legion emblems on their hulls. Instead of the standard diesel engines, these vehicles had been outfitted with electric motors and had additional armor sheets welded onto the front. Unfortunately, even that additional defense wasn't enough to save them from destruction.

I saw a large number of combat robots of Japanese and Chinese origin. The floor was blanketed in shells from their high-speed and high-caliber machineguns. I saw currently inactive turrets with English writing on the walls and floor. At one point, next to a caponier with a heavy Sio-Tu-Kati of my Relict Faction, I saw some jagged German written on the wall in glowing lemon-yellow ink: "Wir sterben, aber wir geben nicht auf!" (We may die, but we will not surrender!)

Eagle Eye skill increased to level one hundred seventeen!

Astrolinguistics skill increased to level one hundred nineteen!

Somewhere around a quarter mile later, we had to turn out of the main corridor and use a detour cut into the ice because the main route was completely blocked. Ahead was just a solid mass of downed tech, pieces of armored spacesuits and bundles of barbed wire. Next to the stairway leading down into the depths of the temple, I discovered another two Sio-Tu-Katis, though it was no simple matter to recognize the Relict Faction tanks in the hardened puddles of metal. One of the heavy tanks had been crushed beneath a huge Meleyephatian walking robot, still frozen atop its vanquished enemy with weapon pointed proudly upward.

There was already repair work underway next to the stairwell – hundreds of eight-legged creatures were fixing the destruction caused by the war, restoring the ice bas reliefs on the walls and sweeping a huge number of firearm shells off the floor.

"That way!" our guide pointed at a downward sloping straight corridor carved into the ice. "Note how the temperature rises the closer we get to the cave."

I already had. Even near the stairwell the temperature was a balmy zero degrees, while up ahead I could clearly hear running water. And that was with a surface temperature of negative two hundred!

The picture we saw a minute later felt strikingly unnatural. There was no artificial lighting to be found in the cave, but nevertheless it was light. Maybe the rays of the bright star were coming in through transparent vaults in the roof, or there were colonies of phosphorescent mold on the walls, but I even turned off my headlight so I could take in the astonishing sight. Water was dripping down from the ice ceiling, even pouring down in streams of transparent liquid and falling into a lake which was flickering with an abundance of small creatures. Red and green seaweed in the shallows. And even plant life on the very shore. The rocks were overgrown with a strange porous spherical plant. The temperature in the cave was forty-five, and the dosimeter on my sleeve started flickering intensely – somewhere nearby there was a source of intense radiation.

My attention to the dosimeter did not escape the Meleyephatian leading our group. Leng Ovaz Ussh pointed a jointed arm at the lake.

"Deep beneath the surface there is a metallic stone asteroid with high content of silicon, iron, uranium and transuranic elements. It fell on Un-Tau around a billion tongs ago and caused this whole natural anomaly."

"An unbelievable sight!" I marveled. "A truly unique place. A real miracle of the Universe. Could I use my Prospector scanning device to record all these wonders? Maybe I'll be able to get closer to solving the greatest mystery of the Universe – what conditions were necessary for life to begin?"

"Yes, of course. But Meleyephatian scientists have conducted all kinds of tests here to try and figure that out and replicate the conditions, yet they have not yet been able to duplicate the miracle. The organic molecules and even amino acids and silicon organics created by harsh radioactivity never form into anything more complex, capable of life and reproducing itself. It must have been a miracle. And it happened right here on Un-Tau."

Nevertheless, I took out the metal tripod and readied the Prospector Scanner. I warned the others go get back to a safe distance, then set the sliders to max for organic materials and radioactivity sources. After that, I put out the geological analyzer's "feet" and stuck them into the ground.

Scanning skill increased to level eighty-seven!

Cartography skill increased to level ninety-eight!

Mineralogy skill increased to level sixty-four!

Mineralogy skill increased to level sixty-five!

Nothing changed. It was still light in the cave and there were little flatworm-like creatures flitting around near the surface of the water. The scanner screen gave me a great view of the large uneven rock two hundred feet beneath the layer of water. It was approximately fifty feet along its longest axis and its width varied from twenty-five to thirty-five feet. My instrument revealed its composition and strong radioactivity. Silicon, iron, magnesium, uranium, plutonium, manganese and strontium. But nothing more. I saw that there were more similar asteroids, both rocky and metallic throughout the comet's ice. And it was not possible to tell what exactly made that one so unique.

I asked permission from Leng Ovaz Ussh to

run another three such scans from different points on the comet's surface and he agreed. Still I must admit that, in this case, I was not so much interested in the cave itself even though I had no doubt remaining that it was a unique natural feature. I was more interested now in the wreckage of hundreds of starships and military hardware strewn about the comet. Blueprints of those could prove very interesting and beneficial.

But then my attention was drawn by little Gerd Soia-Tan La-Varrez. She was behaving strangely. She suddenly gave a groan and fell to her knees. Ayni and Imran ran over to help her, but Leng Ovaz Ussh stopped my friends.

"Don't interfere! Your friend is having an epiphany. She's either seeing a key moment in the future or learning something new. It is a great gift that comes to believers in the Un-Tau temple. Don't rob your companions of this unique gift from the Universe itself!"

And that very moment, I was also overcome. The world around me disappeared, the ice temple and lake disappeared, then went my friends' faces...

All around just darkness and horror. Pain, too. I was severely wounded and bleeding out. My blood was thick and orange for some reason. It spurted out of me with every beat of my twin hearts. Though it wasn't only darkness around me. It was just dark corridors in a totally unfamiliar place. Flooded with water, dangerous and dark. But I could see a light up ahead. I need to hurry to it and drag my lacerated abdomen behind before any more innards spilled out. Behind me meanwhile I could hear a ghastly wailing and squelching on the wet flooded floor. They were closing in on me fast. It was too late to reach my virt pod. The predators would catch me first and tear me to shreds. Then I turned right into a side corridor. I knew it was a dead end. But it had a sturdy metal door I could open and hide behind. There was also weaponry back there. I pictured it. Hundreds and thousands of Annihilators on shelves lining the walls. Those weapons could be used to kill my enemies.

I crawled over to the door and extended a seven-fingered appendage toward the wall panel. Code ##12099, I knew it. And I even managed to punch in the first few symbols before a new wave of pain came over me. Something caught me in its teeth by my already mutilated abdomen and pulled me away from the door. I held onto a wall brace with all my fingers, but I wasn't strong enough. My hand slipped and I was quickly dragged into the darkness. With the last of my strength I unclipped a nearly empty Annihilator from my belt. It had enough charge for one final shot. I turned toward the invar that had me. It was a huge terrifying beast with a large number of clawed appendages and fins. I pointed the weapon at it but noticed another two invars rushing over to join the feast. That was the end. I didn't shoot the beast holding onto me. Instead I placed the weapon to my head. After that, my final wish, acute and utterly unfeasible was for Kung Gnat the Human to learn of my fate. And for him to send someone to the Syam Tro VII Refuge to replace me. After that, the pain vanished, and darkness came over me...

Chapter Twenty-Five

Hall of Visions

"**G**NAT, IS EVERYTHING alright with you?" An alarmed Imran was bustling all around me. Ayni too was sitting at my side on some wet stones covered in greenish brown moss staring at my face with great concern, though it was hard for her to see through my helmet's mirrored faceguard.

I wanted to reassure my friends, but I was just frozen with my mouth slightly open, having seen something unbelievable. Bright threads of light were pouring into the cave from all sides, piercing through the ice walls and disappearing into the depths of the lake. Energy streams of some kind? Or were these mana streams? And how hadn't I noticed them before? Anyway, as soon as I focused my attention on the threads, they disappeared without a trace. I shook my head to drive off the illusion.

Blessing of an unknown nature received. Power of all psionic abilities increased by seven percent. Will last either 10 tongs or until your

first character death.

Attention!!! Your character's Intelligence is not high enough to understand what is happening.

What? My Gnat had an effective Intelligence of forty-six! Very few living creatures could boast of such lofty Intelligence figures. And still that was not enough to understand? How much did I need then?!

I stood up and reassured my friends that I was doing just fine. And I immediately shared the tragic news that Gerd Urgeh Pu-Pu Urgeh our teammate had died in the real world at the far-away Syam Tro VII Refuge and would not be coming back into the game. We had lost the last member of the ancient Relict race. And we all shared the blame for it. The *Tamara the Paladin*'s crew had never made Gerd Urgeh Pu-Pu Urgeh feel like part of the family. Perhaps, had we been friendlier and more insistent with the Relict, spent more time with him and managed to get him out of that deep rut, the Technician would never have gone into the potentially lethal flooded hallways of the refuge to try and fix malfunctioning hardware and bring his dormant compatriots back from their thousand-year slumber.

All my companions looked down dejectedly, agreeing with me.

"Gerd Urgeh Pu-Pu Urgeh thought of me in the last seconds of his life. And he begged me to send a replacement that could get the ancient refuge's systems back up and running. It is very important to him and the Relict race as a whole."

Gerd Ayni the Miyelonian walked in front of me and, looking me right in the eyes, said:

"Captain, please promise me you won't go there yourself! I know you and your foolhardy ways all too well, so I am very worried you might. One loss of life in that dangerous so-called 'refuge' is enough!"

I could read pleading and true concern in my friend's eyes, so I nearly agreed. But still I didn't tie myself down with such a categorical promise, instead trying to hide behind a fog of words. I said the Relict refuge was of interest to me without a doubt. Furthermore, no one else could communicate with the station's artificial intelligence and figure out the complicated mechanisms. But if I were to transfer my physical body to the Syam Tro VII Refuge, it would only be after an assault squadron cleared the ancient corridors of the dangerous beasts that lived inside. However, the Syam Tro VII Refuge was located in the real world, so it would be a definite challenge to send an armed and armored group of troops there...

That wasn't exactly what my tailed girlfriend asked for, but still it took care of most of the Miyelonian's worry. Furthermore, Gerd Soia-Tan took complete hold of our attention, now also coming to her senses and declaring for all to hear:

"Coruler Gnat, I know what happened in the Palace of the Ruling Council of Mage Rulers! Leng Tamara is not at fault! She wasn't even in the room when the explosion took place. There was a big gray-haired man with her from your world. He took the remote detonator away from Tamara and pushed her outside saying his daughter was too young to die. And that he had lived long enough already, so he would take the burden on himself. Tamara also spent some time pounding on a carved door the old man had locked demanding she be let in, then ran for the exit. And that was when the palace exploded. It was that old man that killed all the mages! And the explosives were planted on an order from your wife Gerd Minn-O La-Fin and Mage Diviner Gerd Mac-Peu Un-Roi!"

I squeezed the girl tight, shaken up by the sudden flood of knowledge and tried to reassure her.

"Yes, I know. Minn-O told me what happened in the palace. But she was acting on advice from the Mage Diviner and was convinced to the very end that they were only going to spook the Ruling Council and stop there. To pressure the Mage Rulers and make them vote the right way. Believe me, Minn-O La-Fin never would have done such a thing if she knew how it was all going to turn out. It's true. I checked her thoughts. By the way, that old gray-hair was called Roman Pavlovich. Tamara really was his adopted daughter, and he loved her more than life itself..."

"Coruler Gnat La-Fin," the little sorceress suddenly shifted to a whisper. "Did you know that your wife is a total 'shell?' Gerd Minn-O La-Fin doesn't even have a hint of magical abilities. All her mana actually belongs to the future child. Leng Tamara herself said so."

"Leng Tamara may have been wrong... Though you know something? It doesn't matter. As a native of the magocratic world, you may not understand but my love for Minn-O La-Fin is in no way dependent on whether or not she has magical abilities. And I was already aware my future child would be a powerful sorcerer without Leng Tamara's help."

"I see you two have received your gifts from the Universe and are dazzled," the attendant Leng Ovaz Ussh drew our attention. "Humans, would you like to go further into the depths of the ice temple, or do you need time to process and will go back to your starship? In the Hall of Visions and Hall of Fear, new visions and new knowledge may descend upon pilgrims, but is rare for them to be pleasant or easy to comprehend."

As soon as we heard Gerd Ayni's translation, Gerd Soia-Tan and I traded looks and answered in concert.

"Let's keep going!"

The Hall of Visions turned out to be nothing like the Cave of the Dawn of Life and consisted of a spacious circular room on the tenth under-ice floor. All the walls here were decorated with fanciful ice carvings – a star map as seen from Un-Tau, the sweeping trajectories of planets and other strange objects. And surrounding it all were extensive passages written in Meleyephatian. Gerd Ayni told me that before us were fragments of the sacred writings upheld by renegade nests. For the most part, they were prophecies the renegade nest leaders had received in this very hall.

But the main attraction of the Hall of Visions was not the writing on the walls, but the silvery metal column installed perfectly upright in the middle of the room and lit by bright spotlights. I walked up closer and went a bit to the side because the bright light was blinding even through my helmet's dimming faceguard. I couldn't even believe what I was seeing right away. There were Relict symbols carved on the surface of the column! I walked a circle around it, reading the message.

Leng Ovaz Ussh followed after me and for some reason kept sliding in with comments.

"Human, this column was already here frozen into the ice when Comet Un-Tau was discovered and studied by a Meleyephatian expedition one hundred eighty tongs ago. The language on it belongs to an ancient, long extinct race. The text has only been partially deciphered by Meleyephatian Horde researchers and historians. There is something about divine energy and the alignment of grace, the name of the supreme being they worshipped and some kind of numerals. Most likely, it is a fragment of the ancient race's holy text and the page number it was found on."

"Not at all," I shook my head, very surprised by the absurdity of what the highly placed Meleyephatian just told me. "This says: *'Natural chrono-energy focal point, refracted into three streams by a metallic asteroid that landed on the comet. Intensity at epicenter: one hundred and two units. Energy transmitter for Pyramid recharge installed on instructions of Hierarch Kung Arti-No-No-Arti the Devourer by the team of Gerd Pori-Un-Un-Pori the Listener.'* And next is the date the column was installed. Or rather the retransmitter which redirected the stream of chrono-energy, whatever that is, to a far-off Relict Pyramid data node."

Astrolinguistics skill increased to level one hundred twenty!

I gave it some thought, lined it up with the current date in Relict reckoning and said that the column had been installed forty-eight thousand tongs ago, before the beginning of the Great War between the ancient races.

Scanning skill increased to level eighty-eight!

The interior of the column consisted of a complex device but unfortunately it was inactive by the time I got to it. The Meleyephatians that discovered the ancient Relict artifact had damaged its fragile machinery. They had also moved the column away from the energy focus point and changed its position. I could possibly get the retransmitter up and running again with the Kirsan repair bots, but it was highly unlikely that the Pyramid node this was redirecting energy to was still extant. Furthermore, I understood perfectly well that the Meleyephatians would not allow an outsider to call the shots at their shrine, break an object of pilgrimage out of the ice and crack it open, then put it back in a different way.

"Kung Gnat," our tour guide turned to me, and for the first time I heard notes of intrigue and even respect in his voice. "The Meleyephatian Horde has found several such artifacts in space. For the most part they were dismantled and hauled off to Kharsssh-O, so with the current war they are unavailable. But I have renderings. If you understand the extinct race's language, do you think you could help decipher what's written on the stellae and columns?"

Authority increased to 124!

"Yes, no problem. Send them over. I would just ask that you also indicate where these artifacts were discovered..."

I cut myself off midsentence because just then Gerd Imran was struck by a vision. My Bodyguard suddenly let out a groan and fell to the floor. But he was not a mage! Or did players with no magical gift also have discoveries here? But when I took a step toward my buddy to help, the world before my eyes again went blurry.

It was a familiar place. The Geckho spaceport dispatcher tower. I was in the operations room staring anxiously at locator screens with a large group of humans and Geckho. On the screens were hundreds and thousands of starships flooding into the Solar System. The giant silhouettes of battleships stood out on the backdrop of many small-class ships. There were even a few larger starships. So, the invasion had begun after all! I turned my gaze to the other screen, which was broadcasting a live feed of Earth from a recon satellite. The blue planet was protected by a glimmering energy shield. I had done it!

Blessing of an unknown nature intensified. Power of all psionic abilities increased by fourteen percent. Will last either

10 tongs or until your first character death.
Attention!!! Your character's Intelligence is not high enough to understand what is happening.

I opened my eyes and again saw the glowing thread of some kind of energy stream. This time it was brighter and passing tangentially right through the ice ceiling, breaking off and dispersing into sparks twenty feet away from the improperly installed metal column. Seemingly, the thread was coming from the Cave of the Dawn of Life, or more likely the asteroid on the bottom of the lake. Just like the last time, as soon as I blinked and lost concentration, the vision was gone.

I shook my head, turned and locked eyes with Imran. The Gladiator was sitting on the ice floor and giving me a crazed, wild-eyed stare. The Dagestani muttered something indistinct, but I couldn't understand. It didn't even sound like Russian. But then Imran gulped nervously and repeated it for me.

"Gnat, I'm going to have fourteen children. Five sons and nine daughters. Wow-ee! I saw them all grown up. We were standing together on the observation deck of a skyscraper in Pa-lin-thu. The oldest was wearing a military uniform all weighed down with badges and space fleet admiral epaulettes. I mean, just think, Gnat. Fourteen kids! That must be the biggest achievement of my life!"

Gerd Ayni the Miyelonian next to us couldn't hold back an acrid comment.

"As far as I know about Human biology, it sounds more like your wife's accomplishment. Your part in it isn't all that tricky."

But Imran just waved off the tailed Translator's ribbing good-naturedly.

"You don't understand, orange cat. A large family is something for parents to be proud of! It's too bad my grandfather isn't around anymore. He'd have been proud."

We both stood up and looked at our companions. We stood around for a minute, but neither Gerd Soia-Tan nor Gerd Ayni were overcome by any visions in this odd location. And although the Miyelonian wasn't bothered by that, not expecting a revelation and didn't even especially believe in all this "stupid fortune telling," the little sorceress was clearly feeling hurt. The little one walked a few circles around the metal column, purposely standing exactly where Imran got his vision three times, but nothing happened.

"What are we wasting time for? Let's go on to the next hall!" Gerd Soia-Tan La-Varrez announced and stepped first to leave the Hall of Visions.

Chapter Twenty-Six

The Hall of Fear

THE WAR HAD NEVER reached this far. There were no more traces of battle. The hundreds of rooms for the workers and defenders of the temple remained untouched beneath a forcefield. There were workshops, warehouses, farms growing all kinds of plants and raising some small pupae that looked like maggots used to feed a larger kind of house pet. Residential buildings, a powerplant, a meeting hall, a long-distance comms room, a shooting range and a training arena. A true self-sustaining under-ice city. Furthermore, the atmosphere down here was suitable for breathing, gravity was equalized, and it was a green zone. I suspect it was that very ability to respawn that gave the defenders of the ice temple their commanding advantage over any invading army on Un-Tau. Of course it was a risk and could turn into a death trap if the attackers did manage to capture the under-ice city, but that would just make the Meleyephatians defend their temple all the more staunchly.

"All that live here have disavowed their former lives and dedicated themselves to Comet Un-Tau," the eight-legged tour guide explained to us, pointing his appendages at his many compatriots flitting all around. "Generous donations from pilgrims and renegade nests allow us to upkeep this settlement and want for nothing. The starship flotilla you saw in space was also purchased with donations to the temple and belongs to Un-Tau."

We walked through the workshop or more like fully-fledged factory where a team of Mechanics was hard at work getting some damaged tech back up and running. The Meleyephatians stared at our group in surprise – members of the human race must have been quite infrequent visitors here, if our kind had ever even been here before – but no one was even thinking about stopping us.

Fame increased to 127.

At a certain point, our guide slowed his pace, pressed a jointed leg to his helmet and turned his mobile eyes my direction.

"Kung Gnat, a message has come in from someone called Gerd Ruwana Loki. She represents the Meleyephatian Horde, even though she is a Human by race. Ever heard of her?"

I confirmed my acquaintance with Krong Laa's representative and asked straight away what the woman wanted.

"She requests that Kung Gnat wait for her on Un-Tau and assures him she will make it here in five ummi."

Aw hell! I for one was hoping I had gotten rid of that tiresome observer. Should I tell her I have no time, and am in a hurry? Unfortunately, Gerd Ruwana Loki could easily check that. Furthermore my behavior would look very suspicious, especially after the Psychologist's "accidental" death aboard my frigate. It would be very inconvenient to get into a quarrel with the Meleyephatians now and tear up my hard-won arrangements with the temple defenders. Especially with my *Tamara the Paladin* stationed on Un-Tau and vulnerable on the territory of a potential adversary. I had to promise to wait for Krong Laa's observer.

I also found upsides though. It would give the Army of Earth time to pick up their downed hardware, and me time to study the spaceship wreckage strewn about the comet. Furthermore, I had long been planning to make a big public address to the people of the magocratic world, and it was hard to imagine a better place to make it than the site of the Army of Earth's first triumph. Let them all see that the Kung of Earth was with his army and taking very active part in the events.

We passed through the defensive field and the green zone came to an abrupt end. We found ourselves back in corridors carved into the ice, then on a slope taking us even deeper. There was no light here, so all group members turned on their helmet lights. But then in the distance we saw a bluish glow, and soon we found ourselves in front of a phosphorescent warning on the icy wall.

"This says: 'Separating from group is forbidden. Safeties on, weapons unloaded and stored in inventory. Risk of death!'" Gerd Ayni translated.

When the guide saw our interest in the warning, he explained:

"Up ahead is the Hall of Fear. There, pilgrims come face to face with their greatest fear. Visitors tend to react in all kinds of ways. Some have died on the spot, unable to bare the flood of horror. Some have started blasting at random all around, even shooting their own friends. Some have fallen into uncontrolled panic and run down the labyrinth of dark tunnels leading to the comet's core. And some of them we were not able to find and save before they ran out of air."

By the way, speaking of air... I looked with worry at my pressure gage. Three hours left. But that was in the Listener armor. It had almost twice as much air storage capacity as my companions' spacesuits. That meant my friends would be running very close to empty. One hour and a bit would hardly be enough to make it back to the ship through all the under-ice hallways filled with piles of broken tech. But why didn't Leng Ovaz Ussh warn us about that problem? We could have refilled our air tanks in the green zone, then we wouldn't have had to worry about lack of oxygen. But now we needed to hurry, and I commanded them to keep going.

The Hall of Fear was unlike the Hall of Visions we saw earlier. Here there was no inscribed metal column, no carvings on the walls, not even spotlights. There was one lone reddish glow in the middle of the round room, and you might say that was it. There were also a few pitch-black hallways leading deep into the ice comet in different directions...

We stopped thirty paces from the light source, unable to make up our minds to keep going. I must admit, it was pretty freaky. Furthermore, Leng Ovaz Ussh told us there would be no visions if we stayed in the bright light. The only way was to turn off our helmet lights and slowly approach the red glow in darkness, hoping a sudden epiphany would descend upon us.

"I'm going first!" Gerd Ayni surprised me and everyone else. "The Miyelonians have our own culture, which does not make room for such superstitions. None of these 'discoveries,' or 'gifts from the Universe' will work on me. I don't believe in such fairy tales. So I'm not afraid!"

Not afraid? Well, maybe she was saying that to everyone else, but I could sense my tailed friend's emotional background perfectly well. Plus her knees were quaking like jelly! She wasn't as scared as she was to meet "absolute evil," but her heebie-jeebies were still palpable. On top of that, although Gerd Ayni would never have admitted it, she was hurt and upset by the fact that she was the only one in our group not to get a message from the Universe yet.

"I must not fear. Fear is the mind killer. Fear is the little death..." I heard a familiar quote in my headphones.

Okay then, she had memorized it. By the way, if not for the two blades NPC Dryad Nefertiti had finished working on, would Gerd Ayni Uri-Miayuu be afraid or not? And could a character with full immunity to fear even get a revelation from the Universe in the Hall of Fear?

Before I'd had time to think that thought through, having made it just five steps toward the red light, the Miyelonian suddenly wailed out hysterically and ran off into the darkness, even using her quick movement ability. Stop right there, Whiskers! I was ready for the easily spooked kitty to behave that way and reacted instantly, taking control of Gerd Ayni's mind.

Psionic skill increased to level one hundred fifty-three!

The Translator emerged from the dark corridor a feeble-minded zombie and walked back to the group on shaky legs. Somewhere around the middle of her walk, Ayni managed to overcome the fear and came back to her senses. She looked around and, with ghastly embarrassment and her snout pointed to the floor, started moving all on her own. The proud Miyelonian was horrified in shame for letting other people see her fear. And another thing... I didn't make any comments, but for some reason I knew the Miyelonian's spacesuit was no longer dry.

"She pissed herself out of fear!" I could sense blatant happiness from the little sorceress in the mental message.

"We all have our weaknesses, so don't you dare tell anyone else about Gerd Ayni's little mishap. I'll kick you out of the crew and send you back to Earth! And for that matter, let's see how you handle your fear."

Imran grabbed tightly onto the spacesuit sleeve of the approaching Miyelonian, but there was no need for that anymore. Not raising her head and still staring at the ice floor, the Translator made a confession.

"Captain Gnat, I saw something scary. A rebellion of Prince Hugo supporters rising up simultaneously in one thousand five hundred Trillian star systems! I don't know when it will happen, but the rebellion is inevitable. For the most part, the army will side with the rebels. Civil war. Bloodbaths throughout the Kingdom of the Trillians, rebels will kill 'loyalists,' while supporters of the legal rulers will ruthlessly execute all rebels. And the bloodthirsty Prince has not forgotten the humiliation and suffering you subjected him to. If Gerd Hugo wins the civil war, you will not live! The ruler of the Trillians will do his utmost to find and kill you, Captain Gnat, after torturing you to discover how to control the ancient laboratory. In that bloodthirsty maniac's plans, I am destined to serve as a living plaything. Which he wants to keep for himself and play with to his heart's content, taking pleasure in my pain, fear and despair. Prince Hugo has in fact already put me together a list of seven thousand tortures and humiliations and scheduled them out for ten whole tongs. And he's constantly adding to the list, thinking up more and more new sadistic experiments. He will kill me gruesomely and await my respawn, kill and respawn, and so on an endless number of times. And then, when he tires of that, he wants to cut off my head and sew it to the body of an android to run on metal paws next to my master and forever serve him as Translator..."

Yikes... I agree. That is something to fear. Even Gerd Soia-Tan's eyes went wide in horror after mocking the Miyelonian. I made a generous investment into Magic Points trying to calm my cute companion. I said she just saw one possible line of the probable future, which could easily not come to pass. Especially if we warned the Trillian ruler about his relative's insidious plans and the Prince's rebellion did not come to fruition. I added that I had a basic understanding of lines of the probable future, because I had some experience correcting the very worst of them. And that I had at my disposal a talented Mage Diviner who could tell us how to avoid the ghastly events she'd just described.

I don't know for certain whether it was magic or what I said, but the Miyelonian stopped shaking and gradually calmed down. Nevertheless, after what happened to Gerd Ayni the others cooled their jets a bit. Who would be next to go into the Hall of Fear? And then Gerd Imran took a decisive step forward, heading toward the red light. He approached unhurriedly, even touching the red bulb. Then he shrugged his shoulders and went back to join the others.

"There isn't much I fear in this life. I guess I must be hard to scare."

I went next, handing my Annihilator to the Gladiator just in case. It wasn't that I was afraid of losing control of myself, it truly was just in case.

By the way, what am I even afraid of? That was what I was thinking as I walked up to the only source of light in the Hall of Fear. Some may have feared losing parents or close relatives, but to me all these worries were left in the distant past. I wasn't afraid of school bullies, the dark, heights, or even the dentist. In the real world, there was little that could truly scare me. But what about here in the game? I wasn't scared of the "embodiment of absolute evil," unlike my tailed companion. I had already met Gerd Hugo face to face and defeated him. I wasn't scared of space pirates either. Now my Fame and Authority were so high that pirates were afraid of me. So then what? Anxiety about the future of humanity? Yes, that was definitely present, but it was generalized, not specific so it would be hard to form it into something I could see and hear. Now where did that leave me? Was I not afraid of anything?

That turned out to be not even remotely true.

With the Annihilator in my hands, I slowly and carefully strolled down the hallway of an ancient starship. It was in some way reminiscent of the mobile Relict laboratory. Yes, that's right. There were words written in the ancient race's language on the walls. I was inside the Hierarch's ship! And up ahead was the temporal capsule room, which was my destination. There were many capsules there, a whole thirty, but most of them were open. Only eight were in use, and in them were members of the ancient race awaiting their hour after being lost to time. And there it was – the Hierarch's capsule. The very Relict the Pyramid ordered me to save.

I ordered Valeri and Soia-Tan to provide magic backup and for my other companions to hold their weapons at the ready and not be afraid to use them if the ancient ruler was aggressively inclined. After that, I pressed a button on the panel, opening the temporal capsule.

It was all over in one second. The stream of terror, darkness and power that came crashing down on our group was so powerful I screamed in unbearable agony while all my companions fell dead instantly. I survived a second longer and even tried to use my Annihilator, but the weapon wouldn't shoot. My Listener armor blocked the Annihilator, not letting me shoot the Hierarch! I realized that just before dying. A minute later, the mobile laboratory had accepted a new master and pushed the foreign twinbody frigate out from under its distortion shield and right into the lethal cannons of the Hierarch's ancient cruiser.

Blessing of an unknown nature intensified. Power of all psionic abilities increased by twenty-one percent. Will last either 10 tongs or until your first character death.

Attention!!! Your character's Intelligence is not high enough to understand what is happening.

Mental Fortitude skill increased to level one hundred fifty-three!

Mental Fortitude skill increased to level one hundred fifty-four!

Training skill increased to level fifty-five!

You have reached level one hundred twenty-two!

You have received three skill points (total

points accumulated: six).

I opened my eyes and again noticed a glowing thread of energy. This one went straight, and right into the middle of the Hall of Fear. And disappeared in the space of a second, though that was no surprise.

So that was what brought my vision! My heart started beating fearfully in my chest. I was breathing rapidly as if I'd just taken a fast run. But I didn't speed off into the darkness, fall over or start screaming, instead upholding my dignity in the eyes of my companions. And I even found the strength inside to bow low to the darkness for its extremely useful prediction. And after all, it was indeed possible for me to just waltz into the Hierarch's chamber to try and talk with the ruler of the ancient race. Alright then, now I know that would be a stupid idea and, upon meeting the ancient being, neither a magic link, weaponry or my skills would be any help. There was also the Listener suit I was so accustomed to using it felt like a second skin. In that critical moment, it would betray me and fight on behalf of the Relict ruler. Good to know.

I returned to my friends and said that I had seen my biggest fear and managed to get past it. I took the Annihilator from my bodyguard and put it away. And meanwhile, Gerd Soia-Tan was already on her way into the middle of the Hall of Fear. She stood before the red glow for twenty seconds, after which she turned calmly and walked back to the others in an unhurried pace. No vision? But the little sorceress's first words refuted that theory.

"Her name is Florianna royl Unatari. The one I'll have to fight to the death. She's twenty years old, the blood sister of the White Queen and the apprentice of the Red Queen. She was cruelly maimed by her strict instructor but managed to survive and partially restore her body to health. The personal psionic mage of Emperor Georg the First, the most powerful Truth Seeker in all the Empire and a Master at cutting short unnecessary lives. She has been given the right by the very Emperor to kill without trial or investigation all those she deems a threat to Georg the First. She can read thoughts like me. But unlike me, she is not specialized in the element of fire, but rather death magic. Her favorite move is stopping an adversary's heart. If we can figure out how to defend against such an attack, then maybe I'll stand a chance. Florianna royl Unatari also knows I am coming for her and is preparing for our encounter. And she warned me that our battle can only be one on one. You cannot help me, and she will not be fueled by her minions. Florianna also assured me that she bears no malice toward me, but it's just how things work, so she'll have to kill me."[6]

I fell silent, digesting what she said. She was sounding like a serious opponent. Too powerful for her twenty years. Something incredible must have happened for such a young girl to amass such power. I wasn't surprised she could read thoughts. Psionic sorcerers were often able to do that. But

---

[6] *All aforementioned characters and events are from the* Perimeter Defense *series by Michael Atamanov.*

death magic and stopping hearts? Yes, that warranted some real thought. And meanwhile, Gerd Soia-Tan announced she was planning to go deeper into the comet, to the Hall of Death.

"I really need to get stronger so I can take on such a dangerous adversary," she explained her bizarre intention. "Every vision that comes to me improves my magical abilities, and it was very frustrating not to have that happen in the second hall! So I don't have much of a choice. I have to go into the Hall of Death. And there I will also learn how I will die. Sounds interesting!"

I just shook my head, not agreeing with the tyke's words. Everything before that was one thing, but nothing could make me want to know the circumstances of my own death. Still, of course, I went off to accompany my companion down the dark icy corridors, especially after Leng Ovaz Ussh assured us that there wasn't far to go, just fifty steps.

This one could not in fact be properly labeled a hall. The corridor just came to an abrupt end, severed by a wide crack in the ice. Those wishing to receive the Universe's revelation had to go into the darkness down a narrow set of stairs carved into the ice. Those accompanying them were recommended to wait up on the edge of the chasm. I took a cautious glance over the precipice and down below saw a small dimly lit ledge over a dark crevasse half a mile deep. And that little platform was where pilgrims were supposed to receive this very questionable gift from the Universe.

Gerd Soia-Tan was the only one in the whole group who wanted to go down the dangerous stairway. And although it was nearly impossible to get yourself killed falling in such low gravity, especially considering we were already close to the comet's center of mass, falling into a half-mile-deep crack with no way back up still seemed like an unpleasant prospect.

But the brave girl looked quite cheery as she descended the series of icy steps, stepped onto the platform and spent a minute or so walking around in expectation of a sudden epiphany. I had already started thinking nothing would happen again, when suddenly Gerd Soia-Tan bent severely at the waist then fell to her knees. She was wrenched by a very powerful bout of nausea. Uhh... Barfing in a spacesuit? To put it lightly, not a great idea. But the knowledge that came down on her must have been so burdensome that there was no other way to bear it.

Our companion spent a long time puking her guts out. We waited patiently, just taking the odd anxious glance at the pressure gauges on our oxygen tanks. A mere few minutes later, Gerd Soia-Tan stopped, crawled on all fours over to the stairs and asked someone to come down and help her because she no longer felt strong enough to stand. I ran down to help the kid and picked her up in my arms. Her helmet was all dirty on the inside, and her face looked green.

"And here I was laughing at Ayni..." the little sorceress said barely audibly and chuckled unhappily. "You were right... Captain Gnat... I never should have come down here. It is bad knowledge to have..."

And after that, Gerd Soia-Tan fainted.

Chapter Twenty-Seven

Three Corulers

"**H**OW IS SHE?" Three ummi after we returned from the ice temple, I walked into the med bay along with my ward Tini. The Miyelonian Medic Gerd Mauu-La Mya-Ssa pointed a clawed finger at the sickly pale patient curled up in the fetal position on her hospital bed in a warm set of pajamas.

"She woke up. She is conscious, but practically not speaking. Body temperature is slightly low, but it isn't critical. Her breathing is faint, pulse uneven. Any food she gets down comes right back up, so we had to give her a glucose and vitamin drip. Weakness, overexertion. A few times she woke up screaming, saying her heart stopped or she was being dissolved in acid. She's fixated on the idea that someone is trying to kill her. But outside of that, her body is doing perfectly fine. Ideally, Gerd Soia-Tan should get some rest, two days at least, and experience some positive emotions. Then she'll be good as new."

Positive emotions? I gave Tini a slight push

on the back, and Miyelonian teen looked ashamed, walked up closer to his roommate and handed her a fluffy toy. Green and pink, the seven-tentacled oddity had three eyes.

"Here you go, tailless sister! I bought it back in Serpea just for you. I just never found a good occasion to give it to you. You go ahead and get better soon. It's getting lonely and boring without you in my bunk. I don't even have anyone to beat at cards..."

"Beat?" the little sorceress objected in a soft voice, squeezing the gift to her chest. "Well I'm ahead in the count right now even though you're constantly cheating!"

"Looks who's talking about cheating. You're the one reading thoughts and peeking at cards!"

Soia-Tan couldn't find a response to that. She just started smiling and thanked him for the toy. Tini considered his mission complete and hurried out of med bay, clearly not feeling too comfortable there. I had overheard that the Medic had recently performed an operation on him linked with his coming of age in some way, but I didn't delve into the details. Some mandatory ritual every male Miyelonian had to undergo at his age. By the looks of things, the procedure had not left Tini with the greatest of impressions, though my ward's earring selection had completely changed afterward, which must have meant something.

I then turned my attention to a set of crutches and metal casts in the corner of the room, which Vasha Tushihh had been wearing on his legs until recently.

"Yes, Captain Gnat. Vasha can now walk without any aids. His leg bones are practically healed. For the time being, he shouldn't put too much weight on them, but that's only for the next three days. And by the way, Captain, the Geckho has a high Fame figure. He's just the tiniest bit away from Gerd rank. I would suggest you put some shine on Vasha Tushihh in front of other Geckho or give him a chance to prove himself in combat operations so he can become a high-profile player. That will improve his combat and survival abilities, which would be a boon to our whole team."

"Sound advice, thank you. I'll definitely find a way to raise our tank's Fame. And by the way, how is our Cleopian doing?" I pointed at the sapling under glass with a bright luminescent bulb and automatic watering system. The knotty plant in the ceramic pot now had a few little leaves out and had become noticeably longer and thicker since I smuggled it out of the Serpea prison.

The Medic walked over to the sapling, opened the glass and sprayed its shoots with nutrient mixture from a special spray bottle. He touched the leaves cautiously, then removed a dead branch with scissors and said proudly:

"The Cleopian is growing and becoming stronger. I have read a lot of information on his race recently and am trying to keep strictly to all the instructions. The Cleopian's nervous system is not yet formed and is in an embryonic state while the organism is vegetating. But in fifteen or twenty days, the body will start to grow rapidly and branch out. His nerve cluster count will go up exponentially. And then we need to make sure we don't miss his consciousness 'turning on.' Then memories of his past life will start coming back. It will take just five to seven days before we can make the Cleopian a member of the Relict Faction and provide him an exit point into the real world. Otherwise, the rescued Cleopian will end up stuck in the game that bends reality with no body in the real world."

Soia-Tan called out to me in a weak voice from her bed.

"Coruler Gnat La-Fin, please come over here. I want to tell you what I learned in the Hall of Death."

"Do you really think you should?" I clarified anxiously, aware that the memories could be very hard on the little patient and not wanting to worsen her condition.

"Yes," the little sorceress was determined. "I need to share this information with someone to lighten the load. I saw that I will be killed by your son. A mighty sorcerer, most powerful Archmage and overlord of Humanity. I will cross his wife in some way. Also a very mighty sorceress, no less powerful than your son in abilities, and perhaps even surpassing him. By the way, her name is Deianna royl Unatari, daughter of Emperor Georg the First and the ghastly Red Queen. I will be killed cruelly and painfully. With some ghastly magic that makes the body melt and dissolve. The only thing giving me hope is that it will happen very far in the future. I was very old in the vision that came over me in the Hall of Death. So I have a long life ahead of me. And that's nice..."

Despite the macabre prediction, she found the strength inside to smile. She felt better after sharing the scary information. I then considered it. If Gerd Soia-Tan La-Varrez was fated to live a long life, would she win the duel against Flora royl Unatari? Actually wait. I facepalmed. The duel with the Emperor's psionic would take place in the game that bends reality, where death was not final and characters would respawn. So the vision of death had no impact on the outcome of the duel. And by the way, speaking of cardiac arrest...

I asked the highly experienced Medic if it was possible to prevent such a thing or at the very least get the myocardium functioning again quickly afterward. Gerd Mauu-La Mya-Ssa looked at his patient with worry, took out his tablet and spent a long time studying some figures only he could understand. After that, he assured us the Human girl had nothing wrong with her heart and he could not detect any pathologies or complications. But now that the question had come up, there was a possible solution. He could implant a microcapsule into the pericardial sac, which would restart the muscle tissue in case of sudden cardiac arrest. The only problem was that it was a complex operation requiring certain preparation. Furthermore, after surgical intervention, no matter how delicate, she would need time to recover. Seven days at least, if not ten.

"Alright, get ready to perform the operation," I ordered the Medic and announced to the little sorceress that she could skip training, chores and other obligations for the next ten days. But I did have one thing, or rather favor to ask. But whether she agreed to it or not would need to be decided depending on her physical condition.

"I know what you want to ask me, Captain Gnat," the little patient smiled craftily and set her bare feet on the floor, seemingly having reconsidered moping in pain. "I can help you with your address to the people of the magocratic world."

I had been preparing for this performance a very long time. Ten times I had rewritten and read the text aloud, getting tricky and ambiguous issues agreed on with my companions, several times consulting with my wife Minn-O La-Fin and Chief Advisor Mac-Peu Un-Roi. I even chatted with representatives of the La-Varrez dynasty so the end result wouldn't come as a surprise to them. And finally I thought I was ready.

My Engineers had installed additional lighting in the mobile Relict laboratory's Pyramid Contact Hall, along with a background depicting the ice comet and starship wreckage. Destroying Angel and San-Sano did my hair because my grown-out disheveled black mane and five-o'clock shadow may have been fine for a space adventurer, but they did not play into the image of a respectable Archmage and Coruler of Humanity. And so they cut my hair, evened out my whiskers and gave me a slight upward curl, leaving me with a very tidy wedge beard in place of all my unkempt whiskers. In the matte black armor, I now looked like a Spanish conquistador, though my eyes were glowing with bright blue light. I myself didn't like the look one bit, but San-Sano assured me that it was stylish and respectable, and the people of the magocratic world would like to see the new leader of the First Directory looking like this.

I commanded the two small guard drones to hover nearby so they would sometimes come into frame, drawing the audience's attention. For respectability, I also put a group of four players behind me. To my left was the huge and imposing Vasha Tushihh representing the race of humanity's suzerains and further emphasizing my high status. In contrast was the diminutive Miyelonian Gerd Ayni Uri-Miayuu – let the viewers see that my contact with alien races was nowhere near limited to Geckho alone. Next to the Miyelonian stood Gerd Soia-Tan La-Varrez in her ghastly space-witch garb representing the famed and influential La-Varrez dynasty of Mage Rulers. The kid was hopped up to the gills on stimulants and energy drinks. I really needed her support, and the little sorceress was proud of the mission she'd been entrusted with and eager to help despite her ongoing malaise. And finally, behind me to the right was the very large and striking Gerd T'yu-Pan in exoskeleton armor to represent the people of the magocratic world that did not possess magical abilities. I wanted the billions of viewers to see that my team had room in it for commoners as well.

At the very last moment, I slurped down a mana-restoring slightly alcoholic cocktail because I was planning to make active use of psionics. Plus it would just reduce my stress.

"Let's roll!"

The Engineers had already informed me that although the ruler of the First Directory's speech would be screened throughout the magocratic world, the primary broadcast would be made on a huge monitor installed over Pa-lin-thu central square, and that was what I would see when a comms link was established. But when the light went out for a second and the image appeared, I found myself at a loss for words. No, I mean I was definitely expecting the new Coruler of humanity's speech to attract interest, but there were hundreds of thousands of people on the massive square, if not a million. My speech had been announced in advance, and they could have stayed home to watch the broadcast, but many preferred to gather on the central square of the capital city. The sea of humanity stretched out to a set of skyscrapers that loomed large on the horizon and the crowd was so dense you couldn't swing a cat. I mentally raised my fallen jaw and got myself together.

"Citizens of the First Directory and all people of the magocratic world..."

I was speaking the language of the magocratic world totally fluently now, so I had no linguistic issues. After overcoming the initial anxiety, I started firmly laying out the speech I'd memorized by heart. For starters, I told the sad news that my sister in arms and trusty companion

Tamara the Paladin, who had served as an unwitting catalyst and set in motion long-brewing political processes, had died in battle. The way I told it, she was killed by fanatics that didn't want to go along with her ceasefire with the authorities of the sixteen Directories and insisted on continuing to escalate the conflict.

I named the place and time of her funeral ceremony, then declared a minute of silence in memory of the remarkable girl – a symbol of change and an implacable fighter against all that would wreak injustice. to my satisfaction, the crowd of thousands fell silent. Many fell to their knees. The people loved and nearly worshipped Tamara as a god, considering her the defender of the common citizenry.

After that, with my first decree, I declared all the terrorist groups illegal if they did not lay down their weapons within three hours and set death as the only legal punishment for those that refused to obey! The crowd took that with jubilation. For Tamara's sake, they were willing to tear her murderers limb from limb with their bare hands.

Authority increased to 125!

ATTENTION!!! Your Fame and Authority figures now allow you to increase the number of factions in the Relict military political alliance to eight.

ATTENTION!!! The Relict alliance may now incorporate factions composed of races other than Human.

I dismissed the pop-ups no matter how nice they may have been. It just was not the time. And I got back to my speech. Then I told them about my Army of Earth's victory on the distant ice comet of Un-Tau. It was a historic event, the importance of which was hard to overstate. Humanity had made a name for itself as a prosperous political force to be reckoned with throughout the galaxy. We had fulfilled our duty to our suzerains with honor, gained experience and knowledge and were ready to take on new challenges!

Authority increased to 126!

Authority increased to 127!

Psionic skill increased to level one hundred fifty-four!

Mental Fortitude skill increased to level one hundred fifty-five!

Mysticism skill increased to level one hundred two!

I finally reached the most important part of my speech – the political reforms intended to reduce pent-up tension in the structure of the magocratic world and provide for the further progress and blossoming of all humanity. I told them about the planned two-chamber parliamentary system, for which we would hold elections this year, and where the most prominent and popular representatives of all sixteen Directories would from now on write the laws the planet was to live by.

I told them the Council of Mage Rulers was being curtailed down to eighty members, and that all candidates for the new council would have to be personally confirmed by me. I gave the mage dynasties forty-eight hours to hand over their nominations, after which it would be too late. I said that sixteen candidates for the Council of Mage Rulers I had already confirmed – and that included seven representatives of the influential La-Varrez family political block, which was first to support me and had been a great help getting the new laws agreed upon, while nine of the representatives came from the political block of La-Fin Family vassals. I considered that justified because, although the La-Fin dynasty's authority may have taken a tumble after the death of Archmage Thumor-Anhu La-Fin, it was now not only back to where it was, it had soared higher than ever before.

Finally, I told them about the continuing historical tradition of having three corulers, the most powerful mages of modern times, who would have the authority to exercise control over both parliament and the council of mages. I named myself one of the corulers, which was taken as self-evident and none in the audience opposed. For the second coruler, I announced that the La-Varrez family of Mage Rulers could name a member of their own dynasty. And the seat of the third Coruler of Humanity I announced was still vacant. I said I had offered it to the La-Shin Dynasty, which was so influential and ancient. But over the long days of negotiations, I had yet to receive anything like a concise answer from the new dynasty leader who had come to replace the great Archmage Henri-Huvi La-Shin, nor had I received any help from the La-Shin family when discussing the new laws. And so the La-Shin dynasty had missed its historic chance and would now be reduced to the privileges of a common magical family, on equal footing with all the others, who were also more talkative and on the ball.

Authority increased to 128!

The last part of my speech concerned plans for the future. Our planet's protection guarantee was drawing near to the end, and the coming of an army of invaders had already become an inevitability. But I told them not to give in to panic and work on our defenses with tripled efforts. Earth needed a mighty space fleet, a planetary shield and a large number of anti-space artillery batteries. We also needed a capable, large, and well-equipped army. All that was already under construction in the Relict Faction and other allied factions, but we would need the support of every citizen to be able to provide a safe future for both our current people and their descendants. Furthermore, I assured them we were not alone in space and Earth's influence was growing. We would surely find allies and I promised to take on that task myself.

Fame increased to 128.

Authority increased to 129!

Mysticism skill increased to level one hundred three!

You have reached level one hundred twenty-three!

You have received three skill points (total points accumulated: nine).

And on that note, I finished my grand speech. The second the broadcast was over I fell down on the floor utterly exhausted. Despite all my preparations and the bonuses I got from visiting the

Temple of the Dawn of Life, I still didn't have enough mana. My Endurance Points were also running low. Next to me on the floor, Gerd T'yu-Pan cautiously set the body of the unconscious Gerd Soia-Tan La-Varrez. The kid passed out somewhere around the last third of my speech, though until that point she had been faithfully sharing power and mana with me. And then at the very end, she was just about to collapse, but the Shocktroop standing next to her and aware of what might happen held her upright, so the audience most likely had not noticed.

Yes, it was tough. But I pulled it off!

Chapter Twenty-Eight

First Reaction to the Changes

AFTER THE BIG PERFORMANCE I slept a whole fifteen hours, restoring my depleted forces, emotions and nerves. And right after I woke up, hungry as a bear, I hurried into the common room where my crew just so happened to be eating lunch. I gave a nod to Gerd Ruwana Loki the Horde observer sitting alongside the rest but, despite her desire to talk to me, I took a seat at a different table where my First Mate Gerd Uline Tar was holding a conversation with senior Engineer Orun Va-Mart and a newly minted Gerd, level one hundred fifteen Heavy Robot Operator Vasha Tushihh.

Oh! The Geckho's part in the broadcast to the whole magocratic world had worked as intended! I congratulated my long-standing comrade on the promotion to Gerd and didn't turn down a drink to the occasion. The firewater they poured me was very strong. It was the only kind of alcohol the Geckho consumed, having scorn for anything light such as wine or low-alcohol Miyelonian cocktails. It even made me wince and, following Uline and Vasha's example, I set my cup upside down on the table.

"How is your brother, jealous?" I inquired, to which I was answered that Basha Tushihh was sincerely happy for his twin brother and the first to congratulate him. In fact, the entire Clan Tushihh-Layneh was celebrating the event jubilantly.

But the numerous family unit weren't the only ones to notice my beefy companion.

"I was told that a collection of five silver coins had been produced in the Seventh Directory of Earth in a run of ten million: Kung Gnat La-Fin and his companions – four Gerds of three spacefaring races. And I'm on one of the coins!" the huge furry Geckho's joy was boundless. "I asked T'yu-Pan to get me one as a souvenir. Our boarding team commander promised they would have a newcomer take one into the game that bends reality and bring it to me. I plan to give it to my mother. She's gonna love it!"

"Captain, that is not all the news from the magocratic world," my unexpectedly chatty business partner suddenly interrupted Vasha Tushihh. "My husband Gerd Kosta Dykhsh wrote that the anti-mage uprising has finally died down. Just one implacable group refused to lay down their weapons. Made up of the biggest lowlives, murderers and terrorists to join the rebellion, they're calling themselves 'Death Row.' Everyone else surrendered inside the grace period and was given amnesty."

The uprising had been suppressed? Amazing! This was not the time to fight a civil war. Now the people needed to put all their effort into preparing to turn back an alien invasion.

"The head of the La-Shin family has been overthrown as well," Uline continued to share news. "Relatives of the doddering dynasty leader brought him down and appointed in his stead another more talkative and youthful family member. The La-Varrez dynasty throne is also on highly shaky ground – the young and inexperienced Gerd Sap-Po La-Varrez is in trouble. He has already been removed as faction leader in the game and his being held in a remote castle on an island isolated from the rest of the world. It's rumored the family doesn't want such an inexperienced politician and weak mage to serve as one of the three corulers of humanity. They believe their house leader will too pitiful compared to the other two corulers and do nothing but bring shame on the ancient dynasty. And so the La-Varrez family would like to propose a different candidate than Sap-Po."

"Who?" I inquired, though I had of course already guessed.

"Gerd Soia-Tan La-Varrez. Her Fame and Authority are the highest in the family. But due to her young age, she cannot yet occupy high government posts, so her grandmother is willing to act as regent until her granddaughter comes of age at twenty-one."

I started to smile. The clever old bat! I remembered her from our personal meeting when she talked back to the young faction head shamelessly and even gave Sap-Po a big slap. Alright then, I was not against such an experienced and influential politician being made temporary coruler. All the better, given I wanted to keep Soia-Tan in my crew. And by the way... A plan suddenly formed in my mind. I would have to take little Soia-Tan out of the Relict Faction quickly and put her back with her family. According to the game's algorithms, that would instantly bring my little helper up to Leng status, because she was now the most authoritative member of the La-Varrez Faction. Eight additional stat points (and really probably more because of the "bonus" points the Psionic Mage would almost certainly get when investing in Intelligence, which for her was already far beyond twenty) would allow the little sorceress to grow stronger in very short order. I smiled at the thought. No matter how mighty and ghastly her future opponent Florianna royl Unatari may be, an encounter with a Leng would be a tough challenge.

"Is there anyone else in our crew that can go up in status any time soon?" I asked Gerd Uline Tar, who was now also doing HR duty on the frigate.

My business partner responded without even a second of thought, clearly having already considered this and holding all relevant information in her mind.

"First and foremost, our main Starship Pilot Dmitry Zheltov. He's quite a recognizable player and very close to achieving Gerd status. He's literally just a Fame point or two away. Then our Navigator Ayukh. I have to admit I've been surprised the well-established Navigator had yet to become high-profile after his many years of service in the trade fleet. The only reason I can see is his modesty. Ayukh never goes out for starring roles, always staying behind the scenes. The third would be Destroying Angel. I recently had a deep conversation with her and, among other things, we touched on this topic. Destroying Angel is quite well-known in her native country of Germany, plus she is a very attractive woman. She has even received offers from several men's magazines to do photo shoots. I told her next time to agree so she can bring up her Fame."

Okay then. Not bad at all. The concentration of high-profile players in Team Gnat was now quite high. And soon our crew would start to stand out on a galaxy-wide scale, which would bring up the whole team's Fame. The only thing was that, unfortunately, today's news was not only positive.

"Captain, the malfunctioning equipment we discovered before is getting more serious. Our right power unit has practically given out," Orun Va-Mart the Engineer informed me. "It requires serious repair, and ideally complete replacement. In order to avoid an accident, I have completely turned off the malfunctioning power unit, which has significantly hampered our speed, maneuverability, and made us have to set half the cannons to inactive because they could overload the power grid."

"We can't get it repaired on warranty, because the twinbody's power units are being used in an unapproved configuration as far as the production company is concerned. Really, no repair company that values its reputation would accept the job either. So either we have to get it repaired by an unauthorized service center with no warranty or spend six million crystals to buy a new one," the Trader rattled off the financial scale of our misfortune. "Furthermore, the power unit model we are using is quite rare. It isn't sold everywhere. So we have a limited choice of locations."

I familiarized myself with the list of planets and space stations where we could find ourselves a replacement. One such place caught my eye. Kukun-Dra, the Cyanid homeworld. I had in fact promised to visit it to apologize for the incident with their ambassador on Serpea. Seemingly, the next destination in our space odyssey had been found.

Uline Tar took my words into account and promised to purchase necessary equipment on Kukun-Dra.

"There's one more piece of bad news, Captain. Or rather more like two pieces. As I'm sure you're already aware, Vasily Filippov has left our team, opting to part ways right here on Un-Tau."

Only after that did I notice the Bard's absence. A belated scan showed that Colonel Filippov was not on the ship at all. No, of course I knew the Bard had received an intriguing offer from the Meleyephatian Horde. But to just leave like that, without even talking to his captain? By the looks of things, the colonel must have been offended by something I said or did, though I didn't know what it could have been.

"We need to replace our missing team

member stat! Another Bard or some other class that can hand out bonuses in battle. Someone with experience and at least level one hundred. If possible with Gerd or higher status. Uline, put out a job offer. And announce another vacancy along with it. No urgency, but it would be nice to fill this position, too. We need a player that can provide other team members defense against psionic magic. Race and game class are not important, they just need to be able to do the job. And don't beat around the bush. What's the second piece of bad news?"

Uline looked away and grumbled unhappily, even baring her teeth. She must have found the information worrying or even dangerous.

"The Commander of the Third Strike Fleet is unhappy with you for taking matters into your own hands on Un-Tau. Kung Waid Shishish did not permit the Humans of Earth to exit the war with the Meleyephatian Horde, so he found your actions detrimental to his Authority. You'll have to have a chat with him and somehow mollify him or risk an encounter with this famously quick temper. Otherwise the Army of Earth will not be allowed to leave their rallying point at the Geckho Base and the Tush-Laymeh transport ships sent to pick them up won't be allowed to land."

So there it is... Alright then. I already suspected such complications were possible and was long since prepared for a tough conversation with the Third Strike Fleet Commander. I also had some things to tell Kung Waid Shishish, who had abandoned fifty thousand Humans of my planet to a slaughter without the least bit of support or hope of rescue. And so I promised Uline Tar I would have a talk with the official overlord of Earth and try to smooth over the present misunderstanding.

I did not put off the difficult conversation. Right after lunch, I headed straight into the Pyramid Contact Hall. This time I was put through to the Third Strike Fleet Commander posthaste. As I thought, the huge Geckho was visibly annoyed and threw himself on me with reproach the moment I came on screen. He said that the suzerains control their vassal armies during large joint operations, while the subordinate races are not authorized to make their own independent decisions. Especially such important ones as removing troops from combat positions and exiting the war while allies kept up the fight. He said that my unauthorized decision might have damaged his Authority, and it was only down to my good fortune that it did not, otherwise his fury would have been terrible indeed.

I kept up an iron calm and exaggeratedly respectful attitude toward my superior, did not interrupt the influential Geckho and just sat emotionless while he poured out his complaints. I had already guessed that the quick-tempered Kung had for some reason decided to rein in his harsh principles this time. For some reason he needed me, and the commander did not want to smear me fully into the mud or dole out severe punishments. But Kung Waid Shishish didn't pass up the chance to let out his unhappiness, and spent a long time droning on about the ungrateful Humans and their Kung who had no regard for his sovereign race. Oh well. His stream of cursing didn't affect me all that much. Let him blow of some steam and calm down. Then we could get to business.

"You must have had very good reasons to do something as bold as removing your troops from Un-Tau. Explain yourself, Human!"

Ah, finally the Geckho's monologue came to an end and I was given the chance to justify myself. In fact, I was even surprised my Authority never even once took a dive during the Commander's whole fairly lengthy speech. So I must not have committed any truly serious violations. I suspected the Third Strike Fleet Commander was in fact even happy to have the crisis on Un-Tau over with. Because he had no way of rescuing the Army of Earth from its distressing position, but he also didn't want to acknowledge his own inadequacy. And now he'd put the fear of God into his subject to keep up appearances, and the Commander of the Third Strike Fleet wanted to hear any more or less plausible justification so we could put this whole unpleasant story behind us.

"Of course, my Kung. I did have good reasons to act the way I did. Above all, I was concerned about your Authority because the situation on Un-Tau was becoming more and more critical, while the Third Strike Fleet suffering defeat in such an important landing operation could have left a negative record in your glorious biography. I waited until the last moment to intervene, assuming things were progressing in full accordance with your plan and the Third Strike Fleet would show up unexpectedly when the Meleyephatians believed a win was already in hand and would thus have their guard down. But when my commanders informed me that the army had essentially ceased to exist, and the last of their troops wouldn't hold out longer than an ummi, I decided to show up on the battlefield. Before that, I tried to honestly inform my Kung, but you were very tied up with another important battle, so I couldn't get through."

I didn't tell the highly powerful Geckho off for abandoning my Humans to a slaughter and stuck to milder formulations. With an important look, he nodded. Yes, that was exactly what happened. He was "very busy." That was why he hadn't talked with me before. That explanation was completely satisfactory.

"My frigate's arrival came as a surprise to the Meleyephatian flotilla. I faced the Meleyephatian commander with the threat of unacceptable losses, starting to destroy starships and defensive structures on Un-Tau. And Leng Ovaz Ussh was forced to sue for peace, promising to remove his flotilla's ships from the Geckho warfront and send them to fight our common enemy. Furthermore, the Humans were allowed to take trophies and ships, remove their troops, and given access to Un-Tau at any time, which bears witness to the Army of Earth's military victory, as well as that of the Third Strike Fleet as a whole. My Kung may also pay a personal visit to the under-ice shrine, should he so desire."

That wasn't exactly accurate. I hadn't made any such arrangement with Leng Ovaz Ussh, however it sounded nice as a clear confirmation of our victory. Furthermore, I was absolutely sure that the commander was utterly ambivalent toward Meleyephatian shrines and would not go flying off to check.

"And finally, the most important part. Not long ago, my planet Earth was granted the official right to attack Poko-Poko space station, something of a *casus belli*, an official cause for war. It would be stupid to miss this historic chance. Poko-Poko is a large trading hub and important logistics center located in the sector of space entrusted to your fleet. That station coming under Human control, and thus Geckho control as our suzerains would be an important step toward strengthening the Geckho race's positions in a region of space where they are underrepresented. Furthermore, of the seven co-owners of Poko-Poko, a whole four are Meleyephatians by race, which can be played up in the news as yet another victory for the Geckho and my Kung. And so that was precisely why I removed the Army of Earth and am preparing to capture the space station with the forces now under my command, without any need for the Geckho Third Strike Fleet's ships. But if my Kung is willing to provide support in the form of ships and wishes to share in the military glory, I would only be glad to have such aid from my suzerains."

"Uhh..." for two thirds of my speech, Kung Waid Shishish was just silent, continuing to play his predetermined role, but at the very end I caught him by surprise. "The fact that the Meleyephatians are taking several hundred combat starships away from the front is obviously good news. As a representative of the suzerains, I hereby confirm the understandings reached on Un-Tau and will inform Krong Daveyesh-Pir about this victory of the Geckho race, minor as it may be. Furthermore, the Meleyephatian Horde has removed its ships from Serpea, which has overall improved the situation on the front and returned control over a vassal system to my race. But as for providing ships for an attack on Poko-Poko, I am not yet ready to give a response. I need to think it over. But it is definitely an interesting proposition. Go ahead!"

Nice, he was no longer upset with me, and the Kung no longer had any formal complaints. So now I might find out the reason the fleet commander who was normally so quick to punish was acting agreeable. And an answer did in fact follow.

"I have been informed that you are planning a long voyage for a diplomatic mission. Is that true?"

I tried not to reveal my surprise at how well informed the Geckho was. Alright then, I guess our suzerains had a decent intelligence service.

"Yes, my Kung. And although the mission was given by the leader of the Meleyephatian Horde Krong Laa Ush-Vayzzz, it is also in the Geckho race's interest that I succeed. You need allies in the war against the Composite, who can travel faster than the speed of light and are relentlessly capturing one star system after the next. A force that was capable of stopping the Meleyephatian Horde's expansion would be very nice to have on our side of the barricade. According to Horde intelligence, Emperor Georg the First has a fleet numbering over twenty thousand combat starships..."

Kung Waid Shishish couldn't hide his astonishment and even cleared his throat.

"How much now?!"

I repeated.

"Twenty thousand starships. Among them are almost three hundred battleships. A number of superheavy-class ships have also been spotted."

"Then it's no surprise this Empire was able to stop the Horde's advance. But after hearing those numbers, I'm having serious doubts. Do the Geckho even want such a force in our part of the galaxy? Even if the Empire's ships behave peaceably, they will break the existing system of counterweights, political alliances and basically just upset a delicate balance! The Union of Miyelonian Prides has eight thousand combat ships between four fleets. The Geckho have a bit more, but still not enough to measure our fleet in the tens of thousands. And here comes the empire with twenty thousand ships! And three hundred battleships – only the Trillians can boast of such numbers in their Royal Fleet, or the Horde in its First Fleet."

"When the Composite began their invasion, they had half a million starships and, in all the battles so far, we'd be lucky if they lost even two or three percent of that. In the process, they ground three Meleyephatian Horde fleets to dust. So the great races need such powerful allies. But even if we cannot secure the Empire's support in that war, a peace treaty would allow the Horde to send an additional thousand starships away from their external border to join in the war against the Composite. And although the Horde is at war with the Geckho, the Meleyephatians are currently acting as defense for us on the leading edge of the war with a foreign enemy."

"That is true, Kung Gnat," the normally hot-headed Kung Waid Shishish was surprisingly amenable today. "Okay then, I wish you success in your diplomatic mission. Discussion adjourned!"

Chapter Twenty-Nine

New Team Member

I WAS NOT ABLE to dodge a conversation with Gerd Ruwana Loki. This time the Horde observer was steadfastly awaiting my return from the mobile laboratory in the frigate's shuttle bay. Alright, I couldn't run away from her any longer. At this point it would start seeming silly for a reputable and esteemed Free Captain. I walked up and asked my first question:

"Explain how you got on the frigate. When my frigate was stationed on the comet, you were not yet with us."

"I used the same shuttle that took Colonel Filippov away," the cleanshaven Psychologist smiled cunningly. "It seemed to me that otherwise you might 'forget' me on Un-Tau."

"No, I would not have. I stand by my promises. But it looks like a member of my team will be getting their ass kicked today for a flagrant violation of security protocols."

Without their captain, my officers had made an extremely dangerous decision that could lead to catastrophic consequences – they had revealed the position of the mobile laboratory, first by sending the shuttle down to Un-Tau, then by ferrying the Horde observer back to our frigate. And with the frigate beneath the laboratory's distortion field, we had given ample information to a potential opponent including coordinates, linear dimensions, mass, the peculiarities of its camouflage system and other characteristics of the ancient race's tech. And I was not planning to turn a blind eye to such a violation, intending to harshly punish all involved to avoid something similar happening again in the future.

"Change coordinates! Transport to a random point in this star system!" I sent a mental order to the laboratory's artificial intelligence, and a second later we were brought nearer the star. Very near. It seemed to me we were practically in its corona.

And although the program assured me there was no danger, and the defensive screen would keep the laboratory safe from heat and other forms of radiation, the light was so bright and the load on the gravity compensators so extreme that I nevertheless gave an order to change position again. We were taken to somewhere on the edge of the star system.

Machine Control skill increased to level one hundred twenty-five!

"Paranoia mode engaged?" she chuckled, observing the jumps curiously through a porthole. "Are you also gonna have me searched for espionage devices?"

"I will if I consider it justified..." I muttered in

dismay, already scanning my ship and the Horde representative for any suspicious devices. Nope, all good. At the very least I didn't detect anything new.

"Don't you worry, Kung Gnat, you had nothing to fear. Meleyephatians keep their word and, although your ancient laboratory is of definite interest to the Horde, none of the captains of the seventy-second flotilla could even think to attack you and try to take your rightful property away."

Maybe so, but I was still burning in indignation. The Horde observer sensed that and tried to change the topic.

"I wanted to have a chat about officially joining the crew. It seems to me that you could use a good Psychologist on your team."

"Tell me even one good reason."

"Your team members are leaving," Gerd Ruwana Loki put down a finger on her right hand. It was by the way a well-manicured finger. "The Relict Technician just went into the real world and died there. The Bard left due to pent-up frustration and unhappiness with the state of affairs. In fact, he left without asking or informing the captain, giving you a clear indication of his attitude toward you. And before that, as far as I know, your girlfriend left as well, herself also a member of the *Tamara the Paladin*'s crew."

"Valeri got spooked by the Meleyephatian Horde trying to track her down and wanted to hide from the assassins sent after her and her sister. With the Relict it wasn't all so simple either. He was looking for my support and asked for help. Vasily Andreyevich also wouldn't have left if not for you.

He was just fine until your little chat."

The cleanshaven woman gave a happy smile, revealing a set of even white teeth.

"Just don't start accusing me of sabotage and subversion. Colonel Filippov would have left one way or another. Maybe it would have taken more time, but it was inevitable. You know what was bothering him? No? He was brought into the game as a counterweight to an experienced Strategist from the parallel world and he was planning to become at least as significant a figure. But General Ui-Taka is already a distinguished Leng. He personally led the Army of Earth in battle, earning the deepest respect and the love of its thousands of soldiers. But Vasily Andreyevich... all this time he's been playing his guitar, drinking vodka and entertaining the small team of a space adventurer. It's no surprise the experienced soldier eventually concluded he was capable of more and wasting his time. My conversations with him just moved the decision process along, nothing more."

I could sense that she was right. Yes, the colonel took a bit of rest, got a handle on his thoughts and was now raring to fight and prove his worth as an experienced strategist and commander. But Vasily Andreyevich could not in fact make a name for himself in the crew of a little frigate. And meanwhile, Gerd Ruwana turned on her tablet and showed me the screen.

"A woman has been spotted in the Gilvar Syndicate who facial recognition algorithms have assigned an eighty-seven percent chance of being your girlfriend Valeri. But it isn't her. They just look very alike. This Tailaxian girl is called Dinka-orr-Ayvas-orr-Hunay, Valeri's sister. She is currently first mate on the starship of a famous smuggler, Free Captain Astarta Avakari."

I looked at the Tailaxian's photograph. She really did look similar. The same face shape, the same nose and eyebrows, the same hair color and the very same huge "anime" eyes. But it was not my girlfriend Valeri-Urla.

"So your girlfriend's fears are utterly unfounded," Gerd Ruwana Loki lowered a second finger. "The Meleyephatian Horde knows perfectly well where Dinka can be found. Valeri herself has been detected on planet Shiharsa, the Geckho homeworld. And if the Horde were indeed planning to kill her sister, they would have done so long ago. My presence on the frigate will do nothing to jeopardize the Human you care so deeply for."

"Alright, go on," I returned the tablet. "Any more arguments?"

Gerd Ruwana Loki pointed out the porthole to a distant but still recognizable comet and lowered a third finger.

"You have visited the most important shrine of the Meleyephatian race. The place where all galaxies intersect. A place where players can grow stronger. But out of the whole crew, as far as I know, only four of you personally visited the ice shrine. The rest were either too lazy or frightened and basically found a hundred excuses not to shake up their comfortable lifestyle. But squandering such a unique chance would be just stupid! Sorry to be so frank. But you as captain couldn't find any reason to force your team to get up and drag their asses over to the ice temple. And after all, you could have. And mildly at that, with no pressure or orders, finding the exact right words for each person."

Damn... The Psychologist was right. They all could have stood to get stronger, not only the mages. Gerd Ayni brought up her Agility temporarily until her next death and got bonuses for a few skills. Imran brought up his Strength and temporarily improved his combat abilities. The other team members could also have brought up some stats or skills of their own. Perhaps temporarily, but still it would have been a plus.

"Alright then. You have prepared well for this conversation. Any other arguments?"

She smiled and put down two fingers at once.

"I would no longer be a *pink umot* among your fully fledged crewmembers. I would have more trust and could work many times more effectively. It would be good for you too, Captain Gnat. I have noticed for some reason you are avoiding the Psychologist. Either you're embarrassed or afraid. It's strange. After all, I don't bite. I can be useful and I'm willing to prove it."

What exactly a *pink umot* was, I did not know. It must have been something akin to the earth expression "black sheep." But as for the second remark, I responded.

"I am not afraid. I am just a fairly reserved man, and have a tough time sharing my thoughts with others. Furthermore, I have a few difficult memories there that are hard to get over. The last

Psychologist I opened up to died a terrible death."

When I saw her brows shoot up in surprise, I hurried to add.

"No, no. I was not responsible for her death. There was a biological attack on my former faction's datacenter. In the real world. Many people perished."

"That's frightening to hear. And strange. Earth is currently heralded as a very tranquil place. Unlike the Horde's star systems in the warzone with the Composite. That is of course not an argument in my favor, but I must admit I was planning with time to convince you to add me to the Relict Faction so I could change my exit point into the real world to make sure my body stays safe."

Strange as it may have been, I actually did consider that a strong argument. Even stronger than what she said before. For the first time the Horde observer was acting like a real person with her own interests and worries rather than some robot programmed to serve her Meleyephatian masters.

"And another thing. I know the language of the Meleyephatians – the only one more or less understood by the people of the far-away Empire. They have already shown as much. Yes, I know you have the experienced Translator Gerd Ayni Uri-Miayuu. But she is a Miyelonian by race and it might make the contact more trusting and productive if both sides are represented by Humans only. So I could be useful during the highly important negotiations that will largely define the course of the war with the Composite."

I fell silent, thinking over what was said. I'd rather not. In the end I still preferred my trusty Translator, who I had complete faith in, over a representative of a potentially hostile camp I was barely acquainted with. As if responding to my thoughts, Gerd Ruwana Loki added:

"I assure you, Captain Gnat, if there are any details in the preparation for the negotiations or during the talks themselves that you do not wish to reveal to the Meleyephatian Horde, I can conceal that information from my report. Before the end of my assignment, my loyalty to my captain will surpass my loyalty to the Horde."

"No need for that. I don't expect anything out of you that could place your value to your masters into doubt. Consider me convinced. Welcome to the team. Your pay will be equal to that of a high-profile player. Four thousand Geckho crystals per voyage. Combat missions will be paid separately. If you have any equipment or personal items you need, speak to Gerd Uline Tar. My business partner can provide whatever you desire."

Gerd Ruwana Loki's brows shot upward in surprise.

"It's a pleasure working with you, Captain Gnat. I must admit, the Meleyephatian Horde's conditions are a good deal less generous."

"Go have a talk with the crew. We're going back to Un-Tau so the rest of the crew can also visit the ice shrine. You could stand to visit the temple as well."

"I was on Comet Un-Tau half a tong ago. As a reward from the Horde for a job well done. I even got a vision from the Universe in the Cave of the Dawn of Life. But my bonuses went away after your Jarg 'accidentally' blew me up."

Gerd Ruwana Loki was watching my reaction closely, but I didn't allow any emotions to be reflected on my face. Let her think whatever she likes. The Horde observer had no evidence in either case. I gave a decently long pause and picked back up.

"And let me answer the question you are afraid or embarrassed to ask right now – why have we not yet flown to the highly important negotiations even though we have linked back up with the laboratory which can perform long-distance jumps, and every day of delay leads to more losses for the Horde and a worsening of the situation on the front against the Composite?"

Based on her reaction, I could tell right away I was one hundred percent correct. Before that, Gerd Ruwana Loki had promised not to rush me into the diplomatic mission, but the question was clearly swirling around in the Horde observer's head.

"The main reason: we will be checked and tested to see if we're strong enough to be taken seriously. My companion Gerd Soia-Tan La-Varrez will have to face a powerful psionic in battle. We know that from revelations we got in the ice temple on Un-Tau, as well as other sources. To fail this test would mean putting a big fat 'X' over the success of the diplomatic mission. But Gerd Soia-Tan La-Varrez is not yet ready and will die."

"If that is the only holdup, the Horde can

provide another Psionic Mage with much greater experience and power. We could even scrounge up a Human by race."

To that I responded that, even though she wasn't quite as experienced, it was much more important and valuable to me to have trusted friend than an experienced stranger.

"I have taken that into account, Captain Gnat, and will not rush your preparation. I am willing to train the girl again."

"Since your training began, Gerd Soia-Tan has grown significantly in level and skills, so now she will be able to get through your defenses. But in any case, thank you for offering to help. I'll think about it. But there are two other obstacles. First of all, my frigate needs repair and a new power unit. We cannot show up for the talks in some rust bucket that can barely hobble its way through space. Second, we first have to solve a hostage crisis in Poko-Poko. My Authority as Kung of Earth will suffer very badly if the Human hostages are killed and my Authority is the key defining factor in how other players view me. Including Emperor Georg the First. I cannot allow the highly important diplomatic mission to fall apart merely because I do not have the Authority to convince the Emperor to sign a peace treaty with the Meleyephatian Horde."

"I'm in complete agreement with you there, Captain. But I would like to remind you of an earlier offer to let you repair and modernize your ship at Meleyephatian Horde military facilities. Your frigate is of Meleyephatian origin, so the easiest place to find parts for it is in the Meleyephatian

Horde. It'll be cheaper, too. And you'll find experienced Technicians to help with the repair."

"No need. We have already purchased all the necessary hardware and are prepared to make repairs on our own. But first I need to intercept a crucial crewmember and get them back working for me..."

Chapter Thirty

Three Sisters

"**W**E'RE SORRY, Free Captain Kung Gnat, but you have been denied access to Ponty IV. This is a peaceful station, and you are listed as a wanted space criminal with a danger rating of three. Furthermore, the Gilvar Syndicate has declared you an undesirable element and placed a large bounty on your head. We value our good relationship with our neighbors and have taken note of their warning. The *Tamara the Paladin* will not be allowed to dock at the Ponty IV space station."

Aw hell! The last thing I was expecting was to get stabbed in the back in a star system belonging to the Geckho. Especially considering the fact the Gilvar Syndicate was part of the Meleyephatian Horde and in theory, Geckho should not have been the least bit concerned with their enemy's opinion. But there were clearly a few peculiarities at this station and behind-the-scenes agreements because the Ponty IV system didn't exactly look like it was on the front lines. There was no Geckho fleet, cargo and passengers were crossing the border with an enemy state freely. This was a strange kind of war to put it lightly...

But what should I do now? My friend Valeri's space liner had arrived forty minutes earlier, and I was intending to intercept her in the space port zone before she headed elsewhere and disappeared in the infinitude of space yet again. Furthermore, as far as I understood, Valeri-Urla was heading to the Gilvar Syndicate's systems, which I was banned from visiting after the scandalous bar fight in Serpea. The vengeful captain of the container ship had done everything in his power to ruin my life.

"Captain, see if they'll let you visit the spaceport without your combat frigate entering dock. The dispatchers should let the little shuttle through. They have no basis to refuse it. A blanket ban on visiting a space port requires a danger rating of level six or higher."

The advice came from the experienced Navigator Ayukh, and I did exactly that. After a minute's pause, we had our answer from the dispatchers. A shuttle from our frigate would be allowed to dock, but the visit would be limited to two ummi. Alright then, thanks for that. I took along only Gerd Uline Tar in the four-seat shuttle. Valeri-Urla had long known my business partner. They had spoken a lot and even become good friends, so the Geckho woman's presence was a definite plus.

Our shuttle was let through the defensive field without issue. But I was subjected to enhanced attention in the control zone. They made us walk through several metal-detector-like frames, then searched my inventory. My captain's crystal key was scanned, then that was additionally run through the database. They were clearly looking for a reason to quibble, but I had nothing forbidden on my person, and my documents were entirely in order. I was also acting calm and polite, not giving Ponty IV law enforcement even the slightest basis to find fault. I even complied with the customs worker that demanded I unlock my electronic wallet so he could check my balance, despite the fact that procedure went far outside the bounds of a standard search. The eight million crystals in my account convinced the agents that their "suspicious element" was quite well off and not planning to rob their peaceful visitors. With clear dismay on her mug, the furry Geckho lady returned my things and documents, but I had to surrender my Annihilator and Paralyzer to temporary storage.

I was also recommended not to remove the Null Ring. Otherwise everyone I met would be warned of my pirate status and the massive two-million crystal bounty on my head. Even law-abiding citizens could be seriously tempted by that kind of money. Which was to say nothing of the swashbucklers of every stripe that could also be found on this border station. I confirmed that I had taken that advice into account and only after that were the Trader and I allowed to enter the spaceport.

"I have never before come across such a wary and even prejudiced attitude," admitted my furry friend Uline, who was also subjected to all the aforementioned procedures. "And this isn't some random system in Horde space, this is a Geckho station!"

I agreed that it was a more than strange way of treating us. Of course the Trader and I took into account that Ponty IV was an important border transport hub and the majority of cargo entering the Gilvar Syndicate passed through here, which meant the station's fortunes depended on maintaining good relations with their neighbors. They understood that my open conflict with the by all appearances influential captain from the Gilvar Syndicate would make the local authorities apprehensive. But there was clearly something else my business partner and I had yet to comprehend.

The situation cleared up when Uline and I finished wandering a confusing labyrinth of corridors and studying the signs, emerging into the big arrivals hall where there were many waiting to greet their arriving friends and relatives from a massive liner from the Geckho capital system of Shiharsa. By the way, there were a surprising number of Humans there. No, of course there were also Geckho and Trillians, but I had never seen such a large concentration of Humans anywhere else in space. Though a few of the people caught me by surprise. There were plenty of individuals that had replaced half of their body parts with cybernetics. I saw another group of people who for some reason had wings on their backs. I didn't so much as suspect such people existed before.

"Look, Gnat!" Gerd Uline Tar pointed at a huge wall-sized panoramic armored window. Through it, I could see my frigate the *Tamara the Paladin* a quarter mile from the station not moving and out of the way of the main flow of starship traffic. "What a beautiful ship we have! And the Team Gnat emblem on its silvery hull looks nice and eye-catching, too."

I fully shared my business partner's enthusiasm. The ravening frigate, which was perfectly still as if about to jump looked menacing and even majestic. I supposed the *Tamara the Paladin* was now the very strongest ship in the entire Ponty star system. Furthermore, back on Un-Tau I ordered the emblem designed by my wife Gerd Minn-O La-Fin plastered on both of my twinbody's fuselages – a little flying gnat carrying a huge Annihilator. As for the other emblem I was entitled to use – the Trillian symbol for Execution – I decided against doing that to avoid being associated with the Hive of Tintara after my "mission of epic difficulty." I wanted to forget that whole "absolute evil" story as quickly as possible and certainly didn't want to be associated with the space mafia. But our very own emblem, which was now being viewed by the "wider public" for the first time, was attracting a lot of interest. Humans and members of other spacefaring races were staring wide-eyed and taking pictures of my ship, as well as taking selfies with it in the background.

But then my face went dark. Among the

many Humans awaiting passengers from the ship, I saw one I knew all too well. Denni Marko! A long-time companion of Valeri the Beast Master, who had travelled the galaxy with him for many years. He instigated the very barfight in Blue Glow on Serpea that got me into trouble. And if Denni was here, that meant the space container ship the *Udur Vayeh* would also be on Ponty IV. So there's the real reason they didn't want to let me onto the station! The local authorities were afraid of more turmoil and casualties.

By the way, Denni Marko was not alone. He had two members of the *Udur Vayeh*'s crew with him. My rival was also holding a big bouquet, which I did not like either. It was hard to call the glowing blue branches flowers though. They looked more like coral. But they were clearly intended as a gift for a woman. And I even knew which woman.

By the way, speaking of gifts... I myself had to admit that I not considered it earlier, though I should have. I turned to my furry companion.

"Uline, could you do me a big favor and buy something red and elegant for me to give Valeri? Money is no object. I just want her to like it."

But the desire to buy a present for the gorgeous Tailaxian wasn't my only motivation for sending the Geckho Trader away. I was itching for a serious talk with Denni, and now here he was at the exact wrong time. I didn't know for sure how my rival found out Valeri was coming here, but I certainly did not want him around. And I stepped decisively forward through the crowd.

They spotted me. One of Denni Marko's

companions tugged at his shoulder and said something to him quietly. My former crewmember turned and met eyes with me. He said something to his pals, and they both ran to leave the arrivals hall. By the looks of things, they were going for backup. Soon, this place would be crawling with my opponent's numerous "support group."

But it was not my style to patiently wait for an opponent's move and allow my enemies to prepare. My eyes glimmered with cold blue flame. Just then one of the Humans rushing for the exit – a strapping young lad with a cybernetic implant in place of his left eye – suddenly slowed his pace, then came to a complete halt. He turned around, walked over to the huge Geckho Guard on duty in the arrivals hall and loudly shouted right in his face, practically for all to hear:

"How I loathe your entire race! I can't wait for the Meleyephatian Horde to exterminate you and give the Ponty System to Humans from the Gilvar Syndicate!"

Psionic skill increased to level one hundred fifty-five!

His second companion ran up to stop his comrade from doing anything else stupid, but he also suddenly changed in the face and hawked a loogie right in the Geckho's face. The huge furry giant didn't even use the electroshock baton hanging on his belt. A couple quick pops to the ear and the two troublemakers were rolling on the floor, having lost consciousness along with their front teeth.

Not bad! Two potential enemies down for me.

They wouldn't be on their feet again any time soon, and now they couldn't run for help. Furthermore, the beefy Guard called his comrades via radio and a group of Geckho ran in with professional speed, cuffed the boisterous fellows and carried them to the local law enforcement station. Denni understood exactly what he'd seen. His face went pale and he locked eyes with me.

I then walked unhurriedly over to him and read my rival's thoughts with no shame whatsoever. Above all else, I wanted to know how Denni Marko knew Valeri was coming. If the Tailaxian herself told him out of a desire to reestablish contact then... I had no idea how to act. Fortunately, almost right away I realized that Valeri-Urla had nothing to do with this and didn't even suspect that her one-time admirer was waiting on Ponty IV. Denni though was very concerned about that and afraid of meeting his former friend even more than the menacing Kung walking his way.

Stopping two steps away from the pale Denni Marko, I spent some time staring at the man's silently gaping mouth, then said with a smirk.

"What's wrong? Cat got your tongue? Can't call for help on the radio? Don't worry, you'll be able to talk again in a few hours."

I had a lot more to say to my rival. I wanted to remind him that Miyelonian adolescent Tini had died. I was planning to send a message to the captain of the *Udur Vayeh*. But I stopped myself before saying anything else because the metal gates suddenly slid aside and a whole crowd of new arrivals piled out of the corridor. And one of the very first, wearing a lightweight dark blue spacesuit with the helmet open, was Valeri-Urla walking in a quick pace. Or now actually Gerd Valeri-Urla. I wasn't particularly surprised to see my acquaintance had advanced in status. With the intelligence services of several great spacefaring races searching for you, and even two mighty Krongs aware of your existence, your Fame figure would naturally go up a great deal.

The gorgeous Tailaxian's already huge eyes grew even larger when she saw me and Denni. I wondered who she'd talk to first. But Valeri-Urla just gave us both a curt nod, then stared into the distance behind us and, with a friendly wave and joyful cry, went running forward. I turned around.

I had somehow failed to notice this group of Humans before, but I was wrong to overlook them. Surrounded by four muscular Human bodyguards, there stood a large woman with short head of combed pure white hair wearing a heavy armored spacesuit with additional radiation shielding.

Leng Astarta Avakari. Human. Quarantine Planet Clique. Level-176 Trader.

The very smuggler leader Gerd Ruwana Loki told me about. And right at Astarta's side... if I hadn't been warned Valeri had a sister, I might have thought I was seeing double. Valeri embraced the short Tailaxian with dark hair and the huge eyes of a nocturnal creature. They were identical copies of one another!

Dinka-orr-Ayvas-orr-Hunay. Human. Quarantine Planet Clique. Level-111 Swindler.

As far as I knew, Swindlers had skills that allowed them to hide their character information. But Dinka wasn't the least bit ashamed of her class and in fact put her profession out there for all to see. Valeri was not bothered by her sister's questionable class either, both sisters sharing a warm embrace and sincerely glad to see one another.

The invisible panther Little Sister rubbed up against my leg to show her presence and friendly attitude, decided I'd had enough greeting and hurried off after her master. Denni Marko then shot another glance at me and looked back at the embracing ladies. I didn't even have to use magic. My rival realized all on his own that he was not going to get lucky here, spat on the ground in frustration and threw down his still ungifted bouquet then walked quickly out of the large hall. I didn't stop him.

Just then Gerd Uline Tar walked up with a six-foot-long object wrapped in dark film. She looked at the embracing Tailaxians, thrust the heavy pole into my hand and gave me a little push to the back.

"Go give it to her. Now's the time."

I obediently headed over to my girlfriend, on the way running my Scanning skill to try and figure out what I was carrying. It turned out to be made of stone and quite gnarled in shape. A petrified branch? A mage's staff? I had yet to come to any conclusion before Astarta's guards stood in my path. But that lasted just a brief second. After that, the foursome stepped aside and bowed low before me.

"Kung Gnat..." Leng Astarta Avakari looked curiously at her now mind-controlled bodyguards, then turned her gaze to me. "I've heard a lot about you. I even chipped in for the reward on your head with the other Free Captains from the Gilvar Syndicate. But why are you here? You want your ex-girlfriend back? Well I have an interesting and well-paid job for Valeri which is perfect for her as a Beast Master. Monsters from the Quarantine Planet are in very high demand in the galaxy, and they're a pretty good way to earn money. Plus I have a whole fleet of sixteen starships and intend to offer her the captain's seat on one of them. What could you possibly have to offer your runaway girlfriend?"

"Yeah, sister, come join us!" Dinka eagerly supported her leader. "An interesting life, a whole ocean of adventures and new acquaintances. With your ability to talk to animals, you'll be rich and famous in no time. You can visit old haunts on the Quarantine Planet, and you can even find a mate for Little Sister."

I didn't say anything out loud. Instead of that, I patched into Valeri's thoughts. As if expecting that, she readily picked up the mental conversation.

"And what is your response, Captain Gnat? Intrigue me, take me by surprise." I thought I could even hear open mockery in my girlfriend's emotions. "My childhood memories of Astarta are not the greatest. The smuggler is perfectly happy to engage in slave trading, and once snatched me up to sell.[7] *But still I must admit that overall Leng Astarta is a successful leader who is respected by her subordinates. I requested this meeting myself."*

Ahem... This wouldn't be easy if Valeri herself had already made a decision. I breathed a heavy sigh and fully opened my thoughts for reading.

"You know, I could try all kinds of reasoning, saying I need an experienced psionic I can trust to work with in a mental link. I could say my homeworld of Earth could provide a lot of work for a Beast Master as well. We have begun laying an underwater cable, but now the Naiads are protesting again. We need to reach another agreement. That the issues with the harpies, swamp creatures and forest spirits would also be best settled amicably, rather than with their complete extermination. I could say the Meleyephatian Horde's hunt for you and your sister has been called off and there is no longer any danger. I could even admit that I saw you at my side in the future on the ship of the Relict Hierarch, which means we will reach an agreement if not now then later. But instead, I'll say something different. I need you, Valeri!"

"Why?" her response was instantaneous. *"Yes, Captain Gnat, I am grateful to you for getting rid of my tracking devices, but I believe I have paid you back in full with loyal service, help in dangerous situations and... with my braid. I will also never return to Kasti-Utsh III though I won't hide that I enjoyed my time there with you. And on top of that...*

---

[7] These events take place in the novel *Quarantine Planet* by author Michael Atamanov.

How exciting it was! By the way, let me congratulate my good friend Ayni on the race change. You'll be good together. But that means you already have a favorite in addition to your official wife. So then what would you possibly need me for?"

The mental conversation was not going the way I wanted and was turning down a direction that was quite unfavorable for me. I realized too late that I was using the wrong arguments altogether if I wanted to make Valeri hesitate when her mind was essentially already made up. No gifts, compliments or promises would help me. No, here I had to take into account her peculiar nature, world view and system of values. Use her customary frame of reference, so to speak.

"Valeri, I have heard you say many times that you are a great huntress who knows no equal on the entire Quarantine Planet. Is poaching little beasts for your master Astarta really a path that is worthy of you as a great huntress with three marks on your cheek? Furthermore, you have said many times that you are free and proud, choose your own companions and that the right for a man to be with you must be earned. You were a strong psionic with unique abilities before, and now that you're a Gerd you've become even more powerful. Look around you," I pointed at all the other people in the hall. *"Is anyone here strong enough to have the right to be by your side? No, you are much more powerful than them. And you are also stronger than anyone you would come across on your home Quarantine Planet or in the Gilvar Syndicate. The only one who can defeat you is me!"*

Right then I was finally able to pluck the right string in Valeri's soul. The Beast Master's eyes glimmered with sorcerous fire, her lips spreading into a predatory smirk.

"Prove that is all idle chatter!" Valeri said out loud. "Gnat, I am significantly higher level and more skilled than you, as well as having more experience in magical showdowns. I was no worse than you before, and our fights always either ended in a tie or we were unable to finish. And when I reached Gerd rank, I became much more powerful. You will not outdo me now! But if you can, I will follow you. I promise!"

After that, the words stopped, and the attack started. A strong, concentrated and very professional attack. Valeri-Urla tried to paralyze me. I really did have a hard time instantly finding my footing and defending myself, especially in the first few seconds. Furthermore, I also wasted some force holding back Astarta's four bodyguards. Finally, I set the guards' minds free and concentrated on the main confrontation. Valeri knew me and my quirks all too well, but I understood my opponent's techniques, magical abilities and methods quite well also. I fought back the threat of paralysis, deflected a cunningly veiled attempt to stun me and we started going toe to toe in raw power. It was as if we were moving an invisible wall, each pushing it from our own side. I could of course have used Telekinesis to knock Valeri off her feet and break her concentration. I could have surprised the magess with Disorientation so she couldn't see me, but I considered that cheating. I had to prove with no dishonest maneuvers that I was more powerful as a mage. And I had something to surprise Valeri with.

Once upon a time, it really was a challenge to stand up to her but, over the last three weeks, my Gnat had levelled up from one hundred five to one hundred twenty-two, while my Psionic and Mental Fortitude skills had gone up from one hundred and ten and one hundred twenty to over one hundred fifty. My second specializations in combat skills, the intensive ten-day training program led by Fox the Morphian and the blessing I received from visiting the Un-Tau ice temple also played their part. I was gradually defeating her, relentlessly moving the invisible wall toward the Beast Master. But I didn't need to merely win. I needed to demonstrate total superiority. And then I switched out the Null Ring for the Precursor signet, bringing my Intelligence up by 3. Valeri-Urla herself, as far as I could see, was also using "magic jewelry," so that didn't violate the rules.

Fame increased to 130.

The large audience watching our magic duel gasped in concert when they saw my pirate status and the two-million-crystal bounty on my head. But I tried to abstract myself from the bothersome external factors and concentrate on what mattered most. A little bit more. Just a tiny bit... Victory was already nigh when Valeri-Urla asked Little Sister for help just like during our last duel on Kasti-Utsh III. She asked her to distract me and help her master. But the Shadow Panther was having too much fun licking the marble floor and again refused to intervene.

"Sister, you just spent a whole long voyage sharing your worries and doubts with me, saying you made a big mistake running away from the only man you've ever liked. And so I won't help you now. Wriggle your own way out of it. Or better yet admit defeat and fix your mistake. If you want my opinion, I'm not the only one that needs a strong mate. You do, too. Gnat, you can hear us, right?"

"Yeah, yeah," I greatly embarrassed my rival, at the same time delighting the clever and perceptive panther. *"Thank you, Little Sister. I owe you a bag of treats when you're back on my frigate. And I promise we'll find a strong and handsome mate to pair you with!"*

Mental Fortitude skill increased to level one hundred fifty-six!

But Valeri and her pet weren't the only ones who heard me. Someone else's thoughts also appeared in the "public chat." And it was also a woman, or rather a girl. Gerd Soia-Tan La-Varrez cut into the talk.

"Coruler Gnat La-Fin, what's happening? I can sense you're fighting. Do you need my support?"

"Don't you dare interfere! I thought you were supposed to be getting bedrest after your heart surgery!"

"And who is that?" Valeri-Urla snapped sharply, already down on one knee and bowing her head in defeat, but suddenly raising her eyes in surprise. "You find another magess to go around with you while I was gone?! And she's... a Leng?"

I could sense searing resentment and

jealousy in Valeri's words. So I hurried to explain. I pointed to the *Tamara the Paladin*, still perfectly visible through the panorama window and said my trainee and de facto adopted daughter had joined us. And that she was not supposed to be reading thoughts but recovering from surgery. Then later when she got her strength back, Leng Soia-Tan La-Varrez would be the third mage in our group and, as a trio, we would have the whole galaxy talking about us!

"A lot happened while I was gone..." Gerd Valeri-Urla stood up, though she was reeling and Dinka had to support her sister.

The level-133 Beast Master looked at me, her sister and the now visible panther. With a tender rub of her independent pet's pure white neck, she turned to the lead smuggler, who had been watching the proceedings closely.

"Apologies, Astarta, but Kung Gnat's offer was more persuasive. I'm going with him."

Leng Astarta Avakari said nothing, just flashed her hate-filled eyes at me and turned sharply to leave. The bodyguards hurried after her. Dinka-orr-Ayvas-orr-Hunay gave her sister one last hug, whispered something into her ear then also hurried off after her master.

And only after that did Valeri-Urla notice the long package I was still holding vertically with one end propped up on the floor. The pretty lady asked about the strange thing I had brought as a gift. I unpackaged it. Inside was an emerald green twisted cylinder, transparent and seemingly made of glass. On top of it was some kind of chalice like the kind used to hold essential oils.

"This..." I myself didn't know what I had in my hands, but tried to improvise, "is a decorative candle holder made of obsidian, a volcanic glass. It's a symbol of fertility and health. Young women generally place them in their bedrooms. You can put it in your bunk."

Mineralogy skill increased to level sixty-six!

"Actually this is a sculpture called 'Spiral of Life,' the work of famed Miyelonian artist Murrrash Whisker-Purr. He has an exhibition on Ponty IV right now. By the way, this thing was crazy expensive," Gerd Uline Tar cut in with a comment, but Valeri didn't seem to notice the Geckho woman's statement.

"A candle holder for my bedroom, you say... Put it in your bunk, Captain Gnat. It will give me another reason to drop by sometimes... to admire this work of art. Anyhow, Coruler Gnat La-Fin, no matter how you spin it you defeated me fair and square and, l according to the laws of the magocratic world, I am now your wayedda. For exactly one tong to the day. And after that we'll have to see..."

Chapter Thirty-One

Endless Ocean

"INSTEAD OF KUKUN-DRA, I would have called this planet Endless Ocean," Dmitry Zheltov said, looking down thoughtfully from a height of one hundred miles on the entirely water-covered world.

"Well, in Cyanid Kukun-Dra actually means 'big water,'" Gerd Ayni Uri-Miayuu the Translator chimed in helpfully, also on the captain's bridge just then.

I had invited the Miyelonian here because I thought I might need her help to communicate with the local authorities. Although the Cyanids were Geckho vassals, relatively few of them knew their suzerains' language or used it to communicate. The language of the Cyanids meanwhile – large transparent bubbles that lived on just one planet in the whole galaxy – was known by very few outside the Kukun-Dra system, and the human throat could definitely not reproduce their gurgling speech patterns. But the orange tailed Translator had told me today with pride that she had learned a full ninety-six languages, including that of the Cyanids.

From this altitude, there were no signs of intelligent life, though we had every indication we were currently above the Cyanid capital, a large megalopolis that was home to thirty million. We couldn't even detect any sources of heat, radiation or electromagnetic waves, tell-tale signs of any inhabited planet. And although we had requested landing permission twenty minutes before, we had not yet received a response. Furthermore, where were we supposed to touch down? I did not after all have a submarine, and space frigates were not at all adapted for water landings. Furthermore, there were storms and hurricanes raging down below, and landing in such weather conditions seemed like a very difficult and even risky proposition.

"Send another landing request," I ordered the Navigator. "Just this time let's have Gerd Ayni say everything in Cyanid."

The tailed Miyelonian took the microphone in her hands and gurgled into it, making sounds like flowing water or a boiling kettle for around a minute.

"Look, Captain!" the co-Pilot pointed at a hexagonal platform rising up out of the inky depths. With my good Perception, I could see it without even using the ship's powerful optics, and the instruments further showed that the platform was giving off radio signals at navigation frequency which would allow a landing even in poor visibility. "Looks like they heard us and are providing a landing site."

"Yes," the Translator confirmed. "We are

being told to land on the ocean platform and fasten our ship down so the hurricane raging over the spaceport doesn't blow us into the water."

"A damn 'cozy' spot," Dmitry Zheltov groaned, checking the weather condition map. "Almost right in the middle of the cyclone. But the eye of the hurricane is moving toward the landing site and it is five miles in diameter. Conditions there won't be quite so terrible. The zone of relative calm will be over the platform in twenty-seven minutes. Then we'll have a window of just twenty minutes before we get hit by a powerful typhoon, with wind speeds far in excess of two hundred miles per hour."

"Then don't waste time on idle chatter! Let's get down there!"

The pilot continued grumbling that landing in dense atmosphere on a large planet with just one functioning power unit was hard enough, but he had already commenced maneuvers, and the *Tamara the Paladin* began its descent to Kukun-Dra.

"Well holy crap! Power up defensive field," I demanded of the Starship Pilot a few minutes later when a bright bolt of lightning around two hundred fifty miles long broke free of the planet's atmosphere before our very eyes. I was scared to even imagine how powerful the electric discharge from that thing must have been. "Let's just hope something like that doesn't catch us in midair."

The ship started shaking, and soon Saint Elmo's Fire appeared on our wingtips, bearing witness to the high electromagnetic charge in the atmosphere. But it was all surprisingly smooth, evidence of the masterful abilities of our pilot and his partner. The *Tamara the Paladin* set down gracefully right on the middle of the hexagonal platform rocking in the waves, and the Engineers, Basha and Vasha, and all three Kirsans scurried out to fasten down the starship. As soon they finished the job, the glimmering dome of a forcefield came up over the platform and it started going under the water. A minute later, the force dome and our frigate were entirely beneath the waves. I looked at the external cameras with intrigue and a bit of worry, but it was all calm. No water was getting through.

"There's something I'm not getting," co-Pilot San-Doon Taki-Bu spoke up unconfidently. "Is there any water down there? Or are we going to the bottom of the ocean with no oxygen?"

"Don't worry, there should be breathable air in the spaceport," the orange Miyelonian reassured the co-Pilot. "Cyanids can spend a long time underwater with no discomfort and at very great depth. But historically, they originate from air pockets in subaquatic caves, so those are the conditions they replicate in all their cities. Bubble cities on the bottom of an endless ocean. Furthermore, Kukun-Dra is also inhabited by Geckho. There is even a Union of Miyelonian Prides embassy. They must need to breathe, right?"

That better be true... I must admit, I didn't much want to find myself on the sea floor with no way of leaving a small force dome.

"Depth one hundred fifty feet... Three hundred feet... A thousand feet..." Dmitry Zheltov rattled off when suddenly a brightly glowing advertising billboard came into the camera's frame adorned with an intricate geometric design of bubbles and dispersing waves.

"It says: 'We welcome all guests to the one hundred thirty-eighth galactic antigrav races,'" Gerd Ayni translated, and we all exchanged surprised glances. So what, do the Cyanids hold races underwater?

My Navigator quickly clacked his claws on the keyboard and read aloud that they hold a Challenge Cup regularly on Kukun-Dra, no less than five times per tong. And there any pilot can put their skills to the test against crews from the water world's largest corporations, and elite pilots in service of the royal family. There were three categories of race: solo in fast racing vehicles, duos, and big teams in large shuttles including lots of gunners to ward off the dangerous beasts that lived in the depths of the ocean. In all cases, the vehicles followed an underwater course marked by lights and winding fancifully between rock formations, at times rising to the very surface, and others plummeting to the floor and running through underwater caves. Seven laps, each approximately thirty miles long. The Challenge Cup bore the dramatic name "intergalactic subaquatic races," though almost all pilots that took part in it lived here on Kukun-Dra and were Cyanids by race. In any case, the Challenge Cup was the largest sporting event on the planet, and local interest in it was massive.

Just then, a message appeared on my helmet

display in Geckho.

"The ruler of the Cyanids Kung Bule XXIII extends an official greeting to the Kung of Earth and an invitation for the esteemed Human to watch the subaquatic antigrav races together with him in a VIP box at the capital city central stadium."

I had been invited to watch the underwater races? And really, why not? We were stuck on Kukun-Dra for around three days until my frigate's repair was complete and the Engineers confirmed that both power units were synchronized. Furthermore, I was already planning to visit the local ruler to work out a military and trade agreement between our two races. So this was a great excuse to talk with the Cyanid ruler in an informal setting with no complicated diplomatic protocols. I immediately sent a reply that I would graciously accept the ruler's invitation.

But then another message popped up, forcing me to think seriously.

"Will the Kung of Earth be fielding a team in the race? All Cyanids would be interested to see what the Humans are capable of."

When a highly placed Kung and ruler of their race asks a question like that, it's more of a veiled hint than anything. The ruler of the Cyanids Kung Bule the Twenty-Third was thirsting for a rare spectacle. And refusing the monarch's request would mean starting the negotiations off on a bad foot.

"Ayukh, send information about the Challenge Cup to my screen," I requested and read up on the conditions.

The vehicles used were standardized, but the teams were allowed to make any modifications to the antigravs other than adding thrusters using different physical principles. Weaponry was allowed to be installed but shooting other contestants or the audience was categorically forbidden. Other than that, they had complete liberty both creative and otherwise, and the rules did not forbid ramming or collisions. I considered it.

Sorry, but the light open-cockpit solo racing vehicles were right out. Cyanid pilots could breathe underwater, unlike Humans. And the problems didn't stop at air because space suits were nowhere near intended to withstand such colossal water pressure. And meanwhile, at one point, the track went down to a depth of five miles. For a human, that would spell instant death because any spacesuit would be crushed like a tin can under a tank tread. And loading down the light antigrav with a defensive shield generator and oxygen tanks would make it too heavy, putting my racer at a disadvantage from the get-go.

The large shuttles were probably not a great option either. Although they were protected by a force field, they were relatively slow moving and often attracted attention from sea monsters of all kinds. The track ran directly through dangerous underwater crevices in order to provoke the inhabitants of the sea floor to attack. That made the race quite a sight to behold – something of an underwater biathlon where the life of the whole crew depended on the skill of the gunfighters. I watched a couple shocking videos of gigantic toothy and many-armed monsters attacking shuttles during previous races and honestly admitted to myself that I did not have twenty gunfighters (and that was the minimum according to the rules), even though that was nowhere near a guarantee the monsters' attack would be held back.

The two-seat antigravs though carried a force field generator that could withstand the water pressure and were quick and nimble enough to dodge or escape undersea predators. That was probably the only option for us. By the time the *Tamara the Paladin*'s platform reached the underwater dome of the half-mile-deep spaceport, I had made up my mind.

"Dmitry and Ayukh, in thirty-seven hours... or rather in five ummi, you will be taking part in the Challenge Cup in the two-seat antigrav class. You will be defending our crew's honor and your performance will in many ways define the outcome of my negotiations with the Cyanids."

Both the Human and the Geckho were left speechless and sat there batting their lashes in perfect time, staring at their captain. I suspect only the game rule that they could under no circumstances dispute the decisions of a "high-status" player were keeping them both from making nasty comments about my mental faculties.

"But Captain..." Dmitry Zheltov opened his mouth to speak, but after a prod to the side from his partner, trailed off.

"Anyway..." I said with a clever chuckle, "if either of you chicken out, San-Doon Taki-Bu can take your place. Because I can just sense the co-

Pilot raring for a fight and thirsting to prove himself!"

Dmitry Zheltov and Ayukh exchanged glances, nodded at one another in silence and together announced that they were willing to represent our team in the underwater races.

"Great then! Gerd Uline Tar will purchase a vehicle for you right away. The repair bots and Orun Va-Mart will work on the racing antigrav, so you will be no worse off than the best teams. In fact, you'll probably have better chances, because Cyanids have a lot of mass underwater. They dry out in normal atmosphere, but under the sea their bodies absorb liquid, and each of the two teammates weigh a ton, or even a ton and a half. That means' you will have better maneuvering and speed. So train up, learn the vehicle and the track and onward to victory! I'm going to put a five-million crystal bet on you too, so don't let your captain down!"

All my affairs were wrapped up. The antigravs purchased for underwater racing had been delivered, my Engineers and repair bots rushed straight over like a pack of hungry dogs, each with their own ideas about how to modify it. We had also established coordination with the Army of Earth's troopers. General Leng Ui-Taka, who had lost an eye and right arm in the fighting on Un-Tau, then refused to heal by respawning, told me the first squadrons had already started loading into landing ships and would be arriving to Poko-Poko right on schedule. The mercenaries of the Ak-Viro Boyshey crew (meaning Honor and Freedom in Geckho, according to Gerd Uline Tar they were one of the Geckho race's top private military contractors) had already begun arriving to Poko-Poko in small groups and there were familiarizing themselves with the situation. I then gave the crew all necessary orders and decided to take advantage of the momentary lull to exit into the real world.

Dismissing the standard suggestion to check out my game session statistics, (why look at that when I already had all my figures and an idea of what to shoot for in my head) I opened my virt pod lid. Kasti-Utsh III here I come! With the exception of two short outings for just a minute at a time to reset the time-in-game counter, when had I last been in the real world for a long stretch? I couldn't even recall at first, but it was when Fourth Fleet Commander Kung Keetsie Myau and I threw a barn burner in my hotel suite. I had really been sitting around in the game for too long...

Ayni asked me to wait for her near my virt pod on Kasti-Utsh III, so I didn't go anywhere. Seven minutes later, a barefoot redheaded woman appeared in the corridor, her only clothes consisting of a short pair of shorts, too small for a human woman and thus unbuttoned in the front. It was a provocative and very erotic look.

"Uhh... is something the matter?" My attention toward her clothing did not escape my racially modified girlfriend.

"No, no. It's all very... pretty. Nice to look at. But ladies of my race do not typically go around topless."

"Well, it isn't comfortable of course. I'm a bit chilly with no fur," Ayni said with a shiver.

I went back into the virt pod room, opened a box containing changes of clothing and handed Ayni a warm long-sleeved turtleneck. The diminutive lady practically drowned in it. On her, my top went down to the knee, and she had to roll up the sleeves. Ayni removed her uncomfortable shorts without the slightest embarrassment and set them on the table. She kept on only her ID card, which she wore around her wrist on a chain. She took something else small from her pocket and hid it in a closed fist.

"Where to, captain? We could go check out a professional gladiator tournament and watch the Crystallid champions. Or would you rather go to a restaurant?"

But I didn't want any noisy activities, crowds or attention from those around me. I was tired of the last few days of tension and just wanted to take a break from the hustle and bustle with my pretty girlfriend. And so I suggested to Ayni that we spend a quiet evening together in my suite.

"You're reading my thoughts, not fair," she blushed in embarrassment. "As long as Valeri isn't on the station, that is exactly how I would prefer to spend my time as well."

"Valeri will not be returning to Kasti-Utsh III. She said her Little Sister doesn't do well in a world of plastic and metal. As for a real-world exit point, she chose Novosibirsk. There's a big forest next to the datacenter where she can take Shadow Panther out on walks. A Beast Master should feel right at home there."

"Good news," smiled the redhead. "Then what are we waiting for?"

I embraced my companion with one hand and the two of us headed into the hotel suite. On the way, I noticed the hallways were unusually desolate. There were usually "random" Miyelonians hanging around outside, always on high alert, large and lean.

"They took away your security detail. The First Pride left Kasti-Utsh III together with Kung Keetsie Myau."

I did not know that and had to admit it left me somewhat upset. The First Pride's troops always behaved delicately and didn't get in my way one bit. I had plenty of foes now, and an unguarded hotel room on a populous space station was no longer the safest refuge. And I was assured of that a few minutes later when the door of my deluxe hotel suite swung open. Two steps away from me, a glimmering hologram appeared in midair – a sparkling ball of blue and white somewhere around the size of a basketball. In Miyelonian, but without any emotion or particular vocal features to allow the speaker to be identified, the strange mirage said:

"In ten ummi, I will begin methodically killing hostages. You must quickly choose what is more important to you: a laboratory that holds mysteries you will never solve, or your status as Kung of your *planet, which you will be bound to lose when your reputation falls among your subjects. You know me, I don't like joking around."*

After that, the hologram disappeared and the wall lit up with sparks, melting away and becoming a small plastic device for playing recordings, not suitable for reading information.

Hmm. I know them? That specific part of the message drew my attention most of all. I considered which of my foes could have been behind the kidnapping. The pirate pride of the Bushy Shadow and their leader Big Abi, who had vanished after getting free? But the pirates had basically assured me they were not involved. Or my frigate's former Meleyephatian owner? He was first to come to mind – the experienced spy and saboteur had easily enough capabilities and influence to take the Humans hostage on Poko-Poko.

"Change of plans?" Ayni sighed sadly, also having seen the hologram. "Are we urgently evacuating somewhere else?"

But I was still in no hurry to make such an ill-considered decision. Instead, I took the remote and brought up security camera data on the big screen. In the last four days, there hadn't been any movement in the room. A day before a cleaner had come in, but the small plastic puck was already on the wall. The Miyelonian woman noticed it, but didn't do anything, figuring it was a component of the security system, or a quirk the guest wanted to be there. Meanwhile, all prior footage had been erased. The cautious rogue was trying hard not to reveal themselves.

So the device had been planted in my room five or even more days ago. But that meant the second executed hostage was who the unknown blackmailer was threatening to kill. The problem was I hadn't come to my hotel suite, so the message was not received in time, and I didn't react. Most likely the criminal believed I had left the hotel for good, especially given I had only rented the deluxe suite for one more day, which was not difficult to tell from the hotel's website. I had been planning to extend my booking at the luxurious suite, but now was no longer so sure that was the right decision. Still I decided to stick around and enjoy what I'd already paid for.

"No, we will stay. It is no more dangerous here than any other hotel on the space station. Plus it's much more comfortable and we have a great view out the window."

I walked up to the panorama window with a view of outer space, turned and fell silent midword upon discovering that my girlfriend had already taken off the turtleneck and was now using her teeth to clumsily tear open a condom wrapper. Getting off to a quick start... On the other hand, I had only two ummi to waste, so we did indeed have to get a move on!

Gerd Dmitry Zheltov and Gerd Ayukh were standing in front of me with their heads hanging low, expecting well-deserved reproach from their captain. Yes, they had failed to win. But they certainly held their own in the race. After a frankly weak start and finishing the first lap just thirty-eighth out of two hundred forty antigravs, my crew gradually brought up the tempo and was up in the top ten by lap three. Partially responsible for that change was a mass pile-up in front of them. Two antigravs also got eaten by predators.

By lap five, my guys were up in third and gradually catching up to the two leaders, while by lap seven they were in second, behind only the crew of King Bule the Twenty-Third. On the last turn in the track, my crew made a desperate and risky advance to try and take first, but accidentally collided with the frontrunner, sending both antigravs flying off the track and wasting a ton of time. That led to them finishing in just seventh, while the Cyanid ruler's team finished way back at eleven after hitting some underwater rocks and severely damaging their vehicle. I though had bet that my team would come in the top three prizewinners. Minus five million crystals...

Nevertheless, I was satisfied with my crewmembers' performance. It was entertaining and all they could talk about on the news were the ambitious newcomers throwing down the gauntlet to the acknowledged champions. Even the race's prizewinners drew less attention than Kung Gnat's team. Both players went up in Fame and even hit Gerd status, which was only natural and to be expected. The Cyanid ruler, who proved to be a big fan of competition and reacted emotionally to the race, was also happy that he'd gotten the show he was looking for and wasn't even that upset his team had failed to emerge victorious.

"If they hadn't taken such a risk and just sat back happy with second, I would have been very disappointed. And I even would have started looking for a more ambitious Navigator and Starship Pilot because I only want the best of the best for my team, the kind who would never be satisfied with second place. And as for the money... forget about it! Furthermore, Earth's Humanity has signed long-term trade contracts with the Cyanid race, so I'll come out ahead in the long run. So you did great! You have completely earned your new ranks and will now be even better at your jobs."

The longer I spoke, the more Dmitry and Ayukh raised their heads. By the end, they had started to smile.

"Captain, we were a bit underexperienced. We wasted too much time at the beginning, and it was hard to make it up. But if we get another crack at this race, we'll take the cup for sure!" the Starship Pilot promised.

"The next race is in eight months. Who knows what will be going on in space by then? But if circumstances permit, why not? As captain, I'm all for it."

"The Cyanid ruler Kung Bule the Twenty-Third really liked you," the Miyelonian Translator entered the conversation, having been present at my talks with the monarch. "It was in large part thanks to the positive impression you made that the Humans of Earth were able to ink a military alliance with the Cyanids. The subaquatic race will also be sending deep-water construction specialists to earth. So my captain and I are very proud of you! And I congratulate you both on the promotion to Gerd!"

I looked with intrigue at my tailed girlfriend. Yes, Gerd Ayni Uri-Miayuu had changed a bit since our last interaction on Kasti-Utsh III, which went better than great. She looked more self-confident or something. She used to be more hesitant to speak her mind. She also now had a totally different set of earrings in her ears – the endless constellation of rings and chains had been replaced by gold earrings inlaid with tiny rubies. The Miyelonians in the crew noticed right away, and my assistant was congratulated with quiet whispers that made Gerd Ayni very embarrassed. Then she gathered her courage and headed to Valeri's bunk. I was afraid of potential conflict, but the pair just peacefully discussed the present situation and parted ways the best of friends.

"We can celebrate your higher status later. But now both of you get back to work. The power units are linked, and the ship is ready for takeoff. The dispatchers promise good weather in half an ummi, so we'll be taking off from Kukun-Dra. We're going to check all our systems in space, then jump to the Poko-Poko system. There will be a certified shake-up out there and this time, as Kung of Earth, I don't plan on staying on the sidelines. I will lead the Army of Earth into battle myself!"

Chapter Thirty-Two

Assault on Poko-Poko

"**C**ODE WHITE-BLUE," sounded out on the channel, a signal I had long been expecting that came just in the nick of time because we had only four minutes before the landing ships would be arriving.

"White-blue" meant the Ak-Viro Boyshey mercenaries had broken into the dispatcher area and brought their work to a halt, blocking all stairs and elevators leading to administrative levels as well. But they had not been able to disable the internal defensive systems or external laser artillery. Oh well. We had considered this possibility.

"Gunners, fire!" I placed a marker using Targeting on the distant heavy laser turrets securing the entrance to dock two of Poko-Poko station.

The laser cannon tower vanished in a bright flash of light. The forcefield surrounding the space station couldn't defend against a strike from the quadrupolar destabilizer.

Targeting skill increased to level seventy-eight!

And as for the second, nearer tower, I didn't want to destroy it. If the assault went well, I could use this cannon in the future to defend what would become MY station. The *Tamara the Paladin*, under the ancient laboratory's invisibility field was very near the laser cannon tower, no more than two thousand feet away. So I tried to take control of the cannons. The system rated my chance of success as high – sixty-two percent, but the first two attempts ended in failure, burning up half of my mana for nothing.

"Valeri, Soia-Tan, help me out!"

The ladies joined in the attack with glee, pumping up my mana and sharing their power. The chance of success rocketed up to eighty-one percent. Following my mental order, the automatic system ceased to obey its set algorithms and "changed owner." The three heavy turrets turned in one second and opened fire on a group of station security corvettes, which were not expecting the nasty trick. My Gunners didn't sleep through it through, adding damage from the *Tamara the Paladin*'s five laser cannons. Then half a minute later, the three small defensive starships were no more. Our opponent hadn't managed to make any maneuvers. I suspected the corvette teams had yet to even take combat positions. Furthermore, I "helped" them along by taking out all enemy officers on the starships' bridges.

Targeting skill increased to level seventy-nine!

Electronics skill increased to level one hundred ten!

Psionic skill increased to level one hundred sixty-five!

Disorientation skill increased to level forty-three!

Disorientation skill increased to level forty-four!

Machine Control skill increased to level one hundred twenty-six!

Before the attack, I spent up my nine skill points on Psionic, and the effect of that investment was noticeable. Furthermore, the blessing from the Temple of the Dawn of Life was still in effect, and my effective Psionic level was somewhere around two hundred. I had never before felt like such a powerful mage, and with the support of the Psionic Mage and Beast Master linked to me, I could do the impossible, unaware of the limitations of my power. Even though the players were three miles away, I was totally unhindered in my ability to find and "switch them off," with my much higher Intelligence.

"Captain, group of starships on subscan!" co-Pilot San-Doon Taki-Bu informed me with anxiety in his voice while studying the ship's locator data. "They're approaching fast!"

"Three big cargo ships, a light cruiser and twenty frigates?" I asked hopefully.

"Yes, Captain. And some interceptors."

"They're with us. The Army of Earth and its escort, provided by Kung Waid Shishish."

The Commander of the Third Geckho Strike Fleet decided to come help me capture Poko-Poko so he could share in the military glory of course and bring up his Authority. But it seemed to me that Kung Waid Shishish also wanted to assuage his guilt for abandoning the Human army to the hands of fate on Un-Tau.

To accompany the three large cargo-cum-landing ships, and maintain superiority in near space, Kung Waid Shishish had sent forty starships to take part in the operation: a light cruiser, twenty-two frigates and seventeen interceptors. Not all that many if the going really got tough. But it was plenty of forces to make the Free Captains currently located on Poko-Poko think thrice before joining in.

The Poko-Poko garrison then was made up of thirteen thousand troops. Mercenaries and professional soldiers that lived on Poko-Poko. A very serious force. But the defenders were taken by surprise. Furthermore, some of the players were in the real world. Plus cutting off the barracks and residential areas on the station from the dock zone and administrative floors was the first thing the Ak-Viro Boyshey mercenaries had done, disabling the elevators, severing power cables and blocking all doors.

"Kung Gnat, we're in position!" General Ui-Taka came over the comms channel, and I greeted my ally.

"Commence landing operation! The cannons by dock one are under our control. The forcefield will let you through."

The cargo ships got up as close as possible to the station, just three to five miles away, then the giants started rotating unhurriedly to close the gap and dock. The large starships couldn't properly dock at the space station, but special tunnels had been made for cargo ships to make deliveries and they led deep into the station. That was how the landing troops were planning to get inside. Furthermore, the many shuttles and landing modules were already undocking from the cargo ships *en masse* so they could flood the docks and occupy the most important station zones quickly.

"Friends, forward! Landing troops, best of luck! Combat ships, destroy the two laser cannons on the other side of Poko-Poko and keep watch over both dock exits. I'm really counting on you. No starships can be allowed to leave the station!"

Hundreds of voices roared out in concert on the channel. The troops were overflowing with enthusiasm and raring for a fight. Alright then, part one of the plan had gone off without a hitch. The enemy is disoriented. Their turrets have been neutralized and are not blocking the landing party. The transporters have docked, accordion bridges are connecting them to the openings of the dispatchers' cargo gates, and the Army of Earth are flooding into the station. I thought this time my crew also needed to be on the front lines of the attack and conducting the capture of the docks.

"Gerd Zheltov, forward! Maximum speed, every second counts! Steer the frigate inside the station manually! Show us what you and Gerd Ayukh learned from the underwater race! Take any unoccupied hangar. Gerd T'yu-Pan, boarding team on high alert!"

By the end of the first hour of the assault, the Army of Earth controlled half of Poko-Poko station. We took the docks, dispatcher, administrative and technical floors and entire spaceport zone in one fell swoop. It was very helpful that I declared right away over the station's loudspeaker that all Free Captains and their crews currently on Poko-Poko were at no risk of harm and, after the end of the operation, could leave the station unimpeded even if they were wanted elsewhere in the galaxy. They could also stay and continue their business after establishing it legally and paying taxes to the new owners of the station.

We found just two hundred and four starships of all sorts of classes and designs docked at Poko-Poko station, one hundred sixty of which belonged to Free Captains. Not all of them of course were pirates and wanted criminals, but there were plenty of intrepid cutthroats among them. After addressing the Free Captains, I got a few game messages about successful Fame or Authority checks. Kung Gnat the Human was known to many, and the strength of the army I brought with me was plain to see, as were the forty combat starships maintaining our near-space superiority. And so all the Poko-Poko owners' calls promising generous rewards for whichever Free Captains would stand and defend the station yielded nothing. Considering the balance of forces, good equipment and preparation of the Army of Earth's troops, all four thousand potential enemies opted to sit this one out rather than stand in the way of a government overthrow. That made our main mission much easier to complete.

By the end of the third hour, the Army of Earth had taken control of seven of the station's eleven residential zones, after which somewhere around a third of the Poko-Poko army opted to surrender. It was mainly Miyelonian squads laying down their weapons, which they did in coordination, as if commanded from outside. Most likely, that was exactly the case and the Union of Miyelonian Prides had given that order. There were no truly "independent" stations in outer space, and even known pirate bases such as Medu-Ro IV had some kind of "patron" in the form of one of the great spacefaring races. Here on Poko-Poko, the local corulers transferred a portion of their revenue to the Meleyephatian Horde and the Miyelonians, and the great races turned a blind eye to all the mayhem being wrought here.

But the situation changed with the taking of the Human hostages and my decisive actions. No one wanted to expose themselves as coconspirator to pirates and criminals. The Horde didn't intervene either because it had bigger concerns. The Union of Miyelonian Prides had also staked out a position. It would not stop me and would allow me total freedom. The Geckho meanwhile sent ships to help. The Trillians? Their royal dynasty was grateful to me for warning of the possible insurrection and, as far as I had heard from the news, was currently engaged in negotiations with supporters of Prince Hugo trying to solve the matter peacefully and stop a fully-fledged civil war from taking root. Overall, the rulers of Poko-Poko couldn't count on help from outside, and that completely untied our hands.

The remaining station defenders we managed to split up into three large units of fifteen hundred or two thousand troopers each, trapped in different ends of the station. They didn't want to surrender and were offering fierce resistance. The station's corridors were teeming with red-hot firefights. Human assault squads were advancing with heavy losses, clearing room after room and floor after floor.

I didn't stay on the sidelines either, much like Team Gnat as a whole. We were serving as a skeleton key to open defenses at the hardest sections. My tank group went down straight fire-swept sections of hallway, their excellent armor and linked shields allowing the *Tamara the Paladin*'s troopers to survive where many other squadrons had fallen before and clearing the way for other assault troops. The best laser rifles, heavy infantry resonators, Avashi Shock plasma grenade launching systems... my troopers were dealing out destruction and death. Furthermore, the Small Relict Guard Drones were racing around at the speed of sound, barely visible and destroying everything alive. Unexpectedly, the guard turrets and combat robots also broke down and started to kill the defenders. Wherever Team Gnat showed up, resistance never held out long.

Psionics were also in full effect. Leng Soia-Tan and Gerd Valeri were positively prancing, turning enemies on one another and causing terror. I wasn't far behind them either. The defenders fell into a panic and started killing their own comrades. Officers lost control and ordered their subordinates to surrender, some just killed themselves... Three mages working together in a link was severely OP, and there was no protection against us. Enemy psionics tried to "break through" us, but fat chance! I didn't encounter a single defender that could compare with my Intelligence, and the success of psionic attacks depended most of all on the ratio of Intelligence between opponents. Two corulers of Poko-Poko, Meleyephatians by race, also quickly fizzled out and came under my complete control, laying down their weapons and surrendering to the mercy of the victors.

The only thing was that our mana was burning up very quickly, and the ladies and I needed to fall back, rest up and "recharge." I'd had so many of the mana-restoring cocktails they were making me nauseous and, after the battle, I suspected I was in for severe consequences. But that didn't matter now. We needed to keep up the fight and Team Gnat and myself were constantly needed to aid this or that attack vector.

There were also losses among Team Gnat, but they weren't so frequent. Eduard the Space Commando was in his element and had displayed feats of heroism on the very bleeding edge of the attack, which led to him respawning three times.

Gerd T'yu-Pan also died twice. But neither General Ui-Taka nor I were at all afraid of losses in this operation. During the first minutes of the assault, the Commander of the Army of Earth captured and secured respawn zones where the troopers moved their rez points. And now every fallen trooper was back in the game after fifteen minutes and back in formation not long after that. The defenders also had respawn points on Poko-Poko station, but the Human invaders were just too many. Army of Earth troopers were practically everywhere and keeping a close watch for attempts to respawn. As soon as opponents showed up, they died a quick death, then metal stakes were driven into the floor at their respawn site. Cheap, effective and savage.

An ummi after the assault began, with the Army of Earth in control of eighty-five percent of the station, I got a peace offer from the owners of Poko-Poko.

ATTENTION!!! The Poko-Poko council of seven rulers offers peace on the following terms: Poko-Poko shall pay an indemnity of seventy million crystals, the Humans shall remove their troops from the station. Do you accept? (Yes/No)

Are these guys sane? Just seventy million? Just at the stations docks we had captured forty-two starships in full working order that belonged to the government of Poko-Poko. Eleven cargo ships of various kinds, a Vasta II light cruiser of Crystallid origin, seven frigates (one of them cloaked) and twenty-three interceptors. The value of those trophies alone reached four hundred thirty million crystals at least. Plus we had taken warehouses packed full of all kinds of goods – thousands and thousands of containers we did not yet know the contents of, but with cargo that was probably also worth in the tens of millions of crystals.

If they were offering half a billion crystals as payoff and to release the hostages captured on Poko-Poko, I might have considered it. But with what they did send, I of course chose "No." Yes, there was still fighting, but the intensity was on the downswing. There were less and less station defenders in formation, and few now doubted that the Army of Earth would emerge victorious. So why should I accept such a small slice of reward, when I could take it all?

"Kung Gnat, we have found the hostages' personal effects!" the message came from an old buddy, Gerd Alexander Antipov the Inquisitor from the Human-3 Faction. The "fed" was also here with the Army of Earth and together with a team of expert torturers was busy interrogating prisoners.

"Where?" I asked right away.

"In the hold of a Tolili-Ukh X frigate in cloaker configuration. On a tip we got while interrogating a Miyelonian lady called Gerd Murr-La, one of the seven co-owners of Poko-Poko. The 'big kitty' was drugged out and slept through the beginning of the war. The First Legion guys brought her straight to me in that unresponsive state. I had to get her back to her senses. Gerd Murr-La told me lots of interesting things and I'm sure she has more to say. Both about the Human hostages and other criminal affairs on the station."

Alexander Antipov said the frigate the hostages' things were found on belonged to a Meleyephatian by the name of Kung Maa Tosssh. The Miyelonian druggie said that high-profile Meleyephatian was the eighth co-owner of Poko-Poko station. And maybe even the sole true owner of this whole den of thieves, with the seven "co-owners" acting just as a smokescreen, his obedient puppets.

Horde observer Gerd Ruwana Loki was standing next to me to help conduct negotiations for yet another large squad of Poko-Poko defenders backed into a corner to surrender, when suddenly she stumbled back and covered her mouth with a hand in fear. The Psychologist's eyes went round in horror.

"Captain Gnat, Kung Maa Tosssh isn't just any old Meleyephatian. He is a true legend in the Horde. The very person who uncovered the Morphian plot. The right hand of the ruler of the Meleyephatian Horde Krong Laa. Horde Foreign Intelligence Chief and my immediate superior. Former. Kung Maa was thought to have vanished without a trace ever since the fall of the Throne World, and his replacement has already been appointed."

"Well, looks like your boss has turned up. He was holed up on Poko-Poko. But what did he want with all this?" I gestured vaguely at the station, traces of battle, large number of Army of Earth players and all the rest. "A Human invasion, blackmail, threats. Did Kung Maa really not understand that I would never give him the valuable Relict laboratory and prefer to solve problems by force?"

Gerd Ruwana just shrugged her shoulders without too much confidence.

"I don't know what my boss was plotting. But players at that level don't make mistakes, Kung Gnat. Kung Maa has been alive ten times longer than you. He has vastly more life experience. He was at the head of the Siu Department for a long time, seeking out and exterminating the last of the Morphians. Now the department is closed because there are essentially no Morphians left. But Kung Maa never stopped hunting. And just because you don't comprehend my boss's plans, that does not mean he does not have them. And the frigate was left at dock with its navigation history intact and the hostages' things left out on display. That must mean that Kung Maa wanted you to come to Poko-Poko and find all this."

Just then, Gerd Ayni's Miyelonian voice rang out in my headphones, having been sent as a Translator with a Human envoy to meet the last of the Poko-Poko defenders.

"Kung Gnat, they're surrendering! Every last one. Congratulations! Humanity now has its very own space station!"

ATTENTION!!! Your character has unlocked the Legitimacy parameter. Your current Legitimacy rating is one percent.

That's new. I opened the game guide and read the explanation. I see. The Legitimacy scale showed how far a Kung was from the highest rank in the game of Krong. The level to which Humans and members of other space dwelling races perceived me as the sole ruler of the Human race. Just one percent out of a hundred? I had a long way to go...

There were indeed consequences. I felt like crap, all beat to shit, reduced to a pulp. Not quite as bad as I felt after drinking with the Miyelonians, but still there was nothing good in this half sick state. I wanted to close my eyes and detach from everything that was going on, but there was no way to rest at the moment. After taking Poko-Poko, lots of urgent issues had cropped up and only the Kung of Earth could solve them.

What size garrison would stay behind on the station? How many Humans would be going back to Earth? What to do with the former corulers? Would the regime on Poko-Poko remain loyal to its smugglers, or would the Free Captains have to move on to another station? Could we trust the local units wishing to serve the new authorities? How to divvy up the spoils between the many factions of our planet so no one would take offense? Which members of the Relict Faction should be transferred to Poko-Poko in the real world first?

With a wet towel wrapped around my head, and wearing nothing but my underwear, I was slouching deeply in a levitating leather armchair and staring at an endless list of incoming messages trying to respond to the most import of them. On the chair next to me Gerd Valeri-Urla was "dying," also overtaxed by the recent fighting and never before having spent Magic Points in such a large amount, having completely worn herself out. Little Sister the panther was lying at her master's feet, able to sense how badly she was doing, but totally unable to help.

And although my wayedda was currently wearing nothing but a tight pair of black panties, I was not in the mood to marvel at her beauty and get up to any mischief. I couldn't even find the strength to disagree when Valeri-Urla laid claim to the most luxurious apartments on Poko-Poko as her personal residence an hour earlier, which I had previously declared my property for all to hear. Meanwhile, that same apartment she was also planning to share with me in the real world.

Yes, that's right. I was planning to transfer my physical body from Kasti-Utsh III to Poko-Poko as soon as Human rule was firmly established here in the real world and there was no longer anything to jeopardize my safety. Ayni, Valeri-Urla and the majority of my team were planning on doing the same. It would also be ideal to place a division of at least seven and better ten thousand human troopers on Poko-Poko so none of my foes would be tempted.

The communicator buzzed on the table after I set it down just a minute earlier. Someone wanted to talk to me again.

"Oh, my head..." attempting to reach out for the communicator gave me a beastly headache. "Who's there?"

On the other line was Gerd Ruwana Loki. The Horde observer couldn't hide a happy smile when she saw the Kung of Earth in nothing but boxers and a headband instead of his normal armor suit. Meanwhile, I quickly got myself together and snapped to my usual serious state.

"Kung Gnat, we have the hostages' coordinates. They were saved in Kung Maa's frigate's navigation computer. Seven people. They were in this very star system on their own Omi-Chee space bucket slash yacht, hidden by an invisibility field installed by the kidnappers. They're tied up, sitting in their own excrement, emaciated and badly dehydrated. They're still barely conscious after being given enough sleeping pills and drugs for a horse, but most importantly they're alive. And the death of two of them has been verified. I ordered the hostages sent to the medical center on Poko-Poko."

"Yes, that would be the right thing to do. I admit, I was planning to give the 'golden boys' a good thrashing with whole units of soldiers watching. Hopefully then they'd think with their heads before running off into more dangerous space adventures. But they've had it hard enough. I hope this lesson sticks with them for the rest of their lives."

Gerd Ruwana nodded and fumbled, as if unsure the next piece of news was worth telling.

"Tell me already. I can see something happened."

"Indeed, Kung Gnat. The elderly ruler of the Trillians has stepped down, and that has already been confirmed by Meleyephatian Horde intelligence. He is planning to officially announce his successor in an address to the nation in six ummi. But most Horde political experts have no doubt that, of all the many members of the Par-Poreh dynasty, the monarch will land on Prince Hugo Par-Poreh because he is the most popular among the common people."

Great... Just the thing we needed...

"That isn't all the bad news, Captain Gnat. Information has surfaced that Prince Hugo has signed a military alliance with the Composite and as soon as his coronation ceremony is complete, the Trillians will enter the galactic war on the Composite's side."

I foolishly thought there could be no worse news than that of the imminent enthronement of the bloodthirsty "embodiment of absolute evil." But this news clearly beat all previous records for bad news...

Despite the headache, I stood up and nervously paced the room. I turned to my communicator screen and asked the Horde observer a question.

"Do you know how he pulled it off? After all, the Composite isn't in contact with anyone from our galaxy!"

"We know only about three Composite pilots that were sent to the far-away GG-666 system by an unknown force. They respawned around five ummi later next to the wreckage of their ships. The Trillians saved them from an inevitable death. And Prince Hugo managed to establish mental contact."

Aw hell! And to think I was so glad that my mobile laboratory had taken a few enemy ships with it when making the null transport. If only I could have known where it would lead...

"Valeri, get up! Gerd Ruwana, get in touch with the *Tamara the Paladin*'s entire team. Tell them to hurry back to our starship. Every minute of delay could prove fatal for our entire galaxy. We're flying to the Aysar Cluster in search of new allies!"

Addendum

Crew list of the frigate *Tamara the Paladin*

Players:

1. Kung Gnat. Human. Listener. Captain.

2. Leng Soia-Tan La-Varrez. Human. Psionic Mage. Ward of the captain.

3. Gerd Uline Tar. Geckho. Trader. Captain's First Mate and business partner.

4. Gerd Ayni Uri-Miayuu. Miyelonian. Translator. Authorized representative.

5. Gerd Ayukh. Geckho. Navigator. Senior Officer.

6. Gerd Dmitry Zheltov. Human. Starship Pilot. Main pilot.

7. Gerd Imran. Human. Gladiator. Captain's personal bodyguard.

8. Gerd Mauu-La Mya-Ssa. Miyelonian.

Medic.

9.   Gerd   Ruwana   Loki.   Human. Psychologist. Horde observer.

10.   Gerd Tini Wi-Gnat. Miyelonian. Thief. Ward of the captain.

11.   Gerd T'yu-Pan. Human. Shocktroop. Landing team leader.

12.   Gerd   Uii-Oyeye-Argh-Eeyayo.   Jarg. Analyst.

13.   Gerd Ukh-Meemeesh. Trillian. Gunner.

14.   Gerd   Valeri-Urla.   Human.   Beast Master. Captain's wayedda.

15.   Gerd Vasha Tushihh Geckho. Heavy Robot Operator.

16.   Avan Toi. Geckho. Supercargo.

17.   Amati-Kuis   Ursssh.   Trillian.   Chef-Assassin.

18.   Basha Tushihh. Geckho. Heavy Robot Operator.

19.   Eduard   Boyko.   Human.   Space Commando.
20.   Destroying Angel. Human. Gunfighter.

21.   Grim Reaper. Human. Sniper.

22.   Kisly.   Human.   Machinegunner. Husband to Nefertiti the Dryad.

23.   Orun Va-Mart. Miyelonian. Engineer. Main ship engineer.

24.   San-Doon Taki-Bu. Human. Pilot. Copilot.

25.   San-Sano. Human. Engineer.

26.   Taik Rekh. Geckho. Gunner.

27.   Timka-Vu. Human. Machinegunner.

28.   Svetlana   Vereshchagina.   Human. Assassin. Physical Education Instructor.

Non players:

1.   Kirsan (3x). Mechanoid repair bot. Differentiated by color.
2.   Little Sister. Shadow Panther. Animal. Valeri's Pet.
3.   Nefertiti. NPC-Dryad. Jeweler.

END OF BOOK SEVEN

Want to be the first to know about our latest LitRPG, sci fi and fantasy titles from your favorite authors?

Subscribe to our **New Releases** newsletter:
http://eepurl.com/b7niIL

Thank you for reading *Cause for War!*
If you like what you've read, check out other sci-fi, fantasy
and LitRPG novels published by Magic Dome Books:

Reality Benders LitRPG series by Michael Atamanov:
Countdown
External Threat
Game Changer
Web of Worlds
A Jump into the Unknown
Aces High
Cause for War

**The Dark Herbalist LitRPG series
by Michael Atamanov:**
Video Game Plotline Tester
Stay on the Wing
A Trap for the Potentate
Finding a Body

Perimeter Defense LitRPG series by Michael Atamanov:
Sector Eight
Beyond Death
New Contract
A Game with No Rules

**League of Losers LitRPG Series
by Michael Atamanov:**
A Cat and his Human
In Service of the Pharaoh

**The Way of the Shaman LitRPG series
by Vasily Mahanenko:**
Survival Quest
The Kartoss Gambit
The Secret of the Dark Forest
The Phantom Castle
The Karmadont Chess Set
The Hour of Pain (a bonus short story)
Shaman's Revenge
Clans War

World 99 LitRPG Series by Dan Sugralinov:
Blood of Fate

Adam Online LitRPG Leries by Max Lagno:
Absolute Zero
City of Freedom

Interworld Network LitRPG Series by Dmitry Bilik:
The Time Master
Avatar of Light
The Dark Champion

Rogue Merchant LitRPG Series by Roman Prokofiev:
The Starlight Sword
The Gene of the Ancients
Shadow Seer
Battle for the North
The Devil Archetype

Project Stellar LitRPG Series by Roman Prokofiev:
The Incarnator
The Enchanter
The Tribute
The Rebel
The Archon

Clan Dominance LitRPG Series by Dem Mikhailov:
The Sleepless Ones Book One
The Sleepless Ones Book Two
The Sleepless Ones Book Three
The Sleepless Ones Book Four
The Sleepless Ones Book Five
The Sleepless Ones Book Six

The Neuro LitRPG series by Andrei Livadny:
The Crystal Sphere
The Curse of Rion Castle
The Reapers

Phantom Server LitRPG series by Andrei Livadny:
Edge of Reality
The Outlaw
Black Sun

In order to have new books of the series translated faster, we need your help and support! Please consider leaving a review or spread the word by recommending *Cause for War* to your friends and posting the link on social media. The more people buy the book, the sooner we'll be able to make new translations available.

Thank you!

Till next time!

Made in the USA
Middletown, DE
06 September 2021